HOMEWARD

ALSO BY MARCIE ANNE JENSON:

Whispers of Hope

HOMEWARD

a novel

MARCIE ANNE JENSON

Covenant Communications, Inc.

Cover photograph © 2002 PhotoDisc, Inc.

Cover design copyrighted 2002 by Covenant Communications, Inc.

Published by Covenant Communications, Inc.
American Fork, Utah

Printed in Canada
First Printing: June 2002

08 07 06 05 04 03 02   10 9 8 7 6 5 4 3 2 1

ISBN 1-57734-986-5

Dedication

To my mother and dearest friend, LaRae Jenson Huber. In memory of my grandmothers Delora Rasmussen Jenson and Leona Pomeroy Huber.

Acknowledgements

I must express deep appreciation to the managing editor at Covenant Communications, Shauna Nelson. The gentlest of critics, Shauna has guided and sustained me through the writing, editing, and publication process with her constant encouragement and unwavering optimism. This book would not be if it were not for her. A special thank you to Katie Child for smoothing the rough edges and amazingly perceiving what I was trying to say. I feel deep gratitude for the entire Covenant staff. They make a wonderful team.

I am also grateful to my father, John Talmage Huber, for his belief in this project and for translating the Mapudungun glossary from Spanish to English. Much thanks to my dear friend, Carol Holmes, for her insight and encouragement after reading the first draft. Lastly, unending gratitude to my husband, Gray, for his love and support in the trenches. He'll never know how much I appreciate him.

My cocoon tightens, colors tease,
I'm feeling for the air;
A dim capacity for wings
Degrades the dress I wear.

A power of butterfly must be
The aptitude to fly,
Meadows of majesty concedes
And easy sweeps of sky.

So I must baffle at the hint
And cipher at the sign,
And make much blunder, if at last
I take the clew divine.

By Emily Dickinson

PROLOGUE

Juan Antemil, a graying man in his early fifties, sat at a worn kitchen table in a small, aging farmhouse located in the outskirts of Osorno, Chile. His Book of Mormon lay open to the thirty-second chapter of Alma. Juan studied the ancient prophet's words. On this bright morning, pearls of clouds beaded up over the ocean, and the light wind scarcely whispered of the coming rains. He was home alone. His wife, Marisol, was at the market and his son, Esteban, a graduate student at the university in Santiago, was in Provo, Utah, presenting research on the religious practices of the Mapuche Indians to FARMS, the Foundation for Ancient Research and Mormon Studies. Juan's two daughters, Alicia and Marta, lived close by but were at their own homes caring for husbands and babies.

A sharp knock sounded on the hollow wood of the front door. Juan looked up from the book, scratched his stubble of beard, and reached for his cane. His swollen knee pained him as he stood. He would have to go to the doctor soon and have the fluid drained once more. This knee was a constant reminder of a wild young horse that had bolted years ago. On that occasion, a rope had wrapped around Juan's knee, tripping him, tightening as the horse ran, dragging Juan across the field.

He heard the knock again, louder this time. He hobbled to the door and answered it. Before him stood an old woman, her face a brown mask of wrinkles. A lone, gray braid reached down her back. She wore a thick, worn traveling cloak, the color indistinguishable due to age and dust. Juan, who was mestizo, half Mapuche Indian and half Chilean, sensed what lay behind the mask of age and the toothless smile. He glimpsed the thick silver necklaces bulging beneath the cloak and recognized the *kultrun*, or sacred drum, that was strapped to her back. She was a shaman, or *machi*, a Mapuche Indian holy woman.

Juan stepped back, suddenly on guard. The machi was the icon of the Mapuche culture, and some still believed she could bless or curse at will. Many Christians likened a machi to a witch, for she claimed the power and gift to converse with the gods and the dead. For ages, machis had passed their vast knowledge of herbal lore, healing and cursing rituals, spells and prayers, from one generation to the next. Juan wondered what this machi could want with him.

The memory of another machi filled his mind as scenes from forty-five years before, when he was a child of seven, swept over him. He remembered a time when he was ill with a hacking cough. After dark fell, his father had bundled him in blankets and driven over muddy dirt roads to the reservation.

On the way, Juan's father had explained that the machi only performed the healing ceremony at night, when the evil spirits causing the sickness could be driven away. After they had arrived at his grandfather's *ruka*, or thatched-roof house, they had found the holy woman already there waiting for them.

With an air of authority, the machi had insisted that little Juan lie on the dirt floor. She had blown smoke from a cigarette over him and had rubbed his feverish body with stones and herbs. Then she had given him a hot liquid to drink. She had beaten on the kultrun and had shaken her rattle as she prayed to God for him.

Little Juan had been certain that the magical drink cured him by burning his throat so violently that he would never be able to cough again. The next week, his father had loaded a bag of sugar and a bag of potatoes in his truck to take to the machi in payment for performing the healing ritual.

Before they had left, Juan's mother had not been pleased. "Nonsense," she had said as she nursed the baby. "The Chilean doctor cured the boy, not the Indian witch. If you give away our food, our children will starve!"

His Mapuche father had silently turned his back on his wife and beckoned Juan into the truck. On the way to the reservation, he had explained that if they did not pay, the machi might curse their fields or their health. Despite the payment, the wheat crop had suffered that year, and Juan's baby sister had died in August, the black month. Little Juan had wondered if perhaps the machi knew of his mother's anger. Didn't the Bible say that a gift given grudgingly was not a gift at all?

Juan turned his mind from the past and looked steadily at the woman in front of him. Now, over forty years since his last encounter with a machi, Juan was grateful that his conversion to Mormonism and his faith in Christ had freed him from the Mapuche magic and its accompanying fear.

Without an invitation, the old woman stepped across the threshold into Juan's house. How strange that he still felt this dread! Juan thought of how his child, Esteban, who studied anthropology, was learning all he could about the language and customs of the Mapuche when Juan himself still worked to forget—to break the cords of superstition which bound him.

"Are you Juan Antemil?" the woman asked in her native language, Mapudungun. How did she know he spoke it too?

"Yes, what do you want with me?" Juan answered in Spanish.

"I am looking for a brother and a sister who had no parents," she returned. "I lost them seventeen winters ago. The Catholic father sent me here."

"My wife and I took care of many orphaned children during the winter months. For many years we fed them and gave them shelter. If we could, we found homes for them. Many children came and went."

"I seek a boy called Lautaro and his sister, Mina. Their mother was Mapuche and their father a *winka*, an outsider who came from the northern mines. The father was one of the many who disappeared during the years of Pinochet. The mother was like a hummingbird—her heartbeat quick and wild. Surely, she died. Yet I feel the beat of Mina's heart in the beat of the kultrun. Mina is a woman now and lives beyond the mountains. I do not know what has become of the boy."

"What are these children to you? They are mestizo," Juan said, hoping the woman did not sense his heart beating quickly and heavily in his chest. He knew these two children. His own son had e-mailed him from the United States to confess that he had fallen in love with the girl.

The old woman's black eyes darted, meeting Juan's glance.

"You think the Mapuche do not accept the mestizo. You are right. But in my dreams, God tells me that the soul inside Mina's mestizo body is Mapuche soul. She is a child of the land."

Juan sighed as if he had been defeated in some unseen battle. He remembered how the police had brought these two to his shelter fifteen years ago. Filthy, thin, and scarcely old enough to go to school, they had been living alone under a city bridge, scavenging food from garbage cans. The boy had been sage, wiry, and wild eyed, fiercely protective of the little girl with her frightened, contemplative eyes. They had edged their way into Juan's heart, and he had grieved when the shrieking boy bit him the day the nuns came to take the girl to a convent.

Juan had not been able to comfort Lautaro after his sister was gone. He thought it would be best if the boy left Chile altogether. And so Juan contacted a friend in the United States, a man named Blake Taylor, who had served a mission in Chile years before and had taught Juan the gospel. Juan knew that Blake's sister and brother-in-law longed for children. When Blake came to Chile to facilitate Lautaro's pending adoption, he heard of Mina and visited the Catholic father to plead that the brother and sister remain together. Miraculously, the priest agreed that the girl should be adopted as well. He did all he could to help with the paperwork.

The old woman's voice interrupted Juan's thoughts. "They are my grandchildren," she stated stoically. Juan's expression told her that her search had ended.

He tried to explain. "Their mother was found dead. We couldn't find any grandparents or living relatives," Juan spoke gently. "You should have come here long ago."

"I could not come before," the old woman said simply, as if it explained everything. Did Juan perceive a slight sagging in her countenance? He gazed at her and did not see the dangerous and proud machi, but an old woman weary from a long journey.

"Come and sit." Juan motioned her to the table. He did not relish extending another blow to her, this woman who had spent her life working the magic of herbs and prayer. How could he begin to tell her that her grandson was dead and her granddaughter thousands of miles away in the United States with a different name?

The Mapuche woman sat motionless as Juan described how the police brought the children to his shelter shortly after the rains began fifteen years back. He knew they were Mapuche from the boy's name and the Mapudungun words sprinkled throughout their vocabulary. The boy, Lautaro, was dedicated to his pretty little sister, Mina. When she was taken to a convent, he begged relentlessly for her return.

Juan explained how he had written a letter to an old friend of his, a Californian who had lived in Chile as a Mormon missionary. This missionary knew of a family in the United States who wanted to adopt the children. They were relatives of the missionary. The Catholic father helped arrange things so that the girl could join her brother and be adopted as well.

"*Los misioneros son wesa lonko*," the woman interrupted. Juan recognized *wesa lonko*, the Mapuche term that meant either "crazy" or "possessed by an evil spirit."

"Not this missionary," Juan corrected. "This man was kind and good. His teaching converted me to the Mormon faith. He found a home in the United States for Mina and Lautaro. For many years they were very happy. Then, there was an accident. Lautaro died four years ago."

"How did the boy die?" The machi's face was proud and sternly set as she asked the question.

"He was at the ocean catching fish. He was caring for an injured seagull when a wave threw him into the sea."

"The seagull is a sacred bird to our people," the machi said with her head held high.

"I know," Juan said slowly.

The machi stood up and stretched to her full height. Though she was not very tall, there was a regal quality to her bearing. She looked down her hawklike nose at Juan.

"Chau-chau, the god who is father to us all, wishes Mina to return to me and to her ancestors. He told me this in a dream. The machi dwindle among my people. Perhaps Mina has the gift."

A shudder ran through Juan. Now he understood. This old machi wanted an apprentice, someone to work for her, to gather and grind herbs, to make concoctions and poultices, to become an expert in the Mapuche religion and ways of healing, to become as she was. This young woman would have to possess the gift, to understand the voices of the animals and the rocks, the sky and the stars. And during the *machitun* she must lend her body to be the voice of the dead. At the harvest ceremony the beat of her hand on the kultrun must be strong enough to intercede with the gods. And all the while she would live in poverty. If her strength waned, her own people would shun her.

He too stood, this time without his cane. "Mina is no longer Mapuche. She has a different god now and a different name." Though Juan's voice shook slightly, he spoke clearly and slowly. "She is a Mormon. She is attending a university in the United States. She has a boyfriend. She is well. You must go now." The woman coughed and shook her head. Juan wondered if he heard the sound of tuberculosis within her.

When the coughing subsided, she spoke again. "I am Mina's grandmother. You will contact this wesa lonko Mormon missionary. We will see if he is as kind as you say. He will give this message to Mina. It is her birthright. Do not interfere with the will of God. She must know who she is." The machi reached inside her cloak and brought out a small piece of paper folded into many sections. She placed the paper on top of the opened Book of Mormon. "Mina must come to me before the black month," she said as she turned to go.

CHAPTER 1

EMPTY SPACES

It was an unseasonably warm April evening at the Glenwood apartments in Provo, Utah. The setting sun spread crimson light in the western sky as shadows crept like slender hands across the mountains. Dennie Fletcher stepped out of the shower. She wrapped her long, black hair in a towel and donned a T-shirt and jeans. The doorbell rang.

"Hey, Esteban!" Dennie overheard her roommate, Aimy Tomlinson, through the closed door that separated the front from the back of the apartment. Dennie hurried across the hall into her bedroom.

A moment later, Aimy opened the bedroom door and stuck her head in. "It's your man," she said as she grinned, her short, white-blonde hair framing a lightly freckled, blue-eyed, elfin face. This face was extremely familiar and very dear to Dennie. They had been close friends since they were ten. At the moment, Aimy wore a baggy sweatshirt and shorts. Her slim, freckled legs were pink from the afternoon sun.

Dennie threw her towel at Aimy, who caught it. "My man's on a mission in Florida," Dennie said in a voice soft enough that Esteban couldn't hear.

"Really?" Aimy laughed as she sat down on the bed with a bounce. "Where are you and Esteban going for dinner?"

"The Cougar Eat," Dennie admitted. Aimy pointed to her throat and mocked a gag. Dennie continued, "Aim, life without a car limits one's choices. After we eat, we'll be at the library studying."

"If you want, I'll drop you guys off at the Brick Oven in the Yellow Toy," Aimy offered, referring to her aging Toyota Corolla. "I'll do my baseball rounds while you eat, then pick you up."

"No thanks. We don't mind hoofing it. Meet us at the library later—after your rounds."

Aimy nodded an OK. That evening, Aimy's rounds included driving five boys between the ages of seven and fourteen home from various baseball practices. This was part of her lucrative little business called Pick Me Up. Aimy simply charged five dollars to pick up people's children and drive them anywhere in Provo. She loved that busy mothers who were tired of playing taxi sang her praises. Recently her business had come to include a handful of very elderly clientele who called her *honey* and *sweetheart* and said she was an answer to their prayers. Then there was Augustus Waverly, a handicapped gentleman and her favorite client.

Dennie ran a brush through her hair. Aimy's voice sounded thoughtful when she spoke. "I think Esteban's going to ask you to marry him soon. He doesn't want you to go back to California without a commitment."

Dennie looked up at Aimy with eyes so dark they were almost black. The lids behind them were naturally lighter than the rest of her olive skin, and her ebony eyelashes were long and arched. Dennie's eyes were extraordinary. She shrugged and said softly, "Aim, he knows I don't want to make any commitment until Ron's home from his mission. Plus, Esteban has another year before he finishes his PhD, and I don't think he wants to get married until he's done. Besides, I don't know if he wants to settle here or in Chile."

"Those are just details," Aimy said. "*if you love each other.* Esteban loves you."

"I don't want to move to Chile. You're here, Aimy. And Mom and Dad and Blake and Karin are here. I mean they're in California, in the United States—my home. But most of all, I don't even know if I love Esteban. I thought I loved Ron. "

"Beware of intensity, Density," Aimy remarked. Yet the expression in her eyes didn't echo the lightness of her voice. "Remember, you have two great choices. Think of how you melted the first time you heard Esteban bless the food. His deep Spanish lilt so full of feeling— like what he was doing was absolutely sacred—like he was really talking to Heavenly Father."

"Aim, prayer *is* sacred. We *are* talking to Heavenly Father."

"Right. The rest of us *know* that, but Esteban *feels* it. Plus, the two of you would have such gorgeous, dark-eyed babies."

Dennie laughed and put her finger to her lips, indicating they should speak more quietly. "The man could be listening at the door!" she said, grinning.

"The man's far too polite!" Aimy returned. "A perfect Latin gentleman!"

Dennie smiled as she pulled on her brown leather shoes. A moment later, the girls walked into the living room, where they found the tall, twenty-eight-year-old Chilean graduate student at the chessboard, playing chess against himself.

"My move," he said as he looked up at them, grinning. They laughed.

"Steban," Aimy joked, "If Dennie says *no*, will you marry me?"

"Perhaps after the mish," Esteban returned as he winked at her. The guy was charming.

Aimy sighed dramatically. Her supposed mission was the running joke in the apartment. Ever since she had turned twenty-one in January, she couldn't make up her mind. She'd start filling out the mission papers, change her mind, then get them out again a week later. She had seen a flock of birds once that reminded her of her feelings. Together, they would all fly one way, dark specks against the cobalt blue sky. Then, as if on cue, they switched directions only to reverse course and return to their original direction a moment later.

"To go or not to go, that is the question," she said and exhaled deeply. For the moment she would play the drama queen. Then, her blue eyes became uncharacteristically serious.

"Beware of intensity," Dennie teased gently. "You have two great choices. A mission or Sean."

"I want to meet this Sean," Esteban added, raising his eyebrows.

"You will soon. He's flying here on Tuesday and driving with me back to California," Aimy said. "Esteban, how 'bout if you advise me?"

"My pleasure," Esteban grinned at Aimy. Then he put his arm around Dennie and pulled her close. "I only wish that Dennie trusted my judgment so completely. Perhaps someday . . ." He raised his eyebrows and shoulders in unison.

A few moments later Dennie and Esteban left the apartment and walked down the hallway arm in arm. Although Dennie enjoyed

Esteban's closeness, part of her felt far away. She thought of how very attracted she was to Esteban. He had a warmth, an eagerness of spirit, that sometimes reminded her of her brother. Yet it troubled her to consider that perhaps she cared for Esteban partly because she still ached for her brother who had died.

Esteban was from Chile, the country of her birth. Yet it was a country dim in her memory, much like fog changes the outline of a mountain. She was a citizen of the United States. She had a great relationship with her parents. This was home, and often Esteban felt foreign. And yet, there were other times, sometimes unexpected, when a strange feeling of loneliness and separation crept over her. A collection of past moments sped through Dennie's mind—when she was very small and noticed how dark her own hand looked inside her mother's; a grocery store cashier who gaped at Dennie and her father as if trying to figure out how they could be related; a woman in the ward who lavished praise on her mother for adopting *foreign* children; a game of Truth or Dare at a slumber party where a girl questioned her about her *real* parents. Dennie had never chosen *truth* again.

And yet, through her growing-up years, Thes had been close by, sharing the burden of being different. Until he died. During the terrible days following Thes's death, she felt totally alone. Haunted by guilt, she wondered if she could have prevented his death by telling her parents about his drinking problem. During the dark nights, she dreamt of Chile, of the Andes towering over her like the side of a cradle. In other dreams she stood on the edge of a dark planet all alone; and in one dream she was a little girl again, rocking with laughter as her big brother tried to outrun the clouds.

But it was Ron Babcock, not Esteban, who had broken through her shell of isolation in the months following the loss of Thes. The image of the blonde, blue-eyed missionary filled her mind like a shaft of light. Dennie pictured his wide, easy grin, his long legs and the bounce in his walk. She thought of the evening they hiked with snowshoes in the Sierras, the night in the car when she told him Thes's story and cried in his arms, the Halloween when Ron dyed his hair red with Kool-Aid and they dressed up like Raggedy Anne and Raggedy Andy. She had been able to talk to Ron and laugh with him. Perhaps he wasn't as physically attractive as Esteban, but their vein of friendship ran deep. She missed Ron. But he wouldn't be home for another year. They were both changing. Would the puzzle pieces of their lives fit together once he returned? Could she stand to lose Esteban? Would part of her always feel alone?

The couple crossed the Glenwood and Riviera parking lots, then turned toward the uphill path that led to campus. Halfway along the paved trail, Esteban stopped. He turned to Dennie and touched her cheek. He ran his hand down the length of her hair. "Beautiful Dennie," he said. "What will you become?"

As she walked onto campus with Esteban, a thought struck Dennie. Was loving and marrying Esteban what Heavenly Father had intended for her all along? Was it the closing of a circle that had been drawn when Esteban's father contacted Uncle Blake and arranged for two small orphans to be adopted by a family in California fifteen years ago? Dennie was twenty-one. She needed to know the answer.

Meryl Fletcher went into the den shortly after her husband, Rick, left for work. She sat down at her desk and breathed deeply as she looked at the letters on the computer keyboard in front of her. The blank page on the screen stared at her like a void, empty of words, paragraphs, themes, or heart. No humanity in it, nothing to cry about—or laugh about for that matter. Empty like a vacant lot, or a child not yet conceived. Just space. Empty space that she would fill with song and story.

Her hands were poised with her fingers arched over the keys, almost touching them. She hesitated, unsure of how to begin the first sentence of her first novel, a historical narrative about her *Mayflower* ancestors. She remembered the difficulty she had constructing the first sentence of her last short story—the story that had been accepted by a national literary magazine and had given her courage to attempt this. She had always struggled with beginnings. There was the awkwardness of physical beginnings—her ungainly experience of puberty, not to mention her fumbling wedding night nearly twenty-five years ago. She remembered entering college—that wet-behind-the-ears, floundering, freshman feeling. Her and Rick's first year of marriage had been bumpy too, with neither of them fathoming the skill it took to meld two lives into one.

A thought struck Meryl. Was birth, the beginning of individual life, awkward too? She suspected so—awkward, hard, beautiful, and miraculous all mixed together somehow. Yet she had never given birth or witnessed a child coming into the world. Her two children were adopted. She thought of her forty-five-year-old body—the body that had betrayed her and never conceived a child. Yet this same body had survived premature menopause, an early-stage breast cancer, and the grief following the death of her son. She was not especially toned or coordinated. Yet, she was tallish and somewhat graceful and slender— especially for her age. There were no stretch marks on her abdomen, and the scar from her lumpectomy was almost white now. She both loved and mistrusted this body God had given her.

Back to work, Meryl instructed herself. *Tragedy and Grace—the Story of a* Mayflower *Family.* She typed the title of her novel. Then the telephone rang. The caller I.D. informed her that it was her brother, Blake Taylor. Meryl reached across her desk and answered it with a cheery hello.

"Sis, let's go out for breakfast!"

"Blake, weren't you working last night?"

"Sure was. I just took off my nursing duds and changed into jeans."

"Stay home and get some sleep. Why don't you bring Karin and the kids over for dinner tonight? We'll barbecue hamburgers."

"Meryl, there's something I need to talk to you about first. Alone."

"Is everything OK?"

"Sure. I just had a phone call yesterday. I want to run it by you. How 'bout if I pick you up in a half hour? We can go to Lyons, get one of their pyramid breakfasts."

"Sounds good."

As Meryl turned off the computer and pulled on her socks and shoes, she wondered what Blake's telephone call was all about. Her thoughts skipped back to a different phone call that came on a sunny, wintry day over four years ago. A gentle voice she didn't recognize had informed her that her eighteen-year old son, Theseus Lautaro Fletcher, had died in a tragic accident while fishing at the ocean.

He had been her darling boy—this beautiful, black-haired, dark-eyed son from Chile. Losing him had been so hard. The coast guard had mentioned that they were lucky to have found his body. *Lucky?* Meryl had thought with bitter agony. *I am lucky to have the body of my son?*

Meryl pulled herself back to the present. She gazed at the computer, promising herself she would come back to it this afternoon. She looked around at the den with its worn, chocolate-brown sofa, large, mahogany desk, and bookshelves that reached the ceiling. It was the one room they had not redecorated since she and Rick adopted their two children almost fifteen years ago. The two had been siblings from Chile, a boy and a girl, recently orphaned, and around five and six years old. In Chile they had been called Mina and Lautaro. But before their adoptions were finalized, Rick and Meryl asked them if they wanted to choose new names. Lautaro chose Theseus, the name of the Greek hero in his favorite picture book. They called him Thes.

Mina had wanted to be named after the den, the room the little girl had loved, the room that Meryl sat in now. So, they had chosen Denizen, Dennie for short. Meryl gazed around the shelves at the many books her small daughter had delighted in. Her glance stopped at the worn spine of the one picture book her little boy had devoured. It bore the title *Theseus and the Labyrinth.* She sighed deeply and left the room.

In the hallway, Meryl took her beige cardigan sweater from the closet and slipped it on. She sat down on the living room sofa to wait for Blake. Yet thoughts of Thes's death continued to crowd into her mind. She remembered the night Rick and Blake had dressed Thes's body in the white shirt and navy-black missionary suit they had picked out for his burial. Before sleep that night, in the privacy of their bedroom, she had asked Rick how it went. "I didn't think he would be so stiff and heavy. It was so hard getting his arm through the sleeve." Rick's voice had been like a rasp, scraping the raw surface of his heart.

"It should have been me," Meryl had whispered.

"Meryl, it was right that I dress him," Rick had managed. "I'm his father. And Blake went to Chile and brought Thes and Dennie home to us. Blake loves Thes like his own son."

"I didn't mean that," Meryl remembered weeping. "I meant that I had cancer. I should be the one dead."

Then, Rick had held her tightly and had rubbed her back and stroked her arms. It was as if after handling death, he could not get enough of the feel of life within her.

The next morning before the public viewing, Meryl had gone to the mortuary early to spend a few moments alone with the body—the temple that had housed her son's spirit. She had straightened Thes's collar and tie. She had kissed the skin of his forehead, which felt so little like skin and so much like clay. She had wondered how she could be here, moving through this inconceivable horror. She had wept warm tears on his cold cheek and had felt her utter powerlessness against the inevitability of death. Her son would never speak to her, or laugh with her, or dance with her again. He wouldn't serve a mission. She would not hold his children. Everyone was clay. Everyone.

She had sat down in a chair, weeping, weeping with her head cradled in her knees, weeping and praying to the God of Heaven, the Savior of the world, the giver of life and the only one with enough love to have power over death. Yet, He did not have enough love to save her Thes. Had she been wrong? Was the God of Heaven as cold as the clay which was now her child?

She had lifted her face and looked once more at the form of her son in the casket. There had been a waxen beauty about him, and she had suddenly remembered how she had sung to him and Dennie at bedtime their first night in the United States. "You are my sunshine," she had sung to those little ones who could not speak English. "My only sunshine. You make me happy when clouds are gray. You'll never know, dears, how much I love you. Please don't take my sunshine away." They had slept and she had watched them, stunned at their beauty, their olive-toned skin, silken-black hair, and uniquely molded features. As their chests rose and fell on gentle waves of sleep, she vowed never to forget the preciousness of these two whom God had sent her.

Then, as she had sat by Thes's casket weeping, thinking of her little ones, an image had filled her mind as if placed there by an unseen hand. The image was of the Son of God descending into the cold ocean and lifting her child to light. A feeling of indescribable sacredness had permeated through Meryl as intangible and yet as real as the air she breathed. *Is this what it means to be comforted by angels? Is this the unspeakable gift of the Holy Ghost?* Through the awkward and terrible grief that had followed, Meryl had enclosed that moment in her heart as if it were a pearl clasp fastening the fabric of her soul together.

Now, four years later, Meryl thought of how her soul felt whole again—at least mostly. She loved her husband. Her daughter, Dennie, had flourished and grown to adulthood in a way that was joyous to Meryl. She found creative writing and family history research both challenging and fulfilling. But that didn't mean that there were no empty spaces—times when she ached for her son, days when she longed to be close to her mother, parts of herself that Rick didn't understand, moments of aloneness when secret fears and self-doubts gnawed at the edges of her confidence.

But, Meryl admitted to herself, *there will always be empty spaces. Life is imperfect and this is a telestial world. But isn't that what life is about? Making choices. Finding a way to fill the vacant parts of my own and other people's souls with light.*

CHAPTER 2

IF IT PLEASES GOD

At Lyon's Restaurant, Meryl returned from washing her hands to find her brother sound asleep at the booth, his head lolling cock-eyed against one shoulder. A petite, redheaded waitress, whose torso was shaped something like a bell, guffawed as she set their breakfast on the table. "Has he been working all night?" she asked as she nodded towards Blake.

"Yes, at the hospital," Meryl explained. "He's a nurse in the Med Clinic transplant unit."

"Honey, I know the feeling of being up all night. I worked grave-yard for twenty years," the waitress commiserated before moving on.

With tender amusement Meryl watched her brother as he began to snore. She thought about their relationship. Just fifteen months apart, they had always been close friends. How lonely her life, especially her youth, would have been if it weren't for Blake.

Meryl allowed her brother to sleep as she took a bite of her egg. Her thoughts slipped back to her childhood and to her parents, Ben and Joan Taylor. She and Blake had grown up in Virginia, at the edge of the Blue Ridge Mountains, where the air was heavier than in California and the fall trees against the cobalt blue autumn sky shone like the colors of God's palette.

Meryl had adored her father, a big, quiet man, sturdy and gentle, who worked days as a janitor and nights as a security guard. Yet Meryl had never felt much tenderness toward her mother, a second-grade teacher who was fifteen years younger than her husband. When Meryl was growing up, Joan had been a petite, attractive woman with red hair. She had run her home and classroom with organized efficiency.

Meryl remembered how her mother never yelled and always followed through. As children, she and Blake were well dressed, well fed, and well mannered. Joan read to them every night and took them to Sunday school each week. She smiled regularly, yet the look in her eyes betrayed her tense perfectionism. Thus, her smile seemed out of tune, like a doll's smile with no heart. Joan hugged her children as was her duty, but stiffened within the short embraces. Meryl recalled how her mother's fair skin colored with embarrassment the few times Joan said *I love you.*

Yet Joan had a lovely voice and would sing in the shower fervent hymns that she performed in the Baptist church choir. Sometimes Meryl sat with her back against the bathroom door and listened as her mother's sweet soprano struck her with beauty and pain. She wondered why her mother sang so movingly to the Lord but had no lullabies for her children.

Then, during Meryl's junior year in high school, the parents of her best friend, Beth Hamilton, joined the Mormon Church. Beth, determined to find her own way, discussed Mormonism at length with Joan when the girls were at the Taylors. With her minister's aid, Joan convinced Beth that Joseph Smith was a false prophet. Yet, Meryl's interest piqued, for the story of a young boy praying alone in the woods had reached her heart. She borrowed a Book of Mormon from Beth's parents and began reading. When she came to 3 Nephi, chapter 17, and read of Jesus blessing the people, she wept at the beauty and love within the pages. She prayed that night to know if it was true and was filled with a hunger to know more.

For the next year and a half, Meryl studied in secret the literature provided by the missionaries and the Hamiltons. She had no doubt that her mother would have forbidden this. Deception seemed the only way. Her testimony deepened in the closets of her soul, and she longed to break the doors open and share the gospel with her family.

Shortly after graduation, when Meryl was eighteen, she scheduled her own baptism. She told her parents one rainy evening. Meryl explained how she had read the Book of Mormon and studied the religion for more than a year.

"How could you do this?" her mother said tersely, her hands shaking with frustration.

"Mom, if you would just read the Book of Mormon—" Meryl began.

But Joan's voice rose as sharp as a sword, striking shapeless any additional words her daughter might form. "You have lied to us. You have gone behind our back, defied our trust. Don't ever join this cult. It will bring you misery."

Knowing that more words would deepen the agony, Meryl turned from her mother, stood up, and walked stiffly to her room. She closed the door without turning on a light and lay on her bed, staring out at the darkness.

Later there came a knock at the door. "Come in," Meryl whispered. Her father entered and sat down on the edge of the bed, a dark warm shape in the starless night. Meryl had hoped it was her mother coming to apologize, to mend the wound.

"It will be all right, honey," her father whispered as he patted her arm.

"Not with Mom," she returned softly. He patted her arm again.

"Dad, do you think I should join the Mormon Church?" Meryl asked.

"I don't know as much about God as you or your mother. But I think you should follow your heart. Everything will be all right."

"I know it's the right thing to do, Dad. I believe it's true with every part of me."

Ben Taylor nodded. Then he hugged his grown girl and left the room.

Five days later, with her father's encouragement, Meryl became a member of the Church of Jesus Christ of Latter-day Saints. A year later, Blake joined her in the waters of baptism. Yet her mother became increasingly distant. Meryl thought of how her father, in a rare battle against his wife's will, insisted on supporting Blake on his mission and sending Meryl to BYU.

Three years following Blake's baptism, Meryl married Rick in the Oakland temple. Her parents did not fly out for the wedding. When the couple flew to Virginia for a reception, Meryl noticed that her father, though as quiet as ever, carried a tense, drained look in his eyes. She asked her mother about it. Joan responded that Meryl had broken her daddy's heart. A man such as Ben Taylor deserved to give his daughter away, not be shut out from the Mormon temple. Meryl remembered her mother's words. *I fear that God will punish you*, Joan stated, adding, *You have torn this family apart.*

Now, twenty-five years later, the memory still stung. Meryl wondered if her passion for family history partially stemmed from the distance she felt from her mother. No more harsh words had been said, but their visits had been infrequent over the years. There were always reasons—her mother's job, financial difficulties, or her father's health. Meryl had not done much better—flying to Virginia just twice. She had not even told her parents about her early-stage breast cancer. When Thes died, her parents had been vacationing in Florida, and Meryl had not known how to contact them.

Yet Meryl had heard the saying that when a door closes, a window opens. Blake, her brother, was that window—a support, comfort, and joy to Meryl and her family. If the Church was a gulf separating Meryl from her mother, it was also a bridge of light connecting Meryl and Blake.

Meryl's thoughts trailed away from the past as she looked once more at Blake and thought of how tired he must be, working nights and caring for a young family. He had changed in the four years since his marriage to Karin Parker. His hair—thin, lank, and a light brown—was now gray around the edges. His tall frame had filled out considerably. He looked more like his father now. Blake suddenly jerked awake. An instant later, he chuckled. His eyes hadn't changed—they were still as clear and blue as when they were children. Meryl remembered how Dennie called them flower-blue eyes when she was five, shortly after she learned to speak English.

"The pancakes woke me up," Blake yawned. "They sure smell good."

"Now tell me about this mysterious phone call before you fall asleep again." Meryl smiled at him as she bit into her omelette.

"Actually, there were two calls I wanted to tell you about. The first was from the stake executive secretary. The stake presidency wants to meet with Karin and me tomorrow night. Rumors are flying that Bishop Babcock is going to be released soon. Karin's worried."

"Blake, do you think you'll be the new bishop?"

"I don't know. It seems wrong to even wonder about. Yet the thought won't leave me alone. If it happens, I don't know how Karin will handle it. Ever since I was called into the bishopric last spring, she's had her hands full on Sundays with Chris and the twins. Now, with another baby on the way, it could be the straw that breaks the camel's back."

"More like the metal bat that breaks the camel's back," Meryl teased. Then she added seriously, "Karin's been through a lot, Blake. She's strong. She can handle whatever comes."

Blake was pensive as he went on. "She was such a trooper when Brian and Brandon were born and I had to start working nights to make ends meet. She was so willing to quit work and stay home. It might not make sense, but it seems like the twins at nearly three are harder now than when they were babies. Plus, Chris's father has been calling and insisting on his visitation rights. It's upsetting Chris and is an emotional strain on Karin."

"Blake, wasn't Nicole about the twins' age when she died?" Meryl asked, remembering that Karin had borne two children during her first marriage—Nicole, a girl, and a boy, Christopher. Chris was eleven now and Nicole, if she had lived, would have been twelve.

Blake nodded. "I don't know if Karin has ever completely forgiven herself for Nicole's accident. And now she has two little boys running in every direction. They don't nap anymore. Just keeping them safe is a major stress."

"Not to mention an active eleven-year-old, a difficult pregnancy, and a husband who works nights, sleeps days, and has a major church calling. When do you spend time together?"

"Next to never," Blake sighed. "Let's pray I'm not the next bishop."

"I'm with you," Meryl said as she smiled encouragingly at her brother. "But if you are called, you'll be great."

"That's debatable."

"Come on, you're John Howland-of-the-*Mayflower*'s great, great, great, great, great, great, great grandson. He's also an ancestor of Joseph Smith, Parley P. Pratt, George Bush, and Franklin Delano Roosevelt. With that kind of heritage, how could you be anything other than great?"

"Wasn't he the guy who climbed onto the deck of the *Mayflower* during the middle of a storm and fell into the ocean?"

"That's him." Meryl tried an English accent as she very loosely quoted William Bradford. "*John Howland, a merry and lively young man, fell into the boiling sea. Yet, it pleased God that he caught hold of the halyard which ran out of length, and though he was pulled under many fathoms of water, by grace and a boat hook somehow managed to get himself into the ship again. He became ill for some days afterward.*"

Blake laughed. Then Meryl added seriously, "Blake, if it pleases God to make you bishop, He'll help keep you and Karin afloat."

"I hope so, Sis, I really hope so."

They ate in silence for a moment. Suddenly Blake stopped eating. When he looked up at Meryl, his blue eyes were troubled. "I need to tell you about the other phone call. The really important phone call. It concerns Dennie."

"What about Dennie?" Meryl's forehead creased. She had forgotten all about the other telephone call.

"Juan Antemil called me from Chile. Dennie's Chilean grandmother has surfaced. She's an old Indian woman. She wants Dennie to live on a reservation with her in Chile this spring and summer."

Meryl spoke, her voice urgent. Feelings and questions tumbled over each other. "Blake, I don't want Dennie going to a faraway country over the ocean. I don't want her leaving us. She is sealed to Rick and me. How do we even know if she's really Dennie's biological grandmother?"

Blake shrugged. "We don't know," he said gently.

"Blake, her relationship with Esteban worries me too. There are so many cultural differences. I want to know Dennie is safe and happy. I want to shield her from potential hurt. Is that wrong?"

"Feelings aren't right or wrong, Meryl, they just are. I wonder if Heavenly Father wishes He could shield us, that He could have shielded His beloved, only Begotten Son from hurt. But it would have messed things up in the long run. Free agency is part of the formula for growth and eternal life, and there isn't a way to stop pain when free agency is in place," Blake said simply.

Meryl didn't speak. Right or wrong, she didn't want Dennie going to Chile again. She thought of the petite, dark-eyed five-year-old nestled safely in the crook of her arm. She remembered the small, olive-colored hand that fit so tenderly into her own—and the nimble mind—that bright, sweet spirit that absorbed all of the knowledge and joy Meryl and Rick had to offer.

Then there was the day when six-year-old Dennie had come to her with a small bouquet of flowering weeds from the lot next door. Meryl had kissed her and thanked her, and Dennie had gone back outside. Later that afternoon Meryl had swept and cleaned the kitchen, throwing the weeds out without thinking twice. Before dinner, Dennie had come in and asked if she could have the flowers back. "They are *children flowers*," the child had explained. "Their *mother and father flowers* are still growing in the yard and need them to come home." When Meryl hadn't been able to find the flowering weeds, Dennie had looked at her mother with a forgiving yet worried expression.

Blake reached out and touched his sister's hand, momentarily stopping Meryl's thoughts. "Mer, whatever happens, Dennie will always be your daughter. You and Rick will always be her parents. That is the sealing power."

"I know," Meryl whispered. But she couldn't explain in words, even to her beloved brother, the lingering fear that chilled her.

CHAPTER 3

JEWELS IN MUD PUDDLES

It was early evening when Dennie entered her apartment after spending the afternoon taking finals. She changed into her bathing suit, sleek fitting and emerald green in color. She liked this suit. She surveyed her reflection in the mirror and casually wished that her thighs were slimmer. *Oh well*, Dennie laughed to herself. She compared herself to the girl in the play *Our Town*. Not gorgeous, but pretty enough for "all normal purposes."

Dennie stretched and shook out her hair. It would feel good to swim for an hour before a light dinner. Then she would study for her last final. Tomorrow morning, the semester would be over. She looked forward to the sense of relief, accomplishment, and short-term euphoria.

At the moment Aimy was on her Pick Me Up rounds with Sean, who had arrived last night. Dennie heard two of her other roommates, Rhonda Landon and Kim Squire, cracking up in the kitchen as they played Monopoly with a couple of guys in the ward. The telephone rang.

"Den, it's for you!" Kim called out. "It's your mom!"

Dennie fastened a towel around her waist and tucked her sandals, shorts, and a T-shirt under her arm. She hurried into the kitchen and lifted the telephone lying on the counter.

"Mom," Dennie said.

Dennie couldn't hear her mother's response as one of the guys shouted, "Nooo!" Kim jumped up and hurrahed. Then, she wiggled her hips as she jigged around the room. "Pay up! Park Place is mine! Motels and all!"

"Hang on, Mom," Dennie laughed as she watched Kim. "I'm on my way to the bedroom."

Closing the door behind her, Dennie sat down on the bed. She and her mother chatted cheerfully about Dennie's flight home tomorrow and their plans for the summer. Then, just when Dennie thought the conversation was concluding, the inflection of her mother's voice altered. "Honey, there's one more thing."

"What?" Dennie asked. Dennie's smile fell as she listened to her mother's sweet, soft voice explain that an Indian woman in Chile recently surfaced, claiming to be Dennie's grandmother, desiring to make contact.

"Why would she suddenly show up after all these years?" Dennie questioned.

"I don't know, honey. I'll find out all I can and we'll talk more about this when you are home. Dad and I love you and miss you. We're excited about the summer together."

"Me too," Dennie said. But her voice sounded off-key.

Ten minutes later, as Dennie floated on her back, thinking about everything, questions scorched her. *Why didn't this woman care about me when I was a little girl? What does she want? Letters? Pictures? Money? To come to the United States? To meet me in Chile? What would Thes think if he were still alive?*

After Dennie finished swimming, she climbed out of the pool to find Esteban sitting in a chair, clad in navy dress slacks, a white shirt, and a tie. He watched her, smiling. She sat down in a chair next to him. "How did your meeting go?" she asked as she wrung out her hair and pulled on her T-shirt and shorts.

"Good. The FARMS team wants me to continue my research and report back to them in the fall."

"Great." Dennie smiled.

"You seem . . . what is the word? Busy with other thoughts?"

"Preoccupied?" Dennie suggested.

Esteban nodded. "I've been here watching you swim, but you didn't notice."

Dennie studied her wrinkled, water-soaked fingers. "Esteban, my mom called and told me something concerning my past."

"Let's go on a walk and talk," Esteban suggested.

They strolled together on the grounds of the complex, Esteban's arm around Dennie's shoulders. His sleeves were rolled up, his olive skin contrasting sharply and appealingly with the whiteness of his shirt. Dennie told him about the Indian woman who claimed to be her grandmother. They stopped and sat down on the grass, side by side, Esteban's slacks against Dennie's skin.

"I already knew this," Esteban said, his voice soft in her ear. She smelled of sun and chlorine. He continued speaking. "My father sent me an e-mail a few days ago. Your grandmother is Mapuche Indian, a *machi*."

"A *machi*?" Dennie repeated. The word meant nothing to her.

"A *machi* is a Mapuche healer, usually a woman, and considered holy." Esteban explained. "She is not like other Indian women. She never does domestic work, only the work of the machi. She knows the curative powers of plants and herbs. She knows the ancient, secret prayers and religious rites of the Mapuche people and is said to speak with the voice of the spirits and dream prophetic dreams. Her shamanistic skills are used in a healing ritual called a *machitun*. Members of the community pay the machi for her prayers and healing services. Although the machi has the ability to curse, it is said that she uses her power for good. She is opposite of the witch, the *kalku*. However, if tragedy and sickness occur, sometimes a machi is accused of being a *kalku*."

"And what do *you* think she is, Esteban? A supposed witch or a holy woman?"

"A *machi*, Dennie. There is no other word to describe this woman. And she is your grandmother."

"And is it customary for a *machi* to allow her daughter and grand-children to starve and die in the streets?" Dennie could not keep the bitterness out of her voice. "Because that is what happened, Esteban. My birth mother died of starvation and exposure. Perhaps alcoholism as well. They think she was a prostitute. My brother and I would have probably died too, if the police hadn't found us and taken us to your father. After we were adopted, my brother hoarded food because he knew what hunger was. There are a few things I remember."

A cool April breeze chilled Dennie. She began shaking in her damp swimsuit. Esteban wrapped his arms around her. "Why don't you come to Chile with me and ask your grandmother what happened?" Esteban suggested.

"I don't know," Dennie said and was silent. Esteban continued, "When she grows old, each machi takes an apprentice, a young woman who trains for at least two years to be the next machi. Then, after the training, there is a three-day initiatory ceremony where the young woman is given to the people as their machi. Under the holy canelo tree, the new machi is presented with her sacred tools—her *kultrun*, or drum, and her *wada*, or rattle. She uses these, as well as herbs, to heal and bless the people. Dennie, your grandmother is old and feeble. She has not found an apprentice."

Dennie's head tilted back as she looked at Esteban. A hard, concentrated look entered her eyes. "You think my grandmother wants me to be the new machi, don't you?"

Esteban shrugged and looked at the grass. "It makes no sense. But, my father thinks that might be the case. Your grandmother told him that God spoke and desires you to come. God told her that you have the soul of a Mapuche."

Suddenly Dennie laughed. "Oh, Esteban, she's wrong. I'm as *North* American as apple pie. Can't you just see me, sitting under a tree, shaking a rattle and beating on a drum? I did that in kindergarten."

Esteban kissed her ear. "Perhaps the machi is not completely wrong. Come with me to Chile, Dennie," he said. "Perhaps God really wants you there. Not to become a machi, but to teach a machi the gospel."

Sean sat back in the passenger seat with his fingers woven behind his head and relaxed as he watched his girlfriend drive a giddy, seven-year-old girl to ballet, two sixth-grade boys to baseball practice, and three, gum-chewing preteens to the mall.

"Now we grab a few groceries for my favorite client, Augustus Waverly, before we pick them all up!" Aimy said as she drove her Yellow Toy toward the grocery store. In the supermarket, Sean ran after Aimy as she scampered through the aisles grabbing a TV dinner, a bag of apples, a box of Frosted Flakes, and a half-gallon of milk. "This should hold Wave down," Aimy announced as she paid for the groceries. They speed-walked to the car.

"With this job, you don't need to work out," Sean commented.

"I'm on a schedule, Bucko." Aimy grinned as they climbed in. "Sean, you're going to love Wave. I wanted to hurry so we have a few minutes to spend with him."

As Aimy sped back to Provo, she explained how she was assigned to work with Waverly as part of her clinical experience during fall semester. He had wanted to learn to read, and Aimy was the BYU student assigned to teach him. Before their first tutoring session, she had felt some anxiety. How could she relate to this handicapped, short, bald man with glasses as thick as a peanut butter sandwich? But upon being introduced, he had grasped her hand and shook it warmly. He had then announced that she could call him Waverly. At the conclusion of the session, he had grinned and with sheepish pride confided that he was sixty inches tall, sixty years old, and two hundred and sixty pounds. Aimy had responded by telling him that she was twenty years old, one hundred and twenty pounds, and had twenty cavities. He had slapped his legs and laughed heartily.

"Wave laughs easily," Aimy explained to Sean as she parked in the lot of Waverly's apartment complex. "But he cries easily too. His parents are dead and he doesn't have any brothers or sisters, just a cousin who lives in New York. During our last session Wave got all teary eyed and said that he wished I were his granddaughter. I told him about Pick Me Up and said I ran granddaughter service for free. I visit Wave a couple of times a week—take him to the grocery store and the doctor. Stuff like that."

"That's cool," Sean said. "And very nice."

Once inside the apartment, Aimy stood with her hands on her hip pockets as she watched Sean use the apples to demonstrate how to juggle. He glanced and grinned at Aimy before starting. Her fitted, pale yellow T-shirt contrasted sharply to the bagginess of her worn denim overalls. With no makeup on, she looked younger than her twenty-one years.

Trying to conceal her amazement at Sean's skill, Aimy yawned. Before her eyes he juggled three apples while eating one of the three. Using his mouth like an appendage, he bit the third apple each time it came around. Juice and bits of fruit sprayed out of his mouth as he chewed wildly with eyes focused on the apples, hands juggling steadily—bite, toss, toss, bite, toss, toss . . .

Waverly tried to follow suit. He picked up two apples and threw them high in the air. He stumbled trying to catch the first, and they both hit the linoleum.

"Rats!" Waverly exclaimed. Aimy bent down and picked up the bruised apples.

"He's very talented," Waverly grimaced as he watched Sean with envy.

"He's a show-off," Aimy commented as she grinned at Waverly encouragingly. Augustus Waverly. One year ago she wouldn't have imagined that an elderly, mentally disabled adult would become her dear friend.

The two watched Sean complete his juggling feat by spitting out the third apple's core, then holding the other two apples in the air like they were trophies. Waverly clapped and hurrahed.

Sean winked at Wave and said, "While Aimy's been off getting educated, I've been practicing!" Aimy whisked a broom and dustpan out of the closet and handed them to Sean. "Sweep," she commanded.

"Yes, Highness," Sean mocked. Waverly cracked up, his stomach rolling beneath his T-shirt with laughter.

"Wave," Aimy said after Sean finished tidying the kitchen, "We have to jam. I've got a bunch of kids to pick up."

"Sure. Thanks for getting the groceries." A tinge of loneliness shaded Waverly's voice. As they walked toward the door, Waverly suddenly stuck out his hand and shook Sean's. "I like you. Aimy told me you were funny!"

"Funny, huh! Not handsome? Not charming?" Sean sighed and rolled his eyes. He put his arm around Aimy. "I'm her slave."

Waverly chuckled delightedly. "Her Royal Highness and her slave. That's a good one. Did you know that Aimy is like a granddaughter to me? She is like a shiny jewel in a puddle of mud."

Aimy smiled and kissed Waverly affectionately on the cheek. "Bye, Wave."

"I'll see you the day after tomorrow," Waverly responded. "Six o'clock sharp."

"Great." Aimy waved as she took Sean's hand and whisked him out the door.

"He's a sweet old guy," Sean commented on their way out to the car. "I like him. But why are we stopping by the morning we leave? Maybe we should tell him good-bye sometime tomorrow."

Aimy avoided the question by scrambling into the driver's side of her car, putting the key in the ignition, and revving the engine. Sean hurriedly opened the passenger door and climbed in, closing the door as the car began to move.

"I'm glad you like Waverly," Aimy said, pretending to be casual as she stepped on the gas. "Because I've invited Wave to come with us to California for his summer vacation."

"Really?"

"And I thought it would be a great idea if he stayed in your apartment."

"What? You're kidding, right?"

"Come on, Sean-nee," Aimy cajoled. "He doesn't have a family. He's never seen the Sierras or San Francisco."

"You're serious. You're talking about the whole summer." Sean gaped at Aimy. His scalp looked red against his short, auburn hair.

"Essentially."

"Aimy, I have a microscopically small apartment. Esteban already asked if he could visit for a week or two. I don't have room for everybody and his dog."

"Wave doesn't have a dog. But I might get him one for Christmas."

"Aimy, I think it's great that you're befriending Waverly. But isn't this going too far? Is this some kind of a grandfather wish?"

"No!" Aimy's temperature rose as she wheeled the car into the parking lot of a dance studio. "I want to do something special for him, Sean! His heart is weak. Who knows how many summers he has left! Mom's going to be in Texas for a month, and I didn't think it would be appropriate to have Waverly stay in the house with just me!"

Sean sucked in a deep breath. He hadn't flown to Utah yesterday for a knockdown, drag-out fight with Aimy. They usually proved futile anyhow. "Take it easy," he said, trying to eliminate the frustration in his voice. "I'll think about it. It was just that I was looking forward to twelve hours alone in the car with you. There are a lot of things we need to talk about."

Aimy's mood switched directions. She reached over and kissed Sean. "Sean, we'll have plenty of time alone once we're home. I'll be working for you at Beef Burgers all summer long, remember?"

Sean felt himself softening. He ran his fingers though her short, blonde hair, noticing that it was a bit winter-golden now, not as white-blonde as in the summer. A little girl in a pink leotard bounced out to the car. Aimy exited the Toyota, cheerfully greeted the child, then tucked her into a seat belt while Sean thought of that summer Sunday, nearly four years ago, when he had decided to love Aimy—as if it had been a choice.

It happened in late August. Aimy and her nonmember mother, who had just been released from a drug rehab program, attended fast and testimony meeting. From his pew, Sean had focused on Aimy as she had walked up to the microphone. For a second she had stood there at the pulpit trembling, her shoulders curved forward as if her body insisted she sob.

But instead of breaking, Aimy had thrust her shoulders back and fiercely blinked away her tears. Her voice had not cracked as she had thanked God for her testimony, her friends, her mother, and her bishop. With her blue eyes shiny through a screen of unshed tears, Aimy had looked to Sean like a living candle which, by sheer strength of will, refused to be blown out. Sean had decided at that moment that, although he was a returned missionary and she a wispy girl of seventeen, he wanted nothing more than to be warmed by that fire within Aimy forever. He would wait for her to grow up. Now, four years later, it still hadn't happened, and at times he felt like a glutton for punishment.

Sean sighed as Aimy drove. Once they finished the rounds and were back in the Glenwood parking lot, finally alone, he held Aimy's pixie face between his hands. He kissed her, then sat back and drank in the look of her blue, determined eyes. "Augustus Waverly can stay with me," Sean relented. Then he added, half-joking, "But if he lets gas or snores, he's on the street."

"Thank you, Sean. I'll make it up to you." Aimy's eyes danced and she scurried out of the car before Sean had time to open the door for her. Sean sucked in a deep breath and let it out slowly as he exited the vehicle. He knew that Aimy had had a hard life. She had survived poverty, an abusive stepfather, and a dysfunctional mother. Was that why she seemed intent on eluding him? What was it that Waverly had called her—a diamond in a mud puddle? Was the mud of her past so thick around the diamond of her heart that he might never be able to claim it for his own?

Aimy opened the door to their apartment. Dennie and Esteban sat at the table, eating leftover pizza. But Dennie didn't appear hungry. She had only chewed off a small bite of her piece. In contrast, Esteban's piece was nearly gone. But instead of eating it with his hands, he cut a portion off with a table knife and lifted it to his mouth with a fork.

"Hey, y'all!" Sean announced as he entered the apartment an instant behind Aimy. He reached for his girlfriend and pulled her to him, stretching his arms around her and cupping his hands at her waist. "Did you know that Aimy invited Waverly to spend the summer with us in Grantlin? Wave called her a *diamond in a mud puddle*. What do you think of that!"

"I think it's sweet," Dennie looked up at her friend and smiled, though there was a distracted look in her dark eyes.

"Aimy—a diamond—yes," Esteban added after he swallowed. "This place—a mud puddle—no. Perhaps a pig sty."

Aimy laughed and wiggled free of Sean. Esteban threw his paper plate in the trash, then stood up and stretched. "I'll see you later. Dennie told me she needs to study tonight." Dennie walked him outside to his bike.

"Take care little one," he said as he kissed her. Then he shouldered his backpack and mounted his bike. As he rode away, Dennie noticed how his white shirt shone in the twilight. She headed back toward the apartment.

"I like Esteban," Sean commented when she entered. He put Esteban's fork and knife into the sink. "But I don't trust him. Dennie, I think you should keep writing Ron."

"Ha!" Aimy laughed as she flicked a dish towel at Sean. "That's almost exactly what Esteban said to me!"

"He thinks you should keep writing Ron Babcock?" Sean grabbed the dish towel in the middle of a second flick and used it to pull Aimy to him.

"He wasn't talking about Ron and you know it! But maybe Esteban's right—maybe I shouldn't trust you!" Aimy hung onto the dish towel and was drawn into Sean's arms. She waved to Dennie as they kissed.

Dennie slipped out of the kitchen and into the bedroom. She opened her chemistry book and sat on her bed, a pillow separating her back from the wall. She had to concentrate. If she was going to be a nurse someday, her grades needed to be high. But she felt inexplicably tired. She remembered Ron showing her how to push through walls of exhaustion when they went running together. The second wind would come. Tonight she was determined to push through her personal barrier of weariness and confusion. She would study and put her Mapuche grandmother on the back burner until after tomorrow's final.

Dennie found it difficult to focus, though she forced her eyes on the book for over two hours. Finally she put her book away, donned a summer nightgown, turned off the light, and lay in bed, drained yet unable to sleep.

Sometime later Aimy quietly entered the room.

"I'm awake," Dennie said softly. Aimy noticed a catch in her friend's voice.

"What's wrong?" she asked.

Then, with tears in her eyes, Dennie told Aimy of the machi who claimed to be her grandmother. Aimy hugged Dennie after she finished the story. Then, because Dennie could not sleep, Aimy turned on the lamp and they gave themselves pedicures and manicures. Afterwards, they talked into the wee hours of the morning about the families they hoped to have someday, and the names they would pick out for their children.

The next evening, Esteban drove Dennie to the airport in Aimy's car. On the way to the airport, Dennie sat quietly in the passenger seat while Esteban played Latin love songs on the stereo. He sang along as he drove. She studied their intertwined hands. Esteban's fingers were shorter than one would expect for his height—wide nailed and thickly knuckled. The skin tone was so similar to her own. He stroked her hand with his thumb and continued to sing along with the music. Dennie's Spanish was good and she knew the words. The song was about a lover at sunrise. She heard certain words over and over again—*amante*, lover; and *amanecida*, dawn. She hummed along.

After the song ended, Esteban gently took his hand out of Dennie's and turned off the music. "So, shall I fly to California in two weeks and take you back to Chile with me?" he asked. Dennie folded her hands in her lap, not knowing how to answer. She heard the hum of the tires, the smell of the freeway, of rubber meeting the road. She watched the semi-truck in front of them.

"Come to Chile with me," he said once more.

"I don't think my dad will let me go," Dennie sighed as she spoke. "He won't even let me drive back to California with Aimy. He likes things safe, in control."

"Dennie, you are an adult now and must make your own decisions. Your grandmother is old. My father said that she was coughing, perhaps sick. This might be your only chance to meet her. The Mapuche are a fascinating people, Dennie. I've been studying them for four years, yet I have never been able to get close to a machi. Although my grandfather was Indian, they still consider me a *winka*, an outsider."

"Is this my last chance to meet my grandmother, or your chance to meet a machi?"

Esteban's eyes darkened in frustration, and his voice did not carry its usual warmth when he answered. "How can you say this, Dennie? She is your grandmother, not mine."

"My grandmother is German," Dennie countered. "She was a child in Germany during World War II. She came to my sealing in the temple. Her name is Elsa Hudsfeldt Fletcher."

"There are German settlements in southern Chile," Esteban answered, his sentences parallel to Dennie's, not intersecting. "The Germans took land from the Mapuche. Yet your Chilean father was not Mapuche. Your grandmother told Dad he was *winka*. His Chilean roots were probably European."

"My other grandmother lives in Virginia. She is a descendent of John Howland from the *Mayflower*. I hardly know her. But she is my grandmother, Esteban! Not this woman in Chile!"

"Dennie, why is it so hard for you to accept the fact that you are Chilean?"

"Esteban, I am sealed to my parents. They are my family."

"Yes. But, that is not all of what you are. This Mapuche blood flows in my veins as well. It is the blood of Lehi and Nephi. Dennie, the Mapuche religion and culture have remained intact since before the Europeans came to the New World. There are many similarities to Book of Mormon cultures. I would like to teach you about this. Your grandmother is a machi, and the machi are the spiritual strength of the Mapuche. They keep the culture alive. Yet the people's belief in them is waning. I don't know if this is good or bad for the Mapuche.

Dennie, I want to help this people. Mapuche men are losing themselves in drink. Mapuche girls fill the brothels of Chile. Sometimes it seems as if I can sense these people's tears—tears they are crying because they do not know who they are."

Thoughts of Thes and her birth mother invaded through Dennie's consciousness. Her birth mother had been destitute. Did she sell her body to feed her children? Her brother had become a teenage alcoholic, and Dennie had not been able to help him. Her brother and birth mother had not known or understood their intrinsic worth as children of God.

Esteban continued. "Remember what Sean said—a diamond in a mud puddle. Many Mapuche people have souls like diamonds, but they live their lives as if they were only the mud of Chile."

The two spoke very little the rest of the way. When they stood at the airport gate, waiting for the call that would signal Dennie to board the airplane, she reached up and put her hands on Esteban's shoulders. Looking into his brown eyes, she tried to perceive what was truly inside of him. But she could not see into his soul. Instead, as the light from a window bounced off the darkness of his eyes, she only saw a reflection of herself.

"I'll talk to my parents tonight," she said softly.

"I'll call you tomorrow," he responded as a voice over a microphone announced the final boarding call for Dennie's flight.

Esteban kissed her forehead. "Te quiero." *I love you,* he said as he held her. Dennie kissed him quickly before turning and stepping into the tunnel that led to the airplane. Ten minutes later, as the aircraft sliced through the sky, she took out the manuscript she had printed out that morning, the one her mother had sent her via e-mail. It was the first chapter of the book her mother was writing. It was the story of Dennie Fletcher's *Mayflower* ancestors.

CHAPTER 4

MY LOVE SHALL FOLLOW THEE

London, 1620

Desire Minter smoothed her skirts and took a quick breath as she wiped moisture from her brow. The blonde hair beneath her bonnet felt sticky from the work of cooking supper and tending the fire. Deftly she poked a stick into the blaze and pushed a portion of the embers to the side of the hearth for baking biscuits. Then she added meat to the pot and nourished the flame beneath it with dry wood. With her apron she wiped the moisture from her round face. She was sixteen years old, fair skinned, and more stout than tall.

She turned, and her transparent blue eyes fixed on the mulish hound that stretched on the rug nearby. "I am truly glad to be sailing on the Mayflower *in seven days hence," she said aloud to the dog. The animal yawned, as if it bored him the way she tried to convince herself of the rightness of her fate.*

"Excellent yawn," she replied, flicking a bit of ash his way. Then she went to the dog, knelt down, and rubbed his soft belly while she told him her woes. "Now, I couldn't have stayed in Leyden last year with mother and her new husband, could I? Not with Mr. Roger Symondsen sitting in Father's chair—and Father not even being dead a year. Mr. Symondsen measured every bit of bread I ate! It was a blessing when Mistress Carver took me in to help her. She has been both a mother and a friend to me."

A cheerful voice boomed out from behind the door. "Desire Minter, beware of who might be listening outside!" A young man four years older than Desire entered the house with color in his cheeks. His rust-colored hair and darker beard dripped from the rain. Thin-legged, of average height, and laughing, he bent down near Desire and stroked the dog now stretching blissfully on the earthen floor.

"John Howland, how could you stand outside the door, like a thief, stealing words not meant for any man's ear?" the girl demanded, standing up and smoothing her skirts. Red spots appeared on her round cheeks.

"Perhaps you will favor a man with your conversation rather than a cur." John's eye twinkled teasingly.

"John Howland, do you presume you are that man?" laughed Desire. *"But the Carvers are not here currently. They went to secure provisions for the journey. You must go and come back later. For though you are not a saint, John, I am."*

"Desire," John's voice changed from light to earnest as he stood to face her. *"Spare me a moment. It is you I must speak to before any other. You, the lass who noticed the stone in my heart as I toiled in my brother's drapery shop, the friend who told me about the Separatist Saints and their dream to build lives in the New World as Englishmen and Englishwomen—yet free of the yoke of the English crown."*

"John." As she spoke, Desire wondered if it was remorse that bent her voice to a whisper. *"I set sail next week, and will most likely never see you or the shores of England again."*

"The former is not true, though the latter is!" John spoke in a merry riddle. *"I too am going on the* Mayflower*!"* he explained. *"Despite my age, John Carver has chosen to take me as his indentured servant. Deacon Carver is pious and stern, but it shall be a grand adventure!"* He threw his arms wide as if he would embrace her.

"Master Howland," Desire declared as she ducked away from him, for an instant feigning offense. *"I have lived with the Carvers for more than a year. Deacon Carver is as kind as he is pious; and he is fair, not stern!"* Then she broke into a grin and exclaimed, *"John, I am happy for you!"*

"We shall be merry companions, Desire! We shall sing the jolly songs of England all the way to the New World!"

Desire laughed out loud as John Howland sang and danced about the room:

Let the wealthy and great,
Roll in splendor and state,
I envy them not I declare it.
I'll be my own man, have chicken and ham,

I'll sheer my own fleece and I'll wear it.
So, be jolly now
God speed's the call
Long life and success to all!

Desire heard the murmur of voices in the street. "John." She put her fingers to her lips to caution him, though the timbre of her own voice echoed his gladness. "The elders will not allow us to sing the merry songs of England on the ship. Will you grow weary when we sing the psalms all the way to the New World? Mistress Carver said that the ship is as small as the ocean is wide. And that it is late in the year to begin such a journey. I pray the winds will be favorable. Are you sure you want to come?"

John stopped dancing. He was quiet for a moment as he squatted on the floor once more and rubbed the dog's long ears. As the moment grew somber, Desire recited the psalm her mother used to chant while delivering babies as midwife to the saints in Leyden:

O Lord of Hosts, how amiable are thy Tabernacles
My soul longeth; yea, and fainted for the courts of the Lord
For my heart and my flesh rejoice in the living God.
Yea, the sparrow hath found her a house,
And the swallow a nest for her,
Where she may lay her young
Even by thine altars, O Lord of Hosts
My King and my God.

John's eyes met Desire's, and his voice was calm as still water when he spoke. "The psalms are beautiful too, Desire. The elders are honest men whom I shall learn from. And our friendship shall seem like a spring of fresh water, though all the sea be salty!"

"John Howland, I am glad you are coming!" Desire burst out.

John grinned and raised his auburn eyebrows. "I am no saint, Desire Minter. But, perhaps piety shall rub off from the company I keep as the cur's hair cleaves to my glove." He lifted a gloved hand covered with hairs from the dog. Desire laughed.

"I'm not sure that the suit of piety will fit you, John!" she declared.

"I can change suits as quickly as any of Shakespeare's troupe," John rejoined. "I must go now. Keep a merry heart, Desire. You shall have a friend on the Mayflower!"

Desire returned to tending the fire. As the day turned to evening and outside the sky glowed amber, her thoughts of John Howland were interrupted by a shape in the flames that brought to mind the curved slope of her mother's shoulder. She stared at the blaze and felt the sting of her mother's parting four months ago.

It had been an early morning, with the new sun spreading pink light in the sky, when the company gathered at the docks to bid farewell to those of their congregation heading for England first, and then, the New World.

"Desire," her mother had hissed into her ear, her embrace an iron grip. "The women will need help with childbearing. Remember, if a woman have a strong and hard labor: take four spoonful of another woman's milk, and give it to the woman to drink. If a woman have terrible pain, put the warm wool from a living sheep onto the place of pain."

Then her mother had begun shaking, her grip so tight that it bruised Desire's arms.

"Sarah, what is it?" Roger Symondsen had stepped between the mother and child, sundering the embrace.

"They will have no living sheep, Roger. They shall be intruders and pilgrims in that land. Desire will have no home or hearth."

"Peace, Sarah. Heaven is the only safe harbor. At present, John Carver has given her a home. Give Desire Minter the pocket, Sarah, for we must go."

With red hands, Sarah Symondsen had gained composure and untied a brown cloth pocket, heavy with items, from her waist and tied it around her daughter's. "There are medicines in it, child. And a book of housewifery. Also, the psalms."

"She is no longer a child, Sarah," Roger had said quietly.

"Thank you, Mum," Desire had mumbled, for it seemed her voice would not work properly.

"Our incessant prayers to the Lord will be with you on this hopeful journey," Roger Symondsen had said as if it were an announcement.

"Good-bye, my child." The voice that usually rasped with efficiency shook with emotion. "Though I be bodily absent, my love shall follow thee."

"Good-bye Mother," Desire had uttered as a hotness burned her eyes. How could it be that since her father's death one year ago, she had felt only bitterness towards her own mum?

She closed her eyes and reflected on her own nature. Though she had inherited her mother's capable hands, she had her father's roundness and kindly nature. Yet why did her compassion not extend to this woman who had given her birth? Her father once told her that the years of poverty and exile in Holland caused Desire's mother to become brutally efficient and seemingly indifferent to suffering. "That is not Sarah's true nature," he had said.

Yet, Desire thought as she tended the fire in London, how wrong her good father had been. How differently he would have viewed Sarah had he known how scarce would be her tears at his death and how quickly she would wed another. For these acts in particular, Desire Minter could not forgive her own mother, even if her inability to forgive burned as red as any sin.

Dennie put the manuscript back into her backpack. In another half hour she would land in the Sacramento airport. She reached for one of two books Esteban had given her yesterday and suggested she read as she considered whether or not to travel to Chile. The book was titled *Ul: Four Mapuche Poets.* Dennie read the introduction and learned that *ul* meant "poetry" or "song." The *ul* of the Mapuche included the machi's song, the festival song, the song of disguise, and the sublime or incomparable song. She read bits and pieces of a machi's song: *Speak golden knife. May this city of the echo be a refuge for the ghost.* [1]

Then Dennie glanced through the table of contents and noticed a poem by Leonel Lienlaf called "The Ghost of Lautaro." She turned to it. It was about the legendary warrior, Lautaro, the one whom her brother had been named after. The poem spoke of Lautaro's spirit walking the mountains and the earth, restless, calling to his people.

A chill ran through Dennie. She pulled out the other book, a thick informational work about the history of Chile. She read of how the leaders of the Mapuche were called *Toqui* in times of strife and *Ulmen* in times of peace. The *Toqui* led the warriors, and the *Ulmen* sang the songs of the people.

Then she read of Lautaro. She learned of a young Mapuche boy who was kidnapped by the *conquistadores.* This youth was so intelligent that he was trained to be the page of conquistador Pedro de Valdivia, but when he was barely twenty years old, he escaped and returned to his people.

Lautaro knew the language, weapons, and weaknesses of the enemy. He was chosen as *Toqui.* He taught his warriors how to ride horses. He invented mounted infantry and guerilla warfare tactics. Within a four-year time span, Lautaro secured the southern territories, killed Pedro de Valdivia himself, and pressed north, burning Spanish forts until he reached the gates of Santiago. Only then was he betrayed and killed in his sleep by a traitor.

Dennie put down the book and closed her eyes. In her heart, she said a silent prayer, asking her Heavenly Father what she should do. Was it His will that she travel to Chile? She thought of Desire Minter and John Howland, those whom her mother breathed life into as she put words on a page. The manuscript was like a song, a poem, her mother's *ul*. But as Dennie accepted her adoptive parents' ancestors as her own, was she, in a sense, living a song of disguise? The legendary Lautaro had refused to do this. He had returned to his own people. And Dennie's brother, Theseus Lautaro, had been like a warrior, never forgetting, never able to completely accept what fate handed him. Always he had been driven to run faster than the clouds, to win at almost any cost.

Then a thought entered Dennie's soul and found root there. Of the two of them, Thes was the fighter, the *Toqui*. But Dennie loved peace and song. She was more like the *Ulmen*. She would find the answers to her questions about her and her brother's past. She would learn new songs. She would record their family history. Perhaps, as Esteban envisioned, she would teach as well. But she shivered even as she made the decision. Memories of Chile were as shadows in her mind, and she feared what might lurk in that darkness. *I'll go, Heavenly Father, if it is Thy will*, she whispered. *Please go with me.*

The next morning, Meryl Fletcher put down her scriptures and looked up when her husband emerged from the walk-in closet in his suit and tie. Downstairs they could hear Dennie's voice, but couldn't make out any words. She was talking to Esteban on the telephone. There was a stretch of silence.

"Esteban seems to be doing most of the talking," Rick mentioned. "Dennie's muffins smell good. I hope they're done before I leave."

"They should be," Meryl commented. She thought of how they had picked Dennie up at the Sacramento airport late the previous night. Though Dennie had seemed tired and a bit preoccupied, she had hugged her parents warmly. The house felt complete with her home again. Yet twenty minutes ago when Meryl had walked down the hallway to open the bedroom windows, she had overheard Dennie say something to Esteban about going to Chile.

"Rick," Meryl questioned. "What are we going to do if Dennie decides to go to Chile to meet Esteban's family and this phantom grandmother?"

"She hasn't even mentioned it. Let's cross that bridge when we come to it."

"She's going to mention it. That's what she's talking to Esteban about."

Rick took a deep breath. "If she thinks I will pay for her to fly halfway around the world with some man I don't know or trust, she'll have to think again."

Dennie's unexpected voice at the door caused her father to spin around and her mother to stand up. "Dad, I have thought about this—over and over again. I've prayed about it too. I've decided to go to Chile in two weeks. I'll pay for the ticket with my savings." Rick Fletcher stared at his daughter. She wore black sweatpants and a light green T-shirt. Her dark eyes looked at him with serious intent, and she was not smiling. The sun from the side window gave Dennie's long hair a liquid look—black, shiny, and flowing. Rick knew his daughter was beautiful, and this terrified him.

Dennie went on, addressing both her parents, "I'm an adult now. Not someone to discuss—but someone to discuss things with."

"Then let's discuss." Rick clapped his hands together as if waking himself up. "Dennie, you are an adult, but you are also our child. We only want what is best for you." He hoped his voice sounded reasonable, though he did not feel so inside. He felt frustrated—like he was losing his grip—like his little girl was slipping through his fingers into a shaky realm where he could not follow. His instinct was to close his fist around her, but he did not believe in iron force. She was an adult now. What could he do? His brow furrowed.

"Honey, sit down on the bed by me and let's talk," Meryl offered as she spread the quilt and lowered herself onto it. Dennie sat down next to her mother. Rick turned the desk chair around, took a seat, and faced them.

Meryl, always the peacemaker, began the conversation. "Dad and I just don't think it's safe for you go halfway around the world this summer. We don't know Esteban."

"He plans to spend a week out here before we fly to Chile," Dennie explained. "That way you can get to know him better."

"Are you two *that* serious?" Meryl questioned.

Dennie shrugged. "I guess it's heading that way."

Rick interrogated. "Has he asked you to marry him?"

"No," Dennie said quickly. "I'm not ready for that. I'm still writing Ron. I don't want to marry anybody for a year or two."

"Good!" Rick cut in.

"But going to Chile might cause Esteban to think you are more serious about him than you are," Meryl suggested. "Is that fair to him?"

"I don't know," Dennie answered honestly. "I don't want this trip to be just about Esteban and me. Esteban understands that. The trip is mostly about both of our heritages. I know so little about my birth family, and Esteban has a Mapuche grandfather who has passed away. Right now Esteban is working on a paper for FARMS on the Mapuche Indians—comparing and contrasting their culture to Book of Mormon cultures. The woman who says she's my grandmother is a *machi*—that's a Mapuche holy woman. She's sick. Spending time with her will greatly enhance Esteban's research and it might be my only opportunity to find out about the past."

"Isn't our family enough, Dennie?" Rick asked.

"That's not it, Dad. There are just things I need to know. Questions I need answered."

Meryl cut in. "We're just afraid—afraid you might be hurt. Dennie, when you're a parent, it's hard to let go, to entrust your children in other's hands, to send them off to a foreign country. It's a helpless feeling."

Dennie took her mother's hand and looked into her father's eyes. Rick Fletcher's eyes were the color of honey. His hair used to be the same color, but it was gray now, which made him look older. He had laser surgery last year and no longer wore glasses, except when he read. He was a shade shorter and more compact than his wife. His nose appeared smaller with his glasses gone.

Dennie's mother had aged as well. Dennie thought of how, just last night, Meryl had laughed about the additional touches of gray in her blonde hair, and Dennie had told her that the gray hairs looked like silver lights. But Dennie hadn't mentioned that she had also noticed wrinkles spreading in fine creases around Meryl's eyes and down the sides of her cheeks. Dennie loved her parents, and she had always tried to please them. Defiance did not sit well with her. Her heart pounded as she gathered her thoughts.

"Mom and Dad, you have always been more than enough for me. But when I was a little girl, I used to pretend that I had blonde hair, like you, Mom. I used to imagine when I went to sleep at night that I would wake up with skin as pink as the newborn doves that Grandma Elsa gave us. But different blood flows in my veins. You've always told me to be thankful for who I am, to be proud of myself. But when this grandmother surfaced, I didn't feel proud. I was ashamed. Why was she trying to find me now? Why didn't she care about me when I was a little girl? Didn't she love me?"

"Oh, Dennie, you can't assume that she didn't love you. We don't know that."

"That's why I have to go, Mom—because we don't know. Thes is gone. I'm the only one left. I have to know who we were and where we came from."

Rick Fletcher stared out the window. "You are sealed to us, Dennie. That's all that matters to us. That's all we have to know. I wish that was enough for you."

Dennie felt her eyes sting. "I'm sorry, Dad."

Meryl took her daughter's hand. She said quietly, "Though I be bodily absent, my love shall follow thee."

"What?" Rick said.

"It's a line from my novel," Meryl explained. "Something a mother says to her daughter before the girl sails on the *Mayflower*. Dennie, wherever you go, our love will follow you and be a part of you. We are sealed to each other."

Dennie hugged her mother. She wished she could erase the lines of worry and age from her parents' faces. She and her brother had brought them joy, but they had brought them terrible pain as well. Dennie took a deep breath and forced herself not to weep. "Come downstairs, Dad. The blueberry muffins are done. That's what I came up to tell you."

CHAPTER 5

ANGELS IN THE SAND

Aimy loved the feel of the wheels beneath her as her Yellow Toy cut away the miles and galloped over the salt flats. She remembered when she first learned to drive how she used to be afraid to turn left into traffic. But those days were over now. Driving gave her a feeling of power and independence. She would much rather be on the road than high above the clouds flying in an airplane, feeling as if she had no control. Waverly's snores rumbled from the back seat.

"Well, he snores," Sean remarked from the seat next to her.

"Yeah, he snores," Aimy repeated and she started to giggle. Sean threw a pillow at her.

"Knock it off!" Aimy whispered. "You could cause an accident or wake up Waverly."

"Waking up Wave would be worse," Sean whispered back.

"Say that five times fast," Aimy suggested. Sean took a drink of his soda and massaged his lips before attempting. Afterward, they both cracked up. Then Waverly moaned in his sleep, causing Sean and Aimy to freeze. When his snoring continued, they breathed once more.

"So, are you glad to be leaving Happy Valley?" Sean asked. "BYU is one tough school."

"It's way harder than Grantlin Community College! I had a 4.0 from GCC when I started at BYU last fall. Now I'm lucky to have a 3.0."

"Maybe you should transfer to Sac State. I hear they have a decent Special Education program."

"But Dennie's not at Sac State. I missed her my freshman and sophomore years when she was at BYU and I was at GCC. I felt like I was left behind."

Those were the years we became close, Sean thought. *Those were the years we fell in love. Do you plan on leaving me behind now?* He suddenly felt afraid, afraid of losing the young woman he wanted so much to be his wife. Yet when he spoke, his voice didn't sound afraid, just sarcastic and even bitter. "So, how do I rate? You would rather live with Dennie than me."

Ruffled, Aimy responded. "No, Sean. You know that my grades in high school were crap. I had to work long hours at Beef Burgers, and I couldn't concentrate with Mom strung out all the time. I didn't get straight A's at GCC just so I could live near Dennie. I worked my butt off so I could get accepted at Brigham Young University, so I could be *somebody*!"

"Aimy, you are *somebody*! We have *something*! But we could lose it. I can't wait forever."

"I know. If I go on a mission, we can get married right when I get back. I'll transfer to Sac State and finish there, if that's what you want."

"If that's what *I* want? Don't *you* want it too? And what's this about a mission? You've never mentioned it before. Is it an excuse because maybe you don't want *me* anymore?" Sean sounded incredulous.

"It's not about you, Sean."

"It's not about me?"

"Sean, everything's coming out all wrong. It's just that I want to share the gospel. What's wrong with that?"

"Aimy, you can raise a righteous family. You can teach the gospel to friends in your community. Every member a missionary."

"It's not the same."

"I can't believe this," Sean growled. "I love you and want to marry you, and you want to go on a mission. I thought we had plans."

It made Aimy mad—the way Sean didn't even *try* to understand. Didn't he see that she loved him, but she was afraid of getting married too soon, afraid of losing all she had worked so hard to achieve? She thought of her mother's failed marriages and the years of poverty and want. Her life was not going to be like that! She couldn't stop her voice from rising in a shaking crescendo. "You went on a mission! Girls wait for guys all the time! Why won't you wait for me?"

"Most girls don't wait. Ninety percent of my companions' girl-friends got married while they were on their missions. And I've already waited for four years. We could lose everything. We could lose each other," Sean flashed back.

In the heat of their discussion, they didn't perceive that the snores in the backseat had ceased. But they did hear Waverly's low, embarrassed voice when he said, "Aimy, I have to use the bathroom. Could we stop soon?"

"Sure, Wave," Aimy returned in a valiant effort to keep the edge out of her voice. "There's a rest area in two miles."

For a few moments silence reigned. Then Aimy pulled off the freeway and halted the car in a parking place. "Thanks," Waverly said, smiling tentatively as he slowly climbed out of the car. Then he added, "I love trips."

"I do too!" Aimy forced her biggest grin.

"I'm really loving this trip as well," Sean muttered dismally as he climbed out of the car and shut the door. "I'm thoroughly loving it."

Aimy stood outside the Toyota and watched Sean as he climbed the ramp behind the bathrooms. At the top of the ramp there was a viewing platform. Sean stopped and stared at the miles of white-gray salt fields stretching to the horizon like a surreal desert. A backdrop of blue-gray mountains loomed in the distance, dark shapes cut out against the sky.

As Aimy looked at Sean, something twisted inside of her. She said a silent prayer, for she didn't want to lose him. Yet in a shadowy part of her mind, a basement room in her consciousness, she could not shake her terror of marriage. If only she hadn't seen her mother's relationships turn from romance to meanness and despair. Could she do any better? She looked around her at the barren salt. Lot's wife had looked back on her old life and had become a pillar of salt. Aimy's religion teacher last semester had pointed out that the biblical woman didn't have the faith and strength to start over again.

Aimy ran up the ramp, her hair golden in the sun. "Sean," she gasped when she reached him, her voice low and tentative. "I love you."

He turned and looked at her, wanting to touch her, to hold her, to tell her that he adored her. But instead he said, "Aimy, why do you *really* want to go on a mission? Is it me?"

She prayed as she tried to explain. "No. I was only thirteen when I joined the Church, but it changed my life. It taught me who I was and that Heavenly Father and Jesus really *cared* about me. You don't know what it's like to understand for the first time that someone gave His life for you. It was—I don't know—stunning. Sometimes when I was really afraid, when Mom was half-dead on the couch from drugs or had boyfriends over, it felt like Jesus was wrapping His arms around me, protecting me. I wonder if I should give that back before I settle down forever."

Sean took Aimy's hand. He said quietly, "I can understand that."

"That's not the only reason," she whispered. "I'm afraid that if we married, we would lose what we have. I'm afraid that we wouldn't make it."

Sean put his arm around her. Then he spoke. "Aimy, if we are sealed in the temple, we are bound to each other and to God by a covenant. There aren't any absolute guarantees, but if we are committed to each other forever, we have as much of a chance as anyone. But I have to know if you are willing to take that risk when the time comes, whether it's before or after a mission. I have to know."

"I'm going to figure that out. This summer," Aimy whispered. Then she put her arms around Sean's neck and laid her head on his chest. They held each other until Augustus Waverly hailed them with sweeping waves of his arms and happy shouts from the bottom of the ramp.

Four hours later as Sean drove across the desert, Aimy helped Waverly read the road signs. Together they sounded out a sign that read *Prison Area—Hitchhiking Prohibited.*

Waverly's mouth screwed up in concentration as he thought about the sign for a few minutes. Then Wave broke into a laugh, exclaiming, "Well, they better not let the prisoners hitchhike! They're supposed to be locked up!"

"You're right about that, Buddy," Sean said.

Aimy dozed for a time. She awakened as they approached a group of mobile homes that seemed to have grown up like a handful of weary plants in the middle of the desert. On a hill in the center of this lone, dilapidated bunch was a slightly larger trailer home on a riser. It was painted dark purple, with a cardboard spire and corrugated turrets on each corner.

"Will you look at that!" Waverly exclaimed. "It's a castle."

"No, Wave. It's a fake," Aimy said, feeling suddenly and inexplicably depressed. "It's a cheap home on wheels." *It's like you,* something whispered inside of Aimy. *A piece of nothing, dressed up like a BYU student, pretending to be important.* Aimy shook her head. What was wrong with her? What kind of a person relates to a stupid trailer?

"You're too hard on it. It's a gallant little mobile home with courageous dreams," Sean countered. He looked at her, and there was softness in his eyes as if he understood.

"Like the little engine that could!" Waverly announced.

"Exactly." Sean nodded.

At that moment, Aimy nearly burst with love for the two men sitting in the car with her. "I wonder where the people who live in those mobile homes go shopping!" she said, laughing delightedly. Then, as she looked out the front window, the silver-edged clouds overlaying the sun reminded her of the shape of an angel that a child might make by laying in the sand and moving the surface of the world with her own outstretched arms.

Sunday came and Karin Taylor, over six months pregnant and pink-cheeked beneath her freckles, sat up in her bed at 6:30 in the morning to kiss her husband good-bye. Today he would be ordained as the bishop of the Grantlin First Ward.

Blake bent over her, wearing a white shirt and a suit. After the kiss, she fingered his conservative silk tie. "No Pinnochio tie today?" she teased, referring to a tie constructed of wooden strips that Blake wore regularly two years ago to entertain his seminary students.

"I thought about it," Blake joked. "Maybe next week, when the stake presidency isn't visiting. I could wear my wooden tie and bring my guitar."

"And wear your trench coat. You'll have the youth eating out of your hands," Karin laughed.

"And President Butler questioning his own inspiration," Blake chuckled. "But, seriously, will you be OK getting the kids ready by yourself this morning? Dennie offered to come over. That way it might be easier to make it to sacrament meeting on time."

"I'm fine."

"Sure?"

"Ahh, so the new bishop doesn't want his own wife to miss the announcement?"

"I want at least one person to consent."

"Or dissent," Karin laughed. "Don't worry, Blake. Today I really will be on time. Last night I ironed the boys' clothes, checked my hose for runs, and put the diaper bag and scriptures on the kitchen table. We're A-OK, Bishop. Ready for takeoff."

"Roger, Sister Taylor." He grinned and saluted her before leaving the house.

Karin showered, dressed, and set Sabbath music to play on the stereo. Chris came into the living room already dressed for church. She complimented him and went to wake up the twins. Ten minutes later, as she fed her crew breakfast, she reminded them that Sunday was a special day and they needed to remember to be reverent.

"And today is especially special because Dad's going to be made bishop," Christopher said wisely as he stuffed an entire pancake into his mouth.

Karin gave Chris a look. "Remember, it's *our* secret," she cautioned Brian and Brandon. She hadn't told the twins the news because she didn't want them announcing to the ward that their daddy was bishop. But they seemed much more interested in their pancakes than in the status of the ward's leadership.

"I thought I could depend on you to keep this quiet," she leaned over and whispered to Chris. Then Karin noticed that the lump under Christopher's white shirtsleeve had a long rat's tail.

"So Domino has joined us for breakfast," Karin said, raising her eyebrows. Chris nodded as he chewed.

"Why don't you put him in his cage? We need to leave in twenty minutes."

"Plenty of time, Mom," Chris said with his mouth full. He swallowed and turned to his little brothers. "You guys better be good in church today."

"I good."

"I good too," Brian and Brandon assured their mother and big brother.

"Yeah," Chris said doubtfully.

Fifteen minutes later Karin and the twins were in the entryway, ready to get into the car with time to spare, when Chris ran frantically down the hallway. "Mom, I can't find Domino! I was in my room doing some stuff and forgot he was in my sleeve."

"You should have listened to me at breakfast. We'll find him when we get home," Karin suggested.

Chris planted his feet firmly. "I won't leave until he's safe in his cage. Remember what happened to my goldfish at the wedding reception? I told you *not* to leave them alone in a strange place."

Can't one ever shuck off the past? Karin thought as her mind went back to the day she borrowed Chris's fantail goldfish as decorations for her wedding reception. She had put them on tables in new, fluted-edge, water-filled bowls. They were stone dead when the wedding party arrived at the church after the temple sealing.

"Chris, that was four years ago. Your room *is* strange, but *not* to Domino."

"Please, Mom. You don't want Domino's death on your conscience too."

"Chris, I repented long ago for killing your goldfish."

"Mom, part of repentance is never doing it again."

Karin sighed and threw her hands into the air. She went into Chris's room, lay on her side in dress and heels, stomach protruding, and pulled Domino out from under the bed. A yell came from the kitchen. "Mommy, help! Help!"

Sitting up and practically tossing Domino to Chris, she ran to the kitchen to find Brandon with the refrigerator door open, the remainder of the orange juice spilled all over him. She ordered Chris to clean up the floor and scooped Brandon off to change. Five minutes later they were in the car with a chance of still making it to the church a moment before sacrament meeting started.

"Mommy, I have to go potty!" Brian wailed as she put the key into the ignition.

"Honey, wait until we get to the church," Karin suggested.

"Now, Mommy! It coming."

With a desperate sigh, Karin marched Brian back into the house and into the bathroom. Then, a few moments later, when they finally headed down the driveway, she glanced at the clock in the car's dashboard. Karin groaned, "I can't believe this! We're going to be late! On the one Sunday I promised your dad we would be there on time, we're going to be late!"

"It's OK, Mom," Chris began diplomatically.

"No, it's not OK," Karin cried, her patience depleted and tears of frustration in her eyes. "You guys messed me up. I was ready! I was organized! I did my best! But you guys messed up! If you would listen to me! If you would just do exactly what I say!"

After a silent ten minutes in the car and a mad rush into the church building, sweating, Karin hustled her children into the chapel as the opening song ended. The group made their way to the pew the Fletchers had saved near the front. A look of relief crossed Blake's face as he smiled at his wife from his seat on the stand. Karin nodded to him as she pushed a string of red-orange hair back from her forehead.

On the stand near the bishopric, the stake presidency watched Karin with restrained amusement and some concern as three-year-old Brian twisted his wrist loose from his mother's hand and made a dash for his father. Karin tightened her grip on the other twin, Brandon, while Christopher intercepted a screaming Brian at the deacon's table.

Sister Charity Jones gracefully stationed her imposing frame at the pulpit, breathed into the microphone, and folded her white arms in preparation for the invocation. Like an overgrown reverence child, she stared at Karin, waiting with condescending patience for the Taylor family to settle down.

Chris tickled Brian, turning the small child's tearful screams into equally tearful shrieks of laughter. "I want Daddy! Daddy the bish—" Chris popped his hand over Brian's mouth and pushed him towards the pew. Dennie quickly tore a stick of gum in half and handed it to Brian. Chris removed his hand, and Brian took the gum and popped it into his mouth. Dennie hurriedly gave the other half to Brandon. Brian wriggled out of Chris's arms and nestled into Dennie's lap. Karin took a deep, shuddering breath and mouthed Dennie a *thank you*. Sister Jones ceremoniously closed her eyes and bowed her head, her bun of purple-black hair pointing heavenward.

With his eyes only half-closed, Chris leaned into Dennie and whispered as the prayer began, "Sister Jones's hair turned purple when she tried to get the gray out."

"Who hair is purple?" Brian asked in a loud voice. Dennie put a finger to her lips and pushed down the giggle that was building inside her. Some of the deacons sitting near them were less successful at stifling their laughter. Sister Jones opened one eye, then closed it again as she thanked the Lord for Bishop Babcock "who has served so faithfully," and pled with the Lord to "guide and protect the new bishop and his family whomsoever they might be."

"Mommy, I have to go potty," Brandon pulled on Karin's blouse as the invocation continued.

"No, you don't. You went right before we left," Karin whispered. "You'll be fine."

"No, Brian went potty! I going now."

Karin hurried her little boy out of the chapel as the prayer ended. After helping Brandon use the bathroom, she washed her hands, then took a piece of paper towel and wiped away the stubborn tears still welling in the corners of her eyes. She felt exhausted. She exited the bathroom and walked into the foyer to find Meryl and Dennie waiting for her with Brian in tow.

"Go back in the chapel," Meryl said warmly. "Sit with Chris. We'll take care of the twins today."

Karin hugged her sister-in-law. "Meryl, you're a sweetheart!" She mentally chastised herself for the occasional jealousy she felt over Meryl's calm and steady life. With her own family in Utah, Karin realized she was fortunate to have local relatives as supportive as the Fletchers. She wished Dennie weren't flying off to Chile in ten days. She so enjoyed having her around—Dennie was a darling.

Karin looked around. They were the only ones in the foyer. She shook her head and smiled ruefully to keep from crying. "Isn't the new mother-of-the-ward supposed to walk into the chapel ten minutes before church starts with her kids in a perfect line behind her, tallest to shortest, little arms folded?"

Meryl smiled. "That sounds like a mother duck and her brood, not human beings."

Brian and Brandon commenced quacking.

"Go on, Karin, go back in," Dennie urged. "I have treats for these guys in my purse."

"But you'll miss the sustaining," Karin said to Meryl. "It's not fair for you to miss it."

"It's not fair for *me* to miss it? What about *you?*" Meryl laughed out loud. "Besides, if Dennie can keep these guys under control, I'll follow."

For a second, Karin hesitated, gazing at her restless, tawny-haired sons who were already digging in their cousin's purse. Then she straightened her shoulders and smoothed her child-wrinkled blouse. She dusted a rat hair off her stomach. So what if she were the only woman in the worldwide church who was late on the day her husband was to be sustained as bishop? So what if Sister Jones thought her disruptive? Did it really matter if her attempts at organization turned to shambles and her grasp at dignity fell to disaster? She had a family who loved her and a husband who was charming, kind, and patient, who knew how to laugh with her and work together. She had once been married to a controlling and angry man. She had lost her beautiful little girl nine years ago. She knew the other side of the coin; she knew how deeply difficult life could be.

Karin placed one hand on her stomach and thought of the baby girl growing within her. She opened the chapel door and walked in. She did not waddle down the aisle under the weight of her pregnancy, but stepped gracefully. As she looked up at Blake, her smile shone as bright as her orange hair. She even winked at Charity Jones.

That evening on her way home from a dinner at Meryl's, Karin stopped by the park to let the kids romp before dark fell. Blake was still at the church, meeting with the outgoing bishop. She watched Chris make trains with the twins as the three shrieked down the slide. She wondered if a bishop's wife *should* take her children to the park on the Sabbath. Would people be watching every move they made as a family? She made silly mistakes all the time, and if she were put on a pedestal, she would fall off. Though it was only her first Sunday as the bishop's wife, a part of her felt lonely and separate. She turned to watch the sunset—the crimson, orange, and blue colors gliding in and around the fading sun.

She heard a car approach. Turning toward the road, she saw Blake's car stop behind hers. He got out and walked up to her, his suit on, his tie loosened.

"Hey, Bishop," she greeted him.

"Hey, Sister Taylor." He walked up to her, put his arm around her, and kissed her. Chris bounded over.

"Hey, Dad!"

"Hey, son!" Blake tousled his stepchild's blonde flattop.

"How's your day been?" Blake asked his wife.

"Fine," she said.

"Fine!" Chris snorted. "Ever heard of the mother boating down the River Denial? Dad, Mom totally lost it on the way to church."

Karin laughed. The boy was far too wise these days—a wise guy anyway. Why, just last week, a laid-back Chris had assured her that his homework was under control. Karin, knowing better, had responded that he was boating down that river called Denial.

"Ever heard of the son who pushed his poor mother over Breakdown Falls?" she joked as she cocked her head toward Chris. Her boy grinned.

Bishop Blake Taylor, whose jeans and guitar lay home in the corner of his closet, pretended to strum his suit and tie as he made up a corny, impromptu song. "Let me be your life jacket, your inner tube, your life preserver when you tumble down those Breakdown Falls. Yeah! Yeah! Those Breakdown Falls!"

Chris cracked up and ran to chase his brothers. Blake stood by his wife in the twilight. He thought about the changes facing them. He had switched to working days to facilitate his calling as bishop. Yet this meant no night differential, less money for his family. How would they fare under this new weight? He wondered if he could be the bishop God wanted him to be and the husband and father his family needed at the same time. His workload as a nurse in the hospital's transplant unit was demanding as well. Was there enough of him?

He hadn't married until he was nearly forty. No one had ever seemed quite right. Then Karin stepped into his life, in looks much like his mother—red haired and petite. Yet in spirit so different. Karin was as chatty as his mother was prim, as warm as Joan Taylor was reserved. Was that partly why he loved her—because she was both like and unlike his mother? Whatever the reason, he treasured his wife. Just fifteen minutes ago he had spotted her at the park, looking like an angel standing there in the sand, carrying his daughter within her, her fiery hair as brilliant as the setting sun.

CHAPTER 6

FLY AWAY

"I'd adore Esteban if he didn't want to marry my daughter," Meryl commented as she leaned back in the chair at the Wild Rose styling salon. Moni Tomlinson, Aimy's mother, massaged Meryl's scalp as she shampooed her hair. Meryl continued, "Esteban cooked a beef dish last night for all of us—the Fletchers and Taylors. He called it *carne mechada*. The meat was tenderized in a vinegar marinade and cooked with carrots."

"Mmmm," Moni hummed. "I smelled it all the way across the street."

"It was really good. There're leftovers. I'll drop some by this evening. After dinner, Esteban did the dishes and then played four games of chess with Christopher and one with Rick. You should see that Christopher play, Moni. He beat Esteban two out of four times."

"Little kids are amazing. I remember how Aimy used to beat me at that memory game, the one where you turn over two cards at a time. I was never good at chess though. I couldn't memorize all those little chess pieces and how they moved."

"I'm not much of a chess player either. But Rick and Dennie are decent." Meryl chuckled. "Rick's game with Esteban was pretty intense. It lasted over an hour. Rick pretended to be a good sport, but it bugged him a lot. Maybe partly because Rick and I still can't come to grips with the fact that Esteban's flying to Chile with Dennie in five days. This morning Rick jokingly said that he was going to take Esteban golfing and accidentally hit him in the head with a well-driven golf ball."

Moni laughed and tossed her long, streaked-blonde hair. She wore a low-cut, gypsy-style blouse and tight jeans. Despite her efforts, the weathered lines of her face and the grayness of her teeth betrayed her age and the hardness of her life.

"Our babies are grown up now, that's for sure," Moni commented as she wrapped a towel around Meryl's head. They walked together to Moni's booth. "Did you know that Charity Jones is my next customer? She called and set up an appointment early Monday morning—said she needs help with her color. She usually just has me cut it. You two are the only Mormon women I know, and you're both so different. Charity's overbearing, but she's got spunk. I like that. I figure she'll have me do her hair until she's converted me. Then she'll go on to a different stylist. Doesn't she know that my Aimy has already done everything imaginable to help me 'see the light.'"

"You might as well give in and take the discussions, Moni," Meryl teased. "Aimy's likely to start playing the Book of Mormon tapes in your room while you sleep—so the message will seep into your subconscious."

Moni chuckled and continued chatting as she combed out and cut Meryl's hair. "I think Aimy's gonna settle down soon and marry Sean if she can get this mission stuff out of her head. I'll be glad when my baby's hitched and I know she's taken care of. But, I can see how you feel about Dennie and Esteban. I don't think I'd want Aimy marrying someone and moving to a foreign country where there's poverty and drug dealers all over the place."

Meryl flinched inwardly and responded. "Actually, Chile's one of the cleanest and most modern countries in South America. They say it has a European feel. Drugs are not a huge problem there. Speaking of moving—I hear you might be going to Texas?"

Moni shrugged. "I'm flying out next week and spending awhile with my sister, Joni. She has a friend who's opening up a beauty shop. I can help by doing nails and cutting hair for drop-in customers. With Aimy away at school and thinking of getting married, I get lonely in the house all by myself. Joni says she'd love to have me live with her. I'll see how it goes. The other girls can hold down the fort at this salon."

"I hear that Joni's not the only thing pulling you toward Texas," Meryl pried.

Moni laughed out loud. "What's my baby been telling you?"

"Something about a cowboy named Len."

Moni's eyes shone. "Meryl, Len's the sweetest man I've ever met. My sister's known him for years and he's the real McCoy—there's no meanness in him. I'm done with abusive men. I don't know why I've been attracted to the wrong kind. But Len—Len's as sweet as Aimy's friend, Waverly. Did you know that Waverly gave me a bouquet of flowers when he met me? I think he picked them in the Gleason's yard."

Meryl giggled. The Gleasons lived down the street and were meticulous gardeners. "Now, tell me about Len," Meryl encouraged.

"Len's five feet, ten inches tall, has thick brown hair, and two kids at home. I don't know if I can handle his kids. I need to get to know them better."

"Is there an ex-wife in the picture?"

"No. Len's wife died of breast cancer about two years ago."

The mention of breast cancer caused Meryl to pause. Her yearly mammogram was scheduled for next month. Meryl would never forget the morning five years ago when Dr. Aldrich, her radiologist, had come in and told her something was wrong. He had uncovered calcifications indicating a very strong possibility of intraductal breast cancer. Meryl remembered the shock of the news. At the time she had felt as if she had been shot. However, during the six months that followed, the doctors had treated her cancer successfully with a lumpectomy and radiation therapy. But each year, when her annual mammogram rolled around, she had to face the residue of fear that plagued her.

As this pool of silent thoughts floated through Meryl, Moni finished the cut. She was an artist at work—tapering the hair in front to give it shape, and stacking it in back for more body. Quick and skilled, her fingers maneuvered the scissors, her focus unwavering. She blew Meryl's hair dry and styled it with a round brush. "Don't you look good now!" Moni stepped back and announced when she had finished.

Meryl smiled satisfactorily at her image in the mirror. She would leave her thoughts behind and enjoy the moment. Having her hair done was the closest thing she ever had to a massage, and she enjoyed it. "How come it never looks this good when I blow it dry myself?" she asked.

"Come on now," Moni soothed. "You always look nice. But next time, you've got to let me do a weave. I'll make you drop-dead gorgeous."

"Drop-dead gorgeous? Is that a promise?" Meryl laughed as she wrote the check and handed it to Moni. "Good luck in Texas. When you get back, fill me in."

"Absolutely," Moni said, wishing that she could afford to cut Meryl's hair for free. Meryl and Rick were the best neighbors on God's earth. They had been like family to Aimy, and had helped Moni through rocky times. Years ago when she had been in the hospital from an overdose of prescription drugs and then in a rehab clinic, the Fletchers didn't give up on her. They came to see her nearly every day, even though they were still grieving from Theseus's death. This made her feel human. They hadn't judged her, and their courage had helped Moni get her feet on the ground.

Moni tried to explain some of her feelings in words. "When the kids were little, I always hoped that Aimy would marry Thes—then we'd be related. We'd be the best fairy-godmother grandmas. But Thes died and I got so messed up. Everything was dark and out of control. But you were brave. You got through it and helped Aimy and me too. We made it. Now you're a writer, and I'm doing hair in a reputable salon. Our kids are in college! If I move to Texas, Meryl, I'll miss you and I'll never forget you. Even though I'm not Mormon, I'll pray every day that God sends you blessings for your kindness to me and Aimy."

Meryl squeezed Moni's hand. "Moni, I'll pray that your dreams come true."

"I'll see you in six weeks then—after I fly away to Texas and back home again," Moni said quickly. She didn't want to get emotional now that she had spotted Charity stepping briskly toward the shop. Charity swung the door open, and a gust of wind rushed in.

"Hi Moni! How are you?" Charity greeted the two women. "Meryl, you sure look nice. I hear that Dennie's off to Chile with that handsome Hispanic boy. They sure look nice together. Poor Ron Babcock. He's going to be heartbroken. These boys just shouldn't get so attached before their missions."

"Dennie hasn't made any decisions about marriage yet," Meryl explained, reluctant to go into detail. She was cautious around Charity. Three years ago she had heard a rumor that Charity had discouraged her son, Jeff, from dating Dennie because of Dennie's Chilean blood—because of the color of her skin.

"Well, I guess it can't hurt for Dennie to have one bird in the hand and another in the bush," Charity said. "Our Jeff just became engaged to a girl from Salt Lake named Terry Orlando. She *is* a gem."

"I'm sure she is," Meryl said. "Well, I'd better be going. Bye, Moni. It's nice to see you, Charity."

"Before you go, Meryl, I thought it would be fun if the two of us took Moni to Enrichment next week. What do you say, Moni?"

"I'll have to take a rain check. I'm flying to Texas Wednesday."

"It seems like everybody's flying somewhere these days—you to Texas, Dennie to Chile. I understand that even Christopher Parker is flying to Los Angeles to spend the summer with his real father. I'm sure this situation is difficult for Karin and the bishop."

Meryl didn't elaborate. Moni sensed her friend's discomfort and turned to Charity with her brightest, red-lipstick smile. "Come sit down, Charity." Moni drew her into the shop. "Let's see what we can do to get that purple tint out of your hair."

The next day while Dennie and Esteban toured San Francisco, Meryl proofread the rough draft of Esteban's paper about the Mapuche Indians. She noticed that the young man wrote with intelligence and skill. It was interesting to learn about an indigenous culture, but she couldn't picture her daughter living in a thatch-roofed hut, watching rituals where animals were sacrificed, and calling a woman steeped in superstition her grandmother. Meryl went through the manuscript a second time, tossing aside her personal feelings, with a red pen in hand. She did not soften her comments and criticism over unclear passages or stretched parallels. She wondered how Esteban would react.

She found out the next morning after Esteban read through her comments. He thanked Meryl and asked if they could discuss his manuscript. They sat down at the kitchen table, and together, went through each item. He challenged her on certain points, accepted other suggestions without hesitation, and asked pertinent questions about ways to supplement and strengthen his thematic position. They worked together for over two hours, their minds batting ideas back and forth, thoughts connecting like threads weaving together. When they finished, Esteban graciously expressed appreciation.

Meryl watched him gather the pages of his paper. She noticed his intelligent, dark eyes and his thoughtful, inquisitive brow. How she missed her own dark-eyed son. Memories of helping Thes with his homework swarmed within her. They had sat for hours at this very table. Yet Thes didn't have a quiet, contemplative mind like Esteban, but became easily frustrated when he didn't understand something. She remembered him throwing a book to the floor when he stumbled over words on a page. But Meryl's patience had calmed and encouraged him. They had gone out for ice cream after difficult sessions. Through the labor, Thes had learned to read and understand mathematical operations. He had become a B student.

"Thank you again Sister Fletcher," Esteban said as he stood and pushed the chair in.

"You're welcome," Meryl smiled. "Esteban, when did you become interested in the Mapuche people?"

"All my life I have had two loves: my country and the gospel," Esteban explained. "My research brings the two together. The Mapuche are the ancestry, the very heartbeat of Chile." At that moment, as Meryl heard the passion in Esteban's voice, she had no doubt that he would choose to spend his life in his own country. If she gained this dark-eyed son, her daughter would be far away. It was a high price to pay. Too high.

That evening around the dinner table, as they ate chicken and mashed potatoes, Meryl questioned Esteban more deeply about his family and his nation. Dennie listened tensely. Meryl could tell her daughter considered this an interrogation. Dennie's expression reminded Meryl of when she herself went in for physicals as a small child. Her own mother would stiffen when Meryl asked the doctor about everything in sight. *What is that needle for? Why do you have plastic gloves? Are you going to take blood out of my finger or my arm? Why do you need my blood?* Dennie put her elbow on the table, resting her forehead on her hand as she slowly chewed her food. But Esteban grinned, embracing the opportunity to discuss himself, his family, and his native land.

When Meryl asked Esteban to tell her about his father, he recounted exciting stories about when Juan, as a young man, worked as a *huaso*, or Chilean cowboy, during the springs and summers. Then Esteban went into detail about Juan's labors for *Hogar de Cristo*, The House of Christ, a large charitable organization. "This organization was founded by Padre Alberto Hurtado, a Jesuit priest," Esteban explained. "The padre drove an old pickup truck through the streets of Santiago, rescuing homeless children." He touched Dennie's knee and went on. "*Hogar de Cristo* is the organization that took in little Mina and Lautaro so many years ago."

"Not that many years ago," Rick corrected.

Then Meryl asked Esteban about Chile's geography. She mentioned that she had heard there were many volcanoes and earthquakes. Esteban explained proudly that Chile was the longest country in the world. One poet referred to it as the southern petal of the earth. "And," he continued. "The beautiful Andes Mountains contain over 620 volcanoes, many of them active. There is at least one tremor somewhere in Chile every day!"

Meryl narrowed her question. "What about earthquake fatalities?"

Esteban swallowed his piece of bread and sipped his water before describing a series of quakes in 1960 that struck southern Chile, causing huge tidal waves that swept inland and killed thousands of people. He elaborated on his theory that many Book of Mormon events took place in Chile. The destruction described at the coming of Christ paralleled much of the climatic and geographical phenomena of Chile and the disruptions of the Nazca plate as it pushed into the continent.

"It doesn't sound like the safest place to raise a family," Meryl commented.

"Don't worry, Mom," Dennie cut in. "Esteban has survived in Chile for twenty-eight years. I'm sure I'll be OK for a couple of months."

"And," Esteban said jokingly, "Yesterday I noticed that the people in San Francisco are far more wicked than the people in all of Chile. I'm sure Dennie is in more danger of divine destruction each day she remains in northern California."

Dennie's parents did not share Esteban's levity, but smiled uncomfortably. Then Rick entered the conversation. "Esteban, while we are on the subject of Dennie's safety, I must tell you that I hold you personally responsible for my daughter's well-being while she is gone."

Dennie interrupted tersely. "Dad, I've been living away from home for three years now. I'm twenty-one and responsible for my own well-being."

"Dennie." Rick injected fatherly authority into his voice. "Of course you are a responsible adult. But you are going to a foreign country. I know nothing of what you will face when you step onto a Mapuche reservation. I imagine disease, drinking, perhaps violence. I'm worried. Esteban has studied these people and he assures me that you will be safe. I must trust him, and he must understand how precious your life is to your mother and me."

"Brother Fletcher," Esteban said as he looked into Rick's eyes with a penetration that betrayed the young man's capacity for passion. "I am committed to three things—to God, my country, and to Dennie and her safety. They are the most important things in the world to me." Rick found Esteban's words comforting, but Dennie did not. She wondered if her independence would be swallowed by the desire of this man she cared deeply for, and perhaps loved. Yet, she was unsure.

Her mind slipped to Ron. Once they had attended a concert where the group Rain impersonated the Beatles. On the way home they had cracked up as they sang a medley of Beatles' songs, "Love Me Do," "Yellow Submarine," and "Let it Be." Their hands had been entwined, swinging back and forth in tune with the fun and delight of the music. How would Ron feel if he knew she was going across the world with another man? How would Esteban feel when he found out that she had written her missionary and told him that she was traveling to Chile to meet her grandmother? She had not mentioned her relationship with Esteban in the letter. She had simply sent Ron the Antemil's address so he could write to her there.

The dinner conversation continued as Esteban shared his research with Rick, the man he hoped would be his father-in-law. Esteban described the Mapuche's dedication to their land and their kindness towards their children. He spoke animatedly of their deep spirituality, their belief in constant divine intervention in their lives, and their view of positive and negative forces in the universe.

"They even have legends," he said with glowing eyes, "about a celestial family who directs the lives of the people. The Mapuche participate in rituals for the propitiation of their ancestors. Doesn't this remind you of our temple work for the dead? They believe that those who have passed on can become the sons of God. All of the doors of their huts face east, toward their ancestors, the *pillan*. Did you know that the Angel Moroni statues on our temples face east as well?"

"That's fascinating," Rick said, truly interested.

With that encouragement, Esteban's voice heightened and his hands moved with excitement as he exclaimed, "Brother and Sister Fletcher, don't you see now how wonderful it will be for Dennie to find out about her heritage? It is fall in Chile. Dennie will be with the Mapuche for the *Nillatun*, or harvest festival! Often they sacrifice a lamb at this festival. Her machi grandmother will stand on her *rewe*, her ladder to Heaven. Perhaps Dennie will be able to teach this grandmother and other Mapuche relatives about the gospel and of the true Lamb of God! Perhaps she can share with them the steps toward eternal life. Perhaps this is Dennie's mission!"

"Perhaps," Rick said, thawing though not completely convinced. Meryl just smiled and nodded at Esteban. The young man brimmed with the commitment, passion, and optimism of the young. She respected and envied his emotions. But instead of feeling joyful, she could only think of her own ancestors on the *Mayflower* voyage. Half of their party died that first winter.

Early the next morning, thin light ebbed over the horizon as Dennie and Aimy jogged through their subdivision in sweatshirts and shorts. Dennie's hair was pulled back in a tight ponytail, and the morning breeze fingered through Aimy's short, loose mane.

"Den, I can't believe that I let you talk me into getting up at 6:30 to go jogging with you!" Aimy exclaimed. "Moni is sound asleep in a warm bed."

"Dad's already in the shower. Mom and Esteban were in the kitchen when I left drinking hot cocoa and herbal tea. Don't you love the early morning? Ron always said it was the only time to run."

"It's a great time to sleep too," Aimy commented. As they continued to jog, both young women grew quiet from exertion. Aimy moved well, her breathing steady. Dennie thought about her brother and Ron, how they both had loved to run. But when Thes had run, it had been with a driven will, a purpose in mind, arms pumping at his sides, a race to win, or something to outrun. In contrast, Ron had run for personal development, for self-mastery, finding joy in the sun and wind in his hair or in the stars and clouds above.

Both young women neared the point of exhaustion, needing second winds to gain strength. They kept going, passing the shuttered home with the three German shepherds, the light blue house with the porch swing, the old Victorian two-story with models of the seven dwarves in the yard, and the manicured lawn and flower garden where Waverly had picked Moni's flowers.

They turned east toward the park. Dennie looked up at the sky, trying to keep her mind off of the ache in her chest and the heaviness of her legs. Did Aimy feel as if she were hitting an unseen wall as well? Would they both have the determination to run through their walls of exhaustion? Her brother, Thes, had never seemed to hit a wall when running. He had been so fast. When he was a little kid, he would look up at the clouds or the stars and call out a challenge before he ran. Dennie remembered the night when she was about five and her Chilean mother had died. She and her brother had run away. Only her brother wasn't called Thes then, he was called Lautaro, Lauto.

They had left in the night when it was raining. Lauto's hand had gripped hers like iron. First they had walked—silent like shadows, moving through sheets of rain. Then, a drunken man had taunted them. "I can see you, little ones. God can see you. The devil can see you." Her brother had made her run. She had fallen and her legs had screamed to stop. The rain had slowed. She had looked up to see a hole in the clouds where a star shone through. "Look at the star," her brother had said. "We must run to the star. Then we will be safe." But no matter how fast they had run that night, the star had remained above and beyond.

The sun spread pink and golden light through wisps of clouds. Dennie and Aimy saw the park up ahead. The morning light outlined the edges of the equipment and the slant of the slide with a silver sheen. It made the yellow playground tunnel glow golden and turned the windows of surrounding houses to rose-colored mirrors. Dennie felt a surge of energy come to her legs as she sprinted. She had run through the wall and the second wind was hers! Aimy felt it too and ran alongside.

They slowed when they reached the park. Bending over, they panted with their hands on their thighs. Aimy's legs were freckled and peeling from her attempts to tan. Dennie's legs were heavier than

Aimy's and already a warm brown from the sun.

"Den, let's teeter-totter," Aimy suggested as her breathing lightened. "How long has it been?"

"Too long," Dennie said as they mounted the playground equipment. It felt so natural, going up and down as they talked. They had done this hundreds of times as little girls.

"Are you packed for Chile?" Aimy questioned as she leaned back from the high position and Dennie pushed off.

"Almost. I'm really excited, but I'm really scared too. Esteban is so eager. I've been thinking more about Ron lately. I hate the thought of hurting either of them. I hope I'm doing the right thing."

"You are. When you come back, you'll know what to do next. You'll know if you and Esteban are meant for each other."

"What about you, Aim? Are you still thinking of a mission?"

Aimy shrugged, "I don't know. I'm going to see how the summer goes. Sean and I want to take Wave to San Francisco and Marine World."

"How is Sean adjusting to Wave?"

"They're doing OK. Sometimes Wave talks too much and drives Sean crazy. Plus, Wave is kind of a clean freak, and he's always picking up the apartment. Sean can't find things and Wave can't remember where he put them." Aimy giggled. "Sean says it isn't any worse than living with companions on his mission. Last night, Sean brought up Wave's birthday next month. He suggested we get him wheels—a bike, one of those adult three-wheelers."

"That would be cool," Dennie exclaimed warmly. "Aim, e-mail me this summer! I'm going to be so far away. I'll miss you."

"Me too you," Aimy said as she pointed to herself, held up two fingers, and pointed at Dennie. That had been their secret sign as little girls. *I love you. Me too, you. I miss you. Me too, you. I need you. Me too, you.*

Aimy added, "It's going to be weird with Moni away and the house all to myself. Den, you might have such a wonderful time that you never want to come back."

"And you might have such a great time living alone that you don't want to go on a mission or get married!"

"Let's balance," Aimy suggested as she pushed off the ground as hard as she could and Dennie came crashing down.

Dennie moaned as they leveled the teeter-totter. "We could never balance. I was always heavier than you." They lifted their legs and Dennie's side sank. "And I still am," she added. "That's why you are the one who always suggests trying to balance so you can remind me of my thick thighs."

"That is *not* the reason!" Aimy laughed. "Do you remember that poem your mom wrote about balance? We said it in unison and made it to the district oral language finals in eighth grade."

"Of course I remember." Dennie moved up in the teeter-totter's saddle. Aimy moved back. This movement offset their weight difference, and they repeated the poem as they balanced.

"Balance, by Meryl Fletcher

Spring rain came one day with
The sun shining through showers
Each drop less soft than snow
One year ago, parched with drought
Mountains in flame, we prayed
And hoped for rain.
Not now, with saturated soil and
Reservoirs brimming, we pray
And hope, preparing for floods.
Too fat.
Too thin.
Too much.
Too soon.
Too little.
Too late.
Aching for balance
We fall.
What is the secret of spring storm?
Perhaps, one must live well unbalanced."

After they finished the poem, Aimy slowly dismounted, leaning against the equipment as she let Dennie down softly. "You're mom is so great," Aimy said quietly. "I want to be a mom like that someday."

"I love my mom, but she's not perfect. She's overprotective right now and afraid to let me go. Dad's even worse. I understand how they feel, but it makes everything harder. Moni's cool, Aim. She lets you live your own life. That's a good way to be too."

Aimy shrugged. "I guess. Let's go. I need to get to work."

"And I need to get ready for the adventure of a lifetime."

"You sound like a *Survivor* contestant," Aimy laughed.

"Sometimes I feel like a victim more than a contestant," Dennie commented.

"Come on, Den," Aimy laughed. "Remember Moni's motto after she came back from rehab. *There are no victims, only volunteers.*"

"I'll keep that in mind." Dennie smiled at her friend as they began walking home.

"Den," Aimy commented as they neared their destination. "Speaking of victims versus volunteers—it seems like if you get married, you're volunteering to be a victim. It was like that when Moni married Bill."

"That only happens if you marry the wrong guy," Dennie remarked.

"Or if *he* marries the wrong girl," Aimy mused. "In my case, Sean might be the *victim*." Aimy chuckled wickedly and Dennie cracked up.

"Don't ever change, Aimy, OK?" Dennie said, hugging her best friend before they parted company.

"OK," Aimy said, but inside she hoped that something would change. If she remained status quo, she would never have the guts to get married.

Four days later, charcoal-colored, mascara-filled tears escaped from Moni's eyes when Aimy and Waverly saw her off at the airport. "I should have worn waterproof mascara," Moni said as she dabbed at the tears with her finger.

"What's wrong, Moni?" Aimy asked. She had always called her mother by her first name. "Don't worry about me. I'll be fine."

"I know, Baby, you're always fine. It's just that I've never been a very good mother to you. And now I'm leaving when you've just come home from college." Another brown tear trailed down Moni's cheek. "You don't need me. You've been on your own most of your life. I feel so bad about that." Moni didn't know why all of this stuff was coming out now—right before she stepped on the plane. But when she looked at her daughter, she just couldn't stop the feelings running through her like a downpour that comes from the inside instead of from the sky. "You're so cute and strong, honey. The best kid in the world—the one really good thing in my life!"

Aimy hugged Moni and tried to cheer her up. "When you come back in a month, I'll still be here. The best kid in the world."

"I didn't have a mama when I was little, Aimy. I just went from foster home to foster home. The only person I really had was Joni. So I never learned how to be a good mama to you."

"You did OK, Moni. We're still here. We're still truckin'."

"We'll take a second mortgage out on the house and send you on a mission or give you the biggest wedding reception ever. Whichever you want," Moni told her daughter.

"I just want you to read the Book of Mormon," Aimy said seriously.

"But it's hard for me to get through all those pages," Moni countered. "Maybe you could lend me the tapes."

"I'll send them," Aimy promised.

When it came time for Moni to board, Aimy watched her mom walking toward the gate. The heavy, carry-on bag hung from Moni's shoulder, tilting her posture and tugging at her blouse so that her bra strap showed. From the back Moni looked young with her tight jeans and thin, streaked hair falling down her back. Aimy knew that Moni felt scared—she hated to fly as much as her kid. Moni turned around and waved, putting up a brave front.

"Bye, Moni," Aimy called. She pulled a crumpled Kleenex from her overall pocket and blew her nose. It was her job to take care of Moni. It had been that way for a long time. She became aware of Waverly next to her.

"You are lucky to have such a good mama." Waverly sniffed.

"Maybe so," Aimy said, turning to her friend. "Come on, Wave, chin up. Let's go get a milk shake."

From the front passenger seat of the car, Meryl chatted amicably with Dennie and Esteban as Rick drove to the airport. An observer would have thought that she was happy with the relationship of the young couple in the backseat and content with the adventure on which they were about to embark. Meryl could do this sometimes, this positive act. When her emotions ran high, she tucked them away, exchanging them for short-term feelings—especially when she thought it was best for her daughter.

Perhaps this brief facade wasn't completely honest, or even completely healthy, but Meryl knew cheerfulness felt needful somehow—like washing her face and looking her best on fast Sunday even when her stomach growled and her knees felt weak. Last week Blake had told her that as he watched the congregation from the stand, he felt that he saw a sea of smiles covering up deep problems, isolation, insecurity, and hurt. This had troubled Blake as the bishop. But to Meryl, there seemed to be encouragement in that sea of smiles, like the sun sparkling on the waves, covering the depth of the sea's darkness and power with glimmering hope.

But as he drove, Rick did not hide his feelings so well. When it came right down to it, he didn't want Dennie going to Chile. As he headed toward the Sacramento airport, his frustration vented into impatience with the cars around him. He muttered "idiot" at a driver who cut him off, and a few minutes later let out a mild expletive at the car on his tail. His inability to control his mood irritated Meryl. "Lighten up," she whispered. "You're embarrassing me." He drove steadily and silently the rest of the way.

Meanwhile Dennie and Esteban held hands, stroking each other's fingers with their thumbs. They felt young and wise. They bore patiently the idiosyncrasies of the older adults in the front seat.

Once they were at the airport, a thrill of excitement raced through Dennie. Rick left Esteban to cope with the luggage while he spoke with his daughter. "Take care of yourself," he advised. "Eat right and get enough sleep. Esteban's parents have a computer. E-mail us whenever you can. You have your ticket and passport. Everything is in order. Here's fifteen hundred dollars in traveler's checks for an emergency. If you get sick or just want to come home, call. The tickets are transferable, and I'll make arrangements."

"Thanks, Dad. It's great knowing you're always there."

"When you write, tell us every little thing," Meryl added. "Share your adventure with us."

"I will," Dennie promised. They found four seats in the waiting area near the gate. As they waited, Dennie's foot shook nearly in time with the racing of her heart. The boarding call came. Meryl noticed that Dennie's color had heightened, and she laid a hand on Dennie's forehead. "No fever," she said.

"I'm just excited and nervous," Dennie admitted. She hugged her parents and told them that she loved and appreciated them. Rick held her tightly for a moment, not wanting to let her go. Then Meryl moved Dennie's hair back from her face and kissed her forehead. As she looked at Dennie, she tried to record in her mind each feature of her child.

After the young couple disappeared into the tunnel leading to the airplane, tears sprang into Meryl's eyes. She remembered a day, over fifteen years ago, when Dennie and Thes had stepped out of a similar tunnel. Little Thes had been wide awake, with darting black eyes. Five-year-old Dennie had looked puzzled and sleepy, with a wrinkled pink bow hanging crookedly from her hair. For a moment, time felt to Meryl like a wave, swelling as it neared the shore with experiences, relationships, laughter, and tears, the debris of life, only to topple over, leaving memories as exquisite and fragile as lacy patterns of foam.

Meryl sat very still in a chair, coping with the ache that tore through her. Rick put his arm around his wife and told her that Dennie would be fine. Finally they spoke about where they might enjoy going for dinner. Then they stood up and walked arm in arm toward the exit.

Seated in the airplane, Esteban took Dennie's hand and realized that it was hot and moist, different from its usual soft dryness. "My family will love you, and you will love Chile," Esteban stated.

"Is that a promise?" Dennie asked.

"Oh yes."

"When my brother and I flew here on the airplane, he held his arms out and pretended he was racing the sky," Dennie said quietly. "He used to do that other times too. On his bike and on foot—he would race the clouds." She turned and looked into Esteban's eyes.

"I wish I had known him," Esteban stated.

"Me too," Dennie said. She nearly pointed to herself and raised two fingers, as she would have with Aimy. She felt a twinge, something like homesickness and something like longing, as the airplane raced down the runway. Esteban put his arm around her. The craft swung into the blue, and Dennie closed her eyes and leaned into him.

CHAPTER 7

ARRIVAL

Meryl and Rick drove silently home from the airport after Dennie's plane left. Their thoughts ran in divergent paths. Rick regretted rushing through countless conversations with Dennie over the years. He recalled when she was a teen and he had repeatedly shooed her friends home early in the evenings because he had wanted his sleep. Why hadn't he been more easygoing? He thought of how his little girl used to beg for horses and puppies. He wished he had bought her one. He longed to help her with her homework one more time. He had missed too many opportunities to tuck her in bed at night.

He leaned back, his left hand balancing on the top of the steering wheel. When his daughter came back, he would make up for the missed opportunities—maybe take Dennie out to dinner and to Music Circus in Sacramento. She would laugh when he told a joke, and he would be in tune with her every thought and feeling. Maybe they would even play tennis together. They hadn't done that for a long time. He would let her win. When she came back, he would keep in mind that each moment was precious and fleeting. He would make even the seconds count.

Meryl, on the other hand, wondered how she had become so emotionally involved in her daughter's life that Dennie's departure caused such emptiness. *Is that what it means to be a mother?* she thought, *Giving your time, the best of your life, to your child? Then the hard work ends. It just ends. You stand still and wait to see if all your efforts are enough. Stationary, you watch her move away from you into paths of her own choice, and the buffeting of her own circumstance. The further away, the less ability you possess to aid her, to divert the darts of hurt life sends her way. Still, you care as deeply and worry more, hoping that whatever heartache comes, she will be protected by the shield of your love and feel strength through the power of your prayers. Then, if she chooses the path you foresee for her, wonderful. If not, God bless her.*

Meryl sighed and sat up straighter. She thought of how she had chosen the path of motherhood, not fallen into it. She thought of the vacant rooms in her home. She recalled the days before she had children, that sense of emptiness, of being different from the other women in the Church—of having no role or purpose. She supposed that men felt a similar worthlessness when they lost their jobs and could not support their families. She looked over at Rick's profile and noted the bump in his nose and the firm line of his jaw. He had never experienced the feeling of uselessness. He had always been successful.

She reflected on her joyful excitement when Dennie and Thes came into her life. She became a tributary in the vast river of motherhood. Meryl felt a part of things—soccer and birthday parties, quilts, wallpaper and kid's rooms, Primary and youth activities, Santa Claus shopping in December. Yet even then, she still felt a shadow of difference from other women her age. She sensed a current many would not perceive until their children were grown. She knew what an empty nest felt like.

In response to these feelings, Meryl took literature and poetry classes when her children were young. Occasionally sisters in the ward complimented her on her commitment to personal growth, yet they did not know that it was because she had made a secret vow to herself that she would never be in a position of uselessness again.

It had worked partially, but not completely. Thes was gone. Dennie was living her own life. Meryl flinched at her own weakness, her own fear, loneliness, and sense of loss. But a stubborn part of her balked at the aching. Dennie had to live her own story. Meryl had a life to live too, both folded within and separate from her husband and child. If she wrote and produced, if she kept that creative part of her alive, she could bear the fruit of accomplishment. And perhaps in doing so, she could learn to let Dennie go—even if that going meant her daughter spending a lifetime in Chile with Esteban.

"How are you doing?" Rick asked, interrupting the silence.

"I'm OK. How are you?" Meryl returned.

"I just keep thinking about Dennie and Thes."

"Me too," Meryl said. She reached out and took his hand. Meryl thought about how they had been married a long time. At that moment, silence was enough and as comfortable as conversation.

Five minutes later, he pulled into the Marie Callender's parking lot. "After dinner, let's get a chocolate satin pie," Rick suggested.

"I'm with you," Meryl laughed.

During the descent into Santiago, Dennie blinked her eyes. She felt giddy from sleep deprivation—past the point of exhaustion. Still, she shivered with anticipation. The plane dove into a heavy, dark cloud that hung over the city. Within seconds, the aircraft's wheels met the runway and the roar of engines, brakes, and wind filled Dennie's ears.

"Santiago has a terrible problem with pollution," Esteban explained a few moments later while the plane taxied. "The *cordillera*, the mountain range, traps the air. In the morning the smog is heaviest downtown, but by the afternoon it moves over the wealthy neighborhoods at the base of the mountains. Don't judge our beautiful country by Santiago's pollution. It troubles the rich and the poor. It is democratic pollution."

Dennie smiled at Esteban. His optimism charmed her. He continued, "Next, we go through customs and you will get a card with an identification number. It is called a *carnet*."

Dennie nodded. "I remember. It's as important as my passport. Now, what was your cousin's name again?"

"Carmen Marquez. Miguel is her husband. Carmen is my mother's sister's daughter."

"Are you sure Carmen and Miguel won't mind us staying?" Dennie asked.

"Of course. They are my family."

The plane stopped, and Dennie's heart pounded. The color was high in her cheeks, and her head felt light. She thought of Aimy and the slumber parties of their adolescent years, when they, tipsy with tiredness, giggled until dawn.

She stood up next to Esteban and chatted as they waited for the aisle to clear. "OK. Let me see if I remember our schedule. We spend the next two nights with Carmen and Miguel. Tomorrow, we tour

Santiago. On Saturday we fly to Osorno and stay with your family until Wednesday morning. Then we get up early and spend the day driving to the reservation where my grandmother lives. We stay there for two weeks. Then we go back to civilization for a weekend, and after that, back to the reservation for two more weeks. I can't believe this! I can't believe this is really happening! Wow!"

Esteban grinned. "Yes, my *gringa*!" he exclaimed. "Now we are in Chile! Now we speak *castellano*."

"*¡Choro!*" Dennie responded, showing off the Chilean slang she had studied over the past week. *Cool!* The plane halted. Esteban laughed and kissed her. "Welcome to Chile, Dennie," he said. Then he stood and retrieved their luggage from the overhead bins. She carefully balanced in order to keep from falling back into her seat.

An hour later, with adrenaline no longer pumping through her system, Dennie felt the full weight of exhaustion. They sat on a bench waiting for the *micro*, or bus, which would take them to the Marquez's apartment. In the southern hemisphere it was late fall, nearly winter. Dennie's fingers were red with cold. She pulled her gray fleece jacket closer around her, and she blew on her hands to warm them. Esteban reached over and enveloped her smaller hands in his larger ones. Dennie longed to sleep, but Esteban seemed fine. Dennie wondered if he ever tired.

Esteban was about to say something when the noisy micro neared them, drowning his words. He stood up and motioned to her. Dennie hefted her shoulder bag and coughed as she climbed onto the yellow bus. The stagnant air hung dense with cigarette smoke. Dennie's head spun as she coughed again. She shook her head to steady herself. The driver brusquely handed her a ticket.

"Your *boleto*," Esteban whispered in her ear. His breath was warm on her neck. He added, "Keep it with you in case the bus is checked." She gripped her boleto in her fist while Esteban clenched his ticket between his front teeth because his arms were full of luggage. They pushed their way through the aisle and found seats. The bus teemed with men and women, smoke and chatter. It swerved onto the chilly, dusty streets of Santiago. As the bus rumbled through the sprawling metropolis, Dennie tried to push away the cough and increasing threads of fever that threatened to subdue her optimism.

At the next stop, a pair of hawkers boarded the bus. The first was a burly man wearing dirty clothes and sporting a short beard. In one arm he held a guitar. With his other hand he pulled a young boy onto the bus with him. The child was clad in a torn suit and fraying bow tie. He carried a bag of candy. "Sweets for sale," the young boy's clear, high voice rang out. Esteban and a lady across the aisle bought some candy. Esteban offered a piece to Dennie. "No, thank you," she mouthed. Sticky sweet smells mixed with the odors of smoke and sweat.

The musician eyed Dennie. He inched down the aisle and stopped next to Esteban. "She is a beauty and you a lucky man!" he said loudly. He touched Dennie's cheek. Then he draped his arm around them both and sang a song called *El Hombre Que Yo Mas Quiero*, The Man That I Want the Most. His breath was rancid, and Dennie's head ached. Nausea gripped her. How would she be able to survive the uncivilized reservation when she couldn't tolerate civilized Santiago? Esteban laughed cheerfully and gave the man a few pesos for his performance.

After the musician headed farther down the aisle, Dennie reached up and opened the window. She felt the cold wind in her face as they passed through a poor neighborhood. Dennie gazed at a seedy bar and dirty children playing soccer in the streets. She watched a stocky boy around seven steal the *futbol* from the opposing team and aggressively dribble it. The scene was so achingly familiar that she suddenly felt like weeping. As she reached for Esteban's hand, the bus barreled through the streets without stopping.

Ten minutes later they came to a part of the city near the university filled with businesses and apartment buildings. "Our stop!" Esteban called to the driver. Dennie followed Esteban out of the bus. He shouldered the bulk of their luggage, leaving Dennie with only her backpack to manage. Still, she dragged the three blocks to the apartment building where his cousin lived. The chilly breeze penetrated her as if her warm jacket were a thin cotton nightgown. At the threshold, Esteban took her hand and touched Dennie's cheek. "Your hand is so cold and your cheek so warm. Are you well, little one?"

Dennie smiled and shrugged. "Just tired, I hope." The door opened and Carmen Marquez, a squat, pregnant woman in her midtwenties, greeted Dennie with a kiss on each cheek. She had short hair, smooth, round cheeks, and expressive brown eyes. Laughter brimmed on the edges of her voice as she welcomed them. Miguel, as round and as jolly as his wife, embraced Esteban and commented on Dennie's beautiful hair and the color in her cheeks.

"Only our Esteban could find a lovely LDS Mapuche girl in the United States," Carmen added. "Yet I think you must be mestizo, Dennie. Your eyes and your mouth are Chilean. Only your nose and the shape of your face are Mapuche." Then Carmen turned to Esteban with twinkling eyes. "Cousin, you have gained weight, but you are still a giraffe!"

"And you, Carmita, have gained the perfect kind of weight," Esteban returned, eyeing her swollen stomach. "A treasure within."

"And you bring a treasure." Miguel winked at Esteban. Then he squeezed the muscle in Esteban's forearm. "But you have lost strength, Cousin. We will arm wrestle tonight!"

"Tonight? Yes!" Esteban raised his brows and laughed as he slapped Miguel on the back.

Dennie wondered at this intimacy between Esteban and his cousins. In her family, they were more careful with others. They didn't talk about weight. Out of respect, they left some barriers in place and made room for pools of unspoken feelings and thought.

Moments later, they sat down for a hearty *almuerzo*. Carmen bustled around the table, serving a large salad, then a casserole of beans, squash, and corn. She clucked and teased the men as she dished up their plates. After the meal, they went into the sitting room. Dennie couldn't stop shivering. When she spoke, her Spanish slurred on her tongue. Miguel laughed and teased her, but Carmen's eyes softened with concern.

"Perhaps Dennie should rest," Carmen suggested. "It's been a long trip."

"But what of your abundance of energy?" Miguel asked Esteban. "Did you sin by drinking a Coke on the airplane?"

"No, I'm just very strong!" Esteban grinned and flexed his muscle for Miguel. Then he added more seriously, "Dennie, I lived here with Carmen and Miguel while I attended the university. I can beat Miguel at arm wrestling and Carmen at chess—sometimes anyway. It is good to be back."

"And it is even better to have Dennie here with you," Miguel exclaimed, grinning at Dennie warmly. "Cousin, you must take her to the temple soon."

"We shall see," Esteban replied with a smile. Dennie tried to suppress a cough, but ended up gagging. Carmen brought her a drink of water.

"Come, Dennie," Carmen interrupted. "You must bathe and rest. We will leave the men to their games."

"Carmen, our *gringita* does not know how to use the *califont* and the *estufa*," Esteban said as he affectionately kissed Dennie before moving his arm off of her shoulder.

"Dennie, I will introduce you to Mr. Califont and Miss Estufa." Carmen took Dennie's hand and led her to the bathroom. "The *califont* heats the water," Carmen explained as she lit the pilot light. "You must light it each time you bathe."

Next, Dennie followed Carmen into a small bedroom with a twin bed and nightstand. There was a picture of the Savior on one wall and one of Joseph Smith on the other wall. "This is where Esteban sleeps when he stays with us. But it is your room now. Esteban will sleep on the couch. There is no central heating like in the United States, so we use *estufas*." Carmen showed Dennie how to turn off and on the gas-powered *estufa*. "The *estufa* cannot be left on at night, but you will be warm as you rest this afternoon."

"Thank you," Dennie said.

Carmen grinned at her. "You are our Esteban's *regalona*. We will do our best to spoil you as well!"

Once alone in her room, Dennie took two Advil from her purse. She went into the bathroom and bent her head over the sink, where she swallowed the pills with a gulp of water. She took a short bath before changing into sweats and a sweatshirt to sleep in. Deeply chilled, she wondered if she would ever feel warm again. As she returned to the bedroom, she heard Miguel laugh and cheer. He must have won the arm wrestling match.

"Best two out of three!" Esteban shouted.

Dennie blew her nose and eased onto the pillows. Her head ached. She curled up in bed, pulling the quilt over her. She heard Esteban laugh with his cousins in the other room. Despite their hospitality, she was a stranger and had an overwhelming desire to write to Ron. She nearly got up, then sank back into the pillow. Her head felt so very heavy.

"Dear Esteban, I am a traitor," she whispered to herself. "I love you, but sometimes I'm alone when I'm with you. And Ron, how would you feel if you knew I was traveling across the world with another man?"

Dennie closed her eyes. She was barely asleep when her brother's image rose unbidden before her. He was young again, a boy of eight or ten. *¡Choro!* He laughed at her as he held a soccer ball under his arm. *Mina, you are back in Chile!*

Lauto! her thoughts called to him with his Chilean nickname. *Come back.* She jerked awake and the dream evaporated. She shook violently, and tears were on her cheeks.

Dennie slid onto the floor as a prayer formed in her heart, a feverish and disjointed entreaty. *Dear Heavenly Father. I'm in Chile. I'm afraid. I thought I saw Lautaro for a moment here in this room, a boy again. I miss my family. I'm not strong enough to be alone. Esteban is taking care of me. I'm sick. I want to be strong. Help me. Bless Mom and Dad, Karin, Blake, and the kids. Bless the prophet and the missionaries. Remember Elder Ron. Remember the little boy kicking the futbol in the street. Bless Thes wherever he is. Tell him I still miss him. In Jesus' name, Amen.* Then, when Dennie's consciousness could no longer form words, she climbed into bed as a dizzy, exhausted sleep pressed upon her.

She slept for hours. Carmen didn't awaken her for *la comida*. Then, as darkness embraced Santiago, overlaying even the cloud of smog, Esteban stepped softly into her room, looked at Dennie longingly, kissed her cheek, and turned off the *estufa*.

CHAPTER 8

CONTRASTS

The three days following Dennie's departure, Meryl embraced her resolve. She immersed herself in writing. She became a part of another world as her imagination formed flesh and emotion around names and dates. The people she wrote about became her friends, their voices dallying on the edges of her mind, their faces crossing the darkness of her field of vision when she closed her eyes. They wore bonnets, hats, and scarves. Their eyes smiled at her. They were her ancestors and she felt she knew them. Yet it wasn't only their circumstances that held her captive, but also those individuals who never conceived children.

No vast historical societies of thousands would bear the names of Catherine and John Carver or Desire Minter. But what of *their* sacrifice? Did fruit descend from their souls, though not their bodies? As she wrote, she prayed that her fictional voice would record something of their history, something of their hope, courage, and continuance. Yet when Meryl's fingers flew over the keyboard, she possessed enough self-evaluation to realize that she was not only writing of those who went before, but of herself as well.

"John, have we done right?" Catherine Carver spoke loudly enough that her voice carried through the wind, but not so loudly that it carried to any other than her husband, who stood straight and tall beside her on the deck of the Mayflower. *They were the leaders, the examples—the two who had means to stay and live a comfortable life, yet chose to go and cast their fortunes to God and the sea. Catherine knew that it had been whispered amongst the saints that if Deacon and Mistress Carver supported this endeavor, then certainly it must be right, for the two possessed worldly goods,*

prudence, and godly wisdom. But though others might be fooled, Catherine did not fool herself. She knew that she and John were as fallible as any.

"What do you mean Catherine?" *Deacon Carver questioned his wife as he felt her shoulder level against his. She was a stately woman, handsome, but well acquainted with sorrow. Her green eyes, though rarely merry, were consistently warm.*

"When I was seasick, I wanted to go back to England or to Holland, to safety and comfort. I did not share my thought with the others, but told them to hold fast to what we knew to be God's will. I pray we do not lead them into disaster."

"Catherine, through prayer, with the love of God in our souls, you and I have chosen to go on this voyage. Remember how our hearts burned at the thought of the New World, where there is no crown to dictate how we must worship. It is the Lord's sea and sky. He will hold us safe under the wing of His righteousness. As for the rest of the saints, each made their own decision with the guidance of the Holy Spirit."

But Catherine was not convinced. Only in the brightness of day could she voice the shadows. At night in the crowded hold, with the stench of bodies around her, she had to fill her mind with psalms and prayers in order to survive. Her husband was the stronger vessel. Catherine Carver spoke once more. "My courage wanes, John! We've lost seven precious weeks since leaving London. Our supplies are limited and winter will soon be upon us. The dismissal of the ship* Speedwell *and the contentious stay at Dartmouth seem dire omens to me."

"The* Mayflower *is a good ship. Today the sun shines and the wind is prosperous. The seasickness has passed. God shall lead us. Fear not, Catherine, we shall build a good life, a new life, in a land of milk and honey."

"But John, the strangers on the ship are so different from us. If we live through the journey, can we build a commonwealth together?"

Deacon Carver turned his gaze thoughtfully towards Catherine. His wife spoke truly. Half of the passengers were not members of their faith. His congregation referred to themselves as "saints" and to these others as "strangers." John sighed deeply. A crease formed in his high brow as he thought of each one. Some were contentious. Others knew little of God.

"Catherine," *he said after moments of silent thought.* "Saints or strangers, we are all the working folk of England, not lords or dukes. Each *yearns for freedom from some yoke. I sense that the passengers of this good ship have more in common than we imagine."*

"I pray that you speak truly, John. On my shoulders I feel the weight of the lives of those we take—lively Master Howland, sweet Desire, and the other servants. Was it God's will to bring Desire or my own? I have wished for a daughter as you have for a son. I have watched you with John Howland. Even on this weary journey, his companionship brings you gladness."

Deacon Carver smiled as he thought of John Howland. "I find him to be a hopeful young man of sound limbs and a quick mind. Although he is merry, he is honest. You and I are old to embark on such a journey. He will be a blessing to us."

"John, I would to God that I had given you children."

"God has not given us children, Catherine. Not you. No, John Howland can never be our son, nor Desire our daughter, though our hearts would have it so. But Desire Minter seems to delight in John's companionship. God willing, perhaps they shall be our heirs."

"Your soul is hopeful, husband." Catherine took his hand.

John Carver watched the sea. "I think of the days before I joined the saints, those winter evenings when you and your brother instructed me and prayed for me. The words of the apostle John brought me hope, and with faith I cast my lot with the saints. When this journey was first conceived, I vowed to help. Yet obstacles hedged our way. Then I witnessed the Lord open doors for us. Every part of my soul believes we have chosen the right way."

Moments later, Carver was called into the cabin to counsel with the elders. Catherine remained on deck as the first evening star lit the heavens. With the dome of sky above and the depth of sea beneath, she knew the Mayflower, surrounded by vast ocean, was as small as this lone star in the wilderness of sky. Mistress Carver prayed that the ship's course would be as steady as the rising star, and that the future would shine as brightly.

When Deacon Carver finished his discussions with the elders, he joined his wife once again. Darkness fell and thousands of stars joined the first. The moon shone round and full. The ocean trembled with heaven's light.

"Come, Catherine," he whispered as the bell rang for prayers. He too wished to linger, but it was time to go below and join the others.

As Catherine descended into the hold with her husband behind her, her stomach lurched. She prayed for courage in this damp, dark, rolling *place where she could hardly breathe and was never warm. And she thanked the heavens that John was beside her.*

Instead of touring Santiago, Dennie spent the morning of her second day in Chile lying in bed with a fever. She arose at noon and the house smelled of herbs and chicken. She went into the kitchen to find Carmen painting her fingernails. Soup steamed from a pan on the stove.

"Good morning," Carmen greeted her, smiling. She blew on her nails to dry them. While her nails continued to dry, she asked Dennie how she felt. Dennie answered that she felt all right and that the soup smelled delicious. Carmen laid her hand on Dennie's forehead to check for fever. "A little warm," she said reaching for a jar of pills on the counter. She opened it and gave Dennie one, then poured the girl a cup of milk.

"What is it?" Dennie asked, looking at the round, white pill. She coughed and her throat burned.

"An antibiotic," Carmen explained. "In Chile we buy them at the drugstore. It will help if you have an infection. Take three each day with food for ten days."

"Yes, Dr. Carmen," Dennie remarked with a smile. Dennie took the pill and sat down while Carmen ladled warm soup for the two of them. Next Carmen cut them each a thick slice of bread. The deep red hue of the polish on Carmen's short nails looked like crimson drops on her dimpled fingers.

Dennie's voice rasped as she thanked Carmen. "It is nothing," Carmen smiled as she slowly lowered herself into a chair across from Dennie. She patted Dennie's knee. "Today you save your voice. I will tell you a story."

The story was of Esteban's ninth birthday party. Carmen chuckled, her painted fingers waving, as she described the event. "The guests included five of Esteban's friends and me. His sisters, Alicia and Marta, were also there. After opening gifts, the children went outside to play. Esteban led the boys in mercilessly teasing and chasing the three girls. Finally, Alicia, Marta, and I escaped into the house in tears. Then the boys roamed the countryside, ending up near the stream. It was against the rules to swim in the chilly water, yet

Esteban dared his friends to jump. The entire group stripped off their clothes and took the dare.

"Meanwhile, after drying their tears, the disgruntled feminine trio sought revenge. They went outside in search of the rogues. Hearing laughter near the water, they hid in a thicket and watched the boys' heads bobbing up and down as they played in a deep pool. Alicia ran to the bank and snatched every shred of clothing. The girls raced away and stowed the clothing in the barn. Then they went inside the house and giggled through their tea party.

"An hour later, Esteban's parents wondered where the boys were and went to search for them. They found them in the forbidden water, shaking with cold, their skin wrinkled like little prunes. After hearing of the three demons who had stolen the clothing, Juan laughed so loud that the woods rang with the sound. Marisol marched off to confront the girls. Alicia claimed she had no idea what her mother might be talking about. *Esteban and his friends in the river? Oh goodness, no!*" Carmen stopped for a moment, her plump frame shaking with silent laughter. Then she continued.

"But sweet Marta suggested her mother look in the barn. Marisol went off with a humph, her wide hips swinging in her loose dress. She retrieved the clothes and rescued her son and his guests. After the boys dressed, instead of reprimanding them, the Antemil parents let them bat down a piñata and stuff themselves on sweets. Aghast, Alicia and I suggested that the boys be punished instead of rewarded for their terrible behavior. Juan grinned at his daughter and niece and said that the guests had already paid in full for their crime.

"You will like Esteban's family," Carmen said as she finished the story. "Only pay no attention to Alicia's moods. Alicia is queen bee."

After lunch, Dennie swallowed two more Advil and slept long and peacefully. At four in the afternoon, her fever broke, and she awoke to Esteban standing over her. "Do you feel well enough to see Santiago?" he asked. His smile looked boyish to her. "The wind has blown away the smog," Esteban added.

Dennie nodded. "Let's go."

Forty minutes later, she and Esteban walked holding hands down the *Paseo Ahumada* toward the center of Santiago. The snowcapped Andes rose tall alongside the city. The setting sun bathed the mountain range in pink and orange light. A sweet yet aching sensation swelled within Dennie—the rose-colored peaks looked so familiar, dear and painful. She remembered drawing stylized versions of these mountains in pictures as a little girl.

They passed shops, banks, department stores, and newspaper stands. Young men in business suits and waitresses in miniskirts moved like fluid, silent puppets in the windows of restaurants. They turned down the Alameda, and Esteban pointed out the University of Chile, where he had attended school. He asked if she felt well enough to walk quickly, as he wanted to spend some time on a hill called the *Cerro Santa Lucia* before it grew dark. Dennie nodded and did her best to combat the heaviness of her head and legs. Soon they reached the *cerro*.

They went around to the west side, where a lift took them up the skirt of the hill. When they disembarked, there was a lovely park containing a maze of fountains, pathways, and gardens. "This is where Pedro Valdivia and his one hundred fifty men first camped," Esteban explained. "Valdivia announced he would found the city here. At the time, it was just a rocky outcrop that the Indians called *huelen*, which means 'pain.'" Dennie and Esteban strolled around the hill for a time, holding hands, passing lovers arm in arm. They sat down on a bench as darkness fell. Wind blew through Dennie's hair. Esteban turned her head toward him and kissed her tenderly.

"Aren't you worried about catching my cold?" Dennie asked a moment later. She snuggled into him. He smelled good—warm and clean.

"I have an excellent immune system. *Muy fuerte.*" Esteban grinned. "How do you like the city?"

"It is beautiful," Dennie smiled softly. She felt the chemistry between them.

"Yes," Esteban agreed. "Now that the smog has blown away. " Dennie rested her head on Esteban's shoulder. Stars began to appear in the sky.

"Now I will tell you the story of a man who wanted to be king," Esteban said quietly. "A hundred and fifty years ago, a French man set sail for southern Chile. His name was Orelie-Antoine de Tounens. He carried with him dreams of grandeur. He traveled to Araucania, the land of the Mapuche. Strangely, shortly before he arrived, a great chief named Manil died. As Manil's spirit left his body, he prophesied that a bearded white stranger would lead his people to freedom. The new chief, Quilapan, welcomed Tounens, thinking he was this king, and so the Frenchman's rule began.

"The Patagonian Indians on the other side of the Andes also accepted Tounens as their ruler. Elated by this power, Tounens drew up a constitution for what he called *La Nouvelle France.* However, the Chilean government did not recognize him. He ruled for almost a year until his own servant, Rosales, lured Tounens into a trap where army officials jumped and gagged him and took him to a filthy jail. After spending a few weeks there, Tounens agreed to leave Chile. In my heart I believe that the chief, Manil, was a prophet, and that a bearded white king will lead the Mapuche to freedom someday. The king's name shall be Jesus Christ, and the people will be free from the bondage of death and sin."

Dennie nodded. Esteban looked down at her. His eyes were moist. He cupped her face in his hands, feeling the softness of her skin. "I love you," he whispered into her hair. "This is like a dream for me."

"Me too," Dennie whispered back.

On the way back to Carmen and Miguel's apartment by taxi, with Esteban's arm around her, Dennie looked out the window and was touched by the statue of the Virgin Mary on the Cerro San Cristobal. The white marble shone in a halo of bright lights. There was something in the grace, sweetness, and outreached hands of the Madonna that reminded Dennie of her own mother so far away in the United States.

Early the next morning, Dennie and Esteban boarded a plane that took them from Santiago to Osorno. Dennie coughed throughout the flight, and her ears ached during the ascent and descent. As they neared their destination, Esteban pointed out the Rahue River and the volcanoes in the east. They flew over wooden houses with sharply angled roofs. Dennie noted that the weather of southern Chile was more like the weather of New England in the United States. The farther south one travels, the colder it becomes.

Esteban's entire family, including his brothers-in-law, nieces, and nephews met them at the airport. Dennie smiled and tried to return their embraces, though inwardly she grew weary. Her nose was running again, and she clutched a tissue in her fist as she hugged these strangers. For the drive home, the entire party crowded into a dilapidated van and a worn truck. Despite the cold, Esteban and

Dennie snuggled in the bed of the truck amidst their luggage, with wool blankets wrapped around them. As they approached the crumbling Antemil farmhouse, the sky filled with heavy clouds.

"It doesn't look like much," Esteban commented on their arrival. He jumped out of the truck and helped Dennie down. "But the house has indoor plumbing, heat, electricity, and a computer—luxuries we won't find on the reservation."

"I wonder what we will find," Dennie said aloud. Despite her cold, she breathed in farm smells, animals, fresh air, pungent manure, things both growing and rotting.

That afternoon after a multi-coursed meal, Marisol, gray-haired and brimming with matronly warmth, managed to clean the house, dote on her grandchildren, and chat all at once. She insisted Dennie stay with her and the girls while Esteban and Juan shopped for items for the trip to the reservation. After the men left, Dennie felt drawn to Marta, who was small and slender with a ready smile. Alicia, taller and built much like her mother, smiled less often.

"Come, let's teach Dennie to dance the *cueca*," Marta suggested during a lull in the conversation.

"It depicts the mating rituals of hens and chickens. Dennie won't like it," Alicia stated.

"But it's our national dance," Marta implored.

Dennie glanced at Alicia. "I'd like to try it."

"Then you shall!" Marta exclaimed. She sent her six-year-old, Alejandro, to retrieve the handkerchiefs. Marisol sat down at an old, upright piano. She played and signaled for Marta and Alicia to begin dancing.

"This dance is supposed to be a courtship dance between a man and a woman. We are both women," Alicia complained over the sound of the music.

"Come, the dancers don't even touch each other!" Marta exclaimed, growing disgusted with her sister's attitude. "You, Alicia, are the rooster."

Alicia rolled her eyes and briskly took the handkerchief her sister handed her. She and Marta began dancing toward and around each other, waving the handkerchiefs. Alicia imitated the aggressive, strutting male, and Marta was the shy, flighty female.

Alejandro clapped and stomped to the music. Dennie couldn't help laughing. A few minutes later, Marta insisted that it was Dennie's turn to dance. She danced opposite Alejandro, imitating Marta's fluttering movement, and arched back as she dodged the pursuit of the debonair Alejandro. Alicia's baby girl, Josefina, laughed out loud. Then, during a spirited shuffle away from Alejandro, Dennie suddenly fell into a fit of coughing.

Marisol's fingers stopped on the keys. "It is the foul air of Santiago!" she exclaimed, gazing compassionately at Dennie. "I could not breathe when we lived in that city. Child, you won't be going to the reservation until you are completely well. The machi might perform the machitun over you and try to heal you."

"And Dennie would turn into a duck," Alicia said sarcastically as she picked up Josefina and balanced the child on her hip. "Come, Mother, the machi doesn't want to perform the machitun over Dennie, but to teach Dennie to perform the machitun herself. Hopefully Dennie is adult enough to understand what will be expected of her and strong enough to bend the machi's will. Luckily, the machitun is not fatal!"

Alicia ignored her mother's hushing glare and added with a coy smile, "Dennie, don't let Mama make you frightened of the machi. The Mapuche are harmless. Just beware of the poisonous spiders in the wheat fields." Dennie sensed that Alicia's smile held little warmth, and knew that regardless of whether or not the Mapuche were harmless, Alicia was not, and would be as quick to steal Dennie's clothes as she had been to steal her own brother's so long ago.

Yet Marta was as full of friendly conversation as Alicia was of cynicism. Marta's youngest, two-year-old Juanito, smothered Dennie with kisses as Marta followed Dennie around the house and asked her a hundred things. This sister, just a year younger than Esteban, was especially curious about Thes. Marta repeatedly questioned Dennie about him, explaining that she could not have survived if Esteban had died. She also asked how it felt to be adopted and part of a family who wasn't truly your own. *But they are my own family,* Dennie explained. In the end, she grew nearly as weary of Marta's personal inquiries as of Alicia's caustic glances.

Yet throughout the three-day visit, Dennie enjoyed the sturdy, kind presence of Juan Antemil. In the depth of his dark eyes, Dennie recognized the younger man, an employee of *Hogar de Cristo*, who cared for her and her brother when they were little. Years ago she called him *the jail man,* for even as a very young child she knew that the building that sheltered the thrown-away children of the city was simply an old jail no longer in use. The five-year-old Mina instinctively trusted her *jail man,* and the twenty-one-year-old Dennie still did.

Juan gave both Dennie and Esteban blessings the morning they left for the reservation. Juan's hands, stained and wrinkled by work and age, felt familiar. Dennie, who had been growing increasingly homesick in the Antemil household and increasingly nervous about visiting the Mapuche, found the gentle weight of Juan's hands upon her head calming and comforting. She felt the power of the priesthood as Juan spoke. "Our Father in Heaven, guide her footsteps and lead her soul by still waters. Keep her from harm. Bless and protect her family in the United States."

Finally, under a sky crowded by fleecy white and gray clouds, with volcanic mountains looming in the distance, an awestruck Dennie sat next to Esteban in the aged, four-wheel-drive truck as they drove over bumpy, muddy roads on their way to the reservation. They had been traveling for over four hours, but Dennie did not feel tired. It was as if her senses became more alive with each bend in the road. They passed lakes that reflected the sky and stunning glades of forest with fog and silver cobwebs stretching from bush and tree. Dennie rolled the window down and breathed in the chilly air. It seemed she could smell the life around her. The blue sky and green land danced through and within her.

"Oh, Esteban! It's so beautiful!" she gasped. "There aren't any words to describe it."

"No English or Spanish words," he said. "But the Mapuche have words to describe this place. They have names for everything, even the stones. You will learn so much."

Dennie nodded and smiled inside. She wasn't afraid right now. How could a place of such loveliness be terrifying? The very land whispered of the wonder of those born and bred here. They were called the people of the land and now she understood why. No wonder they loved the land more than gold. And she was one of them. This was why she had come.

She reflected on her own life so full of contrasts. Just a few days ago she had lain in bed, shivering with fever. Just last night, she had been nearly sick with fear. Now she was strong and adventurous.

"I hope we don't get stuck." Esteban's laughter ended Dennie's reflections as they barreled through a deep puddle that sprayed mud over the sides of the truck. "If we do get stuck, we will walk the rest of the way."

"I wouldn't mind." Dennie grinned. "I love this place."

"Enjoy the moment. The western sky is darkening. It will rain soon," Esteban added. They rounded a bend and came upon a grove of unique evergreen trees. Large and stately, the trees' branches worked together to form elegant, umbrella-like shapes. There were four thatch-roofed huts situated throughout the grove.

"Do people live here?" Dennie asked.

"No," Esteban answered. "These huts are communal property. Mapuche families travel here after the harvest festival to gather nuts. These are araucania pines, a tree the Mapuche reverence. Perhaps we will come here again before our adventure is over."

"Why don't we eat lunch here?" Dennie suggested.

"I think we should keep going and eat in the car," Esteban countered. "We need to make it to the reservation by dark. I don't want to be lost in this wilderness when the storm hits."

Two hours later, rain cascaded from the sky. The soaking world darkened as they approached the reservation. Dennie was glad they hadn't stopped. Tired, stiff, and chilled, her earlier optimism slipped away like the sun lost in the storm. Chewing on her lower lip, she stared out the window. Steady rain beat upon the truck as they entered the village. It felt as if this muddy road led into the past.

Smoke rose from windowless, thatch-roofed *rukas,* whose only doors faced east. Dogs barked. Horses and sheep crowded under trees for shelter. Sturdy, round-faced children stood in the rain without blinking as they stared at the truck.

The mud became too deep to drive through, and Esteban stopped the truck. Dennie donned her plastic, orange rain poncho. She and Esteban seeped through the mud to the far ruka. The old machi was already outside. She wore a woolen poncho that looked black in the night rain. Without speaking any greeting, she climbed up a carved wooden pole. It reminded Dennie of a totem pole, standing about five feet tall and fifteen inches thick with carved notches forming steps. Sopping branches of laurel and cinnamon tree surrounded the pole, the machi's *rewe*, her ladder to heaven.

"*Ngillatu mekewi in*," she cried, her voice raised above the cry of the storm.

"She is calling to me, you, herself, and God," Esteban whispered in Dennie's ear, "*Ngillan* refers to the power that allows life as well as the knowledge which preserves it. *Mekewi* is the present, the thing we are doing. *In* means we."[2]

The machi beat upon the sacred drum and continued to pray in a loud voice as lightning lit the sky. In the split second of light, Dennie saw that her poncho was deep blue with geometric patterns of yellow. Rain and tears fell upon her wrinkled, contorted face.

"She says that your mother's spirit now crosses the river of sky to the other world." Esteban's voice was like the wind in Dennie's ear. "Because her daughter's heart now beats in the home of her ancestors."

Dennie leaned into Esteban. Her own heart beat as wildly as the machi's pounding on the kultrun. The power of the storm and the machi terrified her. She said a silent prayer, knowing that even with Heavenly Father's aid, she needed Esteban beside her.

"Stay with me," she whispered to him as she gripped his hand.

"Forever and ever," he whispered back.

The machi climbed down from the rewe and approached Dennie. A thousand wrinkles rimmed her eyes. The toothless old woman stepped so close to Dennie that the young woman instinctively took a step backwards into Esteban, nearly falling.

The machi stared at the girl, face to face. Dennie looked down. Esteban's arms were around her. If Dennie had been able to read the machi's mind, she would have known that the old woman saw her daughter, Pinsha, in the tilt of Dennie's head, the shape of her chin, and the angle at which she leaned into the man with her.

He seems almost to be holding her up, the old woman thought. *She is too much like Pinsha.* The machi's heart shadowed in the thunder. *The girl is weak. She is winka. This child will never be Mapuche or a machi. Why have the gods whispered to bring the girl here? Are they laughing at an old and feeble woman who has no young machi to take her place? I am a fool.* The machi's soaked clothing lay heavy upon her as the proud old woman turned away and walked into her ruka. She heard the voice of the vulture in the wind, and she did not beckon the couple to follow.

Dennie looked down at the mud at her feet. She knew she had not pleased the old woman. She had not passed some test. Unshed tears burned her eyes. Esteban tightened his arms around her.

"Mina." Dennie and Esteban turned to a voice behind them. Standing there was a middle-aged Indian woman. Her hair was matted from the rain. She wore boots and an old coat. Her Spanish was fluent and she smiled as she spoke. "Welcome. I am Maria Callfuhuala, your mother's brother's wife. You are to stay in my ruka." She turned to Esteban. "I spoke to your father a month ago. Tonight, you may sleep inside. Tomorrow, you will find a place to pitch your tent."

As they followed Maria, a spear of lightning filled the sky. A gust blew the hood of Dennie's poncho back. She felt the rain soak her hair and drip down her back. She gained courage in the thrill of the storm. She thought of the machi. Who was this woman really? What in her had been passed on to Dennie? Then her mind flew like wind across the ocean to the warm, sunlit home in California where the mother who loved her sat at a computer, typing out the story of an English ancestry.

CHAPTER 9

DREAMS

John Howland watched the sky, the blue gray clouds layering it like hundreds of frozen waves dissipating as they reached the pink-amber shore of the horizon. This morning, as with each dawn, he had arisen early to help the sailors raise and lower the sails and secure the rigging.

It was done now, and the fair day stretched before him. Soon the company would be on deck, and John would have companionship. He was neither saint nor stranger, rich nor destitute. Yet many sought his company. Because he was merry, children begged him to join them in their games. Because of friendship or love, Desire smiled at him as she and Mistress Carver administered to the sick. Because he was young and restless, indentured youth pulled him aside and whispered of the evils of their servitude. Because his arms and shoulders were strong, Miles Standish spoke to him of soldiery. And because of the intellect in his eye and the compassion of his glance, Deacon Carver read the scriptures with him and taught him the gospel.

But for the moment, John stood alone, and even the sounds of the ship seemed distant as he gazed eastward toward England, toward his own family. He had been raised in the town of Fenstanton, Huntingdonshire, nine miles northwest of Cambridge, on the old Roman road, the son of Margaret and Henry Howland. His father, a yeoman, owned a small farm. Margaret Howland had a Bible and taught her sons and daughters to read. Although the family was not rich, they were bright eyed and hearty. But the farm would never yield enough produce to support the wives and families of each of Henry Howland's four sons. Arthur, the eldest, was the sole heir.

So John had gone to London to seek his fortune. He had tried his hand in his brother Humphrey's drapery shop, but the work of a craftsman was frustrating to John. He yearned to cultivate and work his own land, to feel the sting and stroke of sun, wind, and rain, to harness the elements and cause them to produce. But this would never be, not in merry England, where the gentry owned most of the land and a man's class condemned him to misery. Or so it seemed to John. At night he would wander the streets of London, sometimes stumbling with drink in his belly, sometimes defending the weak with the power of his fists, always helpless under the lash of his dreams.

Then one rainy day, Desire came into the shop with Catherine Carver. Desire did not carry the somber demure of many Puritans. Her eyes twinkled and her cheeks were rosy. Her smile shone like a ray of light. She spoke to John while her mistress looked at cloth. Her affable ways cheered him. The following evening, he spied her wrestling a chicken as she made her way home from the market. He took the bird and carried it for her. He told her how his mother at times put a chicken down the chimney. It would clean out the soot by flapping its wings and flying upwards. They laughed at the ill-fated fowl and spoke of dreams. She told him of her coming journey to the New World, and he entreated her to speak of him to Deacon Carver.

The next morning, Carver sent for John and hired him to do various tasks. The older man was impressed with John's abilities and spoke of taking him on as an indentured servant. And so John, who had always avoided servitude, found freedom in binding himself to this pious and kindly man. Someday, *John vowed,* I will plow my own fields.

Thus, in an instant, the seed was planted that would grow and change John's path forever. After Deacon Carver indentured John to him, John traveled to Fenstanton to bid his family farewell. Humphrey accompanied him. When he reached home, his brothers, Arthur and Henry, clapped him on his back and hugged him fiercely as they wished him well. "When you are rich, John, we will join you!" they laughed. "Are there any pretty maids in the New World?"

"One truly," John answered, grinning.

But Humphrey shook his head and told John it was folly to risk the mighty ocean when he might choose the safety of the drapery shop. Then John's sister, Margaret, wept into her skirts. John sang to her and teased her until she looked up at him. "I shall not see you again, John," she cried, and pushed him away. An instant later, she grabbed him to her in a fierce embrace.

The next day, John's parents bid their son farewell. His mother's

hands shook as she kissed John's cheeks, yet she smiled amidst the tears.
"Good fortune, my boy. May our Lord go with thee."

"Long life, John," his father said, his face weathered, his chin firm,
his eyes blinking rapidly in the sunlight.

On the road to London, the sun shone bright and cool on the green
land. John and Humphrey stopped at a lake for water. While Humphrey
ate his lunch sitting on a rock, John shed his clothing and jumped into
the cold water. Humphrey shook his head as he took another bite of
cheese, thinking that his younger brother was a fool. Even the smallest
child in England knew that swimming and bathing were unhealthy.

Yet as John entered the stretch of blue, the chill of the lake enveloped
and enlivened him. His heart beat quickly. He kicked his legs and stroked
his arms to warm himself. Floating on his back, he looked up at the sky.
He would miss England, but it was his fate to seek a better fortune.
Perhaps someday his family would join him in a new and beautiful land.

He stood on a rock jutting from the lake like a small island. John
stretched out his arms, feeling the tingle of water and wind on his body.
He laughed at Humphrey, who patted a full belly. Then John dove deep
and swam to shore. He imagined that the traces of youth had washed
away, and he was a man ready to resume his journey.

Back on the deck of the Mayflower, *John's thoughts turned away*
from England as six-year-old Wrestling Brewster tugged on his shirtsleeve.
"What is it that creepeth on the ground, his house on his back?" the child
asked. John shrugged and his eyes smiled down at the lad.

"A turtle, sir," the little boy grinned. John laughed long and loud to
delight the child.

"And what is as long as twenty men and as strong as thirty men, but
a hundred men cannot make it stand up?" John returned. The child
shook his head.

"The ship's rigging," John shouted as he picked the child up and
tossed him in the air. The boy's gown fluttered as John caught him under
his arms. He held the boy—heart beating against heart. In a moment of
quiet they heard Wrestling's father, William Brewster, reading the words
of the psalmist before morning prayer:

"Thou dost prepare a table before me in the sight of mine adversaries:
thou dost annoint mine head with oil, and my cup runneth over.

"Doubtless kindness and mercy shall follow me all the days of my life,

and I shall remain a long season in the house of the Lord." [3]

Aimy chewed on the end of her pen as she meticulously went over the details for Waverly's birthday party, then glanced at her watch. She needed to leave for Grantlin Park in ten minutes. She repeated the guest list aloud: Sean, his parents, Meryl and Rick Fletcher, Bishop Taylor and his family. She had even sent an invitation to her mom and Len in Texas—just for the fun of it.

She thought of how everything was set for the barbecue. The coals and lighter fluid were in the car. Sean would bring Beef Burger patties, buns, and fixings. Meryl was bringing a fruit salad and Karin a pasta salad. The ice chest full of soda was in the back of the Yellow Toy. Aimy clicked the button on the end of the pen with her thumb. She wanted things to run smoothly mostly for Wave, but also to impress Sean's mother. Rhea Garrett, a tall, thin woman with short, severe gray hair, was not easily wooed.

Aimy's foot drummed the faded linoleum as she checked off everything else on her list: Meryl would bring the croquet set—Wave loved to play croquet. Sean had Waverly's gift, a three-wheeled adult bike, in the back of his truck. "All set!" Aimy said aloud. "On your mark, get set, go!"

Aimy stood up and went to the refrigerator to get out the cake she had ordered from Costco. It said *Happy Birthday, Waverly* and was decorated with a clown and balloons. She thought of how she had picked it up that morning and a grandmotherish bakery employee had asked her how old Waverly was today.

"Sixty-one," Aimy had answered truthfully. The woman had then looked at Aimy like the girl needed her head examined.

Aimy bent over and lifted the cake, then heard a sound that momentarily froze her—a key in the front door. She stood up straight, her heart pounding. She and Moni were the only people who had keys, and Moni was in Texas. What was going on? The door creaked open.

"Who's there?" Aimy called loudly as she gripped the cardboard sides of the box holding the cake and set it down on the counter. She opened the knife drawer.

"It's just us, Baby! Me and Len! Surprise!" Aimy heard her mother's voice. An instant later, Moni and Len stood in the kitchen, grinning at Aimy like little kids who had just played a huge April Fool's joke.

"But you're in Texas!" Aimy gasped as she gaped at her mother's streaked-blonde hair and wide smile.

Moni giggled. "Not right now! We hopped on an airplane and came on over for the party. When we got the invitation, Len said, 'Let's fly to California and surprise Aimy.' I said, 'Won't it cost too much money?' Len said, 'So what? You only live once!' So, here we are! Joni's taking care of Len's kids. We're flying back tomorrow."

"I can't believe it!" Aimy hugged her mother. "I thought for a second that maybe you died, and your spirit teleported here to say good-bye on its way to heaven."

"No, it's me, Baby, it's the real me!" Moni laughed. Then she introduced Len. He had thin, muscular legs, curved shoulders, a cowboy hat, and deep smile wrinkles around his eyes and mouth. He seemed really nice, but Aimy reserved judgment. As far as good men were concerned, Moni had a low batting average.

"Let's go," Len said as he put his arm around Moni's shoulders. "We don't want to be late for the party."

"Then we're off," Aimy said as she picked up the cake. Moni and Len followed her out into the late afternoon sunlight. Aimy liked the fact that Len opened the door for Moni before the two entered the rental car. It seemed to be a good sign.

When they arrived at the park, Sean was already there. He acted like it was the most natural thing in the world to have Moni and Len skip over from Texas for the party. Sean and Len lit the barbecue while discussing cows, horses, and cuts of beef. Moni and Aimy tied bows and balloons all over the bike. When the guests began arriving, Aimy left to pick up Waverly. A few moments later she arrived at Sean's apartment to find Waverly waiting outside, dressed in his Sunday best.

"You look handsome in that tie," Aimy said. "But you might not need it where we're going."

"Where are we going?" Waverly asked as he hefted himself into the car.

"It's a surprise," Aimy answered as she tied a blindfold around his eyes. Waverly loosened his tie.

"I'm sixty-one today," Waverly commented. "That's very old."

"No, eighty is very old," Aimy corrected. "Sixty-one is a great age."

"Sixty-one years old, two-hundred and sixty-one pounds, and sixty inches tall."

"I'll get you some platform tennis shoes," Aimy said. "Then you'll be sixty-one inches tall."

Waverly chuckled, but when he spoke again his voice was serious. "Aimy, how old do you think I'll be when I die?"

"Probably a hundred, Wave. Don't talk about stuff like that."

They drove the rest of the way to the park as Waverly chattered about past birthdays. Once there, Aimy helped the blindfolded Waverly out of the car. All of the guests, including the twins, waited silently while Aimy positioned Waverly in front of the ribboned three-wheeler.

She untied the blindfold. Waverly blinked his eyes. He burst into tears. The shouts of surprise and the blue, shiny bike covered with balloons and ribbons were more than Augustus Waverly could bear. "All of my dreams have come true!" he exclaimed.

The party proceeded perfectly. The air smelled of spring. People ate and played croquet. Christopher opened a bag of birdseed, taking handfuls and twirling while the seeds arched and sprayed from his fingers. A menagerie of ducks and geese ran over, and Waverly and the twins threw handfuls of seed into the air while Karin took pictures. Afterward, Waverly tried his bike out in the parking lot. Delighted with the front and rear baskets, he put a twin in each and rode. "Now I can go to the store and to work by myself!" he exclaimed.

Waverly stopped riding when dusk fell. Len and Sean pretended they were monsters and chased the little kids through the trees. Blake, Rick, and Waverly joined in by stalking and moaning like zombies. Christopher alternated from chasee to chaser.

Moni laughed as she sat on the grass next to Meryl. "What do you think of Len?" she whispered.

"A keeper," Meryl whispered back, squeezing her neighbor's hand.

"Have you heard from Dennie lately?" Aimy asked Meryl as she joined the women.

"She e-mailed us the day before she left for the reservation. She said she had a cold. Other than that she sounded fine."

"She sent me a note too," Aimy added. "Santiago sounds cool.

And things with Esteban are heating up."

"How so?" Meryl asked.

"While you two chat about Dennie, I'm going to talk to the Garretts," Moni announced. "They look kind of lonely over there, and we might be related someday." Moni lightly nudged her elbow into Aimy's rib cage. Aimy winced.

Moni felt a bit nervous as she approached the Garretts, her hips swaying slightly in her tight, faded Levis. The couple wore buttoned-up polo shirts and crisp, pressed slacks. Thoughts swam in Moni's mind. Would they like her? Would they mind that Aimy wasn't from a regular Mormon family?

"Hi," Moni said.

"Hi," Rhea echoed as Moni pulled up a lawn chair.

"Len and I flew up for the party. We're going back to Texas tomorrow." Moni attempted to make conversation.

"That's nice," Rhea stated.

"When will you be back to stay?" Cliff Garrett asked, exuding friendliness.

"In three weeks. Len and I are talking marriage though, so I'm not sure where I'll be next year."

"How long have you known Len?" Rhea asked politely.

"My sister Joni told me about Len a year ago. At first, I didn't want to meet him. But then I found out he's the sweetest guy on the earth. I'm as crazy about him as Aimy is about your Sean."

Rhea's smile looked strained. The conversation waned. A few minutes later, Rhea alerted her husband that it was time to go. Moni waved Len, Aimy, and Sean over. After the initial good-byes, Aimy and Sean walked the Garretts to the car.

"Are you sure you don't want to stay?" Aimy asked. "Blake brought his guitar."

"Oh, I didn't know *Bishop* Taylor played the guitar." Rhea stated. Aimy wondered if Sean's mother was correcting the way Aimy had referred to Blake. He had been Aimy's seminary teacher and friend for years. She couldn't get used to calling him *bishop*.

"We're going to sing and roast marshmallows. Why don't you stay for a little while?" Sean added. For a moment, his expression seemed to Aimy like a hopeful little boy.

"Son, we would like to stay, but we need to leave," Rhea said. "It was a nice party, Aimy," she added.

"You young folks have a great time," Cliff Garrett grinned. "Aimy, you are a sweetheart." Sean looked visibly disappointed about his parents' departure. Aimy looped her arm through his.

"You have to understand that we are in the middle of spring cleaning. Tomorrow is a workday for *us*," Rhea said. "We also get up at five in the morning to exercise."

Party-pooper, Aimy thought to herself. She smiled falsely and waved good-bye cheerfully. If she was going to marry Sean someday, she'd better get used to it.

Fifteen minutes later, the group gathered around a bonfire. Marshmallows crackled and billowed on sticks. The sticky-faced twins sat on either side of their mother, their eyes bright in the firelight. Len and Moni had their arms around each other. Rick and Meryl held hands. Sean and Aimy cuddled. Christopher sat next to Waverly. Blake picked up his guitar and the group sang Waverly's John Denver favorites while the fire glowed and the smoke rose high in the air. Waverly had a nice voice and knew every word of each song. His voice blended with Blake's, and the others sang along. With Sean's arms around her, listening to Wave's voice, and watching her mother smiling up at Len, Aimy did not wish for a mission, marriage, a degree, or a job. She only wanted that very moment to last—forever and ever.

During her first night with the Mapuche, Dennie's emotions vacillated from fascination to fear. Her stomach squeamish, she longed for electricity, heat, and indoor plumbing. She hardly slept, though her sleeping bag was thick and the mattress beneath it soft. In the morning she felt immeasurably thankful to Esteban both for his presence and for the makeshift bathroom he constructed outside at dawn using tarps held up by poles and trees. Here Dennie washed, shivering in the cold, using basins of warm water that Esteban heated over the fire.

The Callfuhuala family consisted of Maria, her husband Mercurio, and their twelve-year-old daughter, Eva. During breakfast, Dennie ate a small portion of the vegetable and lentil soup that Maria cooked over the fire. Noticing Dennie's hesitance, Eva approached Dennie and shyly offered her apples and milk, calling her *Mina*.

Dennie thanked Eva and returned her smile. Esteban studied the soup as if trying to memorize the ingredients.

Mercurio stared silently at Dennie, his bangs long and matted, his eyes dark and probing. Dennie reddened and was glad Esteban sat beside her. She had no idea what was behind her uncle's glance. Maria seemed to sense Dennie's discomfort and whispered to her guest that Mina reminded her husband of his sister, Pinsha.

After breakfast, Mercurio explained that it was harvest time and there was much work to do. He and his family would be in the fields all day. Esteban asked if he could help. Dennie echoed the offer. Maria smiled and Mercurio nodded.

It was almost an hour's journey by oxcart to the wheat field. The day was overcast, and the mountains loomed gray and white with snow and mist. When they arrived, Dennie watched in wonder as Mercurio harvested the wheat. Though middle-aged and small in stature, he was quick, strong, and lithe. He moved with the same intensity and quickness of purpose that she remembered in her brother. The muscles in his arms tightened as he taught Esteban how to cut the stalks with an iron sickle. "You hold the stalks below the ears with your little finger facing the earth. Here you cut the wheat." Mercurio worked through the field like a machine, leaving ears of wheat in his path. Esteban tried using the second sickle, but his hands were clumsy, and he was sweating, though the day was chilly. Dennie laughed and warned him to be careful or he might cut his fingers instead of the wheat.

Dennie copied Maria and Eva as they followed the men through the field, gathering the cut wheat in armfuls and loading it in the oxcart. After a morning of labor, the cart was full. The family stopped working and ate lunch. Dennie and Esteban accepted the food offered to them by Maria—homemade tortillas and beef that had been spiced and dried. They drank milk sweetened with honey.

After the meal, Maria, accompanied by Eva and Dennie, drove the oxcart to a knoll of flat rock. The women unloaded the ears of wheat. Eva and Dennie were instructed to thresh the wheat while Maria returned to aid the men in the fields. "I must take the sickle from Esteban," she said to Dennie with a shy smile. "The work will go faster."

After her mother left, Eva, who wore short boots, began tramping on the wheat, grinding it into the knoll and thus separating the husks from the kernels. "See, Mina, this is the way," the girl said brightly, her braids swinging and her poncho swaying. "You step like the jilguero bird! He does not hop." Eva sang gaily as she shuffled two steps forward and three steps back, breaking open the kernels. "Beat! Beat my feet. Break these ribs. You and the jilguero bird."[4]

Dennie joined in. It felt good to move, work, and laugh with this sweet and friendly girl. First Eva taught Dennie the Mapuche threshing songs. Then, as the afternoon lengthened, Dennie sang to Eva, bright songs like "California Girls" and "The Yellow Submarine." Eva laughed at the English words and tried to hum along as she stomped on the wheat. When Maria returned with another load, she smiled at the two young women, warmth in her dark eyes.

Later, the sun sank in the west as the weary group made their way back to the ruka. Dennie and Eva rode in the cart with the bags of wheat. The others walked. When they entered the hut, the machi was inside, like a silent shadow, waiting for them. Dennie noticed that Maria's smile faded when she saw the old woman. Solemn-faced, Maria welcomed her mother-in-law and immediately tended the fire and began cooking.

That evening, the only conversation was between the machi and Mercurio. They spoke in Mapudungun, and Dennie could not understand. But she noticed that Esteban was very still, concentrating, digesting each word as he chewed his food. When they had finished eating, the machi stood and stretched up to her full height. She opened her mouth as if she would speak. Though aged, Dennie sensed her grandmother's confidence and power. The woman glanced momentarily at Dennie with stern, bloodshot, unblinking eyes. Then her look fell to Eva and remained there, softer now. She spoke in Spanish so that all could understand. It was an oration, not a conversation.

"This is the dream that awakened me to become a machi," the old woman began. "Two beings came before me. Though I did not know them, I was not afraid. When they walked, they looked like people, but their feet did not touch the ground. They said they were sent by Chau to tell me to continue the ancient rites and to cause the nillantun to be convoked; they who forget Chau shall be unhappy on earth and shall not enter into his kingdom.

"Next, four old men approached dressed like the rainbow. They clothed me with many colors and adorned me with leaves of the canelo. My food was the copihue flower. They took me to the four points of the earth: the east, the north, the west, and the south. They named me Melillanka, meaning, in the voice of the people, *four magic stones.* They told me that I must love my neighbor and cure him from his illness and evil. *Take the herbs of the land,* they said, *and give these to men to drink. Chau has blessed these; do not have any doubt.* Then, they left me and I returned to earth, where I woke up."[5]

After she finished speaking, the old woman went to Eva. She touched her cheek with her wrinkled, leathery hands and kissed the girl's forehead with parched lips. Tears shone in the machi's eyes, and her hands trembled. Eva's eyes were wide, but Dennie couldn't read her thoughts.

"Mother," Maria said softly. "Eva has had *no* dream."

"It will come," the old woman returned, her tone almost a challenge. "And with it a new name. She is the only one." Then the machi signaled Mercurio that it was time to go. Her son rose up and left the ruka with his mother.

After they left, Maria explained that Mercurio would not return that night. Her husband went to aid the machi as she performed the machitun on a woman who was ill from childbirth. "It is time now to prepare for sleep," Maria stated.

Dennie went outside and watched as Esteban pitched his tent on a small hill south of the ruka. Her body ached from work. She had no doubt that she would sleep as soon as her head touched the pillow.

"It looks like you're off the hook as far as becoming the next machi," Esteban said as he pounded a stake into the ground. His voice was light, almost teasing.

Dennie shrugged and said, "She took one look at me and knew it could never be." Esteban nodded. "I don't think she likes me very much," Dennie added.

"It's hard to tell," Esteban commented thoughtfully. "She really wanted you to come. Anyway, Eva's taken with you." He stood up and put his arms around Dennie's waist. "She's not the only one."

Dennie leaned into Esteban. "It's so strange being here. It's the most beautiful place I've ever been—and the scariest. Eva's sweet.

Maria too. I think I will love them before this is over. I don't think Eva wants to be the next machi."

"Who knows?" Esteban shrugged. "To the Mapuche, becoming a machi is a great honor."

A moment later, in the makeshift bathroom, Dennie changed into sweats and a sweatshirt. She kissed Esteban good night before going back into the ruka.

"Esteban es muy guapo." *Esteban is very handsome.* Eva whispered with a giggle when her cousin entered with a flashlight in hand. Dennie smiled and agreed. Eva looked eagerly at the flashlight.

"Here, you keep it," Dennie said, and handed the girl the light. "I have another in my suitcase." Eva beamed, thanking Dennie. Dennie crawled into her sleeping bag and fell immediately asleep despite the intermittent streams of light as Eva clicked the flashlight on and off. That night as Dennie slumbered, she did not dream. Yet the reality surrounding her contained as much adventure, hope, and terror as any night illusion.

CHAPTER 10

THE FINAL THING IN PANDORA'S BOX

"Aimy, Wave wants to go to a funeral!" Sean said as he sidled up to Aimy a week later during a midafternoon lull at Farmer Owen's Beef Burgers. They wore bib overalls and red plaid shirts—the Beef Burger uniform. Aimy's overalls came to just above her knees, while Sean's went to his ankles and had the word *manager* embroidered on the front pocket.

"What?" Aimy looked at Sean in disbelief.

"Our friend, Augustus Waverly, has a morbid streak. He has a *thing* for funerals. When Parley Daniels came by to home teach last week, he asked Wave if there was anything he could do for him. Waverly said to let him know when funerals are scheduled. 'Hmm,' Parley said, 'not many funerals are scheduled in advance.' Then Parley and I laughed and Wave turned red. Anyway, Parley called last night. Brother Jeffrey died. "

"You lie," Aimy said good-naturedly. "There isn't a Brother Jeffrey in the ward." Aimy sprayed cleanser on the counter and started wiping it down. Sean watched her. She was a hard worker and so full of life. He thought about teasing her and asking if she ran off of Energizer batteries. She could go and go and go. He loved her shape—her slim, freckled limbs, the quick, light energy.

"What are you staring at?" Aimy eyed him and aimed her spray bottle towards the middle of his forehead. "Get to work or else!"

"I'm the manager. Talking, watching other people slave, that's my job." Sean grinned. Then he added, "But I wasn't lying about the funeral gig. Brother Jeffrey is Harry Jones's grandfather. He was ninety-eight, and he's been in a rest home for the past fifteen years."

"Really?" Aimy set the cleanser down. Her forehead wrinkled as she mused. "I wonder why Wave likes funerals. I can't stand them."

"Why don't you go ask him? He's right outside."

Aimy gazed out the big glass window at the children's play equipment. Sean had hired Wave to keep that area clean. The only customer at the moment was a young Asian-American mother dipping curly, pigtail fries into barbecue sauce while her children played. She wasn't the usual mom-in-sweats-and-tennis-shoes. She wore gray pants, boots, and a silky, salmon-colored blouse. Her hair was pinned and styled fashionably. A baby in a car seat slept at her feet. She rocked the car seat with the toe of her boot. A boy and a girl around three and four years old played on the equipment.

It seemed like a strange thing to Aimy, looking so good with all those little kids. Aimy thought about how as a teen, she had disliked baby-sitting—whiny, demanding, irritating children. And it bugged her how pretty young women got married and transformed into tired-mommy slobs. *I could never do that,* Aimy had thought a billion times. *I don't have the patience for kids.* But as Aimy observed the young mother, a longing swept through her. She wanted to walk right out there and pick up the sleeping baby, to feel the infant's warmth against her shoulder and the touch of the tiny eyelashes brushing her cheek.

The two children climbed to the top of the slide. They each had a toy car in hand. "Tell us which car is the winner!" they called down to Waverly, who was putting red, yellow, and blue balls back into the ball pit.

"OK!" Wave called back as he stationed himself at the bottom of the slide. The cars zoomed down. When Wave announced the winner, the little girl cheered and the little boy shouted his disappointment.

"Do it again!" Wave suggested. This time the boy ended up victorious and the little girl cried.

"Time to go!" their mother called.

"Not now!" shouted the boy.

"Five more minutes!" wailed the little girl. The baby woke up screaming, and Aimy's urge to hold the child lessened dramatically. A breeze lifted a napkin off the table. Wave scurried over and picked it up. Then he pulled two pieces of candy from his pocket and gave them to the mother, who used them to bribe her children down from the slide. Waverly threw away the garbage on the table, and the young mother smiled Waverly a thank-you as they left.

Aimy turned to Sean. "Wave likes working here. It makes him feel useful. Thanks for hiring him."

"Cheap labor. Besides, I didn't want him hanging around my apartment all day." Sean grinned and Aimy humphed. He laughed and added, "You know I think he's doing a great job. People really like him. The *Grantlin Herald* plans to write an article about him. Great advertising!"

"He's proud of his overall uniform," Aimy said. "When's the funeral anyway?"

"Thursday, 10 A.M."

"Well, Mr. Manager, are you going to take the morning off and go with Wave?"

"No, but I'm giving my favorite employee the morning off to take him."

Aimy winced. "Sean, I hate funerals. Plus, I really need to work. I need the money."

"Why don't we take him together?" Sean suggested. "And think of the money you'll be saving. If there are enough funerals this summer, you won't need to take Wave to Marine World or Great America."

Aimy laughed and flicked the rag at Sean. "Fun-nee!"

"Funerals are fun! Fun! *Fun!*" Sean grinned like a demon and raised his eyebrows a couple of times.

"You are insane!" Aimy cracked up. Then Sean put his hands on Aimy's slim shoulders and rubbed them for a moment before tickling her.

That same afternoon at the Taylor home, the telephone rang. Someone had called a few moments ago, but Karin hadn't answered. The mystery caller hadn't left a message. Karin considered letting this call go as well. She hesitated giving up one of those rare, quiet stretches of time while the twins napped and Chris was at school. Yet she wondered who it might be. Was it the same person who had just called? Karin picked up the telephone. "Hello?"

"Karin."

Her stomach tightened as she recognized the voice. It was her ex-husband, Cory Parker. The story of Pandora's Box, which she had read to the twins before their nap, flew through her mind. Curiosity had been Pandora's tragic flaw, and it seemed that Karin's own curiosity about the telephone call just reopened her box of troubles.

Cory spoke, "I made airline reservations for Chris today. He'll be flying here on June fifth and back on August seventh."

"Cory, we already went over this. Christopher is refusing to go," Karin explained. "Maybe if it were just for a weekend."

"He's coming! The tickets are nonrefundable. He had a great time at Christmas!"

"He was homesick at Christmas. I don't want to force him, Cory. It won't be good for your relationship with him."

"I know what's best for my relationship with my son. I've paid child support for a lot of years. The judge gave us dual custody."

"I think you should consider Chris's feelings."

"Are you talking about *his* feelings or *yours*, Karin? He's never told me that he doesn't want to come."

"He's afraid to, Cory. He's just a little boy."

"He's not a little boy anymore. I'm his father. Let me talk to him."

"He's not home from school yet."

There was silence on the other end, and Karin could feel Cory's anger. Her heart beat faster, and she put her hand on her back as she lowered herself into a kitchen chair. Scenes flashed through her mind as horrible as the demons flying from Pandora's box.

She married Cory right out of high school. He was five years older then Karin—and a returned missionary who had joined the marines. Her parents were wary. They didn't like the way Cory criticized little things about Karin—he didn't like the way she did her hair, her chattering, or her taste in clothes. But first love carries a power of its own, and Karin remained enchanted.

Within two months after their wedding, Karin was pregnant. First came a daughter, Nicole, and then Christopher fourteen months later. Karin staggered beneath the constant needs of her babies and the unceasing criticism of her husband. Depression enveloped her. His wife's weakness frustrated, disappointed, and angered Cory.

With her parent's support, Karin sought professional help. Things improved sporadically. Then, when Nicole was three and Chris a toddler, the family went on a camping trip. Karin perspired as she stood over the fire, cooking some fish Cory had caught. Flies swarmed the fish. She batted them away and heard a truck barreling through the campground. Karin looked up to see a flash of Nicole's bright swimsuit through the distant weeds. She instinctively called out her child's name, not realizing that Nicole was on the far side of the road. Her beautiful, tiny girl ran toward Karin's voice, in front of the truck.

After Nicole's death, Karin drowned in grief and guilt. Cory's criticism turned to cruelty as he pointed all blame in her direction. Her parents came over one day while Cory was at work. They loaded Karin, Chris, and a few of their things into the car and drove away. Karin never went back.

Pulling her mind away from memories and back into her own bright kitchen, Karin's hands shook as she held the telephone. How strange that the human mind could travel back in time, that Cory's voice could bring back the emotion of the past.

"Karin! Are you there?" His voice was loud in the telephone.

"I'm here," she answered.

Then Chris burst in the front door and ran into the kitchen. "Mom, if that's Dad on the phone, tell him I won the chess tournament!" Chris shouted. "Tell him I'll take him on when he gets home!"

Cory's voice was edged with tightly controlled anger. He had heard his son refer to Blake Taylor as *Dad*. "I don't let Chris call Jerry *Mom*. I've asked you not to allow him to call Blake *Dad*."

As Christopher opened the refrigerator to get a snack, Karin carried the telephone into the bathroom and closed the door. She didn't want Chris to overhear. She hated how this conflict shadowed her boy's life, and knew she had to be strong for his sake. She remembered the final item left over in Pandora's box after all of the horrible things had flown into the world. It was *hope*. She took a deep breath.

"Cory, I can't help it if Chris calls Blake *Dad*. That's Chris's choice. For six years, you rarely contacted Chris. Blake is the father in this home—you have to understand that."

"You want to know why I didn't contact Chris?" Cory was yelling now. "Do you know how bad I felt? My baby girl was dead and you took my son away! Do you know what you did to me? Nobody deserves that! This is unbelievable! My kid is going to spend the summer here, Karin. It's my legal right."

Why did a part of her pity Cory? Had his pain at Nicole's passing been as horrible as her own? He had always battled his temper. Was that his fault? But Chris wasn't comfortable around Cory. Chris wanted to be home. Her abdomen cramped violently, and she sat down on the lid of the toilet seat. It cramped again. She had to get off the telephone, had to lie down.

"I have to go. I'm sorry." Karin touched the button, disconnecting them.

Karin went to bed and the cramping stopped. A half hour later, the twins woke up and started jumping on her bed. From the kitchen, Chris yelled for them to be quiet and whined for Karin to help him with homework. Karin stood up and the cramping commenced. She looked at the clock. Blake's shift was nearly over. In tears, Karin called her husband and asked him to come home as soon as he could.

Blake was home within an hour. The boys were watching cartoons when he walked into the door, and he hurried into the bedroom. Karin apologized for worrying him and explained that the cramping had lessened and there wasn't any bleeding. But when he asked how her day had been, she couldn't keep her eyes from filling with tears. As she told him of the conversation with Cory, his jaw formed a hard line—a look so uncharacteristic of Blake Taylor that it caused his wife to stop talking in midsentence.

"Bill Edwards on the high council is a family law specialist. He's out of town this week, but I'll call him Monday," Blake said tightly. "We'll get the custody agreement changed. I won't allow Cory Parker to force Christopher to leave. And he's not going to upset you and endanger your health or our unborn daughter's life."

"But don't you see, Blake?" Karin voice was urgent as she sat up in bed. "Don't you see how Cory feels? He feels like I stole his son away without his consent. I caused his daughter's death. Cory will fight with everything he has to prove I'm not a capable mother, to get custody of Chris. The legal fees could kill us. And look at me—overwhelmed and out of control. This place is a mess. Cory will bring up my postpartum depression and what happened to Nicole. We could lose everything if we reopen the past. We could lose Christopher." Karin felt her stomach turn. She began crying.

Blake put his arms around her. "Honey," he whispered in her ear. "No court in the United States would take Chris away from you. He's been with you every day of his life, and he's a wonderful kid. You're a wonderful mother. Things are going to be fine."

The eleven-year-old boy listening outside the door with his math book under his arm couldn't hear his stepfather's quiet reassurance. But he had heard the rest of the conversation. His mother had caused the death of a sister he couldn't even remember. If he didn't spend the summer with Cory Parker, there might be a trial and the judge might force him to move away. All this stuff was upsetting his mom so much that it could hurt his baby sister before she was even born.

Chris did his homework alone that night, and hardly spoke during dinner. He failed his spelling test the next morning. That afternoon, while staring at the television set, he made up his mind. After dinner, he announced to his mother and his stepfather that he had changed his mind. He wanted to spend the summer with his real father. When they asked why he felt differently, he said that Dennie was getting to know her real grandmother, so he figured he should get to know his father better. Plus he'd get a trip to Disneyland and Universal Studios. His mother hugged him and asked if he were sure. He shrugged her away. Blake repeated the question. "Yeah," Chris said. "Absolutely."

Later that evening they called his father to tell him the news. Cory Parker hurrahed into the telephone. He promised baseball games, soccer and football in the evenings, and trips each weekend. Chris asked if he should bring his chess set. "Nope," Cory Parker said. "Leave it there. I don't play. We'll have better things to do. You'll see!" After the conversation ended, Chris went into his room and threw his chess game against the wall. A pawn and a bishop shattered. The king rolled under the bed, and the queen's head broke off. Then Christopher set to work constructing a huge warship out of tiny Legos.

On the way back from the funeral, Aimy sat in the car's passenger seat next to Sean. Her head throbbed. In the back seat, Waverly cheerfully hummed "I Am a Child of God." Sean joined him. Aimy's nerves were raw. She had hated the funeral. It hadn't held the debilitating sorrow of Thes's four years ago, but it still was sad—and she didn't even know the guy. There had been a flag draped over the casket, and pictures of him when he was young and vital. His grown children had cried when they talked about him. His life was over now. Over. Dead people didn't even look real. They looked like mannequins in a wax museum. Then they were buried. Her head felt like it was about to split open.

"Wave, I don't get it!" she finally burst. The humming ceased. "Funerals stink! How can you stand them? They are so depressing! Don't hum anymore. My head is killing me."

Sean cut in. "Aimy, Wave likes funerals. He really does. It's no big deal."

Aimy glared at Sean. No big deal! Four years ago, Thes's funeral had almost killed her. Thes had been more than a childhood friend—so much more. When she was in fifth grade, he had hidden her in the Fletcher's walled-off garage for four days to protect her from Moni's abusive husband. Two months before Thes had died, when he had been playing football during a championship game, Aimy had grabbed a bullhorn and cheered for him. After he had heard her voice, he had scored a touchdown. The next day he had touched the bruise on her cheek and had given her a rose. He had told her she was too good for that jerk, Brak Meyers, whom she had been dating. When Thes had died, a part of her world had been cut away.

"I'm sorry, Aimy. I didn't know the funeral would make you sad," Waverly said softly.

"Funerals *are* sad, Wave. They always have been and always will be."

"Let's not go anymore."

"How can *you* stand them, Wave?" Aimy repeated.

Waverly shrugged. In the rearview mirror, Sean noticed that his bald head had turned red. Was it from the warmth of the afternoon? Was he embarrassed? Was he ashamed because he had hurt his Princess Aimy?

"Come on, Wave, tell us why," Sean prodded gently. "Everybody likes different things. It's OK. Why do you like funerals?"

"They always say nice things about people," Wave said quietly.

"They do," Sean agreed.

"The music is pretty," Wave added.

"Uh-huh." Sean nodded.

"And people talk about how nice it is to go back to heaven. I like that."

"Me too," Sean said.

"But I don't want to go to funerals anymore," Waverly insisted.

"Listen," Aimy cut in as she leaned her head against the window. "Wave, it's OK if you like funerals. From the sound of things, Sean enjoyed it too. Maybe it's a guy thing."

"Wave, my man, the three of us will go to Great America," Sean said. "But when there's a stiff, it's me and you, buddy!" Upon hearing Sean's words, Aimy couldn't help herself, and she glanced at the two men and had to laugh.

CHAPTER 11

THE GOLDEN COIN

Blake Taylor sat up straight in his bed at five o'clock Monday morning. A dream had awakened him. In the dream, his father had been running toward him, full of youth and vigor. Suddenly his father had crumbled, his leg bent at a strange angle. His mother had appeared at her injured husband's side. She had looked up and called for Blake to help. Blake hurried toward them, but by the time he arrived, his mother's hair had turned white and her face was old. His father's body lay cold and still.

Blake's thoughtful eyes fell on Karin. She snored softly in her sleep. He tucked the blanket around her and climbed out of bed. For a tall, middle-age man, his movements were smooth and silent as he dressed in jeans and a T-shirt. He went into the kitchen and poured a glass of milk. It was close to eight in the morning in Virginia. He thought about how his mother had called him a couple of weeks ago and asked about the kids and Karin's pregnancy. There was no tension separating Blake from his mother like that which existed between her and Meryl. Blake knew that his mother viewed him tenderly. As a child, he had seen beneath her starched demeanor, and had recognized the tenderness in her eyes when she read to him and the love in her touch when she held his hand.

He remembered how Joan had been disturbed rather than angry when he joined the Mormon religion. She assumed that he had been deceived by his sister and had not willfully rebelled against his parents or God. Thus Meryl absorbed most of the blame. Mother and son had written regularly on his mission with the understanding that he would not try to convert her, and she, in turn, would not belittle Mormonism.

His parents had not come to California when he married Karin. But they had visited shortly after the twins were born. It had been a good visit—Joan adept and helpful with the babies, and Ben charmed by Karin's sweet friendliness.

Blake picked up the telephone and dialed the same number he had memorized as a child. Joan answered with a curt *hello*.

"Good morning, Mom," Blake ventured.

"Blake! What a surprise! How are you?" It sounded as if his mother's voice had been injected with cheer.

"Fine. I was thinking about you and Dad. I even dreamed about you."

"Was it a good dream?"

"Hmm," Blake chuckled. "Well, in my dream Dad was running and broke his leg. You called for me to come help."

Joan laughed. "You're dad hasn't run for a long time, and I'm doing just fine. I need to leave in a minute. I'm helping with the school's field day. Then I have two weeks off before I go back to tutor the kids taking summer school."

"You're one busy lady."

"It keeps me out of trouble. How is Karin's pregnancy? How are Christopher and the little boys?"

"Fine. Chris is going to spend most of the summer with his biological father in southern California."

"I don't think that's a good idea, Blake. The boy needs to be home with you and Karin."

"Chris made the choice," Blake said, a shrug in his voice. "We told him he didn't *have* to go."

"I'll keep the boy in my prayers," Joan offered. "How is Meryl?"

"Fine. Did she tell you that Dennie is in Chile?"

"No," his mother answered. "It's been a long time since I've heard from Meryl."

There was an instance of silence where Blake wondered if it would be wise to continue this line of discussion. It had also been a long time since Meryl had heard from her mother. Joan picked up the dangling thread of conversation. "Honey, give the children a hug from Grandma and tell Meryl hello. I need to leave now, but I'll go get Dad to talk for a minute. He'll be glad to hear from you. Good-bye son, and God bless."

"Good-bye Mom," Blake said, but he knew she didn't hear him. She had already gone into the back of the house to get Ben. Blake's parents had never purchased a cordless telephone; his mother claimed they caused brain cancer.

"Son!" Ben's voice boomed onto the line.

"Hi Dad!" Blake raised his voice so that his father could hear. "How are you?"

"Good! How's Meryl?"

"Fine! Dennie's in Chile."

"Dennie's chilled. Is she sick?"

"She's fine, Dad. She's traveling this summer. In the country, Chile."

"Oh." His father still sounded confused. Blake knew that it was difficult for him to hear over the telephone lines.

"Tell Meryl I love her."

"I will, Dad."

"How's your family?"

"Great! The baby's due in a couple of months."

"I'll talk Mother into coming out."

"We'd love that. Dad, I've been called to be bishop."

"You've been called what?"

"Bishop, Dad. I'm a Mormon bishop now."

"A Mormon bishop! Son, I'm proud of you."

"Thanks, Dad. I'd better go now and get ready for work. I love you."

"I love you too, Blake."

Blake put down the telephone. Lines of care etched his face. He had dreamed of his parents joining the Church and had prayed that the rift between his mother and Meryl would mend. It didn't seem that the dream or prayer would come to fruition anytime soon, maybe not even in this life. Blake made a decision. He would continue to pray.

About the time Blake hung up the telephone, Meryl awakened. Rick slumbered next to her. Two memories immediately ran through her conscious mind as if they had been part of her dreams. First, she had a mammogram scheduled for 11:30 that morning, and second, she hadn't received an e-mail from Dennie for over two weeks—ever since the day Dennie had left for the reservation.

Meryl considered how she had checked her messages at eleven the night before. Dennie had *promised* to e-mail home on Saturday or Sunday when she was at the Antemils on a weekend break from the reservation. Meryl fought the urge to run to her computer and look once more.

But she had been obsessive about checking her e-mail all weekend. Perhaps Dennie's plans had changed. Maybe she and Esteban had ended up staying on the reservation. Meryl shook her head briskly to stop her thought patterns. It was almost humorous the way her imagination wreaked havoc by concocting circumstances that could have caused Dennie not to e-mail—earthquakes, volcanoes erupting, or banditos with knives. Even with her best effort, these images dallied on the edges of her mind. *They are fine*, she told herself firmly. *If anything were wrong, Juan Antemil would have sent word. I'll go on a walk and shower. Then I'll check my e-mail.* Meryl got out of bed.

Seconds later, the simulated sound of birds rang from their Nature Awake alarm clock. Rick stretched and his eyes opened sleepily. "Hi," he muttered as he reached over and turned off the alarm.

"Good morning," Meryl returned. She slipped into her navy blue jogging suit. "My mammogram should be over by one. Do you want to meet somewhere for lunch?"

"Sure, where?"

"The Oriental Garden?"

"It's a date. How'd you sleep last night?" Rick knew that his wife was usually restless the nights before her mammogram—not to mention their shared concern over Dennie.

"Better than expected," Meryl smiled at Rick as she tied her tennis shoes. "Maybe someday mammograms will feel routine."

"No doubt." Rick stretched in his white T-shirt and navy blue pajama bottoms. So much navy blue, Meryl contemplated. Was it the color of their conservative life? She gazed at her husband. Though middle age was etched in the lines of Rick's face, his physique was still lean and compact.

Rick did not have the softness of her brother, not physically or emotionally. The tightness of his muscles paralleled his tendency towards perfectionism. This trait had served him well in the professional world. Yet if Meryl could have altered anything about her husband, she would have blessed him with a more easygoing nature.

And she would have made the rendering of tender physical affection more natural to him. He did not seem to need the hugs and touches that meant so much to her.

Early in her marriage Meryl had wondered why she had been attracted to a mate who seemed emotionally more like her mother than her father. Had she done this in a subconscious effort to try to fix something? But as time passed, she had found Rick to be a good listener, and his unwavering dedication to their marriage nourishing.

Years ago, when they had found out about her infertility, they both had been stunned. But after she had cried, fire had filled her eyes, and she had told Rick that if he wanted to leave her, he could. She wouldn't carry the baggage of having messed up *his* plans for *his* life. She was strong. She could make it on her own.

"What are you talking about, Meryl?" His reaction had been both honest and incredulous. "I married you. This isn't *your* problem, it's *our* problem. It's something we deal with. It's part of life." At that moment, Meryl had loved him for the real shock he felt at her words and for the matter-of-fact integrity of his response.

What did it matter if Meryl had to remind Rick to say *I love you* at night and to hold her hand when they went on dates? When she asked him, he tried. It had been like this for twenty-two years. They were comfortably settled in the rhythm of their companionship. Meryl treasured the integrity and constancy of his support while accepting the way he loved.

When Meryl came back from her walk, Rick grinned as he ate cold cereal for breakfast. "So, what's the good news?" she asked.

"An e-mail from Dennie," he remarked. "She's doing fine! She sounds happy. I'm so proud of her!"

Meryl ran to the den. Rick had left the e-mail on the computer screen. The message was long. Meryl read it with a longing for satisfaction that must have been similar to the hunger Esau felt when he devoured his mess of pottage.

Hi Mom and Dad! We spent the weekend at the Antemils. In about two hours Esteban and I leave to drive back to the reservation. After spending two weeks with the Mapuche, I'm both anxious and hesitant to go back. Walking into their village is like stepping into the past.

Sometimes it's really hard though. I long for a shower and clean hair. There's no electricity or plumbing. It's chilly all the time, and the food is strange. There is such little variety. For breakfast and supper the Mapuche eat a tortilla-like bread with a soup or gruel that is cooked in a pot at the hearth. The soup is flavored with salt, chili peppers, and greens. I can't stomach it in the mornings. For the midday meal we usually have a dish made of beans, peas, corn, and potatoes. It's called pisku, *and I sort of like it. We eat beef jerky when we go on day trips. Fresh meat is only eaten on special occasions.*

I'm not used to poverty like this. Sometimes when I watch how hard the people work for so little, especially the women, my heart aches. There is a twelve-year-old girl in the family I'm staying with. Her name is Eva and she has become my dear, little friend. She goes to a small school run by nuns. She is very bright. She reads well and speaks fluent Spanish. I bought some books this weekend that I'm going to give her. When Eva is not in school she tends the sheep or spins wool for her mother, Maria, who weaves beautiful wool ponchos. Sometimes I sense that Eva wants more than life on the reservation. But it will be such a battle.

The lack of sanitation is a challenge every single day. Luckily, Esteban brought some tarps and made me a makeshift bathroom. I'm so thankful for the canned food he packed and for my warm sleeping bag. He's taking good care of me, Dad.

What else would you like to know? Mom, you said to tell you every little thing. I'll try. It rains three out of four days! But that's why the world is so green. It is gorgeous here, and I'm taking lots of pictures. There are mirrorlike lakes reflecting volcanic mountains. I've been in dense forests full of fern, mist, and wildflowers. There are stretches of open space where the Indians farm winter wheat. Esteban and I helped with the harvest the first day we were here. The people live in thatched-roof houses called rukas. *They have only one room and no windows. The hearth is in the center, where a fire always burns. A large pot hangs above the fire.*

The door of the ruka always faces east. This has religious significance because the Pillan, *or glorified ancestors, are said to live eastward. Esteban compares this to phrases in the scriptures referring to eastward in Eden, and to how the statues of Moroni on the temples face east.*

I am staying in the ruka of Maria and Mercurio Callfuhuala. Mercurio is my birth mother's brother. Maria, his wife, came from a different village. The society is patriarchal and partrilocal—women live with their husband's families after marriage. Identity comes through the male line. Esteban sees this as parallel to the family structures in the Book of Mormon. Remember how it used to bug me that Ishmael's daughters had no given names? They were always referred to as daughters or wives of men (the wife of Nephi, etc.). Well, it's kind of like that here.

Now, more about Esteban. He sleeps in a tent that he pitches outside the ruka. He calls himself my sentry, my human guard dog. He puts a thick tarp underneath his tent so he stays mostly dry. It gets so cold though, and at night a dog whines at the front flap of Esteban's tent, begging to come in. Esteban says that if it gets any colder he will invite the dog in for body heat—fleas or not!

I stay warmer than Esteban because I am inside the ruka. It gets smoky though, and sometimes I cough at night and my eyes water. But I'm feeling well. My cold and sore throat are gone. Maybe living so primitively will make me tough! I hope so.

The evenings are fascinating. The oral tradition of the Mapuche is so rich. Families and others in the community talk, sing, and tell stories to work out problems. In the Callfuhuala home, Maria and Mercurio tell Eva tales by firelight and sing to her in their native language. Mercurio's hands are amazing. They move so quickly when he tells a story, almost like the hands of a snake charmer. Sometimes other families will come too. I can't understand much of their conversation since I don't speak Mapudungun. Sometimes the language is even difficult for Esteban to understand, regardless of his years of study. It helps when Eva cuddles up next to me and interprets in Spanish. Although the entire family can speak Spanish, they continue to speak Mapudungun at night to keep their culture alive.

During these evenings, Esteban tries to teach the gospel. He tells our hosts about Joseph Smith and shares stories from The Book of Mormon. They listen to him with nods and smiles. Then Mercurio tells his own tales about talking stones, whispering foxes, and demons within volcanoes. I can tell that it frustrates Esteban—that he feels as if he isn't being taken seriously. I don't know how to help.

It is fall now. We did the most amazing thing last week. We attended the Nillatun, *or harvest festival. The people prepared for it all week by cooking food, shining silver jewelry, patching clothing, and currying and clipping the horses and oxen. I helped Maria as much as I could. But the most fun was helping Mercurio with a beautiful, dark bay horse he calls Namcupan. Esteban tried to groom him, but Namcupan pinned his ears back and bit him. (Esteban has a big bruise on his arm.) But I had been visiting Namcupan every day and feeding him apples, so when I took the soft brush, Namcupan let me groom him. I loved it. Namcupan means* Eagle Lion. *I climbed on him and Mercurio led me around. (Dad, remember when I was little and I would beg you for a horse?)*

Anyway, when it was time to go to the harvest ceremony, we traveled three hours by oxcart to a grassy field in a glade where the ground is never plowed and animals never graze. Oh, Mom and Dad, how do I describe it! Indians came from all over to attend. There were hundreds of people. They set up a carved altar, or rewe *(it's sort of like a small totem pole), in the middle of this circular field (the circle is a very important symbol to the Mapuche). Sacrifices were offered—stuff like grain and then a sheep. I couldn't help crying when they cut off the sheep's ear and bled him. Esteban was so fascinated, but I think that little Eva felt the same way as I did because she held my hand tightly.*

Next, the heart was cut out of the sheep and a bowl of its blood was burned on a sacrificial fire. Then the Mapuche people danced in a slow circle around the altar. Men on horses encircled the field, galloping and shouting. This was supposed to drive evil spirits away.

There was music—whistles of stone and trumpets of bamboo. The machi, my grandmother, beat on her sacred circular drum, or kultrun. *She wore a blue and white poncho the colors of the sky. She climbed the altar and sang to the beat of the kultrun. Eva interpreted for me: "We pray for rain to increase our crops, to multiply our animals. Divine Man with the golden head and you, Divine Woman—Make it rain! We pray to the two great, old persons."* [6]

Mercurio said that there aren't many machis who are as powerful as our grandmother. She is said to have the power to communicate between the earthly world and the spirit world. This communication allows her to motivate the spirit world to action, and thus people are healed or crops are saved. Esteban told me that anciently the machi were men, not women. He thinks this a shadow of what was once priesthood authority.

I don't know. The Mapuche religion seems so different from the true gospel to me. I can tell that my machi grandmother wishes she had never brought me here. She stares at me a lot, but hardly ever speaks to me. She never invites me into her ruka. She rarely comes to Maria's ruka in the evenings. She is aloof, and it makes me feel so strange. I think there is a hard look in her eyes when she watches me. I don't please her. Maybe she thinks that the gods made a mistake in asking me to come.

I asked Maria if the machi is angry with me. Maria said that the machi is sad. There isn't anyone to take her place, and she thinks she is going to die before August, the time called the black month. The machi wondered if I had the spiritual gifts to become a new machi. Now she knows I do not, and she feels foolish. Eva is the machi's only hope.

I asked Maria how a new machi is chosen. Maria explained that they choose themselves. Usually a young girl becomes deathly ill and is miraculously healed by a machi. Or she is struck by lightning and recovers. Then she dreams a dream usually involving a white lamb and a kultrun (the sacred drum). After this she knows that she is called to be the next machi. But this doesn't happen often nowadays. The machi are dying, and young girls are not replacing them. Maria says that the rising generation has little use for the superstitions of the past. They seek Chilean medicine, but my grandmother fights this trend. I asked Maria how she feels about it. But she didn't really answer. She just said that she doesn't know what will happen. Then Maria's eyes followed little Eva's every move as Eva played with her pet lamb. Maria started to say something about Eva, but then she reconsidered and wouldn't go on. I don't think Maria wants Eva to be a machi. But Maria doesn't trust me enough to talk to me about it. Not yet, anyway. I like Maria. I like her shy, smiling ways. She works so hard.

Each day, Esteban and I grow closer. He is so kind to me and very protective. He is a comfort when I feel frightened or alone. It would be so hard if he wasn't here. One day, Esteban and I played chueca, *a kind of hockey, with Eva, her friend Juana, and two young boys. It was raining softly, but I felt so alive as we ran and laughed with a snow-capped volcano in the distance. It was a wonderful time.*

Mom and Dad, this place causes me to think about Thes all the time. Sometimes I feel like I can see him in Mercurio. He is about the same height, and his eyes are similar. Mercurio is slimmer than Thes, and very quick on his feet, hence his name. His father's name, Neuculfilo, means running snakes. I think Thes's quickness must have come from these same genes.

Another strange thing—I've found out that blue is the sacred color of the Mapuche because it is the color of the sky. They speak about how the rivers of sky lead to the Promised Land of the afterlife. Remember how Thes used to race the sky! And the family last name, Callfuhuala, means blue gulls. Thes was trying to get a hook out of a seagull's mouth when he died. This seems so strange to me.

Yesterday during the sacrament, I thought of when Thes died, and I imagined Thes traveling through the rivers of sky to Heavenly Father and Jesus. I cried and when Esteban asked what was wrong, I told him I was so thankful for the gospel. I'm so grateful that the Savior's sacrifice paid the price for all of us. I wish Thes could be here with me, learning about this people. We are of Lehi's lineage. I would like to talk to him about that and about what it is coming to mean to me. But I think maybe he already knows—maybe an angel has shown and explained all of these things to him. I wish that Esteban and I could teach the gospel more effectively to the Mapuche. But it seems like an insurmountable task. Except, perhaps, with Eva. She is so eager to learn. Maybe faith can move mountains of superstition.

I love you both. Esteban was right—it is the adventure of a lifetime. I miss you, but will see you in six weeks. During the next two weeks I hope Maria and Eva will teach me more of the Mapuche way. I wonder if Maria is something like my birth mother. Her eyes are kind and her smile quick. Perhaps she can tell me about my birth mother. But at the same time, I feel so thankful for you, Mom, and you, Dad. I feel such gratitude for the life and family you gave to me. I'm glad my life is not like Maria's. I pray that there is hope for Eva and other children like her.

I will write more in two weeks. I'm going to send a quick note to Aimy. I was hoping there would be a letter from Ron waiting for me at the Antemils, but there wasn't. I feel guilty, still wanting his letters while I grow closer to Esteban. I'm not going to think about marriage right now. I'm going to take it one day at a time. Tell Uncle Blake that he needs to get the Internet so I can e-mail him. Tell Chris that I didn't take a bath for two weeks. He'll be very jealous. E-mail me.

Instead of going all they way back to the Antemil's every two weeks, we will travel to the nearest town every other Saturday. Esteban met a member of the Church there who has a computer. When we go, I'll check my messages and we'll stock up on supplies. It's not as far, so we can go to town and back in a day. Love you mucho! Dennie

Meryl printed out the message. After reading it once more, she folded it carefully and put it in the desk drawer. She sat still for a moment, sorting through conflicting emotions—joy in the woman Dennie was, and renewed heartache at the mention of Thes and the days gone by. Would her Dennie marry Esteban and live in Chile? Was it the Lord's will?

Meryl sighed deeply. *There is something about raising children,* Meryl thought with tears in her eyes, *that is like gold coins produced by a refiner's fire. One side of each glittering piece holds the face of joy, the other side the face of sorrow. Each time a circle of gold is thrown into the air, we do not know on which side it will land. We only pray that it will land in our Savior's hand.*

CHAPTER 12

WHEN ONE MUST

Meryl wiped her tears away when she heard Rick call good-bye from the kitchen. She found a smile and called out, "See you at lunch." A moment later, she heard his car pull out of the driveway.

Taking a deep breath, she lowered herself to the floor, kneeling with her legs tucked under her hips and her hands folded in her lap. Her prayer was honest and open, with some words spoken aloud and others whispered in her heart. It was the prayer of a woman who did not hide her soul from God. When she finished, she felt more acceptance and gratitude. Her daughter was learning so much in addition to being healthy and brave. With God's help, Meryl possessed the strength and skill to make it a day worth living. She looked at the clock, noting that she had an hour before she needed to shower. She turned on her computer and continued her story.

Joan Tilley watched from her bunk as her thirteen-year-old daughter, Elizabeth, carefully placed her eighteen stones, nine shiny and nine dull, into the green silk bag the girl wore around her waist. Mother and daughter had just played a game of Nine Men's Morris. Elizabeth tucked the playing board away.

"Excellent game, Mother." The girl looked up and smiled. Her eyes shone green and bright.

"Excellent for you, Lizzy." Joan smiled back. "Are you champion of the whole ship?"

"Nearly. But I won't play Francis Billington. He carries his father's musket, pretending he is one of Captain Standish's soldiers. If I won the game, I would fear for my life!"

Joan chuckled, and then whispered, "The Billingtons are a contentious family, Lizzy. You are wise to stay away from them."

"Mother, are you well enough to walk on the deck with me today?" Elizabeth asked hopefully.

Joan nodded and sat up to pull her stockings on. A fit of coughing shook her frail frame. Seasickness gripped her. After the coughing stopped, Joan passed a shaky hand over her brow. "I'm sorry, Lizzy," she muttered as she lay back down.

"I'll bring you food, Mother," Elizabeth offered. "To make you strong."

Joan saw the look of hope in the girl's eyes. "A bit of cider and cheese," Joan answered. "And Elizabeth, don't forget to drink some lemon juice. It will protect you against the scurvy."

"And what of you, Mother? Should I bring you some?" the girl questioned. Joan Tilley shook her head. On her way to get the food, Elizabeth passed John Howland sitting in the corner reading the Bible. Engrossed in the book, he did not look up as she walked by.

"Good morrow, Master Howland," Elizabeth said brightly. Perhaps the elders would think her boldness a sin, but Lizzy wanted to challenge John Howland and Desire Minter to a game of Nine Men's Morris. She had not yet played them.

"Good day," John answered, but he didn't look up.

"What portion of the Bible are you reading?" Elizabeth asked.

"Of the miracles of Jesus," John answered as he took his eyes off the page and looked up at Elizabeth. For an instant he studied the young girl. Since the maid was curious, he would return a question. "Do you really believe in God, young miss? Or do you just hope because your parents tell you so?"

Elizabeth's brow creased in thought as she answered, "The Holy Spirit causes me to believe. Surely Jesus came to earth and died that we might have eternal life. Don't you believe it, Sir?"

"I yearn to believe," John said seriously. "And yet, I know not God."

"Then you must read of God and pray to Him," Elizabeth said stoutly. "Then you will know Him."

John grinned as he spoke. "Such simple words of wisdom. What else do you know, Wise Maiden?"

"I know how to play Nine Men's Morris? Do you?"

"Very well," John answered.

"Then you must borrow my board and stones!" Elizabeth announced. "You shall play Desire Minter. Then I will play the winner. Will you do it?"

"Aye," John agreed, grinning. "Let me finish the chapter first. Then Desire and I shall find you. But beware, though you might be wise, when I play Nine Men's Morris I am a serpent!"

Meryl's fingers rested on the keyboard and she looked at the clock. It was after nine and she was still wearing pajamas. After backing up her novel on a disk, Meryl showered and donned beige slacks and a short-sleeved sweater. Then she neatly arranged her hair and make-up. She swallowed her vitamin and calcium pills with a breakfast of wheat toast and grape juice. Ten minutes after breakfast, Meryl drove down Grantlin Boulevard with a Willa Cather novel on the seat next to her. She took note of the blossoming trees and the dome of blue, cloudless sky.

At 10:50 in the morning, she arrived at the Women's Radiology Center in downtown Sacramento. The office girl, immaculately groomed and smiling, greeted her with a cheerful hello and paperwork. The waiting room was spotless—the decorations classic and feminine, as if they whispered *nothing bad can happen here.*

Ten minutes later, Meryl followed the technician, Darcy, into the room with the machine. While the x-rays were taken, the easygoing Darcy, with her white hair, round hips, high cheekbones, and lovely mouth, chatted amicably about the past year. She positioned Meryl for the x-rays. Despite the physical discomfort of the mammogram, Meryl felt calm.

Afterward, Darcy led Meryl to a small room with two chairs and a television set. Meryl knew the instructions by heart as Darcy recited them: *Wait here and watch the video about monthly breast self-exams while Dr. Aldrich reviews the films. Then he'll come in and talk with you about the results.* After Darcy left, Meryl felt a tad rebellious toward the video she had seen once a year for the past five years. She muted the sound and read Willa Cather while it played. The video ended. For an additional fifteen minutes, Meryl continued to read and wait.

Finally, Darcy stepped back into the room. "Meryl," she said and smiled. "I hate to tell you this, but we need to take some more pictures. There's a spot that looks questionable. I don't think it's anything to worry about. Did you use deodorant or powder this morning?" Meryl shook her head.

"Well, come on back. We'll get this over with."

"When do you think we'll be finished?" Meryl asked, looking down at her watch. "I'm supposed to meet my husband for lunch." Even as she spoke evenly, memories of her breast cancer experience five years ago challenged her calm exterior.

"You should be out of here in a half hour. Would you like a few moments to call your husband and tell him you might be late?"

"Yes, please." Meryl reminded herself of little Oliver Twist in the musical. *Yes please. More please.* But she was a grown woman. She did not want more. She had enough of this five years ago—the whispers of cancer, the invasive surgery, the radiation, the concerned, therapeutic glances of medical personnel. She went into the front office to use the telephone. The lovely receptionist was greeting the next patient. Meryl dialed the number, and Rick answered.

"I'm running about thirty minutes late," Meryl explained. "They are going to take additional x-rays. There's some questionable tissue,"

Rick paused, then asked, "What kind of questionable tissue?"

"I don't know."

"I can hardly hear you. Are you OK?" Of course she wasn't OK. But how could she tell him with all of these people around?

"I'm OK."

"Do you want me to come?"

"No. By the time you arrived I would be on my way."

"I'll see you at the restaurant then."

"It's probably not anything."

"I know. I'll be waiting."

"Bye, Rick."

"Bye, Meryl. I love you." Rick wasn't the type to tell his wife that he loved her over the telephone while he was at the office. Meryl knew he was afraid.

Back in the exam room, Darcy showed Meryl the films, including the little dots in the shadow of tissue that concerned the radiologist. "Dr. Aldrich wants these magnified," Darcy explained. "If the edges are smooth, there's nothing to worry about. If bumpy, they are calcifications."

"And?"

"That might indicate a recurrence of the intraductal cancer that you had before."

Meryl took a deep breath. She told herself not to panic, not to be afraid. She had lived through breast cancer treatment before. She could do it again. She held statue-still while Darcy flattened her breast in the jaws of the machine. It was not just uncomfortable this time, it was tight and painful. She held her breath while the pictures were taken. Her hair curled neatly at the nape of her neck, and her eyes did not blink. Yet the whole time she prayed, her soul inaudibly searching for her Father in Heaven, her mind silently seeking a portion of the Savior's courage. In wasn't until after the pictures were taken and she was dressed once more that Meryl noticed the smelling salts on a medical tray near her. Darcy had been concerned that Meryl might faint.

Fifteen minutes later, Meryl recognized the compassionate tilt of Dr. Aldrich's head, the tender angle of his lean jaw, and the concerned crease of his high forehead. She had seen this look before. Only this time, there were gray streaks in the neatly trimmed beard.

"They look like calcifications, Meryl," he said as he put the x-ray pictures over a light with one hand and touched Meryl's hand with the other. Then he pointed to the magnified dots. "See the rough edges and how they are positioned fairly near the surgery clip from five years ago? It looks like some intraductal cancer has recurred. Much like what you had before."

"Is the prognosis the same? What about treatment?" Meryl asked. She knew the questions. She felt as if her past were repeating itself, as if she had swallowed a huge dose of packaged déjà vu. Yet this time she was older and calmer. She knew these people. She was better informed.

"If this is what I think it is, then the prognosis is the same. The cancer is at such an early stage that the cure rates are over ninety percent. After we finish talking, we'll call your surgeon and set up an appointment this week. It's Dr. Toom, isn't it? He'll want to do a biopsy."

Meryl nodded. "Am I looking at the same treatment choices? Another lumpectomy plus radiation therapy, versus a mastectomy and no radiation?"

"Perhaps," Dr. Aldrich said. "But if I were your surgeon, I'd encourage a mastectomy this time. When the breast undergoes radiation therapy, a small portion of the lung is hit as well. I wouldn't advise putting your body through that again. After the mastectomy you would be finished with treatment, unless you opt for breast reconstruction. In California, insurance companies are required to pay for this."

"What about chemotherapy?" Meryl questioned.

Dr. Aldrich shook his head. "There shouldn't be a need unless the pathologist uncovers something I can't see. The possibility that this cancer has spread is almost nil."

No chemotherapy. A mastectomy. A chill went through Meryl. She knew that if she lifted her hand at that moment Dr. Aldrich would see it tremble. How strange that they spoke calmly together about something unimaginably horrible. They spoke of cutting off her breast, of slashing away a part of her so tied to her emotions and her perceptions of herself. It was that portion of her physical being that both she and Rick perceived as beautiful.

"Meryl, are you all right?" Dr. Aldrich asked.

"Not right now. I will be." She spoke honestly.

"I know this is difficult," he said kindly. "Try to remember that you are basically a healthy woman. You are fortunate that both times your cancer was detected in the earliest possible stages."

Meryl nodded.

"Do you have any other questions?" Dr. Aldrich asked.

"Not right now. I might later."

"Feel free to call me anytime. Let's go and make that appointment with Dr. Toom."

Twenty minutes later at the restaurant, Meryl played with her food with a fork. Rick encouraged her to eat. "Everything is going to be OK. We've been through a lot. We'll get through this. Try to eat."

Meryl stared at her soup and cashew chicken dish. She had as little appetite as the seasick Joan Tilley in the book she was writing. "I'll take it home. Maybe I'll be able to eat later." She wished Rick would reach across the table and just hold both of her hands in his.

"Rick, I don't know whether to go through breast reconstruction or not."

"That's up to you."

"Would it bother you having a wife without a breast?"

"I don't know."

"What do you mean you don't know? Could you live with it?"

"Of course I could live with it. I'm married to you. I love you. I just don't know if it would bother me or not. If it did, I'd get over it."

"I feel like you got a bum deal. I couldn't give you children. Now, I'm having a mastectomy. I'll be disfigured. I feel so badly about it." Tears filled Meryl's eyes. She stared at her soup.

Rick reached over and covered his wife's long, elegant fingers. "I didn't get a bum deal," he said quietly. "We have a beautiful daughter."

"I'm not going to tell Dennie."

"Why not?"

"It would upset her. I won't be a ball and chain she must drag around."

Rick didn't know how to answer. He didn't know what to say. He held his wife's hands. He thought her hands were so graceful, so soft to the touch and capable of caring for others. But he didn't tell her. He just waited. She slipped her hands out of his and ate a few bites. She looked up at him and asked, "Are you glad you married me?"

"Yes."

"When will you be home tonight?"

"About six. I meet with a client this afternoon. I have to prepare him for a hearing tomorrow morning. Will you be OK?"

Meryl nodded. "Will you be able to get off on Wednesday for the appointment with Dr. Toom?"

"Absolutely. What are you going to do this afternoon?"

"I'll try working on my manuscript. But I feel so drained. Maybe I'll take a nap first."

"Good idea." Rick motioned the waitress over. She packed the leftovers in small boxes with wire handles while Rick paid the bill. He put his arm around Meryl and walked her to the car.

"I love you," he said. "Don't worry about dinner tonight. I'll pick something up."

"How about a Farmer Owen's beef burger? I'll work on my appetite."

"You've got it." Rick hugged Meryl. Then he said softly, "You aren't going to die, Meryl. I'm so thankful." After the embrace, while he walked away, Meryl touched the damp spot on her cheek. Were the tears Rick's or her own?

"Little Mistress Tilley, your mother sick again, eh?" The hard-eyed, yellow-haired seaman laughed at the thirteen-year-old girl. She emptied the foul contents of the chamber pot into the sea and did not meet his eyes or answer him. Her neck was slim and elegant as she looked away.

The man continued, more loudly now. *"Your mother wanes during fair skies and fresh breeze! Think of what will happen when the storms fly from the west. Dear mum will be meat for fishes!"*

"Please do not jest, sir," Elizabeth muttered. Her green eyes glanced up at him from under her bonnet. Her youthful voice held fear and exhaustion, and the merest shadow of contempt. He touched her bonnet with stained, calloused fingers. Instinctively, Elizabeth shrank away.

He laughed again. *"Then you and your father will die of broken hearts. And I, I shall dine heartily on your hardtack and cheese. My lass in London shall have your bonnet. And after divers days, I shall wind the silks of Master Tilley, your papa, the pious dead weaver, around my waist while I dance!"*

Elizabeth drew herself up. She had to run, throw up, or scream. The sailor laughed again. *"Little peacock, the sharks shall love your sweet taste."*

"We shall not die!" she burst. *"You shall never have what is ours!"*

"I take what I desire. I shall have you!" The sailor bellowed and reached for the girl. Elizabeth fled. John Howland and Desire Minter heard the man's shout and raucous laughter as they sat together playing Elizabeth's game.

"Tis the seaman called Isaac," Desire exclaimed. *"The one who mocked Dorothy Bradford yesterday, causing her to weep so bitterly! He said she would never again see the babe she left in England! Why does he torment us?"*

John answered darkly. *"He delights in taking the people's fear and twisting their souls until they writhe."* John remembered three days ago when Isaac had laughed at Mistress Carver. The cruel sailor had told the lady no children would weep when her body was thrown into the sea because she had none. Catherine had paled. Deacon Carver had reproved Isaac with words of restrained firmness. Then the seaman had cursed bitterly at the Deacon. Upon hearing of this abuse, John Howland's hands had knotted. He had lived on the streets of London. He knew that his own fists were as quick and hard as any man's.

John's eyes had narrowed as he challenged the bully. *"I can deal with the likes of you, Isaac."*

But Deacon Carver had stepped between the two and ordered John into the hold. *"John, if words are his only lash,"* the older man had whispered when they were alone, *"we will turn the other cheek like our own dear Lord and leave his punishment to God."*

John's reverie broke at the sound of Desire gathering up the game. *"Come, John,"* she said. *"We will find and cheer whomever Isaac torments."*

It was Elizabeth they found as they walked the breadth of the ship. She sat, tucked under a railing, leaning back against the ship sobbing.

"Lizzy, what happened?" Desire asked breathlessly. The child spoke haltingly and with tears. As she related the incident, John's hands clenched and unclenched. She had escaped the sailor, yet his threat to the merry young lass was too much to endure. John thought to call on Roger Wilde, the burly manservant Deacon Carver had hired to labor in the fields of the New World. Together they would throw the sailor into the sea. Let others haul him out again, if they chose. Perhaps that would cool his tongue. John turned to go, determination and rage in his eye.

"John, where are you going?" Desire stopped him with a light hand on his arm.

"Master Isaac shall feel the cold sting of the sea!" John muttered.

"John, you mustn't!" Desire burst out. *"For Isaac is a viper. If you threaten him, he will strike! What of you? What of all of us?"*

The girl Elizabeth looked up at him, imploring. Her dismay touched John. She dug her tears away with her fists. John saw that a flash of gold burned in her green eyes. He considered Desire's request and asked. *"What think ye, Miss Tilley? Should we throw him into the sea presently? Or wait until the moon is full and the fish feed at night?"*

"Perhaps we should wait until the moon waxes full," Elizabeth said, gulping. *"Then perchance no one will hear the splash. For my father and uncle, godly men they be, might pull him out before the poor fish have finished their feast."* A small smile pulled at the corners of Elizabeth's mouth as she imagined Isaac's fate. Her wit cooled some of John's anger. This girl had a surprising nature.

"Oh, John is dangerous, Lizzy," Desire exclaimed with a smile. *"You mustn't encourage his wickedness!"*

"Dangerous indeed! To Isaac the sailor!" John exclaimed.

"Come, John," Desire encouraged. "Show Lizzy how bad you are. Dry her tears with one of the songs you heard from Master Shakespeare. Whisper it, though, or we shall all be discovered and the elders might think to throw us into the sea instead of Isaac."

Then, with hair and beard streaked shiny-bronze from the sun, John found he wanted to cheer the child more than to punish Isaac. His eyes danced and his large red hands swayed as he whispered:

When shepherds pipe on oaten straws,
And merry larks are ploughmen's clocks,
When turtles tread, and rooks, and daws,
And maidens bleach their summer smocks
The cuckoo then, on every tree,
Mocks married men; for thus sings he,
  Cuckoo!
Cuckoo, cuckoo—O word of fear,
Unpleasing to a married ear!

"Poor, lonely Master Howland!" Elizabeth laughed when he finished. "With such a wild and scandalous nature, no father will allow his daughter to marry you!"

"We shall see, pretty damsel," John spoke like a prince as he gave Lizzy his hand and helped her to her feet.

"Who won Nine Men's Morris?" Lizzy asked as they walked toward the hold.

"I beat Desire four games of five," John grinned at her. "When shall we play?"

"I must sit with Mother this afternoon," Lizzy said. "Perchance tomorrow."

"Tomorrow it shall be," John exclaimed.

"Lizzy, how fares your mother?" Desire asked.

"Not well," The girl's eyes clouded once more. "She coughs and vomits still."

"Come, let us leave John to his own business." Desire took Elizabeth's arm. "I have powdered cumin in my pocket. There is red wine on the ship. If we mix the two together, it will calm her stomach. Then, for the cough we will combine the powder of betony, the powder of caraway seeds,

the powder of skirret dried, and the powder of pepper. She shall drink this mixed with honey."

"Will it help?" The girl implored, her eyes brimming with tears once more. "Desire, do you think she shall die?"

"No, Lizzy, she shall live," Desire declared, praying that she spoke the truth.

Elizabeth watched as Desire opened her pocket and checked for the ingredients. "Where did you learn so much?" Elizabeth questioned.

"My own mum," Desire returned quickly.

"You must miss her! How do you bear it?"

Desire's blue eyes searched Elizabeth's green ones. "One learns how to, Lizzy, when one must," she said gently.

CHAPTER 13

WALLS

"I have a joke for you!" Karin chatted with her children as she drove them to a field to fly kites. She hoped the outing would change Chris's attitude. He hadn't been himself lately. Irritable and easily annoyed, for the past two weeks he had lashed out repeatedly. Karin wondered what was triggering his moodiness. A foreshadow of puberty perhaps—a simple, growing-up stage that just had to be endured. Yet she wished she hadn't told him about Meryl's cancer diagnosis. Still, it was more probable that the trip to Cory's next week was unsettling him. But he was adamant about going. Perhaps he simply felt bored and lonely with school out. Karin couldn't put her finger on the problem. All she knew was that her usually cheerful, communicative boy brooded, angry and silent. Karin continued, "What did the butter knife say to the piece of toast?"

"Me give up!" Brandon yelled. "Tell me!"

"Do you give up too, Brian?" Karin queried as she looked into the rearview mirror at her little boy. Brian was more hesitant than Brandon, more thoughtful, less quick to demand.

"Wait. Me finking," Brian said with his head between his hands.

"It's thinking, not finking! Learn to talk!" Chris murmured sullenly.

"You not my best friend!" Brian said back, narrowing his eyes at his big brother.

"You aren't my friend at all. You talk like a baby!" Christopher returned. Tears welled in Brian's eyes.

"Bri, you talk great!" Karin countered, offsetting Chris's criticism.

"No, you don't. She's just saying that because she's your mother," Chris cut in.

"Christopher Taylor, that's enough!" Karin's voice was firm. Brian sniffled.

"It's Christopher Parker! Not Christopher Taylor!" Chris responded with venom.

Karin's patience wore thin. She needed to get to the bottom of this. "Is that why you're so mad? Because your name is Parker? Don't you know that you're special, and loved, and part of this family?"

"Me am special too!" Brandon joined the conversation.

"You are not special." Chris turned on his other brother. "There are millions of three-year-old boys in the world. You aren't any more important than any one of them. There is nothing special about you."

"Me am special!" Brandon shrieked.

"Of course you're special. So is Brian. And so is Chris. He's just mad right now." Karin's latter sentence was spoken stringently as she gripped the steering wheel. Her heart beat quickly, her emotions on the edge of control. How could she combat his anger? It seemed to Karin that Christopher tormented the twins until he was disciplined just so he could yell that she and Blake were unfair. The fetus squirmed in her abdomen. She took a deep breath.

Chris scratched the leather seat of the car with his sliver of fingernail. "I'm not special. None of us are special," he said.

The gesture and words seemed so innocent, so simple. Karin's heart ached for Christopher. "Of course you are special, Chris. You're unique and delightful. You are the only person in the universe like you. You are Heavenly Father's dear son, His valiant warrior." Chris didn't respond. Karin reached out to touch him, but he plastered himself against the passenger door.

"Mommy, what the bread and knife say?" Brian whined.

"What?" Karin asked.

"Your joke, Mom. Remember?" Chris snorted dismally. "What did the butter knife say to the piece of toast?"

"Let's jam, man!" Karin finished. Brandon's gales of laughter filled the car. Brian grinned and giggled.

"See." Karin leaned over to Chris while keeping her eyes on the road. "They are special and brilliant. They get the joke."

"Sure," Chris remarked. "Guys, what did the rock say to the house?"

"What?" Brian queried.

"Let's have a drink of milk," Chris answered. The twins threw their heads back and laughed.

"They get that one too," Chris commented sarcastically. Karin stopped the car next to the elementary school's large field.

"I have another one," Karin added, raising her eyebrows at her eldest child's attitude.

Chris ignored his mother and picked his trick kite up off the car floor. He remembered how Dennie gave it to him the year his mom and Blake married. She had told him that it once belonged to Thes. Dennie had explained that although Thes was gone, he was still Chris's cousin because they were all sealed together in the temple, in a huge family tree. But she had been wrong. Chris wasn't sealed to Blake Taylor. He was sealed to Cory Parker. He had believed Dennie when he was seven. But he was eleven now and knew better.

Karin continued, "What did the branches of the tree say to the trunk?"

"Come on, Mom. Let's just leave the car," Chris said as he pushed the unlock button. The twins piled out of the car with their Mickey Mouse kites in hand.

"Chris, that's right!" Karin grinned as she opened her door.

"What's right?"

"Let's leave. That's what the branches said to the tree trunk! See! Proof that you are intuitively brilliant! And special too!"

Chris fought the trace of a smile that might serve as his mother's reward. Well, there was one thing for sure. He was her kid. But what about the sister he used to have? How had his mom caused her death, and why hadn't she ever told him about it? Chris fingered the kite in his hands. He wouldn't think anymore. He would fly his kite.

He ran backward quickly, the yellow and purple kite catching the south wind. Chris gave it more line as it soared upward, and caused it to dip and weave. He ran with his kite, calling directions to his mother as she struggled to get his brothers' kites aloft. Finally, they flew too. He was part of the wind, the sun, the grass, and the flight! For a time, Chris forgot that he was leaving next week for the one place he didn't want to go. He forgot about his dead sister and his dead cousin. He forgot about his Aunt Meryl's cancer. He forgot that he was a Parker, not a Taylor.

When the twins' kites were aloft, Karin turned and watched her golden-haired, eldest son. She marveled at the way he moved, the way his legs had lengthened. He seemed to be feeling better. She could almost perceive the slender, sensitive man he would become— so intelligent and witty that it caused her to shiver. Would he become an angry man as well? No, not her Chris. But why was he so dramatically different? Why was he now intent on spending time with Cory? Why did he push her and Blake away?

Karin sighed. Christopher wasn't the only person separated from her by an unseen wall. Since Meryl's cancer diagnosis, there had been a barrier between them too. Where there used to be talk and laughter, there were stretches of silence. Meryl seemed distracted and had lost weight. Karin wanted to help her, but Meryl didn't seem to want anyone. She resisted Karin's offers to go on walks or to lunch. Her mastectomy was scheduled in two weeks, and she hadn't told Dennie or her parents. When Karin tried to chat casually with Meryl, she felt strained. Karin worried that her casual comments about pregnancy and children might feel as salt on Meryl's wounds. It seemed that Karin awkwardly felt her way down the dark hallway of possible comments to all of the wrong words.

And there were barriers between Karin and her husband too. Blake was bishop now. There were so many walls of confidentiality surrounding him. She felt keenly the change in their relationship— the things he could not share. They were separate in a way they had not been before. And sometimes, she felt strangely jealous—jealous of those who took so much of his time, emotion, prayers, and energy. She needed him. Their children needed him. But she was grateful too; grateful that Blake was worthy and willing to be a bishop, grateful that she had these exhausting, demanding children. It was good to be the center of their universe. And, most of all, she loved the fact that two hearts beat within her body—that of her baby girl and herself.

And other walls were coming down, Karin reflected. Her in-laws had been calling every week. Joan seemed intent on becoming close to her son and daughter-in-law, and had even promised Karin that she and Ben would come out to help when the baby came. Yet Karin had been asked not to tell Joan of Meryl's cancer. She felt a twinge of guilt for withholding information she knew Joan should know.

"Mommy, help! My kite falling," Brandon yelled, snapping Karin out of her thoughts. She continued the work of motherhood.

An hour later, on the way home, the twins fell asleep in the car. The baby moved so much that Karin caught her breath. She reached for Chris's hand and put it on her stomach. The unborn infant stilled. Chris waited in silence, but he did not move his hand. A gentle rolling. A kick. And another.

"Did you feel that, son?" Karin asked. Christopher nodded.

"Sometimes I can feel her heart beat too. It's so cool. Her due date is the week you come back from your father's. I'll try to keep her from coming until you're here. We'll need you, Chris. To keep her safe and warm. It will be hard sometimes with the twins and Dad being bishop. You'll help me, won't you, son?"

Chris nodded again. "I will," he said solemnly. The baby stilled, but the eleven-year-old did not move his hand from his mother's abdomen.

When they were home, Chris went up into his room. He took Domino out of his cage and held the rat gently between his hands. He felt the quick, precious heartbeat and wondered if the baby's heart inside his mother beat just as fast. He taped together a maze of empty paper towel and toilet paper rolls, then put Domino into the entrance. The rat stretched his body longer to navigate the maze. Chris knew it was dark in there, but Domino found his way through the turns to the light at the end, where sunflower seeds awaited him. After Domino's adventure, Chris held him. He hugged Domino gently. Domino licked his hand.

It was as if Meryl moved through each day surrounded by a pillar of glass which both protected and isolated her. If she reached outside it, she feared she would shatter. Her mastectomy was scheduled in two weeks. She struggled to cope with the knowledge that she would be dramatically physically altered for the rest of her life. A part of her would be gone. When Rick held her intimately, what used to bring closeness would now hold the shadows of disease, fear, and loss. She had seeds of death inside her. How could she combat this? How could he?

Another decision loomed near. She had to decide whether or not to have breast reconstruction. If she chose to, a plastic surgeon would insert some kind of bag when the mastectomy was performed. After recovery, and in stages, this bag would be filled with saline. It was a painful and tedious process.

On a Thursday afternoon, Meryl and Rick went to a consultation at the plastic surgery center. They sat together in the waiting room, each thumbing through magazines that held little interest for them. When they were called into the examination room, the décor caused Rick to raise his eyebrows and Meryl to shake her head. On the walls hung posters of beautiful women with reconstructed faces, breasts, lips, stomachs, and thighs.

A petite Asian nurse instructed Meryl to change into a Japanese robe made of deep blue, silken fabric, embroidered with pale stars and moons. "We don't use standard hospital gowns," the young woman explained. "We hope you will be aware of your own beauty."

Rick looked at the medical equipment in the room while Meryl changed. The robe did not fall comfortably on Meryl. She felt clumsy and strange in the attire. A few minutes later, with Rick beside her, the stocky, mustached surgeon instructed Meryl to open the robe. The doctor did measurements and took pictures. Meryl's feet were ice cold. If only the glass walls around her were not transparent.

After Meryl dressed, the surgeon took them into his office and showed them slides of women who had endured mastectomies. They observed before and after pictures, and the steps of reconstructive surgery. The slides were cut off at the neck so they couldn't see the women's heads. As they looked at pictures of headless, topless, one-breasted women, Meryl couldn't stop herself from glancing at Rick, trying to perceive his reaction. But there wasn't a reaction. It was as if his face were carved in stone. Finally they were in the car again, heading toward home.

"What are you going to do?" Rick asked.

"I don't know," Meryl stated.

"It's up to you," he said.

"I don't think I want reconstruction," she added. "I just don't want to go through it. I want it to be over."

"OK," he said. But his face was as expressionless as it had been during the slide show. Meryl thought that this stoic mask covered his horror of what she would become. Yet if she had truly been able to perceive his innermost thoughts, she would have realized that he feared any movement would cause him to weep for her suffering.

That night Meryl slept uneasily. First she dreamt she waited in a beach house, watching out a window as Dennie, a young child in the dream, played in the ocean, wearing a swimsuit similar to the Japanese robe—deep blue with stars and moons. In the beach house, men in white doctor's robes attacked Meryl, but she couldn't scream for fear of frightening Dennie. They carried her body to the sand and left her there, alone and injured. Meryl awakened with a sense of shame and helplessness. She moved closer to Rick. In his sleep, he stretched his arm around her. She prayed silently and tried to sleep once more. Yet sleep eluded her for what seemed like hours. She arose and stepped quietly downstairs. Her computer waited silently and patiently for her fingertips.

In gray moonlight she lies alone
Curled in a womb of sand.
Her weeping hair falls over slender breasts
Harboring seeds of death.
"Take positive control," they urge
"You have treatment choices, options, and hope."
She stares ahead wide-eyed and alone.
Will her choice be terrible enough to kill the death within?
It is morning now.
Her daughter plays in the tide.
Sunlight streaks the black hair silver.
The girl's suit deep blue with stars, her laughter bell-like
The woman does not scream for fear of frightening the child.
She longs to crawl from the beach
Into the arms of her mother, her father
Yet her mother's arms are steel bands.
And her father is old and far away.
Still, the tide comes in.
Dear Father in Heaven,
How can one fight the pull
Of the moon?

It was four in the morning when Meryl left the computer and wandered back upstairs. She offered a silent prayer and tried to sleep

once more, but another nightmare followed her. This time Meryl
dreamt she had leprosy. Dirty rags wrapped around her head. Rick
stared at her, pain in his glance. Her mother gaped at her.
Disappointed. Angry. *God has punished you,* her mother's voiceless
eyes spoke. Meryl awakened, her body draped in cold sweat.

Spring in Virginia's Blue Ridge Mountain region glistened with
wild flowers, blossoms, and a thousand different shades of green. Joan
Taylor tapped her polished nails against the steering wheel as she
drove home from the local elementary school. Each weekday she
volunteered her time to the Grandparent Mentor Program. Today the
child she worked with had pushed her patience—losing his place,
shaking his feet, pushing back on two legs of the chair. And a second-
grader at that! If he had been in Joan's class before she retired, he
would have behaved differently—he would have sat still. And more
important, he would have been reading by now!

Joan drove down and then up the steep hill that led to her home.
Umpteen years ago her kids had named that part of the road The Big
Dip. She pulled into the carport of the two-bedroom, brick house
where she and Ben had lived for thirty-four years. He sat on the
porch swing, stroking their cat, Honeydew, and waiting for her.

As Joan left the car she thought of how she could no longer hide
from the fact that her Ben was an old man. His hand draped across
Honeydew. The skin reminded her of a piece of rubber, stretched beyond
the point of elasticity and then, fitted wrinkled and loose over the thick
finger bones. If only that were the extent of aging. But Ben couldn't hear
well. Plus, a couple of years ago, he had a bout with prostate cancer. And
just last week, the doctor diagnosed congestive heart failure.

Yet Joan didn't mind taking care of him. He was the best thing
that ever happened to her. She wanted him with her as long as God
would allow it. She tried to live the right way, uncomplaining, in
order to keep on the good side of heaven. She hoped her prayers were
heard. She couldn't imagine waking up in the mornings without the
warm bulk of Ben near.

Yet, eventually she realized she would have to face Ben's death and
live with it. What would she do after he was gone? What did she have
left anyway—two middle-age children who had joined the Mormon

Church and moved to the other side of the country? Her daughter, Meryl, had been to blame and was lost to her. Joan hardly knew her grandchildren. But she would try to get to know them better—the little ones anyway. She would visit when Blake's baby was born. She would hold the twin boys who reminded her of her son.

The cat purred. "Hi, honey," Joan said loudly so Ben could hear. She sat down on the swing next to him.

"Who are you talking to, Little General? Me or this cat?" Ben asked, but he didn't put his arm around her or touch her. He continued to stroke Honeydew. He knew from long experience that his wife liked her space.

"Both of you," Joan answered.

"How'd school go?" he asked. She thought of how he'd asked her the same question nearly each weekday since they married.

"The child I taught wiggled and slouched the entire time. He won't be able to learn if he can't sit up straight and tall, and concentrate."

"Hmm," Ben responded with a hint of a twinkle. "You always could get kids to sit up straight. Poor little soldiers."

Joan sniffed and Ben laughed. As they sat in the swing together, their minds moved back forty-five years.

He was a janitor at the school where she received her first teaching job; she was a red-haired slip of a thing, not any bigger than most of the sixth graders. Regardless of her physical stature, she ruled like a general in her classroom. Ben was in his thirties, a hardworking man, shy and lumbering, and as slow of speech as Moses. His first wife had left him after a year of marriage, claiming she couldn't live with a man who wouldn't talk to her.

They first spoke one afternoon when Joan had playground duty. Ben was outside, raking up a pile of leaves. The bully of the school, bigger than Joan and mean as a bulldog, pushed down one of Joan's second-grade students. Joan ordered the boy to the office.

"Make me go, little teacher," he taunted. When she approached him, he put up his fists.

Ben started toward Joan, the rake in one hand and his strides long and quick. "Can I help?" he asked, thinking of how he would like to be a hero to the little lady. But he didn't get the chance. "No, thank you. I'm fine," Joan answered. Then her hand snaked out, as fast as a lizard's tongue, and latched onto the boy's ear. The youth writhed as she marched him toward the building.

"Ryan, don't you dare lay a finger on one of my children again," she stated calmly. "You're going to the principal. Special delivery." Ben laughed to himself as he leaned on his rake. That gal might be little on the outside, but she was darn big on the inside!

The next afternoon, Ben cleaned her classroom extra well and left a note on the chalkboard. He addressed it to the kids. The note asked what they were learning and how they were doing. He signed it *Bennie—the mouse.*

The next morning, Joan thought another teacher or one of the older kids left the note. To model letter writing, she and the class wrote back. The chalkboard correspondence continued for months, and the young teacher became more intrigued as time passed. Ben answered the children's questions from a rodent's perspective, and described life in the mountains—the trees, flowers, and animals, the dangerous escapes and glorious adventures.

Perceiving a sensitive and creative mind behind the messages, Joan decided to find out who it was. One afternoon she left the school and parked the car around the block. Like a thief, she slunk back and peered into the window of her own classroom. Silently, she watched the big, slow-moving janitor chalk words onto the board.

The next week she made it a point to find out what other members of the faculty thought about him. She asked around and learned that he was unmarried and extremely quiet. Most of the female teachers thought him slow-witted but masculine, even attractive.

Then, one fateful afternoon during story time, one of Joan's students threw up. Ben was called. When he walked in, the thirty children stared at him with noses plugged to avoid the rancid odor. He cleaned up the mess with a gray-string mop, and soon the class-room smelled of clean soap. Joan told her class to unplug their noses and fold their hands in their lap. She addressed Ben primly as the children listened. "Mr. Taylor, our class has two friends, a literate mouse who roams the mountains and you. We appreciate Bennie's charming stories. We also appreciate your hard work. We truly value both." The big man's face shaded scarlet, and his full lips stretched into the kindest smile she had ever seen. The petite, red-haired general felt her heart beat slightly faster.

Now, forty-five years later, they were still together, and Ben wouldn't have it any other way. During warm moments she called him *Bennie,* and he still addressed her as *The Little General.* Ben knew she wasn't the perfect wife, that intimacy was sometimes difficult for her. But Ben didn't blame her. He was a patient man. He never forgot the days of their courtship, when her life unfolded before him—she, a rare bloom, her past, weeds congesting the roots.

Joan's father left before she was born. Her mother died of cancer when Joan was six. Joan went to live with her grandparents on a citrus farm in Florida. These were happy years. Joan's grandmother, Eleanor Allen, loved Joan with warmth that breathed life into the reserved, prim child. The elderly woman made Joan angel food cake and called Joan her own sweet angel. Eleanor drew chalk houses on the hard dirt, and together she and Joan decorated them with rose petals. With soft orange clay they clothed plastic, three-inch baby dolls. Eleanor cuddled with Joan each evening as she read to her from the Bible.

Her grandfather, Jacob, introduced Joan to his horse named Sunny, his three cows, two dogs, and menagerie of chickens and peacocks. His oranges tasted as sweet as nectar. Since the chickens ran free in the yard, it was quite a game of hide-and-seek finding the eggs. Joan loved watching Grandpa candle them with a cylinder oatmeal box, a hole cut in the side and a light at the bottom.

Joan never forgot the day her grandfather beheaded a chicken. The child stared in horror as the headless bird briefly ran around the yard. "It's hard to watch now, Punkin," her grandfather called to her, his voice jolly and robust. "But tonight it will be good eatin'!"

Then, one hot summer morning a month before Joan's eleventh birthday, Jacob uncharacteristically slept in. Later, Joan went out with him to do the chores. The air fairly steamed with heat—it was ten in the morning, ninety degrees Fahrenheit, and ninety-percent humidity. Jacob mounted Sunny, and Joan climbed up behind him. On hot days, they liked to ride, rather than walk, out to the barn.

Her grandfather suddenly stopped the mare and told Joan he felt dizzy. Then he fell off the horse. Joan pounded on her grandfather's chest, breathed into his mouth, and shouted for her grandmother.

Jacob had suffered a heart attack. He slipped into a coma and died a few days later.

Joan and her grandmother did OK for a little over a year. They kept each other company. They grieved, ate, worshipped, and worked together. Then Eleanor began forgetting things—she couldn't remember what she was doing or where she was going. Joan had to remind her to take her to school in the mornings.

One night when Joan was at a friend's house, her grandmother went to bed, forgetting that she had pudding cooking on the stove. The dogs barked loud enough for Eleanor to wake up and get out of the farmhouse in time, but the dwelling burned beyond repair. "I feel like that chicken, running around without my head," Eleanor told her granddaughter.

Joan's Uncle Tim intervened. He moved Eleanor into an assisted-living apartment. He took Joan to live with his family in Virginia. They were extremely religious, and he and his wife raised their own five children with unbending authority. They told Joan to think about her life and why her parents were taken from her. Why had the Lord given her this affliction? What sins did Joan need to repent of? Joan spent the next eight years moving carefully around her uncle and aunt while avoiding the roving eyes and hands of her oldest cousin, Jack.

She earned straight A's in high school and worked her own way through college. Heedless of her aunt and uncle's warnings, she threw her Bible away and quit going to church. She talked of getting her first job and earning money to move her grandmother to Virginia with her. But God had different plans, and Eleanor passed away one night just a month after Joan's graduation. Joan's uncle suggested that things might have been different if Joan had remained prayerful and faithful to the Lord.

After her grandmother's death, Joan held onto her sanity like one holds an egg—not so tightly lest it break in one's fingers, but not so loosely lest it shatter to the floor. She started regularly attending the Baptist Church. She prayed and sang in the church choir. This comforted her. She decided never to put her love and trust completely in one human being again. She would only trust in God.

In time she was offered a good job and she met Ben. It seemed the Lord had blessed her for her faithfulness. Ben asked her to marry him. Now, almost half a century later, here they were.

Joan stood up from the porch swing and stretched. "There's a letter on the table for you," Ben said. "From California."

"One of the kids?" Joan asked.

Ben shook his head. "Elsa Fletcher, Rick's mother."

Joan went inside and looked at the letter. Ben followed her. *What did she want?* Joan wondered about this woman who had taken her place as Meryl's mother. Joan opened and read the note.

Dear Joan,

Rick called me last night. Meryl's breast cancer has recurred. I know you haven't been close to Meryl in recent years. But you are her mother and I feel that she needs you. My prayers are with you.

Love,

Elsa

Joan sat down. She handed the letter to Ben. He took his reading glasses from his pocket and read it in silence.

"I'm calling our girl," he said when he finished. "She needs her mama and papa."

Joan's voice rasped as she touched Ben's arm. "The letter says that her breast cancer has recurred. She never even told us when she had breast cancer the first time. She doesn't want us, Ben. She hasn't wanted or needed us since she joined the Mormon Church. Now look what's happened. She couldn't have kids. Her adopted son died. Now she has cancer. I told her once that God would punish her. But there's no satisfaction!" Joan's voice broke.

"If God works like that, I've no stomach for heaven," Ben said shortly.

Ben felt his eyes cloud. His girl was in pain, and he wasn't there to help. He didn't want it this way, but couldn't help wondering if he had done things differently years ago, would things be different today?

He remembered Joan's fury and fear over Meryl's decision to marry in the Mormon temple. He had longed to travel to California and wait outside the temple while his daughter wed. However, Joan had been deeply hurt by Meryl's choice. His wife's membership in the Baptist Church meant the world to her. He had been torn between his wife and his child. Still, Meryl and Blake had begged him to read the Book of Mormon. After long thought, he had decided that he couldn't. He couldn't challenge his wife—couldn't break her spirit. She was his multicolored jewel, his fleeting gem. She was more than he ever hoped to have or thought he deserved. He stood by his little general.

"Perhaps God is punishing me," Joan stated.

Ben shook his head. "No. Life punishes us enough without God interfering."

CHAPTER 14

GIFTS

Friday evening held little promise of excitement for Aimy. She and Wave had agreed to tend the Taylor twins while Blake took Karin out to dinner and a movie in celebration of Karin's birthday. Although Aimy wasn't crazy about Karin, she had scheduled this tedium because of her love and admiration for Bishop Blake. She would do anything for him—even baby-sit. *Besides*, she mused, *Sean is working late and Waverly likes to entertain Brandon and Brian.*

Aimy decided to make the best of it. She loaded a cake mix, a can of frosting, and a Peter Pan video into the Yellow Toy. Then she picked up Waverly.

Once at the Taylor home, after the twins kissed their parents good-bye, Aimy announced that she and Waverly were going to help the twins bake a cake for their mom. The boys clapped with delight. Brandon begged to "hatch" the eggs. Wave laughed and laughed. "Baby chicks hatch out of eggs," he explained knowingly. "People crack them open."

After the cake was in the oven, Aimy cleaned the streams of raw egg white off the counter. Then she joined Wave and the boys in the backyard. Brian ran up to Aimy, took her hand, and led her to a small flower garden. "See," the little boy exclaimed with a smile as he pointed at a lavender rose. "It popped out yesterday!"

"Flowers don't *pop*, they *bloom*," Waverly said wisely. Brandon, who had been scrambling in the bushes, ran over with three large snails on his outstretched palms. He motioned the group to the patio, where two concentric circles had been drawn with sidewalk chalk.

"Snail races!" Brandon yelled. He gave one snail to Wave and one to Brian. Brandon, Brian, and Waverly, following suit, put their snails in the small center circle.

"The snail that gets to the other circle first wins!" Brandon explained. Aimy laughed and watched while Waverly and the twins lay flat on their stomachs to cheer on their snails. When it looked like the race would not end in the near future, Aimy went inside to cook hot dogs for dinner. As the water began to boil, she realized that she was actually having a decent time. The twins were cute.

After the hot dogs were cooked, Aimy ventured back outside and watched Brandon's snail win the race. She told the little boys to come in and wash up, and the two compliantly followed Waverly into the bathroom. While seated at the table, Brian and Brandon ate a few bites of hot dog and a pile of potato chips for dinner. They charmed Aimy with their jokes about trees leaving and toast in a jam. After the meal, they frosted and ate half the cake.

Aimy's next chore was to bathe the boys before they ran through the house with frosting-covered faces and hands. She attracted them by pouring a generous amount of bubble bath in the tub. The boys climbed in, smeared on soap-bubble beards, and called themselves Santa Claus. Their slender chests and dancing eyes touched Aimy. Following the bath, the pajama-clad duo joined Aimy and Waverly on the sofa for stories. While Aimy read, the twins took turns holding the rat, Domino.

"Don't hold Domino too tight," Waverly warned Brandon after Aimy finished the first book.

Brandon scowled at Waverly and responded, "We supposed to give Domino lots of love. Chris is away. Dom is sad."

Wave shook his finger slowly and warned them. "Once I kneeled on a frog. Its guts came out its mouth. My friend left his hamster out in the sun. My cousin squeezed her kitten too hard."

"Did them die?" Brian asked, wide-eyed.

"Yes, kids, they sure did," Waverly said direly. Brandon loosened his grip on the rat. Aimy started the second story in a cheerful voice.

After five stories, Aimy turned on *Peter Pan,* explaining that it was her favorite movie when she was little. Aimy told them that she liked Peter, but Wendy bugged her—the girl was a wimp. She didn't mention that Wendy reminded her of Karin.

The twins fell asleep two-thirds of the way through the movie—Brian in Aimy's arms and Brandon with his head on Waverly's lap. Waverly carried Brandon into bed and came back to finish the movie.

Then Aimy lifted Brian and walked into the bedroom—his weight against her, his little-boy legs dangling, his breath soft and sweet on her neck. She gently laid him down. Aimy sat down on the edge of Brian's bed and stared at him.

Her jaw trembled and she began to cry. Why was she developing this hunger for a baby? Why did a part of her want a child to love forever? She wasn't patient or selfless. She wasn't the kind of person a baby needed. How could she risk bringing a child into the world knowing they might suffer like she had when she was a kid? Marriage was risky enough. Who did she think she was, yearning for a kid?

Waverly's heavy frame filled the doorway. "Aimy, come watch the end of the movie with me."

"I can't, Wave," Aimy sniffled.

"Are you crying?"

"Yeah."

"How come?"

"I'm just sad, Wave. That's all."

"Maybe you can say a prayer. Then you can find a happy thought. Like Michael, John, and Wendy." Waverly suggested.

"I'll try, Wave," Aimy said. "Go back and finish the video. I'm fine." Waverly walked away.

At Waverly's request, Aimy knelt down. *Heavenly Father, what should I do? Should I marry Sean? I don't think I could I be a good wife or a good mother. I'm not that way.* The room was silent but for the deep breathing of the twins. Aimy shook her head. She stood up, knowing her strength would be found in doggedly going on, sticking her chin up and out. She wasn't the nurturing type, but she couldn't let that knowledge break her will, even if it broke her heart.

Aimy walked down the hall. As she passed the bathroom, her eyes caught her own reflection in the mirror. She stopped, for it was as if in an instant, she saw Moni there rather than herself—yet it was not Moni's weakness or mistakes she saw as she stared at her own image, but the sweetness in Moni's eyes, the gentleness of Moni's touch.

Aimy began shaking, and a tingling coursed through her body as words came into her mind. *You are beloved of the Lord. You are as you should be. You can marry Sean. You can be a mother.* Joy coursed through Aimy like an electric current. Her prayer had been answered.

Aimy went into the kitchen and looked at the clock. She had an hour until Sean got off work. She called him and asked him to stop by after he closed Beef Burgers. She told him she had a surprise. To pass the time, Aimy cleaned the entire house.

Finally Sean arrived. While Wave watched another video, Aimy took Sean's hand and led him into the living room. They snuggled on the sofa and Aimy whispered in his ear the words he had been longing to hear, "I found my happy thought. I'm ready to fly. Will you marry me?"

"Yes," Sean shouted. "Yes! You bet! Absolutely!"

The next day, with Sean's arm heavy on her slim shoulders, Aimy watched the Marine World dolphins fly through the air, water streaming from their pewter bodies in chains of silver-white light. She fingered the ring on her finger—the diamond ring that had once belonged to Sean's grandmother.

She pinched herself. She had said *yes* last night. Then this morning, Sean had brought the ring over and had given it to her before they went to Marine World to celebrate—just the two of them. Wave wouldn't hear of coming along. He said he had an engagement surprise for Aimy when she came back home.

The dolphins sped playfully around the pool. Aimy still couldn't believe it—she was engaged. She looked at her ring's old-fashioned setting—the yellow-gold rim with clovers of white gold circling the inside of the band, and a small diamond in a heavy, four-leaf clover setting. She tilted her ring upwards. The dolphins leapt through hoops. Her diamond picked up every color from the sun.

She had been so sure last night—just so positive. Together she and Sean had called her mom. Moni had screamed on the telephone and then cried. *Me and Len are doing good too!* Moni had gasped. *Baby, I'll be home next week. We're going to have so much fun planning our weddings.* Aimy had longed to talk to Dennie. But Dennie didn't have computer access when she was on the reservation.

"Man, those fish can swim!" Sean exclaimed.

"Not fish. Mammals—intelligent mammals," Aimy corrected as she elbowed Sean in the ribs. The dolphins rose into the air in perfect synchrony. The crowd aahhed. Aimy shivered. She had to hold onto her feelings from last night—to use them to push away any doubts. She snuggled close to her fiancé. Their skin touched, sticky from the heat. She smelled sunscreen and the scent of Sean, her Sean.

After the dolphin show, they went out to the car to eat the cold sandwiches they had purchased and thrown into a cooler earlier that morning. When they finished eating, Aimy took Sean's hand and pulled him back into the park to ride the big roller-coasters. Sean grinned and let her lead him, saying that it was too hot to sit in the car and kiss. They spent the afternoon waving their arms above their heads, screaming and laughing as they rode the neon yellow *Medusa*, with its ten upside-down circles, the wooden *Roar*, a coaster so loud the riders could hardly hear their own screams, and the giant *Kong*, jerky enough to shake one to insanity. They were aware only of each other and the thrill of the rides.

On the way home from Marine World, they sat close together in the cab of Sean's truck. For a time they rode quietly down the freeway. The future stretched before them like a vast field filled with sunlight and shadow, too dazzling and uncertain to comprehend. After a time, they discussed their plans. Aimy would go back to BYU for fall semester. She would run Pick Me Up because it was a gold mine during soccer season. Meanwhile, Sean would continue to work at Beef Burgers and take business classes at night. They would marry during Christmas break. Sean offered to move to Provo so that Aimy could finish her degree in special education at BYU.

Aimy kissed Sean's ear. She knew what that offer cost him. Owen, the owner of Beef Burgers, had become ill a year ago and was paying Sean a decent salary. Owen had even offered to eventually sell Sean the restaurant for a minimal price. Aimy told Sean that she would check out the special education programs at Sac State and UCD. Maybe she could transfer.

"Have you told your parents yet?" Aimy asked as they pulled off the freeway into Grantlin.

"No, let's call them together when we get to your place."

Aimy's brow creased. "I'm not exactly your mother's dream of a daughter-in-law," she stated with a frown.

"Mom will be happy for us. She'll grow to love you," Sean said.

"Promise?" Aimy asked doubtfully.

"Cross my heart." Sean grinned.

They pulled into Aimy's driveway and noticed Waverly's bike parked out front. "I wonder why Wave is here," Sean commented.

"My surprise," Aimy reminded him. Waverly bustled out the front door.

"The surprise is ready!" Waverly announced, his cheeks red with excitement. "No peeking, Aimy!" Waverly added as he handed Sean a dish towel to tie around Aimy's eyes.

"What is this, Wave?" Aimy asked with her eyelids squeezed shut under the dish towel. Waverly opened the garage door.

"A surprise!" Waverly repeated. He took Aimy's hand and led her around to the side of her mustard-colored Toyota. Sean followed. There was a moment of silence.

"Can I look now?" Aimy asked.

"You are going to be one *surprised* lady," Sean said with a low, cautionary whistle that Aimy couldn't read.

"Now!" Waverly cried. Aimy pulled off the dish towel. Neon-purple lettering on the side of her car spelled out the words PICK ME UP. She stared at it, openmouthed.

Waverly beamed. "Cool, huh! Do you love it?"

"She likes it so much she's speechless," Sean explained. "Wave, who put those words on Aimy's car?"

"Someone I met at Beef Burgers. He puts signs on cars to advertise people's businesses. I paid him myself."

"How much?" Sean questioned.

"One hundred dollars," Waverly answered proudly. "He gave me a good deal. I told him that Aimy taught me to read. Aimy is like my granddaughter."

Aimy shook herself out of her momentary shock. "Thanks, Wave!" She forced a grin and hugged him. Augustus Waverly beamed. A few moments later he went back inside to finish the show he was watching.

When Waverly was out of earshot, Sean doubled over laughing. "It's an advertisement all right!" he chortled.

Aimy punched him in the stomach. "Sean, what am I going to do? Your mom is going to love having a new daughter-in-law who drives a car around asking people to pick her up!"

Sean sat down on the driveway. He had turned red from a lack of oxygen because he was laughing so hard.

"Sean, stop it!" Aimy gave him a swift kick in the thigh. "How can I get rid of it without hurting Wave's feelings?"

Sean struggled to get himself under control before Aimy kicked him again.

"We'll just put a sentence underneath it: *A transportation service for children, the disabled, and the elderly*," Sean suggested. He started laughing again.

Aimy breathed more evenly. "That'll work," she stated as she studied the letters. Then she smiled with mischief in her eyes. "We could drive it over to your parents' house and announce our engagement."

"Perfect!" Sean jumped up, grinning.

"I'm kidding," Aimy laughed. Sean picked Aimy up and kissed her. In jubilation, he swung her around, her feet lifting off the ground. His ring was on her finger! Their laughter filled the garage like a symphony.

The sky hung dark—the same color as the ashen coals in the hearth of the machi's ruka. Dennie stood at the door, afraid to enter. The wind outside blew fierce and chill.

"The snows will come in a few weeks," Eva mentioned.

"Where is the machi?" Dennie asked.

"She's probably gathering herbs in the woods," Eva answered. The child's hair wound around her forehead in a tight braid, accentuating her dark, thoughtful eyes.

Dennie hesitated, wary to step inside. She was already on the machi's black list. For a moment she wished she had gone to collect araucania nuts with Esteban and Mercurio. But Esteban had been adamant she stay at the ruka due to the threatening weather. The men had left early in the morning and would be gone for four days. They planned to gather nuts from the groves which Dennie and Esteban had passed on their way to the reservation.

Despite Esteban's concern over foul weather, Mercurio had welcomed the strong winds, explaining that only the mature araucania pines, those seventy-five to one hundred-fifty feet tall, bore cones. Strong winds shook the kernels from the cones, allowing the people to gather them. These nuts were essential staples to feed the family during the winter.

Dennie turned her head away from the ruka and gazed up at the dark sky. The wind whipped Dennie's braid into her face, stinging her cheek. She hoped that Esteban and Mercurio found shelter in the grove before the storm broke.

"Come," Eva said, touching Dennie's hand. Dennie carefully followed Eva into the hut. Although it was midday, the ruka was dark inside. Dennie switched on her flashlight. The beam glimmered at bowls of twigs, leaves, and roots. There were bottles of putrid-smelling liquids. Moving deftly as one who knows a place well, Eva found what they looked for—a medium-size wooden box containing leaves from the canelo tree. The box was located in the northeast corner of the hut next to the kultrun. Dennie silently followed her cousin. Eva reached into the box and tucked handfuls of leaves into her sack.

"Do you think we should take them without asking permission? Perhaps we should wait until the machi returns," Dennie suggested.

Eva shook her head. "Mama needs them today. She will boil the canelo leaves with the michai roots and dye the wool bright yellow. It will make a warm poncho and bring a good price at the market."

"But will the machi be angry?"

Eva shook her head. "Grandmother shares all she has with us. She is not like the witches, the *kalku*. She has never cursed anyone. She is kind."

Dennie wasn't sure about that. She often felt that the machi wished to curse her. Dennie squatted down and touched the kultrun with a finger. The leather surface felt supple with wear. She studied the design on the face of the drum—the blue and white parallel lines that intersected at ninety-degree angles.

"Eva, do you know what the pattern on the kultrun means?"

The child looked up at Dennie, her dark eyes luminous, her voice innocent. "The blue and white are the sacred colors of the sky. The drum is divided into the four quarters of the earth—like Esteban's compass. Two are good. The south brings fair winds and good fortune. Pillan, the good ancestors, live in the east. But the north and west are bad. The north is where evil winds come from. The west is where the sun hides and the souls of the dead live."

Dennie spoke in a hushed voice. "What about the small square in the center?"

"It is the heart of the land and of the earth. It is the center of all things. When the heart of the earth beats in harmony with the souls of the living and the dead, the good and evil balance. Then time flows according to the wishes of God."

"Did Grandmother teach you this?" Dennie asked.

Eva nodded. The child spoke. "Yes. I lived here during the summer. Grandmother taught me many things."

"Do you want to be the next machi?"

Eva looked down. "I went once with Grandmother to the *machitun*, the healing ceremony. During it, a strange spirit possessed Grandmother. It seemed bad, evil. I ran away into the forest. Grandmother found me and was very kind. She took me home to my father's ruka. She said that I wasn't yet ready to train as a machi. She said that someday I would come back to her."

"Will you?"

"Grandmother says that she will pray for the sign to be given. Then I will go."

"The sign? She will pray that you become deathly sick and are healed?" Dennie asked, remembering Maria's explanation. "She will pray that you are struck by lightning?"

Eva stared fixedly at the dirt floor of the ruka. "Or maybe I will have a dream." Lightning outside illuminated the ruka, causing eerie shadows.

"Eva, does your mother want you to be a machi?"

Eva looked up at her cousin. "No, Mina. She prays to Jesus that the sign never comes. My mother is Christian."

Dennie looked hard at her cousin. "Eva, I didn't know Maria was Christian."

"She was taught by the nuns when she was small. She told my father after they married. Papa was not pleased. Mama does not speak of it anymore. I am the only one who knows that, in her heart, she still prays to Jesus."

"Eva, are you Christian?" Dennie asked. Eva shrugged. "I don't know if I am Christian. I know that I am Mapuche. But I never dream of being a machi. One night I dreamt of the stories Esteban told about our ancestors with Jesus. I told Mama about the dream. She thinks it was a good dream."

Lightning again. Dennie stood still in astonishment. She had never imagined that Esteban's words nourished hidden seeds in the fertile soils of her aunt's and cousin's souls. Thunder crashed, and a lance of lightning reached toward the ground. "Come," Eva gasped. "We must run home!"

Eva and Dennie ducked out of the ruka and dashed, hand in hand. The barefoot child ran swiftly in an old dress covered by a poncho so tightly woven that it repelled the rain. The young woman wore boots, Arizona jeans, and a Nike jacket. Lightning sliced the heavens above and around them. They were cousins—an Indian girl fearing the future, a young woman finding the past.

Maria smiled in relief as the two entered the ruka. Eva handed her the sack of canelo leaves. Dennie took off her wet jacket. "Sit by the fire." Maria offered an old chair to Dennie as she put the leaves into the iron pot that hung over the hearth.

Dennie hung her jacket on a beam near the fire. Then she went to her backpack and pulled out her Spanish translation of the Book of Mormon. She took it to Maria. "Aunt, would you like this book? It is about Jesus' dealing with your ancestors. It is the sacred record of the stories Esteban tells around the fire. It's like the Bible, a testament of Jesus."

Maria hesitated. Her hands shook.

"A gift for you," Dennie said, holding out the book.

Maria took it and turned it over. She opened it and stared at the words for a few moments.

"It would please me if you read to me while I spin," Maria suggested with a timid smile as she handed the book back to Dennie.

During the next three days, Dennie read to Maria and Eva while they dyed and spun wool. Maria worked silently, only speaking when Dennie stopped, to request that she continue. During the day, the words of the scriptures brought peace to Dennie. But at night she longed for Esteban's comforting presence. Why had he insisted on going with Mercurio? Was he safe?

On the third night, Dennie lay awake in her sleeping bag, a glowing ember alive in the fire, darkness cloaking the corners of the ruka. She had not had a bath in days and felt dirty and itchy. She was so far away from home and so alone. She had been in Chile for over five weeks now.

A noise outside sounded like crying. Was it the wind or a hurt animal? Dennie thought of Thes. Her heart pounded in cadence with the rain. She tried to rest.

Eva coughed repeatedly. Dennie opened her eyes as sleep eluded her. Eva stilled. Dennie thought of how Esteban loved her. She felt confused and isolated, and her thoughts spun. Esteban had insisted on leaving her at the ruka this week. Was it just her safety that concerned him, or did he need time away from her? Did he want her to miss him?

Dennie thought of how the intimacy of their surroundings and her dependence on him fueled Esteban's passion and desire to marry. Sometimes he held her with an intensity that caused her heartbeat to quicken. At such moments she longed to dissolve all walls between them. But this longing continued to frighten her. Did Esteban sense her fear? Occasionally he seemed distant, almost angry.

He wanted her to commit and she couldn't. He wanted her to fast and pray about it. She did. Still, she couldn't forget the clean happiness of Ron's smile, the carefree way they laughed together. She recalled how Ron marveled when she showed him that grass twinkled like stars when the sun struck it at certain angles. She smiled softly when she thought back on the time Ron broke his leg and they raced the handicapped carts around the grocery store laughing, always laughing. Before she could marry Esteban, she had to find out what to do with these memories. Maybe she would know for sure when Esteban came back. She imagined his thrill when he found out that she was reading the Book of Mormon to Maria. Finally Dennie slept.

Morning came and the rain continued. Maria made a breakfast of coarsely ground wheat mixed with hot water. To Eva's delight, Dennie added honey and canned milk to the gruel. Yet Eva's nose ran, and her eyes were not as bright as usual.

"Eva, care for the animals quickly," Maria said after breakfast. "Mina, you must read to me. There's little time."

"But I'll be here for two more weeks," Dennie countered. "Eva can read to you after I leave."

"You don't understand," Maria said. She took up her spinning and motioned for Dennie to begin. Eva coughed as she ran out into the rain.

They were on the Isaiah chapters in 2 Nephi. Yesterday, Dennie had been amazed at how these chapters, which she had always found so obscure, held Maria's attention. The rhythm of Dennie's voice mingled with the whir of the spinning wheel and the drumming of the rain.

And when they shall say unto you: Seek unto them that have familiar spirits, and unto wizards that peep and mutter—should not a people seek unto their God for the living to hear from the dead . . . To the law and to the testimony; and if they speak not according to this word, it is because there is no light in them.

A sob erupted from Maria, a cry from the depths of her soul that seemed to have long been held back.

"Maria, what's wrong?" Dennie exclaimed with concern.

"I am Mapuche," Maria cried. "I am proud to be Mapuche."

"The Mapuche are a wonderful people."

"I am also Christian, but I cannot be Christian. I am the daughter-in-law of the machi. I am proud of my ancestors, of Lautaro who fought for the land, of the machis who heal bodies, who honor good rather than evil. How can I believe in Christ? In the cross that was held before my ancestors like a knife when their lands were taken? Do I dishonor those who have gone before, those whose souls' waters have joined the river of sky?"

"No," Dennie said as she reached out and touched the Indian woman's arm. "The people in the Book of Mormon are your ancestors too. And mine. We are children of Lehi. Let me keep reading. There is so much more." Trembling, Maria nodded. Eva came back into the ruka and cast a look at her mother. The girl shivered and coughed. She sat down and warmed her hands near the fire. Dennie continued.

The people that walked in darkness have seen a great light; they that dwell in the land of the shadow of death, upon them hath the light shined . . . For unto us a child is born, unto us a son is given; and the government shall be upon his shoulder; and his name shall be called, Wonderful, Counselor, The Mighty God, The Everlasting Father, The Prince of Peace.

Maria stopped spinning and closed her eyes. Dennie said a silent prayer for her aunt and asked, "Maria, is it OK if I skip to another part of the Book of Mormon, a part that tells why Jesus is the light of the world?"

Maria nodded, but her eyes remained closed. Was she praying? Dennie turned to Alma 7, verses eleven and twelve. *And he will take upon him death, that he may loose the bands of death which bind his people; and he will take upon him their infirmities, that his bowels may be filled with mercy, according to the flesh, that he may know how to succor his people according to their infirmities.*

Dogs barked. There was wind at the door. Maria opened her eyes, and Dennie turned her head. The Book of Mormon lay open in her lap. But Eva already faced the opening of the ruka, as if expecting something.

The machi, water streaming from her poncho, entered the ruka, her eyes blazing like hot coals. Dennie stood up, meeting the old woman's glare, holding the Book of Mormon in her hands. The machi shouted angry words at Dennie that the young woman could not understand. But one word she heard over and over again: *Pinsha, Pinsha*. The machi uttered a command to Maria in Mapudungun.

"No," Maria said. "No." There was a defiant flash in her eye.

The machi strode to Dennie, grabbed the Book of Mormon, and threw it into the fire. Dennie stepped backwards as if she had been slapped. The machi shouted at Dennie once more. She wheeled around and stalked out of the ruka.

Dennie sat back down, still as stone. Tears ran down Eva's cheeks. Dennie felt as if there was not enough fresh air in the ruka to breathe. But Maria did not cry. She went to the fire, took two long sticks in her hands, and pulled the charred book from the flames. She blew out the embers dancing on the scorched pages, then cooled the book with a damp rag. Dennie watched in silence as Maria wrapped the damaged Book of Mormon in a piece of bright wool, handling it as if it were a precious, living thing. Maria handed the book to Eva. With a spade, Maria knelt and dug a hole in the dirt floor of the ruka.

After she finished digging, still on her knees, Maria looked up at Dennie. "Thank you for this gift. The Mapuche keep sacred things in the earth of their homes. We will keep the Book of Mormon with us. Always." Gently, she took the package from Eva and placed it in the hole, then covered it with dirt. She packed the soil so tightly over it that there wasn't a mark to show where she had used the spade. Maria picked up her spinning. Dennie hazarded the question that haunted her.

"What is *Pinsha*?" she asked, her voice soft and barely audible over the wind that shook the hut. Yet Maria heard the question.

"Your mother," Maria answered. "Your mother was called Pinsha. She was small and pretty like you. Pinsha means hummingbird."

"What happened to my mother?" Dennie asked in a hushed voice.

Maria handed her spinning to Eva. "Pinsha had a dream when she was young. She dreamed two white lambs came from her own body. Her mother thought it was a sign that Pinsha had the soul of a machi. She trained her daughter to be the next machi. Pinsha's hands were quick and skilled.

"Then one summer, a young man, Jacques, visited our village from the northern mines. He lived with our people. He secretly won the heart of Pinsha, the daughter and apprentice of the machi. That year at the Nillatun, Pinsha and Jacques could no longer hide their love. They danced openly. The beat of the kultrun echoed the machi's anger at Pinsha. The next night, Pinsha left with Jacques.

"The next year the crops failed. The people suffered. Children and old ones died. It was said that the gods would not listen to the machi because her daughter, who knew the secrets of our people, had chosen a winka man.

"One spring your mother came back alone with you in her belly and your brother in her arms. She told Mercurio that Jacques was gone, one of the many who disappeared during the years of Pinochet. Pinsha stood outside her mother's ruka and called to the machi, asking to come home, asking for forgiveness. But the machi would not acknowledge her daughter's children. 'They are winka,' she said, turning her back. Pinsha left weeping, not knowing that the machi wept too as she sat with Mercurio in the ruka.

"You see, the machi is not so different from other women, for she has a mother's heart. The following season she asked Mercurio to find Pinsha and see how she fared. He came back with sad tidings. He said that Pinsha worked in a brothel in the city to buy bread for her children, Lautaro and Mina. In sorrow and shame, the machi commanded that Pinsha's name be erased from the memory of our people. But she could not erase the memory of Pinsha from her own heart. Your mother's poncho, woven in blue and white—the poncho she was to wear as a machi, is buried in a steel box in the corner of your grandmother's ruka."

CHAPTER 15

HOW A MAN LIVES

Rick Fletcher waited apprehensively as the day of Meryl's surgery fast approached. Would it be a fulcrum in their lives or a destination? Yet while he waited, he continued to serve his clients with meticulous conscientiousness, and his efforts as ward clerk in church proved flawless. He didn't miss a beat.

But he felt tightness in his jaw every moment of each day. His wife was suffering and he didn't know how to help her. Not completely understanding why she isolated herself, he wondered why this time of trial was so different from others they had passed through. He remembered her initial cancer diagnosis nearly five years ago. She had found strength in his support. When they lost Thes, they had clung to each other for survival.

He had asked her why she was so inward. She said that she didn't want people's pity, she didn't want them to treat her differently, and she didn't want their feelings toward her to be altered.

Did that include him? Was she afraid that his feelings toward her would change—that he wouldn't love her intimately after her surgery? He had tried to reassure her, had told her that he always wanted to be married to her, no matter what. *But how will you feel inside, Rick?* Meryl had asked. *What will your gut reaction be?*

Who cares about gut reactions? He exclaimed. *They come and go like water. You are my wife. That is all that matters.*

But that wasn't all that mattered to Meryl. She lost her appetite. There were new angles in her cheeks. She wrote false, cheerful e-mails to Dennie. There were pools of silence between them. She talked about Thes frequently.

When Rick suggested that they go out of town to a romantic getaway the weekend before her surgery, she declined. She explained that she wanted to stay home—to get as much writing in as she could before the operation. She didn't know how long it would take to recover, to gain the strength to sit at the computer again.

Rick experienced a feeling of disassociation, of drawing apart. She didn't know how long it would be before she could write again? What about him? How long would it be before she was well enough to go away with him, to escape together to a place of beauty and fun? Did that matter to her? But he kept silent. He wouldn't burden her with guilt, not right now.

Then one night past midnight, he awakened to the sensation of Meryl against him. Her body was damp, and she was shaking. She must have had a nightmare. He thought about asking her about it, but how could discussing it help? He put his arm around her.

After that, things were a little better. Sometimes she slept in his arms. She asked him to accompany her on walks in the evenings. Two evenings before her surgery, she said that she had the strangest sensation. *It seems like the whole world belongs to me, Rick,* Meryl had said. *Because I'm alive to perceive it. My eyes, my ears, my senses present a breadth of view—precious, liquid, and fleeting. The air I breathe feels like a miracle, the sunset a vision. Yet I am alone.*

Rick held her elegant hand tightly in his. He would pray for her continually. He would give her a blessing tomorrow. He would do all he could. She was his wife, and he loved her. That night, Meryl stayed up late, typing her manuscript.

One afternoon, John Howland spied Desire and Elizabeth in a corner of the ship laughing. He thought of how yesterday, the girl Elizabeth had beaten him five games of nine at Nine Men's Morris. He had told Lizzy that she reminded him of his sister Margaret, a formidable but delightful opponent. Desire had watched the final game and had cheered for Elizabeth. Perhaps that was why John's concentration had lapsed. Yet John had enjoyed the merriness in Elizabeth's eye at her victory. He feared the child would be sorrowful soon. Her mother's strength continued to wane despite Desire's best efforts.

John walked over to the young women to discover their current jest.

Desire's book of housewifery lay open in her lap.

"Go, John," Desire said with a smile as she hastily closed the book. "A man does not want to hear of housewifery! Your ears are more tuned to Stephen Hopkins's tales of mutiny on his former voyage to the New World."

John's expression turned thoughtful. "I fear that Edward Dotey and Edward Leister, Hopkins's own servants, listen too well to their master's stories of youthful rebellion. They glance at one another secretly when he speaks. I think the two do not want to be servants in the New World."

"Constance Hopkins tells me much of Dotey and Leister," Desire said, thinking of how Constance was her own age, full of mirth and quick to flaunt her own beauty. "She minces about Dotey and Leister, professing love to each— and they are high-spirited and prone to violence. Constance is not wise."

"Constance is as foolish as the rest of her family," John replied. "I fear their servants plot against them."

"But what about you, John?" Elizabeth asked thoughtfully. "You will be a servant in the New World. Do you want to be?"

John looked at the girl. "The scriptures teach that he who serves is greatest of all. I will serve my time and learn all I can from Deacon Carver. Then I shall be more free than before my servitude."

Desire nodded and smiled warmly at John.

The young man clapped his hands. "Now my friends, what do you laugh about so heartily! True friends would not hold back such merriment!"

"Come, Desire, read it to him," Elizabeth's eyes now twinkled. "T'would be good advice for Constance Hopkins."

"Lizzy, I think not," said Desire, her cheeks reddening.

"You think that it would not be good advice for Constance or that you should not read it to John?" Elizabeth asked.

Desire laughed. "It would be fair advice for Constance. But I would not read it to John or any man."

"Then I shall," declared the younger girl. She opened the book, crin-kled her nose, and arched her neck aristocratically as she read. "It is meet that our English housewife be modest inwardly as well as outwardly. In her carriage toward her husband she shall shun all rage, passion, and humour, being directed rather than to direct, always patient, pleasant, amiable, and delightful, never using her anger to abate her husband's evil for this is both monstrous and ugly." Lizzy broke down and finished the

passage giggling. "Desire and I think we are destined to be ugly monsters if we wed!"

"Then the men who marry such ugly monsters shall be thrice blessed," John declared.

"Lizzy," Desire said, her cheeks crimson. "You must be modest if you hope to become an English lady."

"Fie on modesty!" John declared. Then he bowed deeply. "I bid such amiable, pleasant, and delightful English ladies farewell. I must speak with Deacon Carver concerning Dotey and Leister."

After John left, Lizzy pored over the book while Desire stared out to the sea. Desire loved John more with each passing day. Had her own mother ever felt this way about her father?

"Come, Lizzy," Desire said at last. "Let us go and see your mum." As the two started for the hold, Isaac the sailor stepped into their path.

"How fare the Ripe Peach and Little Peacock?" His eyes gleamed with sarcasm and cruelty.

"Our families await us," Desire said quickly as she tried to step around him. He blocked her way, then grabbed her arm and held it tightly.

"They shall wait then," Isaac hissed. With his other hand, he touched Desire's red cheek. "Such a sumptuous treat you shall be for the fishes. Yet I should like to taste you first. Would John Howland eat a peach that has already been bitten into?"

He pulled her body into his. Desire struggled and turned her head from him. "Lizzy, get help," she whispered.

"Aye, Lizzy, get help," Isaac mocked. "By the time Lizzy returns, I will have tasted my peach." Tears of shame and fear blinded Desire.

Hot anger coursed through Elizabeth. "If you touch her, John Howland will kill you!" Lizzy hissed.

"Think ye that I'm afraid of John Howland?" Isaac threw his head back and roared with laughter. But Isaac's laughter stopped at the sound of approaching footsteps. Isaac pushed Desire away. "We will meet again, Sweet Peach."

Elizabeth took Desire's hand and pulled her towards the hold. "We will tell John and he will kill Isaac!" Elizabeth spit out. Tears ran in crooked paths down Desire's cheeks.

"Lizzy," Desire begged. "Please don't tell John. We are nearly halfway *to the New World. When we arrive, the sailor will leave us be and soon return to England with the ship."*

"But Desire, no one is safe with Isaac unchecked." Elizabeth looked into her friend's eyes.

"We shall be less safe if we anger him. It would shame me for John to know," Desire whispered. "Please, Lizzy."

Elizabeth saw the tears in Desire's eyes. She put her arms around the older girl, their bonnets touching. "I won't tell. Not if you don't want me to."

Two mornings later, under blue skies, Isaac the sailor woke up gasping. He screamed aloud, for his head roared with pain. By midmorning the huge, brawny man shook uncontrollably. His flesh burned. The crew's doctor let blood, but to no avail.

Captain Jones sent a man to summon Desire, for it had been rumored about the ship that she had priceless medicine in her pocket and that the maid's knowledge of herbs had healed many on the voyage. The messenger descended into the hold and gave Desire the Captain's word while she ate breakfast. Desire paled at the mention of Isaac the sailor more than at the fear of the disease.

"Desire, will you try to help the sailor?" Deacon Carver asked the speechless young woman. Desire nodded.

"I will go with you," Catherine Carver added.

"And I," John Howland spoke. As the group left the hold for the sun-drenched deck, Desire dared not meet Elizabeth's eyes.

Standing near the sailor's bunk, Desire swallowed and stared at the dying man. He had no power over her now. Ought she to try to make him well? She had the power to hasten his death with the wrong medicines.

Deacon Carver seemed to read her mind. "Child, should we not love our enemies and do good to them that hate us, as our Lord instructed?"

Tears brimmed in Desire's eyes as she looked down at her hands. What would the Carvers think of her if they knew she thought such evil? What did God think?

"Desire," John said as he covered her hands with his. "Do you know how to help this man?"

Desire looked up at John and whispered, "Yes." He nodded. She swallowed, but her voice was firm as she gave instructions. "Take him to the deck. Build a fire there to warm him."

She told the captain of the concoction her mother instructed her to make while her father lay dying of fever. If they could cause Isaac to sweat, then the sickness might decrease. She asked for posset ale, and a sailor brought it. Desire's hands remained steady as she took a few bruised aniseeds within her pocket and mixed them with the ale. "He must sup this," she directed as she joined those on the deck.

Two sailors held the writhing man. The fire flamed hot against the chill, and the salty sea air smelled of smoke. Captain Jones pried the man's mouth open, and John Howland poured the liquid in. Isaac spit and choked on it. Desire's hands shook. The sweat did not come. With her father's illness in her mind, Desire mixed more medicine and helped to stoke the fire. Again and again she tried to save the man's life, battling death as a sailor battles the sea. Yet she did not win. Within two hours, while the group watched, Isaac's breath rattled and the sailor died. Desire stared at the fire, sweat beneath her bonnet, her lips pale and cold.

"Call Elder Brewster," Deacon Carver instructed John Howland. "And let any who choose come onto the deck to pray for the man's soul whilst his body is lowered into the sea."

The Tilleys, the Bradfords, the Brewsters, and a handful of others came to the place where the dead man lay.

"It is an evil omen," Dorothy, Elder Bradford's wife, cried, cowering at the sight of the body. Her own frame convulsed with terror.

"Courage, Dorothy," her husband instructed his young wife firmly. "Witness the just hand of God on a profane man."

Catherine Carver reached her arm around Desire's waist. Lizzy's eyes met Desire's. "I tried to save him," Desire whispered. Lizzy nodded. The group was instructed to close their eyes and bow their heads while the corpse entered the waves. But Elizabeth Tilley's eyes stayed open. Solemnly, she watched the man disappear into the water with a splash and glint of sun. She did not know that John Howland watched her, wondering at the strength of her spirit.

Reverend Brewster's voice raised to heaven in a song of prayer. Elizabeth and John closed their eyes. "Jehovah feedeth me, I shall not lack. In grassy folds, he down doth make me lie. He gently leads me, quiet waters by. He doth return my soul: for his namesake, in paths of justice leads me quietly."

The group dispersed. John looked at Desire. He noticed the redness in her eyes and the heaviness of her carriage. She looked unlike herself, as if the apple of a lass had turned in one day to an old woman.

"Desire?" John asked as he followed her, touching her arm. "Would you speak with me? You sorrow."

"All men die the same, John!" she cried as she turned to him. "Whether they be kind and generous as my father or as wicked as Isaac the sailor. They all die the same."

"But they do not live the same," John said gently.

"It mattereth not in the end."

"It is all that matters, Desire. It is the key."

"The key to what, John?"

"The key to hope. And I think to heaven."

"And to heaven." Desire wept with her forehead on John Howland's shoulder.

That night when all had gone to bed, Elizabeth lay next to her mother, her green eyes open in the darkness. She knew her mother was also awake, for her breathing was light.

"Mother," the girl whispered. "Yesterday I wished Isaac dead. Did God in His justice strike the sailor for his evil treatment of our people? Elder Bradford thinks it is so."

"Perhaps not, child," Joan answered in a hushed voice. "Our Lord rejoices at the death of his obedient children, for He gathers them home as a hen gathereth her chickens under her wing. So it must also be that the heavens weep when a sinful man such as Isaac dies."

"So it must be," Lizzy repeated. After long thought, she too slept.

The next afternoon, the weather changed as fierce storms thundered in from the west. The sails were lowered and the lone ship rode the monstrous waves. The helmsmen desperately tried to turn her toward the wind.

Captain Jones ordered the passengers to stay in the hold. As the Mayflower *pitched and rolled on the open sea, wooden barriers cracked and icy water drenched all those crouched in the bunks below as they huddled together, weeping and praying.*

For days storms pounded the sea. Sickness, stench, and ice-cold fear filled the hold. The cries of women and children echoed in John Howland's ears. Savage waves tore the ship, cracking the Mayflower's *beam. The ocean drenched the people again and again.*

Helpless fury infused John. Where was that Jesus he had read of in the

Bible? The God who answered prayers? The God who stilled the tempest? The God of light? Why did He leave His people powerless? Confusion and doubt filled John as he watched those weaker than him suffer nearly more than they could bear—those whom he had grown to love. But he could not die huddled in filth and terror. Heaven might close its eyes to the storm, but John would not. He would go to the deck and fight this hellish storm before his heart burst with rage and terror!

"Stay with me!" Desire sobbed as John gained his footing.

He held her for a moment. "I must live, Desire, even if I die," he hissed into her ear.

John scrambled out of the hold. On deck, lightning pierced the sky. Sheets of rain struck him; the wind roared in his ears. A mariner frantically motioned him down. But too late. A mountainous wave flipped the boat onto her beam-ends. John was swept into the sea.

He swam and struggled with little hope of winning. He would die and soon find out the measure of heaven. Dark rain, wind, and open sea. Then the words of Jesus came as a voice in his mind. "Peace I leave with you: my peace I give unto you; not as the world giveth, give I unto you. Let not your heart be troubled, nor fear."

John rode a wave as if it took him toward heaven. Yet it did not leave him in the arms of the Lord, but beside some topsail halyard trailing the ship. With a final surge of will, John clutched it, looping it around his body and arms before he was pulled down into the sea and darkness.

Four mariners hauled the lifeless form of John Howland aboard using a boat hook. They carried the man downward into the dark hold, where a weak lantern shone. Deacon Carver took the man in his arms, then lay him down and pounded on his chest, weeping. "John, John! I would have you live. By the grace of our Lord, Jesus Christ, I would have you live!" John coughed, retched, and opened his eyes. The ship heaved.

"He lives!" Deacon Carver shouted at the saints and at the storm! "Thanks be to God! John Howland lives!"

Later, as John lay ill and shaking, Desire held his hand and whispered into his ear. "The key lies in how a man lives, not how he dies. Our Lord would have you live, John!"

Lizzy Tilley crawled across the hold to her friends. Desire held Lizzy to her. Then the girl took John's other hand and pressed it to her cheek. John felt Lizzy's youthful tears—warm strength against the icy rain.

CHAPTER 16

A STILL SMALL VOICE

Eva's cold worsened as the day lengthened. By late afternoon, there were dark shadows beneath her eyes. Rain continued to pour outside. Relief flooded Dennie when Esteban ducked into the ruka shortly before dark. Yet he moved slowly, his body and clothing bedraggled and mud soaked. His bloodshot eyes underscored his weariness.

"Are you all right?" Dennie asked as she walked toward him with extended arms. Esteban took a step back. He didn't seem to want to be touched. He shook from cold, and when his eyes met Dennie's, she sensed restrained anger. Esteban spoke. "Ten miles away from here, the truck is stuck in the mud. We walked. When it stops raining, we'll take the oxen and pull it out."

"Where is my husband?" Maria asked with a furtive glance toward the door of the ruka.

"Despite the storm, the machi was waiting for him on the road. He is speaking with her. What happened while we were gone?"

"You're cold," Dennie said as she turned to Esteban. "Change into dry clothes. Then I'll explain."

"My dry clothes are in the truck," Esteban stated shortly, without looking at her.

Deftly Maria handed Esteban an old shirt, a pair of pants, and a poncho that belonged to her husband. "Do you have more clothing for Mercurio?" Esteban asked before he changed. "He too is soaked to the skin."

Maria nodded, assuring him that they owned one more pair of pants and two other shirts. "The poncho is warm," she added. Esteban thanked Maria politely. He changed in the screened-off corner of the ruka while Maria stirred the soup cooking at the hearth. Eva coughed as she fingered her spinning.

Melancholy enveloped Dennie. Her grandmother hated her. Esteban was angry with her. He couldn't even look at her. How quickly things change, joy suffocated as water douses a fire.

Barefoot, Esteban hung his wet clothes on a beam near the hearth. Mercurio's pants came to Esteban's midcalf. His eyes drifted towards Dennie. He looked away. After lowering himself slowly to the dirt floor, he sat cross-legged, the poncho encircling him. Bearded and masculine, he looked so altered, so remote.

"Tell me what happened," he said as he stared into the fire.

Dennie sat down near him but did not touch him. In this lonely place, right or wrong, fair or unfair, she needed him. The days' events poured from her. Dennie spoke in English, hoping Maria would not be offended. It was their only privacy. Dennie told Esteban of Eva's fear to become the next machi, of Maria's belief in Christ, of reading the Book of Mormon and of the machi's anger.

"I wonder if I should have shared the Book of Mormon. It's caused such contention," Dennie said earnestly.

"Of course you should have given her the Book of Mormon!" Esteban's voice was sharp.

"Why are you angry with me?" Dennie asked.

"I am not angry," Esteban said stoically, each word a stony weight.

"Everything about you is angry," Dennie countered. "Your voice. Your eyes. Everything."

Esteban looked at her as if he were surveying her, examining her. Then he spoke in a tight voice. "In town, I went to Diego's house to check our e-mail. Alicia sent me a message. In it, she mocked me. Two letters from Elder Babcock await you at my home."

Dennie reached out and touched Esteban's hand. "But you knew I was writing Ron."

Esteban pulled his hand away. "I did not think you would write him in Chile. I have been a fool. I hoped to make you part of my family, and you gave another man my address! He sends you loving letters at my father's house. How could you do this? How could you shame me like this? Alicia laughs at us! She says that I should have listened to her long ago, that you are like all of the other gringas in the United States. That you are spoiled and selfish, that you do not know how to love."

Dennie looked away. She didn't know how to answer him, didn't know how to explain. "Alicia is wrong," she said quietly.

Esteban's voice was acid. "I can't go on like this, only giving and getting nothing in return."

"I'm sorry," Dennie whispered. "I don't know what to do."

"That is all you can say? That you are sorry! That you don't know what to do? After how I have loved you?" Esteban's voice shook.

There was a noise at the entrance to the hut. Dennie glanced at Maria and saw fear in the woman's eyes.

Mercurio stepped inside the ruka, mud dripping from him. He stood, his back as straight as the machi's rewe. His eyes burned like dark lava, like Thes's eyes used to look when he was angry.

Mercurio spoke sternly to Maria in Mapudungun. Maria bowed her head. Mercurio turned to Esteban. "I'm sorry my friend, but Mina is no longer welcome here. She must leave as soon as we pull the truck out of the mud."

Esteban nodded silently and looked at his hands. There was pain in his eyes.

"Eva," Mercurio continued. "You will go to your grandmother now. Your training begins tonight. You shall be the next machi. It is an honor."

"No, papa. Please." Eva sank into her chair.

"Go now!" Mercurio shouted. "The machi awaits you!"

"I won't!" Eva looked up at her father with defiant tears in her eyes. She held on to the sides of her chair. Mercurio stepped to her and slapped her hard across the face. The chair rocked. He pulled her from the chair and threw her to the floor. Maria bent over on her stool, her face in her hands.

Without speaking, Eva stood, wrapped her poncho around her, and fled the hut, her red, flushed cheeks cooled by tears. Mercurio looked at his wife. Her sorrow seemed to increase his frustration. He kicked the legs of the stool.

"Please don't hurt her. It's my fault!" Dennie cried as she ran to Maria. Mercurio's anger turned towards Dennie. He raised his hand as if to strike her. She called Esteban's name, but Esteban did not respond. Yet Dennie's fearful voice reached Mercurio and withered his rage. He stood stone-still, breathing hard, staring at his hand as if it were not a part of him, as if it were venom. He lowered his hand, but his voice lashed out, "The machi is right. You are like Pinsha. Sorrow and confusion follow your footsteps like vultures follow the dying."

Dennie's voice shook as she spoke. "Maybe I am like Pinsha. But you are not like my father. He would never strike his child. And you are not like my Uncle Blake. His voice does not wound." She turned from Mercurio and looked at Esteban. Her words came chill and low. "And my brother, Lautaro, would not have sat silently, watching."

Esteban continued to stare at the fire. Dennie knew there was grief in him, but there was pride too. She felt as if the hut were closing in on her, the anger and sorrow of those around her suffocating her. She couldn't stay, yet she had nowhere to go. She turned and went to her partitioned corner of the ruka, crawled into her sleeping bag, and buried her head in the pillow. There she wept and prayed.

The next day the rain continued. The four adults moved about silently and separately. Mercurio fed the animals. Maria spun with downcast eyes. Esteban stoked the fire in the hearth. Dennie stared at a novel in her dim corner of the ruka. She could not concentrate on the words. She could not forget about Eva—in her grandmother's ruka, all alone.

Dennie wanted to go home, yet Mercurio's words stung her. *Sorrow followed her.* She closed her eyes and thought of her bright California home, of BYU football games, of her parents, and of Aimy and Ron. Esteban pushed aside the partition. His hand held a lantern, the light in it burning brightly. He placed it beside Dennie, but did not speak to her.

That evening the rain lessened. Dennie stayed in her corner. She drank a can of pop and ate a granola bar for dinner. She heard the machi's voice outside speaking to Mercurio in Mapudungun.

A few moments later, Esteban opened the partition and looked down at Dennie. He spoke gently. "The machi came looking for Eva. Eva never went to the machi's ruka. The old woman thought Mercurio neglected to send her. The rest of us are going to search the reservation for Eva. She is probably with Juana or another family. You are to stay here in case she returns."

"She might be in the forest," Dennie said urgently.

"We'll search the reservation first."

"Esteban, she's sick," Dennie whispered.

"I know," he said. He turned and left before Dennie could speak again. But as Dennie sat in the shadows waiting and praying, her heart beat with fear. She felt certain that Eva wasn't on the reservation but had hidden outside somewhere—alone, ill, and frightened. Eva had no bright California home to fix her mind on. This reservation, this hut, this family was all Eva had, and it had crumbled beneath her. And Dennie's presence had hastened the crumbling. This knowledge broke Dennie's heart.

As darkness fell, panic rose within Dennie. She couldn't stand the silence of the hut any longer. She felt driven to help her cousin, to find Eva before the night passed. Dennie pulled on a coat, found her flashlight, and left the ruka. Although the rain had ceased, it was cold and windy.

She stumbled through the brush toward the forest, calling Eva's name, begging her to come home, and promising to help her. No human voice answered Dennie, only the lash and cry of the wind. Dennie wrapped her arms around herself, the T-shirt beneath her coat drenched with sweat, her teeth chattering. She tripped over the root of a tree and fell, tasting mud and blood.

She began to cry, her tears mixing with the wet earth. Her task was hopeless. She didn't know the forest and would only become lost in her search. She was powerless to protect her cousin. Why hadn't she listened to her parents? She had hurt Maria and Esteban. She had destroyed Eva's life. She shouldn't have come. Ever. Were she and her brother Pinsha's lambs? One was dead, the other weeping in the mud. Truly sorrow followed them like vultures trailed the dying.

Time passed—perhaps twenty minutes, perhaps an hour. Finally Dennie's tears stopped, and she huddled beneath the tree, motionless and chilled, empty of strength or will. Finally, she pulled herself into a sitting position, her back against the trunk. She had to make her way back to the ruka. But before going, she whispered a desperate prayer for Eva. After her prayer, Dennie looked up. Between the branches of the tree she saw the sky. There was a break in the clouds directly above her head, and through this break a lone star shone.

She thought of the night Pinsha died. Lautaro's words filled her mind. "Run toward the star, Mina. When we reach it, we will be safe."

Then a feeling of calm encompassed Dennie, as clear and concrete as writing on a stone tablet, as mild as the eye of a storm. The winds of her soul whispered a message, and Dennie realized that truth sometimes seemed a dichotomy—that she was solitary, but not alone.

For as she sat under the sacred canelo tree with the star above her, she was Mina Callfuhuala, the daughter of the outcast Pinsha—Pinsha, the sweet hummingbird, the beloved child of the machi. She was also the child of the faceless Jacques, a passionate man who believed in romance and freedom. And she had a brother. Her brother was Lautaro Callfuhuala, named for a Mapuche warrior, a blue gull racing the sky. But they were also Denizen and Theseus Fletcher, the blessed and precious children of Meryl and Richard Fletcher, descendants of those saints who crossed the plains and the sea.

They had been sealed together in the temple, in concentric circles, in strings of light. A scripture she had read in seminary long ago came to her mind. *If ye receive a child in my name, so ye also receive me.* A promise from her Savior, a description of the gift the Fletchers had given her—of the home of love and the gospel of Jesus Christ.

The cost for her presence there had been great, the toll of human pain and suffering almost unbearable. But the product was love, the kind of love in the Savior's voice when He called the Nephite children to Him, the kind of love that encircled them with fire and angels, the kind of love that broke down prison walls.

She heard a rustling and footsteps. Dennie stood up. Could it be Eva? She called out and ran toward the noise. A moment later she saw Esteban walking toward her.

"Have you found Eva?" Dennie asked.

Esteban shook his head. "Mercurio is saddling Namcupan. He has promised Maria that he will search the forest until he finds Eva."

"She's out there somewhere," Dennie said quietly. "Under the same sky. I think that Heavenly Father will protect her."

"I hope so, *regalona*," Esteban said. "Forgive me. Please forgive me."

"I forgive you," Dennie said quietly as she looked into Esteban's eyes. But she did not take Esteban's arm, though he offered it to her. She was no longer his *regalona*, his pampered one. She was Denizen Mina Callfuhuala Fletcher. She belonged to her Father in Heaven and to her Lord, Jesus Christ. Her birth mother, her adoptive parents, her brother, her Savior—they had paid a price for the existence, safety, and salvation of her soul. She could and would stand alone, for she was not alone—their love was within her, encircling her.

She walked back to the hut beside him. When she entered the ruka, Dennie walked straight to Maria and put her hand on her shoulder. "I love you," she whispered. "I will pray for you and Eva."

Dennie then changed into dry clothing. Maria washed and dressed the cuts on Dennie's face. The two women sat up late by the hearth, hand in hand. The prayers in their hearts surrounded them like a shield of hope as they asked their God to keep Eva safe and bring her home.

Morning came. Clouds rising above the ocean moved toward the Andes, layering the sky. The day lengthened, and Maria asked Dennie if God had forgotten them. "No," Dennie answered. "He never forgets."

Finally, near evening, Mercurio returned with the limp form of Eva slumped in the saddle in front of him. He dismounted carefully, tenderly, carrying his precious burden toward the entrance of the ruka. Maria ran to him gasping. "My child! My child is dead?"

Mercurio shook his head. "She is alive." Maria touched Eva's burning cheeks. A barking cough shook the girl. Her eyes opened and closed again from an unfathomable weight.

Gently, Mercurio carried Eva into the ruka and laid his daughter on the earthen floor near the fire. He turned to Esteban. "Get the machi," he said. "Tell her the child's breath comes painfully and she burns with fever."

"But she needs a doctor," Dennie challenged her uncle. "We must take her to town. To the hospital."

Mercurio looked over at Dennie. This time there was no anger in his eyes, only sorrow. He shook his head. "The machitun will be performed. My daughter is the hope of our people, of the living and the dead. She is all we have left. Only Eva can fill the dark place left by Pinsha. There is no choice. You do not understand. You are winka."

Esteban put his hand on Mercurio's shoulder. "I will get the machi."

Dennie followed Esteban out of the ruka. "Should I take Namcupan and ride for a doctor?"

Esteban shook his head. "It's too far. No doctor would come. We have to respect Mercurio. Eva is his child."

"But she might die, Esteban," Dennie choked. "I believe that Heavenly Father means for us to save her."

"The truck is in the mud. Only Mercurio can get Eva to the hospital, and he will only do this with the machi's permission. Thus, I get the machi and we pray."

Dennie nodded. While Esteban was gone, Dennie watched Maria massage Eva's feverish body. She bathed it in water tinctured with fragrant leaves. Then she covered Eva with clean sheep pelts, the fur side next to her body. The child's breath rasped painfully, her mouth and cheeks bright red, her skin soft and lovely and fragile.

Outside, Mercurio shouted as he galloped Namcupan in a tight circle around the ruka. He was the son of the machi, encircling his home, driving away the evil spirits which sought his child's life. As he rode, the sun sank in the heavens and the river of blue sky turned fire red while a stream of light like a golden chain balanced on the edge of the horizon.

Blake Taylor left the hospital after his shift and drove toward the airport. He was the bishop, the spiritual leader of nearly three hundred people, yet at times he felt as if he couldn't focus, as if his mind pulled him in a cacophony of different directions. There was the ward—people without callings and presidents of auxiliaries battling for the same individuals to fill their empty slots. There were struggling youth and marriages cracking under constant pressure. There was his job in the transplant unit, the politics, the life and death struggles of his patients, the triumph and despair of their families. And of course, his family—Chris far away and Karin battling to keep her chin up. But it was Meryl, his beloved sister, who held his thoughts at the moment.

Soon he would meet his parents' plane. They were coming because Meryl was having a mastectomy tomorrow. Yet Meryl wouldn't know they were here. Blake had made the decision to keep their presence a secret until after her surgery. Yet he was a wise enough man to know that his judgment was fallible, and this realization troubled him.

He remembered explaining his feelings to his mother on the telephone a week ago, aching at the knowledge that each sentence hurt her. *Mom, don't tell Meryl you're coming. Patients need to go into surgery feeling as calm as possible. They simply do better and recover sooner. Study after study has proven it. The hospital provides soft music and heated blankets to help.*

It's just that we don't know how your coming will affect Meryl. It could cause more stress. I don't think we should risk throwing a wrench into Meryl's psyche right now. She's too fragile. After the surgery, you and Dad can visit her and comfort her. It will be wonderful. But not before.

After the conversation, Blake had wondered if his mother's pride would be wounded, causing them to stay in Virginia. His mother was an enigma to him. He loved her, but he could not predict her reactions or gauge her temper.

Yet Joan Taylor had called back the next day to give her son their flight schedule. They would arrive the evening before Meryl's operation and stay until Blake's daughter was born. Maybe they could help Karin with the twins in the interim. They agreed to keep their presence a secret until after Meryl's surgery. They wanted to do whatever was best for her.

However, regardless of his parents' consent, the deception of their arrival rubbed like a pebble in Blake's shoe. He hadn't even told Rick about his parents' impending arrival. He thought of how later tonight, he would go over to the Fletcher home and join Rick in giving Meryl a priesthood blessing. Would he feel as if he had betrayed her? Tomorrow he would make up for it. While he was at work, he would keep tabs on his sister—talk to the anesthesiologist and make sure that her nurses didn't make any mistakes. He wasn't taking any chances. He had worked at a hospital too many years, had seen too much.

Blake's digital phone rang. He picked it up and heard Karin's voice greeting him. "Hi, honey," he said. One of the twins shrieked in the background.

"Are you ready for your in-laws?" Blake asked.

"As ready as I'll ever be," Karin replied. "I paid Aimy and Waverly to help. Aimy cleaned with me while Wave played with the twins. The house looks pretty good. Chicken is in the oven."

"Great."

Karin was quiet for a few seconds. Then she spoke of the worry that clouded her mind, even overshadowing her anxiety about Meryl's surgery and her nervousness at her in-laws' arrival. "I still can't get ahold of Chris. I promised to talk to him every two days, and it's been two weeks. Jerry made up another lame excuse about Chris playing outside with a friend. She said she'll have him call back. But he never does. Blake, what's happening?"

"Maybe he's just busy having fun."

"But it doesn't make sense. I know he would want to talk to us, if for no other reason than to find out how Domino is doing."

"If we don't get through by next week, I'll go down there and check it out."

"And leave me with your parents?" Karin laughed a bit nervously.

"Do you think you'd survive?" Blake heard something drop and crash. A child's voice leapt into laughter.

"Would *your parents* survive?" Karin returned. Another crash. A shriek. Karin continued. "I'd better to go and find out what the partners in crime are destroying."

"Good luck," Blake said. "Let's hope my parents don't bring anything breakable."

"Or valuable," Karin added.

"Or take-a-part-able," Blake said.

"Or open-able."

"Or swallow-able," Blake added. Karin laughed out loud. Squeals and screams reigned in the background. "Adios, amigo," Karin said.

"Bye, honey." Blake hung up the telephone. As he exited the freeway, he took a deep breath and offered a silent prayer for his wife, his sister, and his mother—the three women who held his heart.

At ten that night, while Rick showered, Meryl readied herself for bed. She savored a long drink of water, the feel of the cool liquid sliding down her throat. She wouldn't be able to eat or drink anything else until after her surgery. Her hand shook ever so slightly as she put the glass down. Thoughts of the coming day crowded into her mind. She sat down on the edge of her bed and took a deep breath. In an effort to calm down, she thought of the blessing Rick and Blake had given her earlier in the evening.

Blessed with peace and health, Meryl also recalled the comfort of promises made in the blessing. *These trials will soon be over, and you will have many, many years to live and rejoice with your loved ones.* Her soul had calmed when Rick assured her of her family's concern and desire to strengthen and assist her. He had also blessed the surgeon and anesthesiologist with knowledge and skill, then had counseled her, *Exercise faith. Be not troubled nor afraid. You are a beloved daughter of God.*

"Are you in bed?" Rick's voice came from the bathroom.

"In a few minutes. I'm going downstairs to say a prayer in the den," Meryl answered. As she stepped softly down the steps, Meryl felt the carpet nap on her bare toes. *At least tomorrow the surgery will be over*, she thought. *No more waiting. No more psychological acrobatics to escape thoughts of the inevitable.*

Inwardly, she went over the next day's agenda. Unless there were complications, she would stay only one night in the hospital. Then she would come home to her beige carpet, her green-and-yellow-flowered bedspread, her chocolate-colored couch in the den, the pictures of her children on the walls, her computer, her manuscript, perhaps an e-mail from Dennie, and her husband. *Her husband.* How would Rick deal with all of this? How would it change their relationship? Would she loathe her own body? Would he?

She battled tears struggling to surface. Once in the den, Meryl knelt down. She began to pray—she planned to thank Heavenly Father for her blessings and to seek comfort and strength. But peace would not come, and anxiety encompassed her. She practiced relaxation techniques she had learned in a book about breast cancer. She tried to clear her mind so that it would fill with the Holy Spirit.

But instead, a haunting image rose into her thoughts, outside of her conscious control. It was an image of herself with her head wrapped in filthy rags that covered diseased, cankered flesh—it was the nightmare that she had pushed away weeks ago. In the dream, Rick could not hide his fear of the image; her mother had shunned it. But here it was again in the last instance, beckoning Meryl to face the reality of sorrow.

"Heavenly Father, help me," she pled.

I shall not leave thee comfortless. The words were like fire in her mind. Meryl closed her eyes and breathed deeply. The cankered figure stood in the shadow of her consciousness. And then—then—Meryl knew what to do. She imagined herself healthy and whole, next to her own diseased image. "What can I do to help you?" she whispered.

Take off my bandages, her own injured spirit spoke to Meryl's heart.

With her soul reaching to bridge the space between fear and faith, between man and God, Meryl imagined herself gently undoing the filthy wraps. What was found there amazed her, for under those rags she discovered no cancer, no leprosy, no hideous features, only light and indescribable beauty—and the radiance of a woman's face containing enough compassion, joy, and faith to cross the chasm separating earth and heaven, life and death. This was the image of one made clean through faith in the Lord Jesus Christ. She knew beyond doubt and fear that this was the heritage of the children of God. Meryl's hands opened and her heartbeat slowed. The image slipped away. She opened her eyes, her soul satiated with peace.

Upstairs, Rick waited for his wife. An hour passed. The house was quiet. He wondered if was possible that she had fallen asleep. Should he go to her? Did she need his comfort, or would he be interrupting her prayer? Rick stood up and ventured down the stairs. When he looked into the den, he saw his wife in a corner, kneeling.

"Meryl, are you OK?" Rick asked as he entered the room.

"Yes," Meryl said truthfully.

"Do you want to come upstairs with me?" Rick questioned. Meryl nodded. He went to her, reached out his hand. She took it as she stood.

With her husband's arm around her shoulders and her arm around his waist, they walked up the stairs together. That night, Meryl slept with her head on Rick's chest and the sound of his heartbeat in her ear.

CHAPTER 17

YOU ARE MY SUNSHINE

Cory Parker watched his son, Chris, out of the corner of his eye while reading the newspaper. The boy was engrossed in a book titled *Mrs. Frisby and the Rats of Nimh*. There was a picture of a mouse in a dress on the front.

Cory felt confident that the decision he had made a few weeks ago was right. It was definitely time to gain full custody of Christopher. *Fortunately*, Cory reasoned, *Jerry adores Chris, and the boy clearly needs his father.* Chris's enjoyment of board games, books, and animals irritated Cory. He didn't necessarily feel that these activities were wrong in themselves, but in Christopher they accentuated the softness Cory had noticed around the boy's mouth and in his eyes. He was too much like his mother—weak. From Cory's perspective, Karin's weakness had caused her depression, Nicole's death, and the divorce.

Cory instinctively knew that there was another side of his boy, a side just waiting to come out. When they played soccer or football together, Chris's features changed, his jaw tightened, and he was quick on his feet. There was mettle in his son, and Cory, a former marine and current police officer, knew how to bring out the iron in a man.

Whatever it took, he would find a way for Chris to remain with him. His boy would learn to be strong. It would be hard for Karin to accept, and a part of Cory felt badly about that. *But*, he rationalized, *she left me, not the other way around. Fortunately, she has a husband and kids to help her cope.*

A week previous, Cory had visited with an attorney named Keith Halverson, a family law specialist whom a fellow officer had referred him to. Halverson had explained that if Chris were happy living with

Cory and chose to stay, they had it made in court. They would simply have to prove that he and Jerry had as much to offer the child as his family in Grantlin. It should be a slam dunk.

So Cory and Jerry kept Chris busy having a great time. They went to baseball games, Disneyland, Universal Studios, and San Diego. They also got caller ID. When Karin's number lit up the telephone, they carried it into the bedroom before answering it. They created excuses, saying Chris was busy, and always neglected to tell Christopher that his mother had called.

When Chris asked to call home, they put his request off. It was deceptive, and Cory valued honesty; he viewed himself as a forthright man. But he didn't see a better way, and he was convinced that these deceptions would make it easier for Christopher in the long run. *Besides*, Cory reasoned, *in a crisis, Abraham pretended Sarah was his sister, and Abraham certainly didn't tell Isaac whom he planned to sacrifice as they walked up the mountain. In the Book of Mormon, Nephi deceived Zoram by pretending to be Laban. Dishonesty isn't usually right, but it is sometimes necessary. Difficult circumstances call for uncomfortable action, as long as my motives are correct. Christopher belongs here with me, not in Grantlin. The sooner the boy feels that way, the better.*

The next morning, a Tuesday that Cory had off, he decided it was time to talk to Chris about this decision. Cory waited until he and Chris were in the car on the way to sign Christopher up for a two-week football camp hosted by the local high school. As he drove, Cory explained how he and Jerry had decided that Chris should stay with them. Chris would be happier here. It would be better for everyone. Cory pointed out that Chris's family in Grantlin really didn't have time for him. "Sure, Karin and Blake care about you," Cory stated kindly. "But, son, they have a family of their own. Even though they love you, you must realize that you are a burden. Jerry and I need you and you need us. You are the center of our lives. Our lawyer is certain that the judge will agree. We belong together. We are a family."

Christopher was quiet and teary eyed as he listened to his father. "Come on, bud," Cory supplicated. He put his hand on his son's shoulder. "You'll get used to it. It's hard switching schools, but you'll have Jer and me supporting you. Football camp starts next week. You'll meet some guys there and have friends before school starts."

"I want to talk to my mom," Chris said.

"That's understandable. We'll call her on Saturday when the rates are lower. Together we'll explain everything to her," Cory stated matter-of-factly. "She might seem upset, but it will be the best for everyone in the long run."

"Maybe I don't want to play football," Chris said.

"Can't hurt to sign up. That way you'll have the option. Afterward we'll get some ice cream."

Christopher began to cry. Cory pulled the car over and hugged him. He could be patient now, but once he had custody, he would teach his son to be a man. He would teach the boy the importance of strength, attitude, and respect.

Meryl's surgery went better than she expected, with no nausea, confusion, or sluggishness following the anesthesia. Her nurses were kind and sensitive, and the pain was manageable. Blake trailed in and out of her room every couple of hours, dressed in his hospital duds, checking her chart and medication. Rick was by her side constantly, giving her sips of pop to drink, helping her to the bathroom, and holding her hand.

At 6:30 in the evening, Meryl lay alone in the hospital room while Rick went to get some dinner. Gazing down at the left side of her chest where the hospital sheet bulged with ice packs and gauze instead of flesh and blood, a sense of loss and aloneness flooded her. She closed her eyes, shutting out the world and wondering how these feelings could still plague her after the spiritual gift she had experienced last night. Maybe it was the medication and the pain. She considered how strange and inconsistent the rivers of human emotion ran.

Thoughts of her introversion during the past weeks came into Meryl's mind. She had shielded herself from everyone, even those she loved. She knew that a mastectomy was not something to be ashamed of, yet she was ashamed. Questions haunted her. Was it a shame borne of pride and fear? She longed for another woman to share her thoughts with.

She missed her beautiful daughter, Dennie. She ached for the mother who had turned away the day of her conversion. Yet she realized that her mother had been distant long before that moment. Was

Meryl's membership in the Church simply a cloak covering the fact that there was something inside Meryl that was unlovable? Yet her father truly loved her. So did Blake and Rick. Dennie loved her, but Dennie was so far away.

Meryl's thoughts turned to Karin. During the past weeks, she had pushed aside Karin's warmth. Was it because Karin's fruitfulness, femininity, and wholeness caused Meryl anguish? Tears crept down her cheeks.

"Meryl, are you OK?" Candace, a young nurse with short, dark hair, put her hand over Meryl's. Meryl nodded. Candace added, "You have a visitor."

"Who?" Meryl asked.

"Moni Tomlinson."

"Good."

The nurse handed Meryl a tissue, and Meryl wiped her eyes. She thought of how a few days ago, Moni had come home from Texas, beaming with an engagement ring. Meryl in turn had told Moni about her breast cancer. She had confided in Moni when she couldn't talk to her daughter, her sister-in-law, her visiting teachers, or her own mother.

Yet she had cried in Moni's arms—Moni, a nonmember, a hairdresser, and a rehabilitated drug addict. Was it because Moni understood the need to be beautiful, to be loved? Moni had walked the path of weakness, fear, and pride. Moni had endured suffering, loss, and violent abuse. Moni knew the score of pain. Meryl found strength in the grip of Moni's hand in hers.

Moni smiled down at Meryl. She brushed her streaked-blonde hair out of her eyes. "How you doing?"

"Pretty good." Meryl smiled up at her friend.

"When do you leave this place?'

"Tomorrow. I can't wait."

"I set up an appointment for you in my shop ten days from today. I am going to give you a weave and a perm. You're pretty now. But when I'm finished, you will be gorgeous."

"Promise?" Meryl asked softly.

"Yeah, I promise." Moni blinked back tears. She bent down and kissed Meryl's cheek.

"You tired?" Moni asked.

"A little bit." Meryl nodded. "Has Aimy heard from Dennie?"

"Not this week. How 'bout you?"

"Nope. Sometimes Dennie doesn't make it into town where there's a computer."

"You'll hear from her next week."

"I know. She's coming home in a few weeks. I can't wait."

"I'll bet. Aimy can't wait either."

"Is Aimy still happy about her engagement?"

Moni nodded. "I hope and pray. Then sometimes everything falls into place. But sometimes it doesn't. I keep my fingers crossed. I check Aimy's horoscope and mine every day. I know it doesn't mean anything really, but it makes me feel better. I can hardly believe my baby's getting married. I wish I could be in the temple with her. But I'm listening to the Book of Mormon tapes. I'll be waiting outside."

"That will mean a lot to her. I wish my mom had been waiting outside."

"The elders came over last night and gave me a copy of my family tree. They said something about Isaiah and turning the hearts of the fathers to the children."

Meryl smiled. "And?"

Moni chuckled and went on. "I noticed that the scripture says that the hearts of the *fathers* need turning, not the hearts of the *mothers*. My take on it is that God realizes that our hearts are already turned to our kids every minute of every day. Let's just hope that the earth isn't wasted because the dads and kids can't get their own hearts turned around right."

Meryl laughed. Pain sliced through her chest. Moni noticed the color drain from her friend's face.

"Hey, sweetie, I'm going to go. I'll bring you over some chicken soup tomorrow after you get home."

"Thanks," Meryl said as Moni squeezed her hand.

After Moni left, the nurse came in and gave Meryl a pain pill. The drug made Meryl drowsy. Rick returned. She felt Rick's dry lips on her cheek and she heard him tell her good night before she sank into sleep.

Joan Taylor awakened at six in the morning. For a sleep-filled instant, she didn't know where she was. Then memory returned. She was in Blake's home, lying in her grandson Brandon's twin bed. Ben slept in the other bed across the room. The little boys slumbered in Christopher's room. The house was still.

Joan lifted a pile of clothes off a chair and found her purse. After tiptoeing softly down the hall and into the bathroom, she dressed and fixed her hair. She didn't want to wake up Ben. He needed his sleep. She was certain that Blake would bring Ben to the hospital in a couple of hours when he went to work. After Joan put on her lipstick, she opened the bathroom door and was on her way. But there stood Ben in the hallway, already dressed and waiting.

"Let's go, Little General," he said quietly. "Let's go see our girl."

As Joan drove the rental car to the hospital, her mind was on Meryl—her baby girl—long fingers, soft skin, no hair—so sweet and affectionate. Joan had been stunned by her preciousness. But the love she had felt for her baby had frightened her. Then Blake had come, adding to the danger.

When one loved too much, when one's heart wrapped too tightly around another, any other, one was in peril. They could leave at any moment. Joan's mother had. So had her grandparents. Although she treasured her family, she hadn't been able to give herself fully to loving them, not any of them—Ben, Meryl, or Blake. Only God could be loved fully. Only God would always be there.

Yet Joan had tried to be a good mother, to fill their needs, to teach them right from wrong. She had given them a stable home. She had fiercely protected them. And her children had been so bright and good, like their father. They had been fine.

Then had come Meryl's first day of kindergarten. A little boy had wet his pants, and Meryl had cried for him. Joan had known at that moment that her daughter was overly sensitive, too empathetic for her own good. You couldn't hurt for every other person, or you'd always be bleeding. She had to find a way to make Meryl stronger, less fragile. So with Meryl, she had withheld even more of herself, telling herself it was for Meryl's good, that it would help her to stand on her own two feet, to be independent. Joan had figured that Meryl knew she was loved—how could she not know when her clothes were always pressed, her face wiped clean, her hair combed, and her lessons paid for?

Yet as Joan drove over the flat California landscape, as the sun rose and spread pink and orange light into the wide sky, she wondered. Had she been wrong all along in the way she had raised Meryl? Was that why Meryl had made mistakes? Was that why she had been wooed by the Mormon Church? Was it too late to talk to Meryl about it?

At the hospital, Meryl awakened. She was sore, so sore. A nurse entered the room. Meryl swallowed a pain pill.

Twenty minutes later, a cheery orderly came with a breakfast tray. Rick called. He would be there in an hour to be with her until it was time to go home. The hospital psychologist, Anne Kilpatrick, stepped into the room. She was short and stocky, with crisp, gray hair. Something about her keen, determined eyes reminded Meryl of Charity Jones.

Anne asked Meryl how she was doing. They chatted for a while. Then Anne explained that there was one more thing she wanted Meryl to do before she was discharged. Meryl was to look in the mirror at the incision, at her body. Anne pointed out that this was routine procedure for breast cancer patients at the hospital.

Meryl looked back at Anne. "Everything is so raw."

"Just try." Anne patted Meryl's arm matter-of-factly. "The incision will be red now, the flesh around it perhaps bruised or discolored. That will disappear as you heal. For the time being, I just want to make sure you'll be able to change the dressing and take care of yourself. Acceptance will come."

"OK," Meryl said. She was compliant, always compliant. It was as if she were programmed that way.

Anne went into the bathroom and wheeled out a portable mirror. She set it up by Meryl's bed, then put her hand on Meryl's shoulder. "You're fine. I'll go out of the room, and you just sit up and take a look. Call me if you need me."

Meryl sat up slowly. It hurt to move. Carefully, she untied the hospital gown, yet kept it closed around her. There was a knock at the door. Anne's voice. "I just found out that your mother has been waiting down the hall. She has offered to be with you right now. Would you like her to come in? I think the support would be helpful, but it's up to you."

Meryl's heart beat quickly. Her mother? Then she realized that Anne must be referring to Elsa, Rick's mother. Meryl recalled that

Elsa had promised to drive up from the Bay Area sometime today in order to be available for Meryl when Rick went back to work tomorrow. With gratitude, Meryl realized that Elsa must have arisen at five in the morning to arrive so early.

But did she want Elsa with her at this moment? Did she want Elsa to witness the intimacy of this loss? Meryl thought of the blessing Rick and Blake had given her. She had been told that her family would stand by her, that they would be with her to strengthen her. Perhaps Heavenly Father had inspired Elsa to come now, to strengthen her at this moment. She would let Elsa come in and allow her to be near. Meryl would look at the incision quickly. Then they would talk and comfort each other.

"Come in," Meryl said. The door opened and closed. Meryl faced the mirror rather than the woman who entered the room. "Let me get this over with, then we can chat," Meryl commented as cheerfully as pain would allow. She opened the hospital gown. She looked into the mirror at the incision. It was not a horrible gash. It was a neat, clean, thin line— red, but not fiery. Her chest moved with each breath. And because the cancerous lesion had been deep within her breast, necessitating the excising of muscles covering the rib cage, Meryl visibly saw, beneath skin and ribs, the pulsating of her heart, vulnerable and miraculous.

Timidly, Meryl put her hand to her chest. She remembered how Dennie as a child had called her to come and hold Elsa's doves. *You can feel their heartbeats!* Dennie had gasped. *Mama, Mama! You can feel their heartbeat! Come and hold them!* And Meryl had. They were Elsa's doves. How appropriate that Elsa was here now.

Meryl's mind turned to her mother-in-law—Elsa Hudsfeldt Fletcher, that incorrigible German woman had always treated Meryl like her own daughter. Elsa with her accent, her flowing dresses, her shiny gray hair—Elsa, who had been at the temple when they married, who had rejoiced when their children had been sealed to them, who had wept at Thes's funeral. Elsa had lived in Germany as a little girl during the war. She had lost her husband to a stroke thirty years ago. She had told Meryl many stories of heartbreak and courage.

"Elsa," Meryl said turning. "Look. I can see my heartbeat."

But the woman standing behind her wasn't her mother-in-law. Petite frame. Reddish-gray hair. Recognition interrupted Meryl's thoughts. Painfully she closed her gown. It was literally her mother. Her own mother, Joan Taylor.

Meryl spoke slowly. "I thought you were Elsa."

"I know that," Joan said.

"No one told me you were coming." Meryl slowly sat down on the bed. She could have wept, but she would not. Not in front of her mother.

"Elsa wrote and told us about the cancer."

"When did you get here?"

"Two days ago. Blake suggested I wait until after your surgery to visit. I think he would have preferred to delay the surprise until after you came home from the hospital. But I wanted to see you."

Meryl lay down. Each breath was painful. She stared up at the ceiling. When she spoke, she couldn't keep the bitterness out of her voice. "Why did you want to see me, Mother? And what do you see? A deformed body? A slash across my chest? My punishment by the hand of God. But it isn't like that, Mother. God hasn't punished me. He has stood by my side through all of this. He has comforted me. He has been my strength."

Joan Taylor could not find the words to answer.

After a stretch of silence, Meryl spoke. "Did Dad stay alone in Virginia?"

"He's here," Joan said. "Out in the lobby."

"Daddy's here? He's really here?"

Joan nodded. "I'll get him." She stood up and walked away from her daughter without having touched her.

A moment later, at the threshold of the room, Meryl heard her father's voice singing, singing the same song she used to sing to her own children. "You are my sunshine, my only sunshine. You make me happy when clouds are gray."

"Daddy." Meryl wept. Ben Taylor entered the room and hobbled over to his sweet girl.

As he stroked her hand, he finished the song. What neither of them knew was that outside the door, bent over in sorrow, Joan whispered the words along with him. "I dreamt I held you in my arms. When I awakened I was mistaken. And I hung my head and I cried."

CHAPTER 18

THE TURNING OF HEARTS

A continent away, Esteban and the machi arrived at the ruka as the sun set. Mercurio reined in Namcupan. With a lean sweep of his legs, he dismounted and handed the reins to Esteban. The machi set up her rewe outside the door of the hut. She turned to her son. "It is the sign. With Chau's help, she shall live."

After entering the ruka, the machi greeted Maria with the same words. "It is the sign. With Chau's help, the child shall live."

The machi did not look into the corner of the ruka where Dennie sat with the partition pulled back, watching. Yet the old woman knew Dennie was there. After taking care of Namcupan, Esteban ducked into the hut and sat down near Dennie. Neither of them dared speak.

The machi went to Eva. She stooped down and kissed the child's cheek. Above Eva's head, in line with the body, the machi planted a canelo twig in the earthen floor. She planted laurel and cinnamon at Eva's feet. Mercurio, acting as her liaison, warmed the kultrun near the fire, making the leather taut. He handed the drum to his mother.

She chanted as she beat on the kultrun. Her eyes closed, the incantation monotonous, interrupted only by an occasional high-pitched wail at the end of a stanza. Mercurio threw straw on the fire and the machi passed her hand through the flames and waved them over Eva. She splashed a liquid from a wooden bowl on the child's head and chest. The machi wore a black stone on a leather thong about her neck. She lifted the stone over her head and massaged Eva's body with it.

Once more, she beat on her kultrun as dark shadows filled the hut, the only light being the fire illuminating the machi's profile. She prayed to Nenechen, the supreme being, to Chau, the god who fathered the Mapuche, to the spirits of the north, south, east, and west. The beating of the drum ceased, the flames hissed.

The machi's features altered as if she had changed. She looked younger, stern, and warlike. Her voice was high, almost a shriek, as she spoke rapidly in Mapudungun. Mercurio's eyes bore into her as if he consumed each word. Then, the machi jumped up, moving deftly as if she were young, jumping from one side of Eva to the other, shaking her rattle. With a shout she ran from the ruka. Mercurio followed her. Beside her rewe, the old machi collapsed in her son's arms.

Mercurio carried his mother away from the star-blazed night into the shadowy ruka. When the machi came to, she asked her son to repeat the words she had uttered while in the trance. She leaned against her son, shaking and exhausted.

Mercurio's voice repeated her words slowly and stoically—in Spanish, as if he wanted everyone to understand. "You said that evil spirits seek Eva's life. Their power is great. But the power of the pillan is great too. If the magic of the machi is strong enough, the fever will break by tomorrow noon. If not, Eva will die." Mercurio let go of his mother and went back outside, in desperate need of fresh air and open sky.

That night, the old woman stayed in her son's ruka. She sat near the hearth, wrapped in the sacred blue and white poncho of her calling, listening to the rasp of her granddaughter's breath. For many hours Dennie could not sleep. She felt a need to breathe for Eva, to protect her. Suddenly, the machi's head turned. She looked at Dennie. Dennie saw the hearth's firelight reflected in the depths of her grandmother's ebony eyes. Her grandmother's eyes bore into her own. In the darkness, they stared at each other, the two who shared the same genes but not the same dreams. Neither would look down nor away. Then finally, the machi's look softened and Dennie understood her thought as clearly as if it had been spoken. Dennie could sleep. The machi would watch over Eva tonight.

When Dennie awakened the next morning, Esteban and Mercurio were gone. "They left before daybreak," Maria answered Dennie's questioning eyes as she bathed Eva with cool water. The machi rocked back and forth, muttering. Maria spoke once more. "They took the oxen in order to pull the truck from the mud."

Hours passed as the sun moved across the sky. Eva's fever did not break. The child's eyes were bloodshot, and she hardly had enough breath to cough. Maria ministered unceasingly to her. The machi went outside the hut, climbed upon her rewe, and prayed.

As the sun rose to the center of the sky, the old woman climbed down from the rewe. She entered the hut and took one look at her feverish granddaughter beneath the sheepskin. She did not pray or beat on her kultrun, for she knew that the evil spirits had won the battle. Her efforts were in vain, and Eva would die. An anguished cry rose from her lips.

Then the machi took Eva into her arms and rocked her as she sang a Mapuche lullaby, the same one she sang to Pinsha when she was a baby. "Sleep, sleep, little one. As the fox comes to take the chickens, so he can also come to take you. The lion comes. The tiger too. I will weep. I will weep. Sleep, sleep, little one, sleep." Tears ran down the machi's leathery face, filling the countless wrinkles.

While the machi rocked Eva, Maria folded her arms and stared toward the entrance of the ruka, which glowed in the sunlight. The three women heard the truck's engine. Gently, the machi lowered Eva and stood. Maria went and took her child's hand.

Dennie approached her grandmother from behind. She touched her shoulder. The machi flinched and turned to look at her, but Dennie did not see a proud machi, but an old Indian woman with swollen eyes. A mother. A warrior. A healer. A grandmother. One defeated.

Dennie spoke in Spanish, with her back straight and her eyes grim and determined. "I beg permission to take Eva to the hospital. Pinsha is dead. Lautaro is dead. Let me try to save Eva. Perhaps that is why God sent me here."

The old woman looked at the girl. The old woman was the machi. She spoke to the spirits of the four winds. She knew their voices. They blew within her. She felt the heartbeat of the world when she pounded the kultrun. But Pinsha's heart had beat inside of her own body. This child's heart had beat within Pinsha. The gods had summoned this girl to her. Was it a test? In which direction did betrayal lie?

Mercurio entered the hut. Mercurio with his quick hands and lean frame. Mercurio who was growing old. Maria's numbness broke, and she wept in her husband's arms. Dennie continued to stand tall and straight before the machi. "Please, Grandmother."

The machi looked down. She remembered Pinsha standing outside her hut long ago, her belly swollen with this girl in it, biting her lip until it bled, with tears on her cheeks and a son in her arms. "Please, Mother." Her lambs. Pinsha's lambs. But the machi had turned away from the hummingbird and the perfect lambs. Death followed them as vultures trail the suffering.

But death did not find one of them. Mina had survived and was a woman now, requesting permission to save a life with fearless, unrelenting compassion and patience. The machi looked up and met the eyes of Mina, the child named after the far-off mines. Pinsha's gem. Pinsha's source and fortune. Within the eyes of Mina, the old woman saw the look and strength of a machi. The machi would have Eva live. Was it possible that Mina was her only hope in saving the child?

But Mina was winka, Christian, Mormon. All of these forces threatened to destroy the sacred religion of the Mapuche that the machi had covenanted to uphold. Mina's father, Jacques, was the machi's enemy. He had stolen her daughter away. Had the gods sent Mina to save Eva? Or was Eva dying because Mina had come? Winds of confusion blew within the machi's soul, threatening to tear her apart.

"Grandmother, I beg your permission to try to save Eva's life." Mina's voice again. The machi looked from Mina to Eva, who lay half-conscious on the white sheep's pelt. One granddaughter pleading for the other. The old woman shook violently. She crouched down, choking on sorrow, confusion, and fear.

But the tree that upheld the machi's soul did not break; it bowed to the winds of change, for it bore but one seed. And this seed was the machi's love for Eva. With a cry, the old woman took off the black stone that hung on a thong around her neck and put it on the ground in front of Dennie. "Go. Take Eva. Go." Then she stood. With her back bent like something broken and leaving her kultrun and rewe behind, the old woman left the hut and walked slowly and haltingly away.

After the machi left, Mercurio's strong, quick hands shook with fatigue and fear. He spoke to Esteban. "Go quickly. I will follow in the oxcart in case you can't get through. First I must give the animals food and water."

Dennie turned to Maria, who was already dressing Eva in a warm dress and stockings. With what strength Eva had, she clung to her mother. The bed of the truck was packed high with supplies and cans of gas. There was only room for the driver and two passengers on the cab's bench seat.

"Maria, ride with Eva in the truck," Dennie said. "I'll come with Mercurio."

"No, Mina," Maria shook her head. "There are two hospitals. Don't take Eva to the clinic."

"I don't understand," Dennie said.

"I'll explain on the way." Esteban moved quickly, checking for blankets and water. He went into the ruka and brought out Dennie's bags. He loaded them into the truck. He turned to Dennie. "Let's go. Eva's weak. The hospital is five hours away."

Dennie sat in the middle of the truck's bench seat. Gently, Mercurio lifted Eva next to her. He picked up the black stone and put it around Eva's neck. Maria covered her daughter with a hand-woven blanket.

"Papai," Eva whimpered. *Mama.*

"Tami piuke am," Maria uttered. *Heart soul's reflection.* The girl's body convulsed with coughing. Afterward, she weakly laid her head on the pillow in Dennie's lap. Mercurio shut the door, and Esteban put the truck into gear. Maria and Mercurio stared after them.

Esteban drove as quickly as he could, plunging the truck through water, praying that the tires wouldn't get stuck, hoping that no time would be lost. Dennie sensed that each bump in the road was painful to the feverish girl in her arms. A coarse wheeze, almost a whine, accompanied Eva's every breath.

"Why wouldn't Maria come?" Dennie asked.

"There is a public clinic and a private hospital. Two different places." Esteban shook his head, his eyes dark and focused on the road ahead. "The public clinic gives substandard care. Many of the sick who enter never come out again. The Mapuche fear it. The hospital is modern, and the doctors there save many lives. But they usually won't touch an Indio. They would never get paid. But with you here, a citizen of Los Estados Unidos, it is possible."

"They *will* treat Eva," Dennie stated, her eyes set with determination.

"Yes, gringa, you convinced a machi to send her beloved grand-child with a winka. I believe you can convince a Chilean doctor to treat Eva," Esteban said quietly.

The hours passed slowly. The truck lurched and shook over the bumpy road. Dennie stroked Eva's hair. She wanted to weep for Eva's pain, for her moans and voiceless sobs. But she did not. She sang to Eva instead. "I am a Child of God," "As I Have Loved You," "Tell Me the Stories of Jesus," "I Wonder When He Comes Again," and "You Are My Sunshine."

Esteban stopped once to give Eva a blessing. He didn't have any olive oil, nor was there another priesthood holder to aid him. With his hands laid upon Eva's head, and in the name of Jesus Christ, he blessed her to live and breathe until they obtained medical help.

Evening approached. Ribbons of brilliant light, golden, red, blue, and pink, streamed through the heavens. They passed a lake so still that it reflected every color of the sky. Two waterfowl, like black dots, flew next to each other in a straight line, a foot above the surface of the water. The water lay so motionless and clear that it looked as if there were no earth, only four birds skimming in perfect symmetry through two inverted skies.

Watching it, Esteban spoke, "The Mapuche believe that the first human soul was thrown out of the sky, out of the rivers of color."

Dennie did not answer. Her hand was on Eva's pulse that beat so quickly—too quickly.

"Hurry, Esteban, hurry," Dennie begged. Thirty minutes later, they were on paved road. Esteban drove the truck as though it were an ambulance.

Finally they arrived at the hospital, a tall, stone building. Esteban carried Eva in. Dennie walked quickly up to the front desk, oblivious to the pain in her stomach, the stabbing ache in her back and legs, and the dryness of her mouth.

"I'm Denizen Mina Fletcher," she said in English, standing straight and tall as she pulled out her passport and carnet and laid them on the counter. "This is my cousin," Dennie pointed to Eva. "She is very ill and needs a doctor."

The woman's shrewd eyes passed from Dennie, a foreign do-gooder in well-fitting jeans and a warm jacket, to the sick child wrapped in Mapuche garb. "Your cousin?" She said skeptically. "You are both dirty enough. Does your cousin have insurance?"

Dennie took out her packet of traveler's checks. She still had over a thousand dollars. "No. I will pay for it," Dennie said. "If this isn't enough, my parents in the United States will send more."

"One moment," the receptionist said. She took Dennie's money and passport with her into a back room. A hefty man with a trim mustache came back with the receptionist. He looked at Eva and Esteban. He spoke to Dennie. "You will stay until her treatment is complete? You will pay for this? You will sign the papers?"

"Yes," Dennie said. He nodded to the receptionist.

Moments later, Eva was whisked onto a gurney. A mask covered her face, and a machine breathed for her. An IV was inserted into the vein of her arm. Dennie stayed close, holding Eva's hand, and wiping tears of terror from the child's eyes.

Hours later, while Eva slept, a kind doctor assured Dennie that they were doing all they could for Eva. They had her on oxygen and were treating the pneumonia and infection with intravenous antibiotics. He recommended that Dennie eat and rest.

In the reception area, Dennie found Esteban waiting for her with *sopaipillas pasadas*, servings of pumpkin bread covered with warm caramel sauce. She ate a few bites, but couldn't enjoy the warm sweetness. She felt dizzy from exhaustion.

"Are Mercurio and Maria here yet?" Dennie's speech slurred.

"I'm going to go and look for them," Esteban stated. "And find rooms to sleep in."

Dennie nodded and spoke. "Will the hospital let me stay here in Eva's room? Eva's scared."

"I'll check," Esteban said. "Sit down and rest." Dennie curled up in a large armchair. Twenty minutes passed. Dennie dozed. Esteban, led by a nurse, strode wearily back into the waiting room, carrying a bag of Dennie's clothes. The nurse tapped Dennie's shoulder. Groggy and disoriented, Dennie sat up. They followed the nurse into Eva's room. Eva lay still in the bed with the oxygen mask over her face. The nurse handed Dennie a towel and soap. "Please wash in there," she instructed, pointing to the bathroom.

"Thank you," Dennie returned. After she showered and changed into clean sweats and a sweatshirt, Dennie found that a cot had been wheeled into the corner of Eva's room. Esteban was already gone.

Dennie kissed Eva's forehead. Then she curled up on the cot and immediately fell asleep.

When Dennie awakened, it was early morning. She was covered by something heavy and warm. She looked down at the garment blanketing her. It was woolen and handmade, the weave tight and the yarn coarse, with a blue background as deep and dark as the eastern sky at the edge of night. Geometric stars and moons swirled white patterns in the weave. It was a Mapuche poncho.

Dennie looked around the room and saw Maria sitting in a chair beside Eva. Maria smiled at Dennie shyly. The oxygen mask was still over Eva's face, but the girl seemed to be sleeping more comfortably. The Indian woman, with her braided hair and old dress and boots, looked out of place in the modern hospital.

"How is Eva?" Dennie asked quietly as she pulled the poncho tightly around her shoulders and sat up.

"Her breath comes easier," Maria answered. "The doctor said the medicine is helping. Thank you."

Dennie smiled. "This poncho is beautiful," she said. "And warm. Did you make it?"

Maria shook her head. "No. Your grandmother sent it with us to give to you. This poncho belonged to your mother, to Pinsha. It is the poncho of a machi. It is yours now."

"Why did she give it to me? Did she give it to me because the holy women are dying? Because there won't be anyone like Pinsha to wear this after the machi is gone?" Dennie asked, tears springing to her eyes at the thought of a way of life crumbling, leaving an old woman powerless and alone.

"She gave it to you because you are no longer winka. You saved Eva's life. You are *Mapuche*, a child of the earth, the land. One of us," Maria answered.

Dennie nodded and buried her head in the nap of the poncho. She breathed in the woolen scent—old, dusty, and sweet. She left a trace of her tears.

That day, Eva continued to improve. Esteban drove thirty minutes to Diego's home to send e-mail messages to their parents. When he came back to the hospital, he told Dennie that a message had awaited him. Carmen had suffered a miscarriage and lost her and Miguel's child.

"I'm so sorry," Dennie said.

Esteban went on grimly. "It is said that bad things happen in threes. I wonder what the next will be? I have a motel room down the street. I must go and call my cousin."

Dennie looked up at him. "Can I come with you? I want to call home and tell my parents about Eva and the cost of the hospital stay." Esteban nodded, yet the distance between them was tangible.

As they walked through the drizzle toward the entrance of the motel, a group of young men whistled, and an elderly couple raised their eyebrows and smiled knowingly at them. These people saw a handsome, stately young man and a beautiful girl wrapped warmly in a brilliant Mapuche poncho, one the young man probably paid much money for.

"Why are we attracting so much attention?" Dennie asked.

"They think we are newlyweds or lovers." Esteban laughed wryly but without mirth. "In Chile motels are different. Hotels or establishments specifically marked *motel de turismo* are like the places you find in Los Estados Unidos. But motels are strictly for honeymooners or people having an affair. Last night, I was too tired to care. After Mercurio and his family were settled, camped in a field on the edge of town, I found the room closest to the hospital, even though it was a motel and I had no sweetheart with me."

Dennie felt her cheeks redden as they entered Esteban's room. She looked around at the hot tub and cozy fireplace. If things had worked out differently, if she had married Esteban, perhaps they would have honeymooned in a place like this. But deep within her, she now knew that would never occur. Esteban gazed at her briefly. Was he gauging her reaction? Was there longing in his glance? Esteban didn't try to talk to her about it or to touch her. He made no effort to bridge the distance between them. He went to the telephone and called his cousin.

Dennie watched Esteban's face as he spoke to Carmen and Miguel. She saw the empathetic look in his eyes, heard the concern in his voice as he expressed consolation, love, and hope. He was a good man. She hadn't been fair to him. He needed someone who could be part of his family completely. She knew she must remain separate, though a part of her ached at the thought.

After Esteban hung up the telephone, he handed it to Dennie. "Your turn," he said. Dennie dialed, and her father answered. So much had happened in the weeks since she had heard his voice. Relief and gladness rose within her. Dennie's eyes stung.

"Hello?" he said again.

"Daddy, it's me."

"Dennie! Sweetheart! Are you all right?"

"Yes. It—it's just so good to hear your voice. So much has happened."

The connection was clear. Dennie told her father the events that had transpired over the past five days. He assured her that he was willing to pay Eva's hospital bill—that Dennie had done the right thing—that he was proud of her.

"Dad, can I talk to Mom? Is she there?"

"She's resting right now, Dennie. She had surgery two days ago."

Dennie sat down on the edge of the bed to steady herself. Her father assured her that her mother was fine. He explained that the breast cancer had recurred, but had been caught at an early, curable stage. Dennie's mother had undergone a mastectomy.

Dennie gripped the telephone. As a little girl, she had leaned against her mother's breast for comfort, for love. Her mother's breast. Beloved. Diseased. Discarded. The image of the machi entered Dennie's mind. The image of Pinsha. Beloved. Diseased. Discarded. They had come so close to losing Eva. Yet she hadn't even known that her mother was in danger. "Dad, why didn't anyone tell me?"

"Dennie, it was your mom's decision. She hardly told anyone. Grandma Fletcher told Grandma and Grandpa Taylor. They flew here and surprised Mom."

"But Dad, no one *told* me."

"Mom didn't want to worry you. She didn't want you to come home before you were ready."

"Are you sure she's OK?"

"Positive."

"Could I talk to her?"

"Let me go and see if she's awake. Hang on."

A few minutes later, Dennie heard her mother's tentative, musical voice. "Dennie?"

"Mama." Dennie started to cry.

"Sweetheart, don't cry. Everything's fine."

"Mom, I wish I had known. I wish I had been there for you."

"I know, honey, I know."

"Mom, I love you. Why didn't you tell me?"

The line was quiet for a moment as Meryl tried to form words for her thoughts.

"Dennie, I've been thinking about the doves that Grandma Elsa raised. Remember how we examined their shells after the babies hatched? There were peck marks on the inside of the shell where the chick was trying to get out. We expected that. But we were surprised to find a pattern of circular peck marks on the outside of the shell—where the parent dove pecked, helping her little one. We laughed and said how they were responsible parents. I guess I wanted to be a responsible parent too. I didn't want to trap you in some kind of a shell formed by my own weakness and flaws. I wanted you to be able to soar, to become who Heavenly Father meant you to be. In doing so, I built a shell around myself."

"Mom, I don't know if I will ever soar. But I know one thing. A part of me has changed. And when I'm finished here, I want to come home."

A week passed. Joan Taylor went into Meryl's den to pass some time. Ben was napping on the couch in the living room and Meryl was upstairs resting. They had just had lunch with Meryl—chicken salad sandwiches and peas. In a few minutes Joan would awaken Ben and they would go back to Blake's home. It disappointed Joan the way Meryl remained quiet and distant toward her. But Meryl was healing and Ben wanted to spend time each day with her, so Joan would continue to bring Ben over every morning and try not to get in the way or wear out her welcome.

Joan surveyed the shelves of ceiling-high books on three walls of the den. It was more of a library, really. She thought of how there was one thing that hadn't changed through all of the years—her daughter's love of books. She remembered Meryl reading while she ate her after-school snack. Joan pictured her little girl sitting on a swing in the backyard with a book balanced in one hand, the other hand holding the swing's chain, the Blue Ridge Mountains behind her.

On one shelf, Joan noticed a row of books that she had purchased for Meryl over twenty-five years ago—*The Boxcar Children, Anne of*

Green Gables, *Little Women*, *The Chronicles of Narnia*, *Trixie Belden*, and *Nancy Drew*. She touched each book and thought of how Meryl used to call each one of them *her friend*. But Meryl had never called her mother *her friend*.

To combat the melancholy seeping into Joan, she turned away from the shelves and stepped toward the desk. As she tapped her fingernail on the dark wood, she gazed at the pile of papers sitting next to the computer. The top paper bore the words *Tragedy and Grace—the Story of a* Mayflower *Family*. Meryl was the author.

Curious, Joan picked up the stack of papers and flipped through a few pages. She recognized the name John Howland. Meryl had sent Joan pedigree charts four years ago, and had highlighted Howland as Joan's *Mayflower* ancestor.

Joan sat down on the chocolate-brown couch. She leaned back and began reading the story. Ben and Meryl slept long and peacefully. Hours later, Joan came to the final pages:

The day's first tender, pink light illuminated the eastern sky, but the lookout on the Mayflower *gazed westward. Desire awakened in the bunks below. How much longer could she endure the stink of close quarters, the rocking of the sea, the hardtack? Her pocket was nearly empty of medicines. Two weeks ago she had administered to Missus Hopkins, who safely delivered a son, Oceanus. Six days ago, young William Butten died.*

The sailor on lookout saw a faint dark line below the horizon, parallel to the starboard bow. "Land ahoy!" he cried. Within moments, men, women, and children crowded the deck! Land. A New World! The Mayflower *rang with the joy.*

"Land, John! Land to walk on, to run on, to till, and to build homes on! Where will we anchor?" Desire exclaimed as she skipped to John Howland's side.

John shrugged. His look did not echo the rejoicing of the rest of the company. "I fear that whenever we anchor, it will be too soon. There is mutiny afoot," he whispered darkly. "Last night, Dotey, Leister, and other servants came to me and said that if we bound together in a secret oath, we would gain our own liberty when we came ashore. For none have power to command us here, the patent being for Virginia, not New England."

"Oh, John, what are they planning?" Desire asked urgently.

"To secure weapons in the night. To rebel. To murder if it comes to that."

"What can we do?"

John shook his head. *"I would rather be murdered by Dotey and his lot than be a traitor to the man who is as a father to me. Yet, though I shun the rebels' violence, I understand their desire to govern themselves."*

Reverend Brewster's voice interrupted John and Desire as he spoke to the company. *"Listen, my beloved friends and fellow travelers, to the words of the prophet Isaiah, for surely this is the heritage of the people of the Lord: 'Therefore ye shall go out with joy, and be led forth with peace; the mountains and the hills shall break forth before you into joy, and all the trees of the field shall clap their hands.'"*

"Pursue peace, John," Desire whispered. *"If you can."* John nodded and took Desire's hand as the sun washed the sky with the colors of dawn.

That morning, as Captain Jones sailed the ship south, looking for a harbor, John and Deacon Carver huddled together in a corner of the ship. Edward Dotey cast a dire glance their way but did nothing. As the two men conferenced, the Mayflower *met with treacherous waters and shrieking gusts of wind. John, who usually possessed more energetic will than fruitless worry, felt a chill run through him. Would they come so close only to lose all in the end?*

"So many are sick. There is mutiny on board. Will even the ocean turn against us?" he exclaimed to Deacon Carver.

"Peace, John," Deacon Carver said. *"Though the powers of darkness combine to destroy us, God's will shall prevail."* They bowed their heads and sought the Lord's guidance through prayer while Captain Jones headed the Mayflower *north once more.*

By evening, a gentle breeze blew and they came upon a calm, safe harbor. Chains rattled as the anchor was lowered! As night approached, Deacon Carver called a meeting with the twelve leaders of the company and invited John Howland to join them in the captain's cabin.

After opening the meeting with prayer, Carver asked John to speak to the group. John explained the danger of mutiny and the desire of the young and ambitious servants to govern themselves. William Bradford saw no hope but to sadly charge the rebel servants with treason and duly punish them.

"Is there no other way?" Reverend Brewster questioned. *"On this journey, God hath preserved all our lives—even those with rebellious and*

ambitious natures."

"No one will string up my servants!" Stephen Hopkins exclaimed. "I need them to build and till. You don't kill a horse for kicking at his stall."

"Perhaps the horse will kick his master," Bradford challenged.

Deacon Carver interrupted. "Truly we need every able-bodied man. It will do no good to throw the malcontents into the sea. Let us rely on our Lord and our own reason. At the suggestion of my servant, John Howland, I recommend we draft a document, which combines ourselves into a body politic. It would guarantee each man the right to elect a governor and to aid in the framing and enacting of just and equal laws for the general good of the Colony.

"Tonight, John Howland will speak to the mutinous faction about the importance of government and unity. He will gather information about their willingness to sign this compact. I pray that it will satisfy those longing for freedom while it organizes and aids us all."

Thus, under the leadership of John Carver, the Mayflower Compact was written. That evening, John Howland met with Dotey, Leister, and the other male servants. He explained that the document would grant them the rights of men once their servitude ended. The majority of young man clasped his hand and welcomed his leadership. Dotey's and Leister's eyes shone bright with scorn, but they did not argue.

The next morning dawned, Saturday, November 11, 1620. All of the men of the Mayflower, *including servants, were called together and the compact was read aloud to them. It was explained that after signing, they would have the right to cast a vote to elect a governor. A cheer arose amongst the men.*

The first to sign the document were twelve men of substance, the wealthiest and most influential of the group. Deacon John Carver's signature led the rest. John Howland's was the thirteenth name on the compact, for although he was an indentured servant, he was honored for his leadership in the path of unity rather than division. After John, twenty-six goodmen signed. Finally, Edward Dotey and Edward Leister added their names to the document, knowing that without John Howland, their rebellion would not succeed. Then Deacon Carver was elected governor by saints and strangers alike—the first man, perhaps in all of history, to be so chosen in a free election.

After the meeting, when all had breakfasted, the Pilgrim company, both men and women, met once more on the deck of the Mayflower. *John winked at Desire and Elizabeth. Then he shouldered a musket and climbed into the small boat on its way ashore with sixteen armed men under the command of Miles Standish.*

"Be safe, John," Desire called. When John turned to look at her and wave, Standish shouted at him to act like a soldier. John, in a merry mood, laughed.

Elizabeth wrinkled her nose and whispered to Desire, "I shall call Captain Standish 'Captain Shrimp' for his shortness, red hair, and flaming temper! Desire, do you think it right that no women signed the compact?"

Desire smiled. "An amiable English lady does not ask such questions, Lizzy. Yet if it were my choice, I would sign as well."

While the men were gone, Desire ministered the last of her medicine to the sick. Lizzy stood on the deck of the Mayflower, *her eyes drinking in the look of the New World. The shore and line of trees looked as if it would never end.*

Dorothy Bradford approached her. Her eyes were bloodshot and held a strange and wild look. "What do you see, Elizabeth Tilley?"

"A New World, Mistress Bradford, with beach, mist, and endless forest," Elizabeth answered eagerly.

"That's not what I see," Dorothy Bradford whispered. "I see before us a hideous and desolate wilderness, full of wild beasts and wild men and a mighty ocean on the other side, a gulf separating us from all of the civil parts of the world, from hope itself."

"It isn't so different from Holland or England," Elizabeth insisted. "The same sun is in the heavens above our heads, the same firm earth beneath our feet."

"The sun burns chill this time of year, and the earth is too cold to plow," Dorothy Bradford said as she looked at the girl with pity in her eyes.

That evening, the exploration party returned to the Mayflower *with a boatload of juniper. They announced that they had met no Indians but had found excellent black earth and thick forest. On the deck of the ship they built fires with the juniper, which smelled pungent and fragrant. The smoke burned high like incense, reaching the heavens.*

Catherine Carver's voice rang clear as she began singing a psalm. "Oh, hearken Lord, unto our voice when lifted in a cry. As incense let our prayers be directed in thine holy eye." John, Desire, and others joined in.

After the singing, William Bradford opened his arms wide and shouted toward the heavens. "May not and ought not the children of those here rightly say: Our fathers were Englishmen which came over this great ocean, and were ready to perish in the wilderness; but they cried unto the Lord, and He heard their voice and looked on their adversity! Let them therefore praise the Lord, because He is good: and His mercies endure forever. Let them confess before the Lord His loving kindness and His wonderful works before the sons of men!"

"Hear! Hear!" shouted John Howland.

"Amen and Amen!" Deacon Carver's voice joined him.

Joan Tilley lay in the hold, listening. She felt ill tonight, and her legs were swollen. She feared the scurvy, for she had given most of her lemon juice to Lizzy. She pulled herself up into a sitting position, then stood and walked slowly to the opening of the hold and looked out.

There, Joan saw her daughter's green eyes blaze in the firelight with life and hope, the strength of youth. And a promise flowed into her heart as warm as mother's milk and as sweet as honey. Elizabeth was whole. Elizabeth would live. Her child would see the excellent black earth blossom.

Joan Taylor held the manuscript to her heart. Tears of compassion for people long dead pricked her eyes. Her own daughter brought this story to life. Joan blinked the tears away.

She thought of how when Meryl was little, Joan had wanted her to be strong and independent. She had forced Meryl to stand alone. And Meryl had. She had defied her mother's will and joined the Mormon Church. However, it was this very church, The Church of Jesus Christ of Latter-day Saints, as Meryl called it, that triggered Meryl's interest in genealogy. It brought about this beautiful story.

Questions assaulted Joan. Could it be that Meryl's conversion to the Mormon Church was a sign of strength and independence rather than rebellion and blasphemy? Was it God's plan that Meryl change religions? Could there be more than one path to heaven?

Inwardly shaking, Joan reflected on these questions. Then she thought of her evening walks back home in Virginia. For years, like a creature of habit, Joan strolled in the same direction around the block, seeing the same familiar angles of trees, houses, and walkways. Then, one evening last fall, she presumptuously strolled the opposite way. To her delight, every flower, leaf, and structure looked different and fresh, like a new and hidden neighborhood waiting to be discovered.

Joan looked up at the sound of footsteps at the door. Meryl stood before her wearing an oversized, button-down cotton shirt and jeans. It was the first day since her surgery that she had put mascara on.

"Did you read it?" she asked her mother.

Joan nodded. "I hope that's OK. How are you feeling?"

"Much better today," Meryl answered. Joan noticed the wary look in Meryl's eyes. Perhaps Meryl's emotional distance wasn't so much a lack of love for her mother as it was a lack of trust in her. The thought struck Joan like a revelation. How much had Joan lost in shunning Meryl's conversion to Mormonism, in blaming Meryl for tearing the family apart?

"I'm glad you're feeling better," Joan said. "Is Dad still sleeping?"

Meryl nodded. She sat down in the desk chair rather than next to her mother. "What do you think of it?" Meryl asked, glancing at the manuscript.

"It's well written. Fascinating. Moving."

"Thank you," Meryl said.

"It made me wonder about some things. Do you feel well enough to answer some questions?" Joan asked. "I keep wondering about what's real and what's not real. Are all of these people historical characters?"

Meryl nodded. "The only name I made up was that of Isaac the sailor. But he is based on a real person. In his history of Plymouth Plantation, William Bradford mentions a profane, brawny, and malicious seaman who torments the passengers, especially the women. Bradford felt it was God's justice when the man suddenly died."

"Hmmm," Joan mused. "Bradford's interpretation makes sense to me. Elizabeth Tilley ended up marrying John Howland, didn't she?"

Meryl nodded. "Yes. Elizabeth Tilley is our ancestor."

"Did John really have a romance with Desire? What happened?"

"Some historians think that at one time John was Desire's suitor. But things changed during that first winter. All of Elizabeth's family died—her parents, and her uncle and aunt. As an orphan, she was taken into the Carver household. Then, in the spring, Governor Carver died after suffering a stroke while working in a cornfield. His wife, Catherine, died a few weeks later. At this time, John became the head of the family and eventually Carver's heir. Thus, the family consisted of John, Desire, Elizabeth, and a couple of servants.

"A few years later, Desire returned to England. No one knows exactly why. At that time, her stepfather had died and her mother had remarried. John wed Elizabeth and they named their first daughter Desire due to their affection for Desire Minter. It isn't clear whether this wedding took place before or after Desire left. Whatever happened, it is a historical fact that these three principled, young pilgrims were bound together by their love for each other."

"Meryl, what about the Mayflower Compact? Did John Howland really help put that together?"

"We don't know details of his exact role. But he was the thirteenth man to sign the compact, right after the most wealthy and influential passengers. This is strange because the other indentured servants signed last. One fictionalized account I read makes John the bad guy, the leader of the historical mutiny. But Bradford doesn't mention any names, and all of his references to Howland are positive. So why was John invited to sign before the goodmen of the company, the heads of families, when he was younger than many and an indentured servant? Personally, I think John Carver and John Howland were key men in unifying the Pilgrim Company. Carver was elected governor by the entire company, and John's name is on the Mayflower Compact in a place of honor."

Joan grinned. "I think you're right. Did he really almost drown?"

"Yes," Meryl spoke eagerly now. "Bradford talks about how he fell off the ship and was pulled under many fathoms of water and lived by the grace of God. Franklin D. Roosevelt, George Bush, and Joseph Smith are among the thousands and thousands of John and Elizabeth's descendants. I think, in God's plan, it was really important that John Howland live."

Meryl waited for her mother's reaction. Would she counter her statement about Joseph Smith?

"And you and I," Joan said.

"You and I?" Meryl questioned.

"We are also his descendants. I guess it's important that we are alive too."

"Yes, Mother, I guess we're meant to be here too," Meryl smiled almost ruefully. This conversation with her mother was strange and hopeful.

"Meryl," her mother said looking down at her fingernails. "Sometimes I make mistakes. Sometimes I'm wrong about things."

Meryl knew her mother was trying to apologize and her heart softened. "Me too, Mother."

"You asked what I saw at the hospital when I looked at your incision. I didn't see punishment, Meryl. I only saw your heartbeat. Your precious heart." Tears welled in Joan's eyes.

"It's OK," Meryl said softly. She pulled a Kleenex out of the box on the desk and stood to hand it to Joan. Meryl reseated herself on the couch next to her mother.

"Meryl," Joan looked up at her daughter and changed the subject. "Did John Howland have red hair?"

Meryl laughed, and her smile reached her eyes. "I don't know. The pilgrims didn't allow their portraits to be painted. They thought it was vain. I gave him red hair because of you."

CHAPTER 19

COMING HOME

A week passed. It was 8:30 in the morning. Aimy decided to check her e-mail before she went to Sean's apartment to pick up Waverly. Sean had to work, but she and Wave had the day off. She planned to take Wave to the ocean.

As Aimy waited for her computer to boot up, she thought of how Dennie was coming home in two days. It would be great to see her again. During the past couple of weeks, Aimy had missed her best friend more than ever. Also, Aimy was dying to know what was up with Esteban. Dennie's last e-mail had been so short—just a congratulations to Aimy and Sean, and a few sentences stating that a lot of things had happened and that they would talk when Dennie came home.

Aimy typed in her password and looked at her messages. There was a bunch of junk mail and something from a Jerry Parker. She wondered who that was. Aimy opened the file, and her eyes shifted to the last line. It was from Christopher Parker. *Jerry Parker must be his stepmother.* But how did Chris get her address? Then Aimy remembered.

Over a month ago, before Chris left to visit his father in southern California, Dennie had sent an e-mail message to Christopher via Aimy. The Taylors didn't have the Internet. It had been a friendly note, describing some of Dennie's adventures with the Mapuche Indians and wishing Chris a fun summer with his father. Aimy had printed out the e-mail and given it to Chris the Sunday before he left. He must have taken that paper with him. The printout had Aimy's e-mail address on it. She read the message.

Hi, Aimy. Cory, my dad, says I have to stay here and live with him. He says that the judge agrees. I guess Mom and Blake are too busy to take care of me. He says it will be better for everybody. I hate it. I hate it so bad. I want to go home. Could you check on Domino? Jerry is calling me for breakfast. She doesn't know I'm using her computer. See ya. Chris Parker Taylor

Aimy stared at the computer screen. It didn't make any sense. Karin had been trying to get hold of Chris. Then she understood. Chris needed help.

Aimy thought about Chris as she printed the message. She had known the kid since he was four. She remembered how he had nearly ruined her baptism by almost drowning. The little boy had climbed down into the font following the service. Thes had pulled him out— Thes the hero, Thes the memory, Thes who was never afraid to go out on a limb for the people he cared about. Chris was eleven now. She thought of his flaxen hair, his irrepressible smile, and his great sense of humor.

Eleven years old. Aimy's mind went back in time to when she was that age. She had run away from home, from her stepfather's sexual and physical abuse. She had not needed to run very far. She had gone across the street to Dennie and Thes, her best friends. They had hidden her in a walled-off portion of their garage, not even telling their parents. While the entire town searched, Dennie and Thes had brought her food, books, and games. During the two days Aimy had been hidden, her stepfather had disappeared, exiting her and Moni's lives forever. If Dennie and Thes hadn't done that for her, things would have been different. So much worse.

Aimy took the paper into the kitchen to show her mother. Moni's eyes darkened as she read it. "You need to get ahold of Blake and Karin Taylor fast. They need to get Chris back here. One thing I know about custody battles is that whoever has the kid living with them has the best chance."

Aimy called the Taylors and read the e-mail to Karin over the telephone. During the shocked moment that followed, Aimy's heart softened toward Karin. The woman had a lot to deal with. Her in-laws were staying with her—that couldn't possibly be fun. Aimy thought of Sean's mom. Although she was polite to her future daughter-in-law, it was common knowledge that she wasn't exactly dancing and cheering about their engagement. Aimy also knew that Karin had been having contractions lately and was supposed to stay in bed for the next three weeks.

When Karin spoke, her voice shook with rage and fear. "I've tried to call Chris so many times! They never let me through! They *will* have to send Chris home, won't they? They *will* let me talk to him?"

Aimy heard Sesame Street and crying kids in the background. Karin mentioned that her in-laws were grocery shopping. They would be back in about an hour.

"I'll come right over," Aimy offered. "I'll watch the boys while you call Blake. You guys can go see an attorney or whatever you need to do."

"Oh Aimy, thank you," Karin exclaimed on the verge of tears. "You are an angel."

If you only knew, Aimy thought. *I'm more like Tinkerbelle criticizing poor Wendy. But that's going to change.* "Hang on," Aimy said and she hung up the phone. She told Moni where she was going, grabbed her purse, and ran out to the Yellow Toy.

While Aimy was on her way, Karin made a telephone call. But it wasn't to Blake. She called her ex-husband's home. Jerry answered.

"Let me speak to Chris." Karin's voice was strained and demanding.

Jerry told her that Chris was at the local high school at an all-day football camp. Cory would pick him up about 5:30, on his way home from his shift. Karin could try calling back this evening, but she might miss them because Cory was playing in a baseball game.

Karin hung up and called the police precinct where Cory worked. She explained that there was an emergency regarding Officer Parker's son. She refused to give her name. They put her through.

"Who is this? Is Chris all right?" There was genuine fear in Cory's voice as he spoke into the telephone.

"No, Chris is not all right. Put Chris on a plane tonight. He's coming home."

"Karin?"

"Yeah." Her voice was ice. But Cory knew it would crack under pressure.

"What are you talking about?"

"I'm talking about how you are keeping him there against his will."

"You're crazy, Karin. I've got work to do."

"He's e-mailed one of his friends. You've told him he has to stay there and live with you. You've lied to him. Send him home or I'm calling the police."

"Karin, I am the police. Don't make this any harder. Christopher needs me. He's staying here. He's happy here. You have your hands full with your other kids."

"In my book, this is kidnapping."

"Don't be ridiculous, Karin. I have dual custody. I'm his father."

"You won't get away with this."

"If you want to fight it, I'll see you in court."

"Please, don't do this, Cory. Chris will end up hating you."

"I don't have to listen to this." Cory Parker hung up the telephone.

By the time Aimy arrived, Karin had already talked to Blake and was on the telephone with their attorney. After the call she turned to Aimy, her face pale and stunned. "He said it could take weeks to get Chris back. It might have to go through the courts. I wish I could just drive down there and get him. But it's six hours away, and Cory won't let us anywhere near Christopher."

"Karin, I have an idea," Aimy said.

Fifteen minutes later, Aimy was barreling south on Interstate 5 with Waverly in the seat next to her and a caged rat in the back. She figured that if she made good time, she could be at Chris's football camp by three in the afternoon. She would pick up Chris and be on her way before Cory Parker knew his son was missing.

She was pretty sure she could trick the football coach into letting her take Chris, but she was nervous about the trip back to Grantlin. Parker was a cop and would come after Chris as soon as he found out what happened. However, by that time, Blake would be in southern California driving the Fletcher's Tahoe. Aimy planned to rendezvous with him at an exit an hour away from the high school. Then, Aimy, Chris, and Wave would drive the rest of the way with Blake. Cory Parker wouldn't recognize the Fletcher's car.

Aimy hated the thought of abandoning her vehicle. She imagined Cory Parker, enraged, smashing the windows with a club. Poor Yellow Toy. But a bright yellow Toyota with the words Pick Me Up—*A*

Service for Children, the Elderly, and the Disabled was just too obvious as a kidnap vehicle. Still, Aimy was grateful for the words printed on the side. They might prove her ace in the hole. She stepped on the gas.

Her optimism waned as the day lengthened. It was terribly hot, and Waverly wasn't feeling well. He complained of an ache in his chest. As she neared the Los Angeles area, the traffic thickened. It was nearly 3:30 when she exited the freeway.

She stopped at a gas station and asked directions to Emery High. While Wave waited in the car, she went into the bathroom, brushed her hair, and redid her makeup. She hated losing the time, but it was important she looked fresh and professional.

It was almost four when they found the high school where Chris was supposedly practicing. Aimy eyed a bunch of kids Chris's size practicing in a field. She thought of how they must be roasting in their pads and helmets. She turned her car around and parked so the sign on the side was visible.

There were a couple of coaches milling around, and Aimy strode purposefully up to a mustached man who wasn't currently yelling at the boys. She couldn't tell if Chris was among the players on the field—they all looked similar in uniform.

"Hi," Aimy said. "I'm here to pick up Christopher Parker."

"Chris, your ride's here!" the man called. He looked at Aimy— sizing her up, noticing her shapely legs, her easygoing, confident stance. He added, "Hang on while I get his emergency card. I just need to see your driver's license and verify your name." The coach walked toward a pile of gear.

Aimy watched nervously as one of the boys pulled off his helmet and sipped a drink out of his water bottle. His sweaty blonde hair lay flattened on his scalp. It was Christopher, but he looked older. Different. His eyes latched onto Aimy. He ran over to her.

"Aimy?" The boy stared at her, incredulous.

"Chris," she whispered under her breath. "I got your e-mail. I'm here to take to home—to Blake and Karin. Your mom has been trying to get ahold of you for weeks. I'll explain more in the car. Domino's in the back seat. Play it cool. We'll see if we can figure out how to get you out of here."

The coach met Aimy and Chris at the car with the emergency card in hand. "The Parkers only have their names on the card."

Aimy smiled with disarming charm while Chis climbed into her car. "They didn't tell you? I run a transportation service." Aimy nodded toward her car. "I'm supposed to take Chris to a baseball game his father's playing in tonight."

"I'm not supposed to release these kids to just anybody. Wait a few minutes while I get my cell phone and check with his parents."

Aimy looked at her watch. "Listen, I'm on a tight time schedule. The Parkers are probably already at the game. I really can't wait for you to try to track them down. I've got a disabled man in the car who has an appointment at the hospital in twenty minutes. I could come back and get Christopher after I drop my other client off. Hopefully he won't miss too much of his dad's game."

Chris leaned out the window. "Come on, Aimy. Let's go. We'll be late. Dad'll be ticked." Waverly moaned and held his stomach.

"You know this little lady?" the coach asked Chris.

"Yeah. She's like my chauffeur."

"Get out of here then." The coach grinned and waved them away. As they drove down Elkhorn Boulevard toward the freeway, Aimy handed Chris her cell phone and told him to call his mom. With Domino in one hand and the telephone in the other, Chris listened to his mother tell him how much she loved him. Karin told him how she had tried to get ahold of him over and over again, but just couldn't get through. She reassured her son that they wanted and needed him—always. Karin went on to explain that Blake would meet Chris at a rest stop in about an hour, and she would see him at ten that night.

When they reached the rest stop, Sean was with Blake. Both men bolted from the car. Blake picked Chris up in a huge bear hug and swung him around, tears in his eyes.

Aimy turned to Sean. "What are you doing here?" She grinned. "I thought you had to work tonight."

"I couldn't let my fiancée run a kidnapping scam all by herself. You make a pretty good-looking criminal!"

"Undercover agent. Spy," Aimy corrected him. She smiled as they kissed.

Their bishop cleared his throat, interrupting their embrace. "Aimy," he said. "I don't think we have to worry about the police. I have paper-work from my attorney, Bill Edwards, stating that Karin and I are

Chris's primary legal guardians and you had our permission to pick Chris up from football practice. Bill has a good friend in law enforcement, and they've already contacted Cory Parker's precinct. If they try to treat this as a kidnapping, they won't get anywhere. Anyway, what I'm saying is that I think you're safe driving your car home."

"Yes!" Aimy shouted. Under the pink, smog-filled sky, she did a victory dance around her Pick Me Up mobile. Augustus Waverly sat in the back seat and clapped.

Meryl climbed out of the bathtub at nine that evening. She dried herself and draped a loose, short-sleeved summer robe around her. She took off the shower cap and shook out her hair. Moni had frosted and cut it yesterday. Meryl looked at her hair in the mirror, satisfied with the color and fullness. Dennie would be home the day after tomorrow, and it was important to Meryl to look nice as a signal to Dennie that things were all right.

It had been fourteen days since her surgery. Although she was still sore and somewhat tired in the evenings, all in all she was amazed at how fast her body was recovering. Meryl was also glad that things were going well with her mother. They had agreed to disagree about religion. Although they weren't close, they were communicating and getting to know each other again. They had even gone shopping together for loose clothing that Meryl could wear until she had healed enough to be fitted with a prosthesis. Meryl went into the bedroom to dress.

Rick watched her as she retrieved clothing from her drawers and sat down on the edge of the bed. He thought she looked pretty tonight, her hair deep gold in the lamplight, her calves and fingers slender. He sat down next to her and began rubbing her arms and back.

"What are your motives?" Meryl said lightly, smiling. Yet inside she was serious. She really wanted to know. Was he acting attracted to her to comfort her? Or did he really feel this way?

"Entirely selfish," Rick answered as he kissed her hair.

The telephone rang. "Should we answer it?" Meryl asked.

"Maybe we better," Rick sighed. "It could be Dennie."

It rang again. Meryl picked up the receiver.

She was surprised when she heard Karin's voice on the other end. "I'm so glad you answered," her sister-in-law exclaimed. Meryl wondered what was wrong. Just a few hours ago they had received a phone call from Blake saying that he was on his way home with Chris and all was well. Had something happened?

Karin went on, "My water broke. Joan is taking me to the hospital. Ben will stay here with the boys."

"Are you OK? Is there anything I can do?" Meryl asked.

"Could you come and hold my hand through the delivery? Blake's gone. My mom's in Utah. Are you strong enough?" Karin was crying.

"I would love to be there. I'll meet you at the hospital." Meryl said good-bye and hung up the telephone. She told Rick what was happening as she dressed.

"Are you sure you're up to this?" Rick asked.

"Yes," Meryl said softly.

"Come on then, I'll drive you to the hospital."

On the way to the hospital, Meryl turned to her husband. "Oh, Rick," she exclaimed. "I've never witnessed a birth." He reached over and held her hand.

At the hospital, Karin's labor progressed quickly. Meryl and Joan accompanied her into the delivery room. As Karin strained to bring her daughter into the world, Meryl found that she had been right—birth was awkward, hard, beautiful, and miraculous. But she wasn't prepared for her own emotions, for the love and empathy that saturated her like a warm liquid. New independent life was coming into the world. Karin gripped Meryl's hand and pushed with all the physical and mental energy of her being.

Joan stood back, apart. Yet she wept when the top of the head was visible. She, too, had borne a daughter. The infant moved through a dark tunnel toward life. Then the child emerged—thin, wrinkled, with dark, damp hair, barely six pounds, a few weeks premature. Healthy. Screaming the first breaths of life. A human being. A child of God.

"We're going to name her Meryl after you, and call her Meri," Karin whispered. "Blake and I were waiting until after she was born to tell you."

Meryl's eyes filled with tears. How lucky little Meri was to have such parents! Her father would adore her. This child was surrounded by love from the moment of her birth, by her mother, her grandmother, and her aunt. She was born in a hospital with doctors and nurses ready to bend to her every need. Karin's exhausted breathing filled the room. A nurse placed the baby in her arms.

Meryl looked at her mother. Joan was crying. Was she remembering a similar moment when Meryl was born? But back then, they put women out for delivery. Had she cried the first time she held Meryl? Meryl knew that she was so different from her mother, yet they were inseparably connected. Meryl motioned Joan toward her. "Mom, did you hear that her name is Meryl, after me?"

"It's a good name," Joan said. Meryl put one arm around her mother and the other around Karin and the baby.

After the embrace, Meryl went to the nursery while Karin and Joan called Blake. Meryl helped a nurse clean the wet film off of Meri. The child shrieked at the touch of the sponge. As Meryl gently washed her body, she thought of how Meri was alone now, separate in a sense, no longer in her mother's world of dark warmth, tucked beneath the beat of her heart. The baby felt her own pain and would fight her own battles. She would struggle with fear, pride, and selfishness. That was the natural man, an inevitable part of being human. But Meri also had a seed of divinity within her, the ability to learn to love selflessly, the heritage of spirit children of God. Would this child gain faith in her Savior? Would she allow the seed of faith to grow? Would she pass it on to other generations?

They dried the baby and the nurse wrapped her tightly in a pink blanket and put a pink, knit cap on her head. She asked Meryl if she would like to rock Meri while Karin rested. Meryl nodded. As the child was placed in Meryl's arms, Meryl stared in awe at the closed eyes, the perfect nose and lips. She sat down in a rocking chair and held her. As she rested within the rhythm of the rocker and felt the infant's cheek, not against her breast, but against her heart, Meryl's thoughts flew to her own daughter, to Dennie.

Years ago another woman labored, without medication to dull the pain. Another baby was held against an anxious breast. But there was no security. No doctors, no nurses, no grandparents, no army of support waiting in the wings. At that moment, did Pinsha's heart quake? Was it dark outside or raining? Did the stench of poverty fill her nostrils as she struggled to breathe? Did she fear for her baby girl, for her small son, and for herself?

Meryl hoped that armies of unseen angels encircled her at that birth moment, taking the place of family, doctors, and nurses, driving the forces of darkness away for a time, gracing her with glimpses of her children's worth, whispering promises of a Being of ultimate light who greeted all those who, at the end of their journey, had learned to love.

Meryl thought of Thes, the son she had lost—of her own pain and of her testimony. She knew that birth and death were mirrored reflections of one another, both terrifying and illuminating, their purpose to define the children of God, to allow human beings to bear fruit from the seeds of love. That was why temple work was so important. And family history. And bearing children. It was essential that the divine seed of selflessness, of love, be recognized and passed from one generation to another while the spirit children of God resided in their selfish, human flesh—ragged bodies struggling to survive. Yet for all their self-centeredness and weakness, within their souls they harbored the seeds of charity. They were God's children, and they must pass that seed from one generation to the next. That was their hope. Their meaning. Their survival.

The baby startled in her sleep. Meryl reached out and held little Meri's hand. Somewhere, Dennie was on her way home. Meryl was not barren. The earth would not be wasted at His coming, but would be a fruitful field.

It was early morning when Dennie awakened from a light sleep, the sun blazing yellow and orange through the narrow airplane window. She looked out and saw the pale moon in the new sky, a circular wraith about to disappear under waves of light. A few hours before, Dennie, unable to sleep and feeling imprisoned in the cramped seat, had gazed through the same thick pane. At that time, the moon had reigned king—full and round, spreading lovely, ghostly light over sea and clouds.

The tall man next to her, with a wide forehead and eyes that crowded his nose, snored with his head cocked toward Dennie, his breath, sweet and rancid at the same time—night breath mixed with spearmint gum. He was Jim Carter, Wrigley Gum's chief sales representative in the southern hemisphere. Yesterday evening after takeoff, he had introduced himself and offered Dennie scores of gum samples. She had chewed and commented on them until her teeth grew sore. Then she had stuffed the remainder in the outside zipper compartment of her backpack.

With that thought, Dennie moved her seat into the upright position and reached for her backpack. A piece of gum would lighten her morning breath. Her movement caused Jim to slightly startle and resume sleep in a different position, with his head facing the closed eyes of the stiff woman on his right. Dennie smiled to herself. As she fumbled in her pack for a piece of gum, Dennie's fingers caught the corners of two envelopes. Carefully she pulled them out. Her letters from Ron. Unopened.

She felt their lightness in her hands, their weight in her life. Dennie closed her eyes. Her mind went back to the moment Esteban handed them to her—just before she stepped onto the airplane, just before he kissed her good-bye.

She and Esteban had flown from Osorno to Santiago together, the fabric of their relationship lined with seams of politeness. They spoke of the goodness of the Bolanos family, members of the Church who lived near the hospital and had allowed Dennie and Maria to stay with them while Eva recovered. The talked of how good Eva looked when the doctor told them she was well enough to return to the reservation. That was the day, as if by God's design, the rains had stopped. Mercurio had smiled when he tucked his wife and daughter into the oxcart for the long drive home.

This line of conversation continued until after they disembarked and Esteban walked Dennie to the gate where her next flight would take her all the way to San Francisco. He planned to spend a few more days with Carmen and Miguel.

"Do you think I should have gone back to the reservation with Eva and her family?" Dennie asked Esteban. "Should I have said good-bye to my grandmother?"

Esteban shrugged and remained silent, his eyes focused on some distant point. Dennie continued, talking more to herself than to the man beside her. "When I woke up in the hospital with my mother's poncho around me, I felt like that was the machi's way of saying good-bye. I didn't want to change that. Maybe I can bring Eva to the United States someday. I want to help her get an education. I want her dreams to come true."

Esteban's eyes shifted back to Dennie, and he nodded and smiled. She looked at him—clean shaven, white teeth, beautiful smile. She would not forget him. "That would be good," he said. "When the time is right, my father or I will go back to the reservation. We'll make sure that the Callfuhualas learn more of the gospel."

"Thank you," she said, emotion tugging at her throat, making it almost impossible to speak. She had gained much and lost much in the past weeks.

Esteban took her hands in his. The two of them had not touched since Eva's illness. His eyes were shining. Were they unshed tears? "Dennie," he asked. "Did you find what you sought?"

Dennie nodded. "I found out about myself, about the person I might have been. And the Mapuche people, the children of Lehi. They are my people. Maria, Eva, Mercurio. The machi. Pinsha—the mother I hardly remember. Now their lives are part of mine. Their stories are written in my heart."

Esteban nodded once more. "I'm glad."

Then Dennie choked, a cry rising within her. "But Esteban, you didn't find what you looked for. And in finding myself, I must say good-bye to you. Forever."

Esteban held her close and stroked her hair. When he spoke, his voice was soft. "I know," he whispered. "I know that now."

He let go of her and took two slim, unopened envelopes from his pocket. "These are the letters from Elder Babcock," he said as he handed them to her. "I shouldn't have waited until the last moment to give them to you. Forgive me."

"There is nothing to forgive," Dennie said. "Only to appreciate."

It was time to go, the last boarding call. Dennie bit her lip. Her finger touched where it bled. "It's hard to say good-bye," she whispered.

Esteban looked at her. To her, his eyes were not mirrors anymore. In them she saw passion and sorrow and peace. *"Good-bye, Gringa. Dear Gringa."*

"Good-bye, Esteban," she said. He kissed her lightly and quickly. "Hurry, or you'll miss your plane."

She shouldered her backpack and stepped toward the gate. Before entering the tunnel, she turned around. He waved to her.

She entered the plane and cried during takeoff. Then, an hour into flight, she blew her nose, wiped her eyes, and sipped a Sprite. Jim Carter introduced himself. Did he give her gum to comfort and distract her as she had given her nephews gum in church that Sunday when Blake was called as bishop? That was only a couple of months ago, and yet it seemed like a lifetime ago. Dennie opened a stick of gum and put it in her mouth. She would tell Aimy that gum was a gift from God. "I'm going home," Dennie whispered. Then she opened the letters in her lap.

They were newsy and cheerful, as were all of Ron's letters. He wrote of the people he was teaching. He bore his testimony. He signed them *With love, Elder Ron.* But it was the final *P.S.* that held her gaze. *Dennie, I've heard through the ward grapevine that you have a boyfriend, that he's from Chile, and he went there with you. If things have changed, if you are in love with someone else, it's OK. Well, maybe not OK with me, but I understand. Anyway, I want your life to be wonderful. No matter what.*

Whatever happens between us, I've given my life to the Lord for these two years and I know that's the right decision. I'm sure that you will make the right decision for you. If you're engaged, please write. It will be harder, if I'm the last person to know. My prayers are with you. Love, Elder Ron.

Dennie spent the next two hours of her flight writing to Ron. *Dear Elder Ron, I'm not engaged,* she began. She described her months in Chile, and told him about the Mapuche people and about her own past. She told him of her biological family. She explained briefly that Esteban was her friend now, not her boyfriend, and that they didn't plan on seeing each other again. She closed it with *See you later. Love, Dennie.* Then she slept soundly until the plane descended near the Golden Gate Bridge into the gleaming port of San Francisco. One more flight, one more takeoff and landing, and she would be in Sacramento. Anticipation and joy filled her. Her parents. Aimy. Uncle Blake and Karin. The hot sun. The brown summer fields. Home.

Yet she wasn't the same person. Would they understand that? She knew of a different world, and it existed within her, and this existence altered the shape of her soul as if she were clay in God's fingers, and He would mold her into a woman, not a child.

Two hours later, Meryl sensed a change in her daughter the moment she glimpsed Dennie in the tunnel, walking through the airport gate. She wondered if the others sensed it too—Aimy, jumping up and down, flashing her engagement ring; Rick and Elsa smiling and waving with all of the pride of a father and grandmother;

Meryl's own parents, standing to the side, ready to greet the child they hardly knew. But Dennie wasn't a child now. Did they see that? She was a woman—straight and strong as a young tree, as soft as the wind, as constant and elusive as the moon.

Dennie hugged her mother first, tenderly and gently. "Mom, you look different. Beautiful," she said as they held each other.

"Moni did my hair." Meryl laughed through her tears.

"It makes you look younger," Dennie whispered.

"And you seem older," Meryl countered. "You are a beautiful woman, Denizen. Welcome home!"

As they stood together, the seconds seemed to slow and shimmer like light. Rick hugged his daughter. Grandma Elsa smiled and kissed Dennie's cheeks. Grandpa Taylor shook Dennie's hand and told her, haltingly, about the new baby, Meri. Grandma Taylor hugged her quickly. "I look forward to hearing about your trip," she said.

"Density, Density, Density," Aimy exclaimed as she embraced her friend and showed her the four-leaf-clover engagement ring. "I have so much to tell you. Sean and I have settled on December 27 as our wedding date. My mission's going to have to wait until I'm sixty or so. You'll be my maid of honor, of course. Oh, by the way, I ran a kidnapping scam a few days ago to rescue Christopher from Cory Parker." Aimy cracked up at the confused look in Dennie's eyes. "I'll explain it all later. How I've missed you!"

"Me too, you." Dennie smiled into her best friend's eyes.

As Dennie looked around at those she loved, she thought of how this was the second time she had flown away from Chile and had walked through an airplane tunnel. The first time she had been so young, with Thes holding her hand, neither child fathoming the family and friends that awaited them.

There would be more departures, more homecomings, more journeys until on some future final journey she would find Thes at the end of the road. Perhaps her parents and grandparents would be there already, waiting with Thes, clad in the light of the Lord—her Fletcher relatives on one side, her Mapuche family on the other. She and Thes would reach out their hands and join the two together until they formed a ring of living light, joining and encircling those who had come before and those who would come after, forever and ever.

EPILOGUE

The machi fell ill during the snow and freezing rains, during August, the black month. But her spirit lingered in her ragged body until the spring. Maria and Eva cared for her tenderly with all the skill they possessed.

On an early September morning, Mercurio saddled Namcupan and rode far into the forest. He found what he looked for—an ancient, sacred tree with a wide trunk and sound wood. The next day, with other men, he cut it down and hauled the trunk home by oxcart. The wood was charred and the trunk bisected lengthwise. Then Mercurio worked day and night, hollowing out both sides with an ax to form a coffin.

One evening in mid-October, the old woman's heart stopped beating. The kultrun lay silently by her side. Maria dressed the still body in the garb and ornaments of the machi. Eva placed the black stone around her grandmother's neck.

Juan Antemil was one of the four hundred individuals who made the long journey to the reservation for the funeral rites. He came partly for his son, who was in northern Chile meeting the family of a new girlfriend. But he came mostly for the two grandchildren of the machi, for Lautaro and Mina, whom he had sent to the United States so long ago.

At dawn the sun highlighted the frost on the mountains. Then the light bore onward until it lay on the unplowed, fallow field where a solemn procession bore the body of their machi. She was lain on a bier in the center of the field, her body as still and appearing as chiseled as a carved rewe.

The kultrun, along with flowers, laurel, and cinnamon branches, were placed in the hollowed tree about her body. Two elderly male cousins began an oration, called a *weupin*, a dialogue between humans and their noble dead. They expounded upon the machi's ancestry, and praised her skill, goodness, and power. They spoke of *kumepiuke*, of goodness or pureness of heart.

The seed of her soul would go on in Eva and Dennie, the wind of God's will blowing them to other climes and lands. The machi was now a noble ancestor. To Juan, she had become holy. The green, unplowed field was alive with crimson, bell-shaped copihue lilies. Green and red—the colors of Christmas. The colors which represented eternal life and the blood of Juan's Lord.

Maria Callfuhuala stood with tears in her eyes as she held Eva's hand. Her thoughts ran parallel to Juan's. In her mind's eye she saw the design on the kultrun as it lay by the still body of Melillanka, her mother-in-law. Surely, the love of Maria's god would penetrate the four quarters of the earth, for the Savior's heart beat in cadence with the joy and sorrow of every soul and every people through all time.

[1] Cecilia Vicuña in *Ul: Four Mapuche Poets* explains bits and pieces of the machi's song. Pp. 15, 19.

[2] Vicuña, p. 19.

[3] Wording for biblical passages taken from the 1599 Geneva Bible. The *Mayflower* pilgrims did not use the King James version of the Bible. (Spelling of biblical passages has been modernized.)

[4] This Mapuche song was recorded by Sister M. Inez Hilger in *Araucanian Child Life and its Cultural Background.* Pp. 182-183.

[5] This fictional dream parallels an actual machi's dream as recorded by Hilger, p. 113.

[6] Quote from *Mapuche—Seeds of the Chilean Soul*, p. 91.

BIBLIOGRAPHY

Note: For me, one of the most intriguing aspects of constructing this novel was the personal learning that took place as I researched the Mapuche Native American culture of Chile as well as the 1620 Mayflower Pilgrim company. I found the following works especially helpful and extend grateful acknowledgement. Of course, any inaccuracies within my novel or liberties with language are completely my own.

Mapuche/Chile:

Faron, Louis C, 1968, *The Mapuche Indians of* Chile (Holt, Rinehart and Winston, Inc.), Reissued in 1968 with changes by Waveland Press, Inc.

Hilger, Sister Inez, 1957, *Araucanian Child Life and its Cultural Background.* Washington, D.C.: Smithsonian Miscellaneous Collection, vol. 133.

Mcbride, George Mc., 1936, *Chile: Land and Society.* (New York: American Geographical Society Research Series), no. 19.

Perrottet, Tony (editor), 1998, *Insight Guides: Chile.* APA Publications.

Port of History Museum and Museo Chileno de Arte Precolombino, 1992, *Mapuche: Seeds of the Chilean Soul.*

Roraff, Susan and Camacho, Laura, 1998, *Culture Shock! Chile*. Times Editions Pte Ltd.

Titiev, Mischa, 1951, *Araucanian Culture in Transition*. Occasional Contributions, Museum of Anthropology, no. 15. (Ann Arbor: The University of Michigan.)

Vicuña, Cecilia (editor), 1998, *Ul: Four Mapuche Poets—Elicura Chihuailaf, Leonel Lienlaf, Jaime Luis Huenun, Graciela Huinao*. Translated by John Bierhorst. Poetry in Indigenous Language series. Americas Society: Latin American Literary Review Press.

Mayflower/Plymouth Colony:

Bradford, William, *Of Plymouth Plantation 1620-1647*. Available in many editions.

Demos, John, 2000, *A Little Commonweatlth—Family Life in Plymouth Colony* (Oxford University Press.)

Deetz, James and Deetz, Patricia Scott, 2000, *The Times of Their Lives: life, love, and death in Plymouth* Colony (Anchor, a division of Random House, Inc.)

Hart Faux, Jocelyn, 1994, *Our Mayflower Ancestors and Their Descendants: Ten Generations from Howland-Tilley to Henderson-*Howell (Linrose Publishing Co.)

Johnson, Caleb, 1995-2000, Mayflower Web Pages. Aol.com/calebj/mayflower.html.

Markham, Gervase, first edition published in 1615, *The English Housewife*. Current edition edited by Michael R. Best (McGill-Queen's University Press), 1998.

The Geneva Bible. 1599 edition.

Willison, George F. 1945, *Saints and Strangers* (Reynal & Hitchcock), New York.

White, Elizabeth Pearson, 1993, *John Howland of the Mayflower, volume 2: The First Five Generations: Documented Descendants Through his second child John Howland and his wife, Mary Lee.* Picton Press.

ABOUT THE AUTHOR

MARCIE ANNE JENSON, a graduate of Brigham Young University, spends most of her time juggling the joys and challenges of being a wife and mother. "In some ways I'm a bit like my character, Meryl Fletcher," she admits with a smile. "I'm a breast cancer survivor and a descendant of John Howland. Yet my everyday life is much like Karin Taylor's. My husband is very busy, my home often chaotic, and my four children amazing, energetic, exhausting, and wonderful."

In addition to writing novels, Marcie enjoys reading great literature, going camping and to the theater, oil painting, and horseback riding. She has served in numerous leadership and teaching positions in the Primary, Young Women, and Relief Society organizations. For several years she taught elementary school and worked as a reading and math tutor.

Marcie's first novel with Covenant Communications, *Whispers of Hope*, came out in the fall of 2000 and is a prequel to *Homeward*. Her publication credits include an article in the *Ensign*, and stories and poetry in the *New Era* and the *Friend*.

Marcie currently resides in Elk Grove, California with her husband, Gray, and her children, Jamie, Matthew, Brett, and Michelle. Additions to the family include a Doberman, Sofie, a thoroughbred horse, Courtney, and a rat, Domino.

Marcie welcomes readers comments. You can write to her in care of Covenant Communications, Box 416, American Fork, Utah 84003-0416.

An excerpt from Carol Warburton's . . .

Edge of Night

Tamsin Yeager
Massachusetts—1858

The morning when I first saw Caleb Tremayne is permanently etched into my memory, the strokes as bold and vivid as those of the Flemish masters. Although the edges have blurred over the years, the colors and sounds remain, muted but beautiful, like a rich tapestry displayed under old glass. In my mind I see the golden orb of the sun in a cloudless sky gilding leaf-shawled trees so they shimmered and glowed like coins spilling from a leather purse. A soft breeze blew in from the ocean, rippling the leaves and setting the flowers dancing.

I think I knew even then that something that would change my life forever was about to happen. All of my senses were primed as if they were waves about to hurl themselves at the sand.

The cool tang of the ocean was everywhere—salty and lobster-spawned and wonderful. I remember looking down at the cove from the wooded bluff. The tide was out, leaving a sickle of beach fringed with boulders and sun-bleached logs. The sight never failed to lift my spirits, the cobalt blue water stretching to the horizon, its satin sheen flecked with whitecaps.

From the bluff, I had access to the best of two worlds: the cove with its treasures of sea creatures and circling white gulls, and the wooded headland butting into the Atlantic, lush with every kind of tree and shrub imaginable.

I came there often to sit on a knoll, feet bare, the sun warming my tension-knotted shoulders. That day I stood on the bluff, wind tugging my long skirt, the sound of the crashing waves banishing the cloying smell of Mother's sickroom.

Mother had been unwell for the past five years, being taken with a raging fever that so weakened her delicate constitution she was left an invalid. Even so, she remained her sweet self, finding delight in sipping tea laced with cream and sugar out of fine china cups, listening as I described a flight of ducks or the amusing antics of the garrulous squirrel living under the woodshed. But her greatest pleasure was in my younger sister Clarissa and myself. The three of us spent our days reading together, or listening while Clarissa played the pianoforte.

Thus was our life until the morning when we had wakened to find Clarissa gone and only a note to tell us she was eloping with Jacob Mueller, a nearby farmer's son—though he was much more than that to me. The shock of her sudden departure brought on a return of Mother's fever. As her health further declined, so did her mind and pleasant nature.

The past night had been especially bad. She had tossed restlessly, her twig-thin fingers scratching the counterpane quilt while she whimpered and called for Father, who'd been dead for six years.

"Hush, he'll be here soon," I had whispered, rising to take one of her fragile hands and hold it against my cheek. "Rest now. Your Tamsin is here." I sang to her then, the same sweet lullaby she had sung to me when I'd been frightened or fretful. "Hush little baby, don't you cry . . ."

I cared for her throughout the night, and when Betsy, a neighbor's maid, thoughtfully came to relieve me, I took my gray shawl and fled the house, needing sunlight and glittering water more than I needed sleep.

I lingered on the bluff, the wind tangling my dark, unbound hair, reveling in the few moments of snatched freedom. My mind drifted back to the time when we'd all been together—Mother, Father, my three older sisters, Clarissa, and me. We'd lived on a farm thirty miles inland from Mickelboro, Massachusetts. Father wasn't wealthy, but he had provided enough for Mother to have someone to cook and do the heavy cleaning. With a perspective acquired by time and maturity, I can see now that Father pampered Mother. She was the kind of woman who was easy to pamper, with her fragile beauty and graceful movements that made other women seem awkward and plain. Mother's people were upper class, acquainted with good books and schooled in the social graces. Frederick Yeager's people were as common as the rich brown earth—hard-working Germans, stubbornly clinging to old ways and old language. Although Father was born in Pennsylvania, he spoke with a heavy German accent and sometimes forgot his manners and sopped up the last of his supper with a scrap of bread. Still, his blonde good looks made it easy to see why Mother had chosen him, but I think Father always felt like a man who'd won a beautiful bird and didn't quite know what to do with her.

Even so, they were happy. Children know such things, can sense it in nuance and gesture and touch. Father pampered us as well. Instead of milking cows or helping in the fields like some men's daughters, we were allowed the luxury of books and lessons on the pianoforte, both supplied by Mother and augmented by the schoolmaster who sometimes boarded in our home.

I sighed and started down the path to the cove, not wanting to think of the devastating changes that had taken place since then. The sun had burned away much of the fog, though a few isolated patches still hung in gauzy tendrils among the trees. The path was steep and sometimes slippery, passing through a stand of white birches before it twisted between slabs of granite. It was as familiar to me as the rooms of my home, with a scrubby, wind-stunted pine waiting like an old friend at the last curve in the path.

I stopped to rest, leaning against the rough trunk of the pine to gaze out at the sea, whose power to fascinate pulsed through the air like something breathing and alive. The ocean was unusually calm. Gulls and cormorants wheeled and banked close to the water, and the little boat making its way past the breakers hardly seemed to move.

It was then that I saw him: a tall, dark-haired man striding across the sand to the scattered logs and rocks. There was something watchful about him. Watchful and cautious. I crouched behind a boulder, curiosity and surprise my primary emotions. In all my years of coming there, I'd never seen anyone on the beach before. My curiosity melded with shivers of nervousness prompted by the stark isolation of the beach and Mother's repeated warning that going off by myself would one day lead to grief.

Such didn't prevent me from watching the man's approach. Even in his haste there was a catlike grace to him. When he reached a log, he turned to look back at a boat, his stance one of taut concern as he watched its slow progress toward a larger vessel. I strained to identify the boat's occupants, wondering if they were people I knew, but distance and the shimmer of sunlight made it impossible to see. My attention jerked back to the man when he raised his hand in farewell and stooped to pick up a satchel by the logs. Fitting the strap over a muscular shoulder, he started toward me. His legs ate up the distance, brown boots scraping on sand and shingle.

I'd lived six of my twenty-one years along this coast, and I prided myself in knowing everyone in the vicinity. This man was a stranger, with his thick black hair falling over heavy brows, high-ridged cheekbones, and a squared-off chin. He was a man of the outdoors, perhaps a fisherman or a laborer from a farm, his face and neck tanned to the rich color of rawhide with sun creases at the corners of his dark eyes. He was a man in his prime, perhaps five or six years older than I.

My mind assimilated all of this in the space of a breath, as his black hair blowing in the wind, loose-fitting white linen shirt, and coarse woven trousers were but quick impressions. I crouched lower and felt a prickle of excitement as he hurried by, my heart pounding while questions whirled through my mind. Who was he? Had the boat brought him to the cove, or had he helped to launch it? And why hadn't they chosen the larger town of Lobster Harbor, just eight miles distance, with its wharf and easier access to the sea? Not knowing the answers, my mind returned to the man's wet boots and water-darkened trousers. The stranger and the boat went together. But how and why? The puzzle momentarily banished worry about Mother. I welcomed the change and pulled it around me like a warm quilt on a cold New England night.

———•———

But I had little time to think about the man or the boat. On my return home, while still making my way through the orchard that edged our backyard, Betsy ran to meet me, her hair coming loose and the lines in her scarred face registering worry.

"Hurry, oh, do hurry miss. Your mother's taken bad. Deacon Mickelson sent James for the doctor."

I lifted my long skirt and ran, forgetting the need to be circumspect, my stocking-clad legs bared to the knees, paying no heed to Amos Mickelson and his wife, Hester, standing at the door.

"I never should have left her," I cried, though what more I could have done I didn't know. All of Dr. Field's instructions had been followed to the letter, including the purging and daily doses of nitros. Was it all for naught?

I brushed passed the Mickelsons without speaking, only dimly aware that they followed me into the bedroom. Hester Mickelson's soft, "I'm sorry . . . so very sorry," was scarcely audible above the sound of Mother's harsh breathing.

I dropped to my knees by her bed. Death was all around us, hovering in the morning air, waiting to slip through the glass panes of the window. I wanted to hold it back, flail at it with my hands. *Please God, don't take her. She's all I have left. Don't leave me alone.* My tears made it difficult to see her clearly. Why hadn't I kissed her before I left, told her how much I loved her? As I gazed at Mother's gaunt, sunken cheeks and heard the rattle struggling up through the ropey cords in her throat, I felt a sudden desire to cling to her, laugh with her, love her: all the things in which we had once delighted. What would I ever do without her?